**W9-AUV-256**

## DATE DUE

| NOV 0 7 2020 | | | |
|---|---|---|---|
| | | | |
| | | | |
| | | | |
| | | | |
| | | | |
| | | | |
| | | | |
| | | | |
| | | | |
| | | | |
| | | | |
| | | | Demco |

# LOST

# A HOUSE OF NIGHT
## OTHER WORLD
### NOVEL

# LOST

#1 *NEW YORK TIMES* AND *USA TODAY* BESTSELLING AUTHORS

# P. C. CAST + KRISTIN CAST

BLACK
STONE
PUBLISHING

Printed in the United States of America

First edition: 2018
ISBN 978-1-5384-4074-2
Young Adult Fiction / Romance / General

1 3 5 7 9 10 8 6 4 2

CIP data for this book is available
from the Library of Congress

Blackstone Publishing
31 Mistletoe Rd.
Ashland, OR 97520

www.BlackstonePublishing.com

Dear Readers,

Welcome to another House of Night Other World adventure! I can't wait for you to follow Other Kevin to his world and discover all the cool and crazy happenings over there. But first, I need to take a moment to explain part of my writing methodology, and why that should mean anything to you right now.

I'm a character-driven author. That means that even though I outline, plot, and plan every book and series, as soon as I create characters and breathe life into them all of my well-made plans usually explode. A prime example of this is in *Untamed*, the fourth House of Night book. In that book I introduced a new character, James Stark. I'd created him to be the love of Stevie Rae's life, but the moment he met Zoey he showed me he definitely was not going to follow my plan. And, of course, that ended up being a good thing because Rephaim is definitely Stevie Rae's forever guy/birdboy.

Why am I telling you this? Well, for those of you who read the excerpt of *Lost* that was in *Loved* it's important. You see, I hadn't begun writing *Lost* when I wrote that excerpt. All I knew at that time was that Zoey was going to follow Other Kevin to his world. So, I wrote a scene that worked with what I knew. But when I began actually writing *Lost*, Zoey told me that what I'd written in the excerpt was as wrong as when I'd created Stark for Stevie Rae!

For a while I tried to fit that scene into the book I was writing. I agonized over it because it simply was not working. It didn't reflect Zoey's true motivations, but it had already been published! You guys had already read it! What was I supposed to do?

Thankfully, Kristin came to my rescue. She told me I should rewrite the scene to make it work, and then I should simply tell you guys what happened. Easy peasy! Kristin is often right, and this was no exception.

So, there you have it! The excerpt you read in *Loved* is vaguely like the finished scene, but only vaguely, and now you know why. The lesson here, for me and for other authors who write character-driven novels, is not to try to force a scene before the foundation for the book has been set and the characters in that book are fully actualized, or you'll be writing embarrassing letters to your readers explaining why things "suddenly" changed.

I hope you enjoy this Other World adventure. I sincerely enjoyed writing it for you. And remember, you are powerful—your choices matter—*you matter.*

> I wish you love, always love …
> P. C.

# 1

## *Other Kevin*

The instant Kevin passed between worlds, he felt it: that awful, panicked sense of being lost. The strangeness that was the effect of Zoey's spell—the one which had pulled him from and then returned him to his own world—was overwhelming. The feeling of being hopelessly lost was so strong, so urgent, that it took him back to a spring day when he was seven years old and he'd gone shopping with his mom at the Seventy-First Street Super Target in Tulsa. He'd wandered away while his mom and his sisters had been looking at girl clothes. The next thing he knew, he was sitting in the middle of the home appliances department sobbing uncontrollably.

This was the same awful feeling, only now there would be no friendly employee to comfort him while waiting for his mom to respond to the lost-child page. Yeah, he was a fully Changed vampyre—a lieutenant in the Red Army—but there definitely were times he wished someone would save him.

"Not possible, Kev. Get it together," he muttered to himself.

With a great *whoosh*, like an exhalation of breath, the bizarre hole between worlds disappeared, leaving only a rowan tree, out of place with its greenery, in the space where the tear in the fabric between worlds had been. As his lifeline to his sister Zoey—and her world, which had felt more like home than his own—closed, Kevin wished more than anything else that he could devolve to his seven-year-old self, sit down, and cry for his mommy to save him.

But he wasn't a child anymore, and his mother had stopped being a mommy years ago, so Kevin did what he'd told himself to do—he got himself together. He reassuringly touched the pouch that hung from the leather cord around his neck and took comfort that it had made the trip with him. He checked the inside pocket of his jacket to be sure the copy of Neferet's journal was still there, and then he studied his surroundings.

It was dark, just as it had been when he'd left Zo's world, and cold—though here there wasn't any snow covering the winter-brown grass. He looked to his right. There was no stone wall enclosing High Priestess Neferet's tomb. There was only a rocky grotto and a small, half-frozen pond.

*Because in this world Neferet is free and in charge.* Just the thought had his stress level spiking.

Kevin cracked his knuckles as he lifted his gaze and followed the ridge overlooking the grotto. Sure enough, ancient oaks formed a backdrop to huge clumps of sleeping azaleas.

"This is definitely Woodward Park, but not the one I just left." Kevin sighed. *Okay, one thing at a time—that's all I can do—but I have to actually* do *something, and not just stand here cracking my knuckles and feeling miserable.*

Kevin did have a plan, but it was one that made his stomach clench with nerves. He needed to see someone, and he wasn't sure how well it would go over. People were the same yet disturbingly different here, and he hadn't seen her in over a year.

What if she wouldn't see him at all? Or worse, what if she saw him, but rejected him—refused to see he was different than the others and wouldn't invite him in? *Then what the heck will I do? And how will I bear it if she turns her back on me?*

"I have to take the chance. If I want to try to make things right I don't have much choice. I need allies, and she's the best one I can think of," Kevin told himself as he made his way across the brittle brown grass to the sidewalk that edged Twenty-First Street and bordered the park. Walking quickly, he turned right, heading up the little rise in the street for the soft glow ahead that was Utica Square.

It was a short walk to the upscale stores and restaurants that made up the square, though Kev found himself wishing it would take him longer. Utica's big old four-faced clock, which stood proudly in front of the Russell Stover Candies store, said that it was past midnight, but the square was humming with activity. Since Neferet had taken control of Tulsa and most of the Midwest, human business hours had changed drastically to reflect the fact that vampyres, not humans, were in charge. Utica Square's stores, as well as *any* store or restaurant in Tulsa and the surrounding area that vampyres might want to patronize, opened at dusk and closed at sunrise.

There were, of course, a few stores that opened for humans during the day—mostly groceries, gas stations, and other necessities. But compared to vampyre-patronized businesses, they were shabby remnants of a dying past.

This cold Christmas Eve, Utica Square was dressed with lights—not in celebration of Christmas, but rather because Neferet liked everything to look bright and shiny and beautiful on the surface, no matter what went on just under the pretty veneer.

Blue vampyres and fledglings passed Kevin on the sidewalk, hardly giving him a look, which he found comforting. If an alert had been sounded when he, General Dominick, and the others from his Red Army squad had gone missing, Sons of Erebus Warriors would have been posted at all public venues in Tulsa and Kevin would definitely have been stopped.

The few humans who were out and about reacted normally to

him as well. They didn't make eye contact and gave him a wide berth, leaving the sidewalk or darting into whatever restaurant or boutique was close by to avoid him and the possibility that he was hungry enough to snatch one of them up and have a quick bite. Though Neferet's "official" stance was to discourage red vamps feeding on humans in public, the truth was the only reason the High Priestess wanted the Red Army to show any self-control was that public feeding tended to cause panic. Neferet considered human panic ugly and distracting. So, basically, if it happened … well, it happened. There were usually no consequences for the vamps except a mild verbal rebuke.

It used to upset Kevin that humans were so obviously and justifiably terrified of him, but this night it relieved him. He knew he smelled different—or, specifically, not grave-like—since Nyx had gifted him with his humanity again, but the people of Tulsa were so used to monsters in the night they didn't get close enough to him to realize he was no longer the boogeyman.

Kev didn't let his guard down, though. He considered taking the bus to the depot where his car was parked, but just the thought of facing ravenous red fledglings and curious red vampyres had his stomach clenching. What the heck would he tell them when the inevitable happened—when they realized he'd irrevocably Changed? He needed time and a plan.

But mostly Kevin needed help.

He could easily walk the block to the House of Night, but there was no help waiting there, and he had no desire to return to *this* House of Night. Not now. Not after he'd spent time at the *other* House of Night, where his sister was High Priestess and humans were welcome as friends, not abused as slaves and walking blood refrigerators.

There was only one place Kevin wanted to go, and only one person he wanted to see. Again, his hand went to the lump that rested under his shirt near his heart. He pressed his palm against the little hand-beaded leather bag, finding comfort in its presence.

Kevin made his way through Utica Square to the rear of the village-like shopping center, past Fleming's Steakhouse and Ihloff Salon to the darker, quieter parking lot beyond. It was crowded, so it didn't take long for Kevin to find what he needed.

A lone man, human and well-dressed, wove his way quickly through the cars, heading to the parking spaces that faced the Italian villa–style condos rising like an out-of-place piece of the Mediterranean that had been wrenched from the Amalfi Coast and plopped down in midtown Tulsa.

Silently, Kevin followed him. When his remote key beeped, unlocking the Audi SUV, Kevin stepped from the shadows to face the man.

"Good evening," Kevin said.

The man's eyes went huge and round and his face blanched to bone white. He held out the packages in his hands as part offering, part shield. "P-please! I have a family at home. Please don't bite me. I'll give you anything else you want, but my kids need me, and I don't want to die."

Kevin's stomach roiled. He hated this. He hated that just the sight of his red vampyre Mark instantly created a sense of fear and panic in humans. Kevin stared into the man's eyes and spoke slowly, gently.

"I'm not going to hurt you. You don't need to be afraid." The man instantly quieted. "You're not under a vampyre's protection?" Kevin asked as he glanced at the man's unmarked hand. Blue vamps had taken to tattooing crescent moons on the hands of humans under their protection so that hungry red vamps knew they were off-limits.

"Not a specific vampyre," the man spoke as if from a dream as Kevin's will held him, rooted in place and unable to do anything except what Kevin commanded.

"But you do something that protects you?"

The man nodded sleepily. "I own Harvard Meats. On the corner of Fifteenth and Harvard."

"Oh, sure, I know the place." And Kevin did. This man didn't need to be under the protection of a specific vampyre because his business—being the butcher who provided the best meats in town to the House of Night and their favorite restaurants—was protection in itself. "Okay, here's what I want you to do. Give me your keys. Are you within walking distance of your home?"

The man nodded again. "I live at Thirteenth and Columbia."

"Good. You'll need to walk home. Tomorrow report your SUV missing. Tell them you think it was high school kids—from Union," Kevin added as an afterthought. He'd grown up in Broken Arrow. BA and Union were major rivals, and he had to hide his grin at this small payback for Union winning the last state football championship.

"I'll report it stolen. By Union kids. Tomorrow," the man repeated by rote, handing Kevin his keys.

Kevin hesitated, calling the man back as he turned, moving mechanically, to begin walking home. "Hey, uh, do you need anything from your SUV?"

The man blinked at him, as if he didn't understand the question.

"Is there anything in your SUV that you should take home with you?" Kevin rephrased the question, looking into the man's eyes, increasing his control over him.

"Yes. My laptop," the man said immediately, though his voice still had a dreamy tone to it. "And a few more gifts for the kids."

"Take them," Kevin said. "Hurry."

The man moved quickly, opening the back door and taking out a slim laptop and a bag full of wrapped packages. Then he turned back to Kevin, waiting to be told what to do next.

"Go home now. Fast. Don't talk to anyone. If you get stopped by a Warrior tell him you are on the business of a lieutenant of the Red Army."

"I am on the business of a lieutenant of the Red Army."

"One more thing. This is going to be your best Christmas ever. Actually, it's going to be your best year ever. You're going to show your wife and kids how much you love them every day, and you're going to be sure that you and your family are invaluable to the House of Night by choosing special cuts of meat only for Neferet." Kevin paused, thinking, and then added, "Marinate the meat in a red wine sauce. Neferet really likes her red wine. Understand?"

"I understand."

"Okay, now go. Fast!"

The man rushed away, clutching the laptop and the bag of presents to his chest as if they were all made of gold.

Humming the Broken Arrow fight song softly to himself, Kevin got in the Audi. He took a moment to appreciate the nice interior before starting the car and pulling out of Utica Square. And then he was on his way to the Muskogee Turnpike, which was just a short skip from downtown Tulsa. Once he headed south on the turnpike, Kevin turned up 98.5 and attempted to let Blake Shelton's familiar Okie twang soothe his nerves.

Kevin wasn't exactly sure what he was going to do, but he was exactly sure who he needed to see to get help figuring it out.

The hour-and-a-half drive whizzed by, and soon Kevin was pulling off the highway and winding around an old two-lane until he came to the gravel and dirt road driveway that divided sleeping lavender fields and led to a familiar stone cottage with a wide front porch.

His stomach did nervous flip-flops as he cracked his knuckles and then raised his fist to knock on the door.

Kevin paused. What if she wouldn't invite him in?

He swallowed that terrible thought just as the door opened before he could even knock.

"Hi, G-ma Redbird! It's me. Kevin."

The only sign of shock the old woman gave was a slight pinking of her brown cheeks.

"It has been a while, but I do recognize my own family," G-ma said. She made no move to invite him in. "What can I do for you, Kevin?"

"I need your help. Actually, I need more than your help. I need a plan. It's a lot to explain. Could I please come in?"

"I get no pleasure in saying this, but no. You may not come in. I see that you made the Change."

"Yeah, months ago. I'm sorry I haven't come to see you until now, but you know why I didn't. I had to be sure I could control myself. Well, I'm sure now, and the reason I'm sure is incredible."

"I'm sorry, Kevin. Today is not my day to die, and even were it, I would not want to meet the Great Goddess after my grandson turned me into a ravenous monster. No. Please leave, child. You are breaking my heart, and it is already in more pieces than I can count." Sadly, slowly, Grandma Redbird began to turn from the door.

"Wait, G-ma. Please look at this first." Kevin lifted the medicine bag from around his neck and held it so that Grandma Redbird could get a good look at it.

Her brow wrinkled in confusion. "That is mine. But, I'm wearing it …" Her hand lifted automatically, going to the leather cord that held an identical medicine bag around her neck.

"G-ma, you gave it to me."

"No, Kevin." She lifted the identical beaded bag. "*This* is mine. That one, well, it is a strangely similar copy."

Kevin couldn't cross the barrier of her doorway unless he was invited in, but the bag definitely could. "Here, look at it. You'll see." He tossed it to her, and G-ma caught it easily.

He watched her open the little bag and pour the contents into her palm. There was a purple amethyst crystal and a piece of raw turquoise shaped like a perfect heart, as well as a sprig of lavender, the breast feather of a dove, and a spoonful of red dirt. The last thing that fell out of the bag was a rolled-up strip of lavender-scented paper.

With steady hands, G-ma Redbird unrolled the paper to reveal two words, written in her strong cursive script.

*Trust Kevin.*

G-ma's sharp brown eyes found his. "Where did you get this?"

"Like I said, from you. In another version of our world. After Zoey called me there and Aphrodite and Nyx restored my humanity.

G-ma, it's a long story, but I swear on Zoey's memory that you did give this to me and told me to go to you and show you. I need you, G-ma. I don't know where else to go or who else I can turn to. Will you please let me come in? I won't hurt you. I won't ever hurt you."

Sylvia Redbird studied Kevin carefully. Then her gaze fell, once again, to the two words written in her own hand on the stationery she made for herself there on the lavender farm that grew such fragrant, unique plants that the vampyres left her in peace—as long as she kept providing them with the lavender products Neferet so enjoyed.

"Kevin, I would like to invite you into my home." The old woman stepped back, holding the door open for her grandson.

He entered the cottage and took a deep breath of air scented with childhood memories. Through the tears flooding his eyes he grinned at his g-ma. "Do I smell lavender chocolate-chip cookies?"

"You do, indeed. Would you like some?"

"More than almost anything," Kevin said. "But first, could I please have a hug?"

"Oh, u-we-tsi, that would bring me great pleasure!"

Kevin held open his arms, and his tiny, loving, beautiful g-ma stepped into his embrace. And suddenly he found himself sobbing as she held him and patted his back gently, while he released the sorrow and loneliness and regret at having to leave his sister and return to a world filled with struggle and fear.

"It will all be okay now, u-we-tsi. It will be okay. I am here. I am here …"

## 2

# *Other Kevin*

"G-ma, these cookies are the best in *any* world!"

Grandma Redbird smiled fondly at Kevin. "You have restored my joy in making them. I have no idea how Neferet found out about them, but several months ago her Blue Army goons showed up here, insisting that I fill a weekly order of two dozen cookies—for the High Priestess herself. I thought it odd, but it did help insure my safety, and while they were here they also put in a standing order for my soaps and lotions ..." Her words trailed off as understanding bloomed over her face. "*You* did this!"

Kevin squirmed and grabbed another cookie. "Well, yeah. Everyone knows your lavender is the best in Oklahoma. Your soaps and lotions are awesome, and your cookies are special and delicious. I figured if Neferet knew about them, she would want them. She's all about getting things no one else has, and no one else has your recipe."

"I don't use a recipe."

"Exactly! They're something only you can make. So, I mentioned it to a Warrior who is mated to the priestess who brings Neferet her nightly snacks. I knew all she had to do was try a cookie and she'd be hooked. Apparently, Neferet has a sweet tooth. The soaps and lotions were a bonus."

Grandma Redbird didn't speak for several moments. She studied her grandson as if he was a puzzle she'd just figured out. "You were different. Even before you were pulled into that Other World."

Kevin nodded, speaking around a mouthful of cookie. "I kept thinking that would change—that someday I'd wake up and not be able to control my hunger at all. But it didn't happen."

Grandma's work-worn hand pressed against his cheek. "Oh, u-we-tsi, I wish you had come to me then."

"I couldn't, G-ma. I was super scared of turning into a monster." Kevin stared down at the ancient wooden table. "I couldn't risk hurting you."

"So, from afar you made sure I would be one of the safe ones— the protected ones."

Kevin nodded.

"Thank you," she said simply.

When Kevin was sure he wouldn't dissolve into big, blubbery tears again, he met her gentle brown eyes and smiled. "It's the least I could do after you lost Zoey. I know she was always your favorite."

"Zoey and I were close from the moment she was born, but that is often the way of it with grandmothers and granddaughters. That does not mean I loved her more than I love you."

Kevin felt tears fill his eyes again and he blinked hard to keep them from overflowing. "Really?"

"I give you my word. It was easier to be close to Zoeybird. She wanted to cook with me, to garden with me, and to learn the ways of our people."

"And I wanted to play video games and tell fart jokes with my friends," Kevin said sardonically.

Grandma Redbird's smile was warm with understanding. "You simply wanted to be a boy. There is no fault in that."

"I know I can't fill the place left by Zo, but I want us to be close. I—I need you, G-ma."

The old woman pressed her hand over her grandson's. "I am here for you. I will always be here for you. You will never be alone again, my u-we-tsi."

For the first time since he realized that he had to return to his world—had to somehow lead the Resistance into defeating Neferet—Kevin felt a little of the terrible weight that had settled over his body lift. "Thank you, G-ma. That makes everything better."

"I am glad. Now, I have a few questions perhaps you can help me with."

"Totally! Ask away and I'll munch cookies."

"That is a fine idea. So, you're telling me that our Zoeybird is alive in this alternative world from which you just returned?"

"I am. And she is. Well, she isn't *exactly* our Zo. But close enough. Close like that Grandma Redbird is almost exactly you too. It's weird. Nice, but weird."

Grandma sat across from him, pouring herself a cup of fragrant lavender tea from the timeworn iron pot she'd used for as long as Kevin could remember.

"Let me make sure I understand. In that world Zoey is High Priestess, and in charge. There is no Neferet, and—"

"Neferet is there," Kevin interrupted. "She's magickally sealed inside the grotto in Woodward Park."

"That's right," Grandma Redbird nodded. "You said she'd become immortal?"

"Yeah. I don't really understand that part very well, but I believe Zo and her crew. They said she'd tried to make herself Goddess of Tulsa and went totally bat-shit crazy and killed bunches of people—humans and vamps. Uh, sorry 'bout the language, G-ma."

She waved away his apology. "Sometimes strong language is required. Your description is valid."

"Thanks, G-ma." Kevin pointed at the copy of the journal

Zoey had given him before he left her world. "Zo told me that explains a lot about Neferet's past and her motivations. She and her friends discovered Neferet's history is a weak spot for her. Zo thought that maybe we could find something in there that might help us defeat her here too."

"That does make sense. So, Neferet is entombed. Zoey is in charge. And she has opened the Tulsa House of Night to humans? Truly?"

"Yep! You should see it—human kids were actually playing with red and blue fledglings in the snow. It was bizarre, but crazy cool, and Zo had her crew—they call themselves the Nerd Herd …" Kevin paused as his grandma giggled like a girl. "She had her Nerd Herd initiate human-student programs like the one in Tulsa all over the US. Apparently, it's going pretty well, which is one reason why she was super worried when it seemed like Neferet might be stirring. She knew humans would be her second target."

"Because Zoey herself would be her first?"

"Yep. They're enemies. Um, G-ma, when I explained to Zo how she died here, she told me that she was positive Neferet had killed her, because in her world Neferet had killed two vamp professors the exact same way, though she staged the murders to look like the People of Faith did it."

Grandma Redbird paled at the mention of her granddaughter's gruesome death. Kevin reached across the table and squeezed her hand. "It's okay, G-ma. Just remember that she's still alive. She's just not here anymore."

The old woman nodded briskly and sipped her tea, obviously composing herself. "Neferet's plan in both worlds was to create a war between humans and vampyres?"

"Yep."

"Zoey and her … Nerd Herd were responsible for stopping her in that other world?"

"Yep again," Kevin said.

"Well done, Zoeybird," Grandma Redbird said softly. "That

other world—Zoey's world—sounds like a lovely place."

"It is. Christmas decorations all over—humans and vamps mingling—G-ma, they even turned the Tulsa depot into a cool restaurant run by vamps. Humans pack it full every night." Kevin quickly decided to leave out the additional detail about how red vamps and fledglings from this world had destroyed the restaurant and eaten everyone. G-ma didn't need that sadness.

"Truly?" she said with wonderment.

"Absolutely! Zo told me they even have a farmers' market on the House of Night school grounds every week, and the campus is completely open to humans for it."

"That is, indeed, magickal," she said. "Why ever did you return here?"

"I had to. I'm Zoey."

"U-we-tsi, you're going to have to explain better than that."

"G-ma, just like Zo in that world, I have an affinity for all five of the elements."

Her eyes widened in happy surprise. "Oh, Kevin! That is lovely news."

"Well, yes and no. Yes, because it's cool and a sign of Nyx's favor. Hey, I almost forgot to tell you! Zo's fully Changed tattoo is just like mine—only hers is blue, of course. But she also has a bunch of other tattoos—like on her palms, around her waist, down her back, across the top of her chest."

"She went to a tattoo artist? It sounds beautiful, but it would certainly take quite a bit of time."

"No, G-ma, Nyx gave her the tattoos as a sign that she was on the right path." Kevin sighed. "I'm kinda hoping Nyx might help me out like that too. At least I'd know I was doing the right thing."

"And what is this right thing you'd do?"

Kevin didn't hesitate. "That brings me to the not-so-lovely part. Because I have an affinity for all five elements like Zo, that means I also have the Goddess-given responsibilities she does. G-ma, I have to defeat Neferet like Zo did in her world and set the balance of Light and Darkness right again."

Grandma Redbird didn't miss a beat. "And how do you plan on doing that?"

"No clue, G-ma. I have no clue." He grinned cheekily at her. "But I'll bet you can help me come up with a plan."

"If I can't I know who can. Kevin, what do you know about the Resistance?"

"I'm a lieutenant in Neferet's Red Army. Our only mission right now is to find and eliminate every member of the Resistance."

"You being a lieutenant might help. Do you have access to information like where Neferet believes the Resistance is hiding and how they smuggle people out of the Midwest to safety?"

"Not really. Strategy is left to Neferet, the generals in the Blue Army, and the Sons of Erebus Warriors. Even us red vamps who manage to retain enough of our humanity to be made officers aren't included in planning. Basically, Neferet's Warriors use us like we're mindless weapons. When I first made the Change, I overheard General Stark talking about the Red Army. He called us expendables."

"General Stark sounds despicable."

"In this world, yep, he is. In Zo's world he's her Oathbound Warrior and mate—a really good guy."

That had Grandma Redbird looking thoughtful.

"And General Stark isn't wrong. All he has to do is just point the Red Army in a direction and set us loose." Kevin shuddered. "Most red vampyres are mindless eating machines bent on devouring everything in their path."

"That is actually good for us," G-ma said.

"Huh?" Kevin said, sounding a lot like his sister.

"Well, if this General Stark is a good guy in Zoeybird's world, then at his core there is goodness. Perhaps he can be reached. And you're an officer. You have access to come and go easily from the House of Night, correct?"

"Yeah, I guess. But only between sunset and sunrise. During the day we're all banished to the tunnels under the depot."

"But no one at the House of Night—not one vampyre—would imagine that you are on the side of the Resistance."

Kevin sat up straighter. "You're right, G-ma! That wouldn't even occur to them. They don't usually include officers of the Red Army in their strategy meetings, but they wouldn't notice if I was there, just standing around waiting to be given orders." He grinned. "I could learn all sorts of stuff!" He hesitated, and his grin slid away. "Except I don't smell right, and they would notice that."

G-ma's eyes glittered mischievously. "Let me worry about that, u-we-tsi."

"Ugh, okay. So, is that our plan? You make me stinky again, and I spy on the House of Night and find out stuff about the Resistance? Then we'll have to figure out where they are hiding before the army finds them and tell the Resistance whatever I learn."

"Finding them is not a problem."

"G-ma! Are you part of the Resistance?"

"As Martin Luther King Jr. put it so succinctly, 'The ultimate tragedy is not the oppression and cruelty by the bad people, but the silence over that by the good people.' I will not be silenced."

"Holy shit, G-ma, you *are* part of the Resistance!"

"I am proud to say, yes, I am."

"They'd kill you if they caught you. Sheesh, G-ma. Neferet wouldn't care that you're just one old woman. You'd die," Kevin said.

"I am aware of that, but, Kevin, if I stood by and did nothing my spirit would die."

Kevin sighed heavily. "Mine too. That's why I came back. I have to do something, and I think I'm the only one who can."

"That's very brave of you, u-we-tsi."

"Nah, doing the right thing isn't brave. It's just what decent people do," Kevin said.

"Indeed."

"I want you to take me to them," Kevin said firmly.

"Them?"

"The Resistance. I want to talk with them—tell them what happened to me in Zo's world."

"I'm not sure that will work. They may only see an enemy when they look at you," G-ma said. "What might work better is for you to spy—report to me—and I'll take them the information."

"That would be fine, if it wasn't for Aphrodite," Kevin said.

"Aphrodite? The Greek Goddess of Love?"

Kevin grinned impishly. "I sure think she is, but I guess *technically* she's a Prophetess and not a goddess."

"Child, you are making no sense."

"Sorry, G-ma. It's simple, really. In Zo's world there is a Prophetess of Nyx named Aphrodite who has the power to grant second chances. Because of her, none of the red fledglings or red vampyres there have lost their humanity. She's in this world too."

"Oh, Great Goddess! If only that could happen in this world as well!" G-ma exclaimed.

"Yeah, if humanity is returned to the soldiers in the Red Army, Neferet loses her weapons," Kevin said. "In Zo's world Aphrodite and I had a connection." He paused, ignoring the fact that his cheeks felt super warm. "She, um, told me to find her other self in this world, and that *she'd* love me too." Grandma Redbird's brows lifted, but she said nothing. Kevin cleared his throat and continued. "Also, Zo said I have to put together my own circle—basically, my version of her Nerd Herd. I already know that at least two of the vampyres I need to recruit are blue—and are at the Tulsa House of Night right now."

"But, u-we-tsi, the Resistance is filled with many blue vampyres. Can you not just use them for your circle?"

"I guess, but Zo's Nerd Herd is different—just like her—just like me. They have affinities for their elements too."

"Which makes her circle more powerful than a regular one," G-ma said.

"Yeah. Do you see why I have to do more than just spy for the Resistance?"

"I do. And because I do, I am much more hopeful about our chances for success than I was just minutes ago." Grandma Redbird glanced out the front picture window. "Dawn is already pinkening the horizon. We will sleep, u-we-tsi, and tomorrow—tomorrow we go to the Resistance."

"Okie dokie, G-ma," Kevin said bravely before he shoved another cookie in his face and thought, *Ah, hell ...*

# 3

# *Other Kevin*

"Sap-a-loop-ah? Really, G-ma? Talk about the middle of nowhere," Kevin said as G-ma directed him to exit the Turner Turnpike.

"Kevin, pronounce it correctly."

"Fine. *Sapulpa.* Still—really, G'ma? Why here?"

"Because, as you said—middle of nowhere. Which is an excellent place for the headquarters of the Resistance, as Sapulpa is only about thirty minutes from downtown Tulsa. Close enough to be useful, but still a rural town with nothing to interest vampyres except several ranches that grow some of the best alfalfa in the state."

"So, they have just enough going on to be protected by Neferet, but not enough going on to interest her into actually hanging out here or anything."

"Exactly. Take a left at the next light. That's South Hickory. Then follow this road for about a mile until we go through a couple of stop signs. After the smoke shop look for Lone Star Road and turn right onto it."

"Where the heck are you taking us, G-ma?"

She smiled seraphically. "To one of those lovely little alfalfa ranches, u-we-tsi."

They wound along Lone Star Road, passing rolling fields, some left fallow to ready for the spring planting, and some already green with winter wheat. As per usual for Oklahoma, the houses went from gorgeous almost-mansions to crappy trailers, and back to mansions.

"Hey, check it out, G-ma. It's the Okie white-trash trifecta—a trailer house, an above-ground pool, *and* an old mattress those pit bulls are using as a bed—all in one yard."

Grandma Redbird's nose wrinkled. "I believe those are boxers, not pitties, Kevin."

"My mistake. That's what I get for stereotyping."

"Well, it was definitely a good guess. Slow down, now. See on your right where that pretty white fencing begins?"

"Yep."

"There's a gate just beyond it. Pull in, roll down your window, and press the intercom button. I will do the talking."

Kevin did as he was told, turning into a lane that was blocked by a large iron gate. He did a quick glance around as his window rolled down and saw that the easy, tidy look of the little ranch didn't tell the entire truth.

The gate, like the well-tended white fence, was threaded with several strands of thick conductive wire. Kevin's eyes followed the wires.

"That's a super-serious electric fence, G-ma."

"Yes, I am aware of that. Press the intercom, please."

Kevin pressed the white button next to the speaker and a little red light lit up, drawing attention to the high-tech camera pointed their way.

"Who's there?" came a woman's sharp voice punctuated by a symphony of yapping dogs.

"Sylvia Redbird. I hear you have a litter of puppies. I'd like to take a look at them, if you still have one for sale."

There was a pause, and then, "I see a red vampyre with you."

Grandma Redbird slid over and stuck her head beside Kevin's. "It's me, Tina. This is my grandson, Kevin."

"Red vampyres are not welcome on my property or in my home."

"This red vampyre is different. I give you my word on it," said Grandma.

"Of course you do. You're under his control. No. You may not enter my property. You may not enter my home."

"Tina, send Babos out here."

"Dogs hate red vampyres. She'll snarl and bark and upset the whole pack," replied the tinny voice.

"She's gonna love me. Promise, ma'am," Kevin said.

"You'll be glad you took the chance," Grandma added.

"Fine. But when she barks and goes crazy, I'm going to be very upset with you, Sylvia. And I'm bringing my .45 with me. One false move and, grandson or not, I'll take that vamp's head off his neck."

"As well you should, Tina," replied Grandma Redbird calmly.

"Be there in a sec."

The intercom connection clicked off as the gate swung open.

"Don't drive onto her property," said G-ma. "Let's just get out of the car." She caught his gaze with hers. "The dog is going to like you, isn't she?"

Kevin grinned. "They used to—before I was Marked. And then at Zo's House of Night there was this cool yellow lab named Duchess. She *loved* me. So, I'm thinking we'll be fine."

The sound of a Polaris' motor getting closer and closer had Grandma Redbird sighing. "Well, it is too late now if we're wrong."

"We're not wrong, G-ma. Watch. I can handle this part. Dogs are awesomesauce!" Kevin walked around to the front of the car and stood just outside the property line before the open gate.

The Polaris roared up, sliding to a stop in front of them. Kevin had to squint against the glare of the vehicle's lights, but he could see a short woman—probably somewhere around his g-ma's age. She had a crazy mane of wavy silver-gray hair with streaks of deep purples, pinks, and blues scattered through it. She was old, but her body was still trim, which was obvious because she was wearing yoga pants tucked into turquoise cowboy boots, and a sweatshirt that proclaimed **KALE** in Yale-styled letters. Holding a cocked .45, she got lithely out of the Polaris, followed by a small, black brindle terrier.

"Hello, Tina. This is my grandson, Kevin."

"Good evening, ma'am," Kevin said politely.

"We'll see how good it is," the old woman grumbled.

"Hey! It's a Scottie dog!" Kevin exclaimed. "I've always wanted one of them. I think they're the coolest little dogs ever."

Tina's green eyes studied Kevin. "You don't sound like a red vampyre."

"That's because I'm a different kind of red vampyre," he said.

"A good kind," Grandma added.

"Impossible," said Tina.

"Show her, u-we-tsi."

Kevin crouched and smiled at the little terrier. "Hey there, little girl! You're super pretty. Wanna come here and let me pet you?"

The dog studied him as carefully as the woman at her side.

"Her name is Babos."

"Babos—that's a cool name. Hi, Babos." He held out his hand. "Come here, girl."

The little dog hesitated, ears pricked at Kevin. She lifted her head and sniffed the air.

"Sorry I don't have any treats for you. I'll know better next time. But I promise that I'm a pretty good chin scratcher." He made chin-scratching motions with his fingers. "Come here, Babos. Give me a try."

The Scottie tilted her head, sniffed the air again, and then with a little huff she trotted directly to Kevin, who smiled and told her she was the smartest, prettiest, sweetest Scottie girl he'd ever seen, while he fulfilled his promise and scratched her bearded chin as she wagged her tail enthusiastically.

"Huh. Would never have believed it if I hadn't seen it with my own eyes," said Tina. "What is he?"

"I told you. He's my grandson. And he's going to change everything."

(

"You seriously have a Scottie ranch!" Kevin couldn't stop himself from gawking as he and Grandma Redbird followed Tina into the sprawling ranch-style home. As they entered through the garage, a bevy of short, brick-shaped terriers, ranging in color from blond and wheat to black and black brindle, mobbed them. Kevin tried to count, but when he hit fifteen he gave up. "Um, G-ma, were you serious about the puppies? Man, I hope so."

Tina smiled at him then—the first time she'd done more than look at him like he was a bug staked on a display board. "I don't have puppies right now, but I will in a few weeks."

"It's code, u-we-tsi. Humans or blue vampyres, and even blue fledglings who are allied with the Resistance, come to Tina's ranch and ask for puppies."

"But what they're really asking for is sanctuary," Tina said.

"Hope someday I can get a puppy," Kevin mumbled as he crouched and thoroughly enjoyed being mauled by a herd of Scottie dogs.

"Why is he different?" Tina asked.

"That, my friend, is a long story that we'd rather not take time for at this moment, as the Resistance is going to need that explanation as well. Are they here?"

Tina nodded. "On the top of the ridge. You know where the hunting blinds are, in those trees adjacent to that flat, grassy easement?"

"I do."

"Some of them are in the blinds. Some are working on trying to expand a little cave-like area they discovered just a day or so ago among the rocks on the side of the ridge. They arrived last night, with a few refugees they need to smuggle out—mostly women and children. There's a winter storm brewing. They thought they'd be safe on the ridge—at least for a few days."

Grandma Redbird sighed. "They're too vulnerable in those blinds. There's so little shelter in them. I know vampyres are resistant to the cold weather, but it's just awful that they have to run from place to place like they do. The stress of not having a truly safe place must wear on them."

"That's why they were so excited to find the cave," Tina agreed. "But Dragon told me that right now it can only hold about five people, and that's if they don't mind being crowded together. They're working on expanding it, but you know that ridge is mostly rock and hard red dirt. It's slow going, especially in the middle of winter."

"Wait, did you say Dragon? As in Dragon Lankford?" Kevin said.

"Yes. Dragon Lankford used to be the Tulsa House of Night's Swordmaster—before Neferet began the war," Tina said.

"Is his mate, Anastasia, here too?" Kevin asked, excitement lifting his voice.

Tina nodded. "She is."

"G-ma! Zoey told me to find Dragon and Anastasia Lankford—that they could help me for sure."

"Then we are on the right path," G-ma said with a smile.

"Man, I hope so." Kevin stood after giving the Scotties one more group petting. "So, you were saying that the Resistance doesn't really have a headquarters?"

"They did have a headquarters, but that was before Lenobia and Travis were trailed, trapped, and killed—along with their horses …" Tina's words broke off as she tried to compose herself, obviously too upset to continue.

Grandma Redbird reached out to her, hugging Tina sympathetically, and then finished explaining for her. "Lenobia and Travis had created a headquarters for the Resistance in the middle of Keystone National Park. It's more than seven hundred acres, and except for the areas near Keystone Lake and Dam, it's wild and undeveloped, even though it's only about an hour from downtown Tulsa to the park. It was an excellent place for a rough camp, especially as Lenobia managed to smuggle several horses out of the House of Night when she and Travis left for good. Someone betrayed them. Lenobia and Travis stayed with the horses, drawing the Red Army away from the rest of the Resistance and the innocents they were helping to safety. They were slaughtered. Lenobia, Travis, the Resistance members, the innocents, and every single horse."

Kevin bowed his head, sadness and regret filling him.

"You were there, weren't you?" Tina's voice was filled with gravel.

"No. And I thank Nyx for that. I was still a fledgling when that happened, and fledglings are never part of an actual deployment. They're not good weapons yet. They have to be fully Changed before enough of their humanity is wiped out for them to be dangerous *and* expendable." He grimaced in disgust. "I heard about the slaughter, though. My general, his name was Dominick, gloated about the victory. It—it made me sick. It still makes me sick."

"I'm glad you weren't there," Tina said, her voice still shaky. "I don't believe I could bear having you in my home had you been involved in that. Lenobia was a good friend. And those horses …" She shuddered. "I can't think about what the Red Army did to them."

"I'm sorry," was all Kevin could think to say.

"Show me. Don't tell me. Help us stop Neferet and the misery she's unleashed upon this world, and I'll believe you're truly sorry," said Tina.

"I will. I promise."

Tina nodded briskly and then motioned for them to follow her into the fragrant kitchen. With the herd of Scottie dogs trotting around their feet, Grandma Redbird and Kevin made their way slowly after Tina, careful not to step on paws.

"I imagine you'll want to be on your way to join them quickly?"

"Yes. That would be best," Grandma Redbird said.

"Actually, you're going to save me a trip. I baked a dozen loaves of bread and finished canning my blackberry jam. Never knew vampyres loved fresh bread and jam so much before Neferet changed our world, but they certainly do."

Kevin's mouth was watering as he watched Tina finish packing the bundles of fresh homemade bread and jam into canvas bags.

"Who doesn't like homemade bread?" he said. "And yours smells incredible."

Tina stopped to look at him. She shook her head. "It's tough to get used to it."

"It?" Kevin asked.

"I suppose *you* is a better word than *it*. What I meant is it's tough to get used to having a red vampyre who acts like a normal, rational person in my kitchen." She snorted and added, "It's almost worth going out with you in the cold and dark to see their reaction."

"I don't expect that it'll be easy for them to accept me," Kevin said.

"You want the truth?"

Kevin nodded.

"It'll take a miracle for them to accept you."

"That's okay." Kevin grinned at her. "I have it on good authority that Nyx is in the miracle business."

"For your sake I hope so." Tina returned to packing the canvas bags.

"For all of our sakes, I hope so," Grandma Redbird said.

"Okay, Miracle Kevin, help me carry these."

Tina loaded Kevin down with as many bags as he could carry, leaving only one for his grandma. Then they followed Tina out the back door and past a built-in pool from which mist was rising like forgotten spirits.

"That looks awesome!" Kevin said.

Tina smiled. "That and the Scotties are my two major indulgences. Well, if you don't count my love of craft beer and pasta. I keep that pool heated all winter. It's a beautiful thing to float in it and stare through the mist up at the stars. Makes me forget how messed up our world has become."

"My friend, would it help to tell you that because of what has happened to Kevin, we have a real chance at defeating Neferet?" Grandma Redbird said.

"Sylvia, I would love to believe we could go back to how it used to be."

"How about more than that?" Kevin spoke up. Both women trained curious looks on him. "How about a world where humans and vampyres are truly allies and friends? Like the two of you are with the Resistance. It's more than possible. I've seen it. It can work, and it makes for a world that's better than what we had here before Neferet started the war."

"You're not from around here, are you, son?"

"Actually, I am. Let's just say I've traveled a lot recently."

"I want Kevin's world," Grandma Redbird said, smiling fondly at her grandson.

"Well, your world sounds good, son. But I'd settle for peace."

"Ma'am, my g-ma taught me not to settle," said Kevin, sending a cheeky grin to his grandma.

"He's a little fresh, but I believe I shall keep him," said Sylvia Redbird.

"I'll tell you what—if you can get the Resistance to trust and accept you, I might believe in that world of yours," said Tina. "*And* I might fix you up with a Scottie pup."

Kevin's grin was like sunrise. "Promise?"

"As long as we're not at war and you give her or him a good home—yes, I promise."

"Deal!" Kevin said.

"Deal," agreed Tina. "Okay, pack the bags in here and take this Polaris."

She opened the hatch of the metal box strapped in where the back seats should have been. Kevin loaded the bags inside after Tina moved the blankets, boxes of matches, and baggies of blood …

"Blood!" Kevin exclaimed. "We're taking them blood?"

"Of course," Tina said, nonplussed. "Vampyres can't live on bread and jam alone."

"But—blood!"

Tina cocked her head. "Young man, in this world where you say humans and vampyres reside as friends, did they also cure the fact that vampyres must have human blood to live?"

"Um, no."

"So, humans there must be fine with vamps drinking blood, correct?" "Yes, I suppose so," Kevin said.

"Well, I'm vegan. I really don't see much difference between drinking human blood and eating a rare steak or a bloody rack of lamb." She shrugged. "I wouldn't do either, but to each his own."

"Who *are* you?" Kevin blurted.

"Just a retired English teacher. Once you teach at a public high school for a couple of decades, not much rattles you."

"Obviously. I wish I could've been in your classroom. I'll bet you weren't boring," Kevin said.

"I'll bet I wasn't either," Tina said. Then she surprised him by giving him a quick hug. "Stay safe. And remember our deal."

"No way am I forgetting that you promised me a puppy!"

"Sylvia, you remember how to get to the ridge, don't you?"

"Oh, I believe so. I seem to recall that we just kept taking right turns," said Grandma.

"That's it. Remember to take care at the gate. You touch that electric wire and it'll fry you."

"I remember," said Grandma. She motioned for Kevin to get behind the wheel. "You're driving, u-we-tsi."

"Slow and steady," Tina said as Kevin started the Polaris. "We've left those old oil trails rough, especially after what happened at Keystone. You'll have to stop and move logs a few times. That's on purpose."

28

"I thought you were under Neferet's protection because of your alfalfa crops," said Grandma Redbird.

"I am, but lately the dogs have been alerting in the middle of the night, and it's not at Dragon and our group. I think the Blue Army has been sniffing around here. Be sure you let Dragon know that."

"I will," said Grandma.

"When you come to the downed tree that's too big to move from the path, that's when you'll be questioned," Tina said.

"I have my code phrase. I am ready," said Grandma.

Tina shook her head. "You know they're going to believe you're under the influence of a red vampyre. They may attack before you can convince them otherwise."

"Then I'll just have to be smarter and faster than they are," said the old woman.

Tina smiled wryly. "Good luck."

"Thank you, ma'am," said Kevin.

"You don't have to thank me for helping the Resistance, son. It's the right thing to do."

"I wasn't thanking you for that. I was thanking you for trusting me—for inviting me in."

"I see. Don't thank me. Just don't make me regret trusting you."

"I won't. I promise."

Kevin put the Polaris into gear and headed in the direction his g-ma pointed—toward a barely discernible dirt path that disappeared into the darkness of the Oklahoma ridge. If he hadn't needed to keep both hands on the wheel to maneuver around ruts and rocks, he would have been cracking the hell out of his knuckles.

# 4

## *Zoey*

"Zoey! Oh, good we found you. Do you have a sec?" a familiar voice shouted from somewhere down the hall.

I forced myself not to sigh, plastered a smile on my face, and turned as Damien and Other Jack wove their way through the busy hallway to me. Then they caught up with me and my smile became genuine.

"Hi, Damien and Jack. Are you two settling in okay? Anything you need?" I asked. The happiness that radiated from them made my heavy heart feel lighter—if only for a moment.

"Ohmygoddess! Everything here is just so fab!" Other Jack gushed, gazing up at Damien with big, love-filled eyes.

Damien's grin was for Jack, but he included me in it, sharing the joy. "Z, we have everything we need—each other."

"And this *awesomesauce* world," Jack added.

"Yes, what Jack said. Actually, we wanted to see if *we* could help *you*," Damien said.

"Well, sure. But what do you mean?"

"We'd like to be involved in the redecoration of the Depot Restaurant," Damien said.

Jack was nodding like a bobblehead doll, though I have to admit he's a lot cuter than your average bobblehead.

"Have you talked to Kramisha? That's really her project," I said.

"We didn't want to until we cleared our idea with you," Damien said.

When both of them just stood there grinning at me, I nudged. "Okay, well, what's the idea?"

"You're gonna love it!" Jack was hopping up and down in barely controlled excitement.

"We should tell her," Damien said.

"Yepper, we should!" Jack said.

And then neither of them told me.

I resisted the urge to strangle both of their ridiculously happy necks, which Damien must have sensed because he cleared his throat and explained.

"So, you know Kramisha already decided to redecorate the restaurant as a big band–era dinner club, right?"

"Yeah, right. We all thought that was a great idea," I said.

"It is, which is why we wanted to bring in some dinner-club specialists," Damien said.

"The gays!" Jack cheered.

"'The gays'?" Now I was totally confused.

"Actually, it would be more accurate to say the LGBTQ community," said Damien. "I went by the Equality Center—you know it's not far from the depot, don't you?"

"Yeah, of course. OKEQ is less than a mile away on Fourth Street. I was there just the other day talking about partnering with them on the next More Color Art Show. I was going to announce it in our next newsletter," I said.

"We know," Jack said. "Toby told us when we were talking about our other idea."

I felt like I was ping-ponging back and forth between the two of them, so I focused on Damien. "Explain, please."

31

"It's simple. Toby Jenkins, the center's director—"

"Yeah, I know Toby," I nodded.

"He's a history buff, and he was thrilled to hear that we're turning the restaurant into a dinner club. He'd like to help us make it not just a beautiful venue with good food and music. He can help us make it *historically accurate*. As in being sure the stage, dance floor, tables, linens, and even the waitstaff's uniforms all are so much like the big band era that people will really feel as if they're stepping back in time when they spend an evening at our restaurant," Damien said.

"That does sound cool," I said. "Which reminds me, Toby told me he has a list of contractors who are proequality and, of course, those are the only contractors we should be hiring. He was going to share that list with me, and then, well …" My words trailed off as we all thought about the events of the past few days.

"Hey, no problem, Z," Damien said kindly. "We'll take care of it for you."

"Yeah, you've had a lot going on. Let us help you with this," said Jack.

"Thank you. Both of you. Yes, I'd appreciate your help, and I think your idea to bring in Toby, and anyone he recommends, is fantastic. Tell Kramisha you definitely have my approval."

"Yippee!" Jack clapped.

"You won't be sorry, Z. The restaurant is going to be spectacular," said Damien. He paused and caught me with his wise gaze. "You look tired."

"Yoga is excellent for stress relief," Jack said. "In my other world, before all that really horrid stuff started to happen, I was a certified yoga instructor. Would you like me to take you through some meditative stretches?"

"Um, not this second," I said. "But if you'd like to teach a few yoga classes here at school I think that would be great."

"Oh. My. Goddess! *Really?* Are you kidding? Would you really let me?"

How could anyone not love this kid? He was like a sparkling unicorn. "Yep, I'll totally let you. Let me get with the School Council and we'll figure out where we can add your class."

Jack hurled himself into my arms, almost knocking me over. "Thank you! Thank you! May I play music? Yoga is always better with music. And hot yoga! Can we have hot yoga too?"

I disentangled myself from Jack. "Sure. Hot yoga sounds good," I lied. *Hot* yoga? Like regular yoga isn't hard enough? "Get a syllabus together, with a supply list, so that I can let the Council know exactly what you need, and we'll figure something out."

"That's great, Z." Damien was still studying me over Jack's exuberant head. "But it looks like you need some rest and stress relief *now*."

"You couldn't be more right," I said. "Which is why I gotta go. I'm on my way to get some barn therapy."

Relief softened Damien's worried expression. "Oh, that's excellent! Grooming Persephone always relaxes you. Have fun. And if anyone asks where you are, I'll tell them you're at the depot."

"That would be wonderful. I just need an hour or so to myself."

"It's yours." Damien put his arm around Jack. "Come on. Let's go talk to Kramisha, and then we can give Toby the good news."

Talking animatedly with their heads together, Jack and Damien headed for the front of the House of Night. I watched them go, trying to hold on to some of the happiness they exuded.

It didn't work. They left and all I felt was tired and sad. Again.

*Come on, Z. Get yourself together and snap out of it! Kevin is back where he has to be, and that's that. That world needs him. In* this *world Heath is dead. Your mom is dead. And we actually defeated Neferet. Get a grip!*

Mentally shaking myself I headed out the back door of the school, turned left, and followed the sidewalk to the rear entrance of the equestrian center. I walked fast, barely nodding to the fledglings who greeted me. I just needed some time alone—some time to relax and not think too much.

The instant I opened the door to the stables I drew a deep breath, inhaling the comforting scents of horse and hay. The class had started, and I could hear Lenobia in the arena, telling her current group of third formers, or freshmen, that horses are *not* big dogs, which had me grinning with nostalgia as I made my way to Persephone's stall. As soon as the roan mare saw me she called a low, rumbly greeting.

"Well, hi right back at you, pretty girl! How are you?" I grabbed the currycomb; a wide, soft brush; and a hoof pick from the cubby outside her stall—as well as a handful of the peppermint treats that were her favorites—and slipped inside with her. Persephone nuzzled me, obviously looking for the candies, which I offered her. I smiled and kissed her wide forehead as she delicately lipped the peppermints from my palm. After I snuggled her some more and kissed her velvet muzzle, the mare returned to her feed and I got to work.

I love grooming horses—Persephone in particular. And her positive energy worked quickly on me. Soon, my mind was empty of everything except braiding her mane and tail, and being sure her hooves were free of even the smallest pebbles.

"Persephone, pretty girl, I wish I could get my hair to shine the way your coat does," I said, resting my chin against her wide, warm neck. She cocked one leg, sighed, and looked very much like she was going to take a nap. I glanced between the stall bars at the stable clock. "Ugh. About twenty minutes and this period will be over and fledglings will be swarming everywhere." What I wouldn't give to be a fledgling again, without a care in the world.

I started to move toward the door to put away the brushes when Persephone sighed again, and, with a very satisfied grunt, curled her long legs under her and plopped down in the middle of her straw-filled stall.

"So, you were serious about that nap, huh?" I turned to the door and then hesitated. "Why the hell not? Maybe some rest will help me snap out of this terrible mood." I dropped the brushes and went to

Persephone. The sweet mare barely opened an eye when I curled up with her, just behind her front legs, resting against her warm belly. "I'm probably not going to actually sleep, though. I haven't been getting much sleep lately," I told her through a giant yawn. Then I put my head on her shoulder, closed my eyes, and went straight to sleep.

(

*Knock! Knock! Knock!* Someone was banging on my door.

*My door? Wait. I'm in the stables with Persephone. Are they banging on my stall door?*

I lifted my head. Dark—it was really, *really* dark. How could it be that dark in the stables?

*Knock! Knock! Knock!*

"Okay, okay! I'm coming!" I said.

*I said? But I didn't say anything.*

A light clicked on and I jumped in shock.

I wasn't in the stables. I was in the dorm. In my old room, but it only kinda looked like my old room. My stuff was there, but the twin bed on the other side of the room was empty. Stevie Rae was nowhere. None of her stuff was there, either. It was like she didn't exist.

*Knock! Knock! Knock!*

"Hey, I'm getting dressed! Sheesh! Hang on!"

I watched a version of myself pull on jeans and a black-and-gold Broken Arrow Tigers sweatshirt.

*What the hell?*

I felt super dizzy and sick, and then my confusion started to clear when I saw that my body was almost completely transparent, and I was hovering a little above the bed.

Then I got it! *Ohhh, I'm asleep. This is a dream—a dream about fledgling me.* Which actually made sense. I mean, I was so stressed out that I was hiding in the barn, napping with my horse, pretty much wishing I was a carefree fledgling. No big surprise I was dreaming that I was a fledgling again.

Only *I* wasn't the fledgling. I was the observer of me, the fledgling.

Okay, so, fine. Dreams are freaky. I looked around the semi-familiar room as "Zoey" hurried to the door. *If Kalona shows up—again—I'm waking up this time. Right away.*

Dream Zoey paused in front of the little mirror over the sink and tried to smooth back her bed head, and I got my first good look at her face.

*Wait, that's wrong. This fledgling Zoey has a regular Mark, like all the other fledglings.*

But, again, I rationalized that that wasn't a big deal. I mean, if I was dreaming about escaping stress by being a fledgling, I definitely didn't want to be the only fledgling with a colored-in Mark. Again.

Dream Zoey opened the door a crack. I saw her body jerk in surprise, and then she stepped back so that she could open the door all the way—*to reveal Neferet standing in the hallway.*

"Ah, hell! Run! This is a sucky dream!" I shouted.

But Dream Z didn't hear me—neither did smarmy Dream Neferet.

"High Priestess! Hello. I, um, would you like to come in?" Dream Zoey asked lamely.

"No! Don't let her into your room!" But, again, neither of them heard me.

"Oh, no, my dear. I am sorry to wake you, as the sun hasn't quite set yet, but I'm afraid you have a rather distraught visitor," said Dream Neferet with sickeningly fake niceness.

"F off, Neferet!" I yelled. Of course they didn't hear me, so I sighed and waited to see what dream weirdness would happen next—and I seriously reconsidered my anticussing stance.

"A distraught visitor? I'm sorry, High Priestess, but I don't understand."

"It's your stepfather. He's rather ..." Neferet paused and

grimaced in obvious dislike, "insistent that you speak with him. He mentioned something about your immortal soul."

"Oh, ugh! Him," Dream me said, and I echoed the thought. *Just tell her to tell him to go away and never come back!*

But Dream Zoey seemed younger and nicer than me—or maybe just younger and more naïve. "Okay, I'll talk to him."

"Excellent. I will escort you to him and remain with you. He really is an unpleasant man."

"Yeah, he sure is, and thanks for staying with me."

Neferet motioned for Dream Zoey to follow her, which she did even though I was yelling, "No, don't go!"

And when Dream Z closed the door I felt myself float after her *and right through the closed door.*

"Okay, this is the weirdest dream I've ever had," I spoke aloud to myself as I drifted after Dream me and Neferet, who were chatting nonchalantly together like Dream Neferet was actually a decent High Priestess and Dream Zoey was just a newly Marked fledgling—kinda like when I'd first been Marked and Neferet had seemed like a mother to me.

I'd been *very* wrong about that, but this was just a dream. It was supposed to be strange.

And the House of Night looked strange too. It seemed somehow darker and emptier than my always-busy, never-sleeping school. In the year since my friends and I had taken over, we'd expanded the human/fledgling program so much that there was usually something going on at all hours.

Not so here. Everything was silent, and the fading light of the setting sun did nothing to alleviate the sense of gloom.

"Um, aren't we going the wrong way?" My dream-self's question pulled my attention back to her and I saw that Neferet had led Dream Zoey out a back door of the school, instead of toward the administrative offices in the front of the main building.

"Oh, I apologize. I should have explained. Your stepfather

refuses to enter campus. One of the Warriors discovered him lurking outside the east wall." Neferet paused and gave my dream-self a big, pretend smile. "That didn't sound very charitable of me. I should have chosen another word than *lurk*."

Dream Zoey's cheeks blazed pink and she shook her head in disgust. "No, that's the perfect word. And I'm the one who needs to apologize. Again. My stepfather is awful. A total religious hypocrite, filled with hate and judgment." Dream me shuddered. "Getting Marked and being able to move away from him was a relief. I'll talk to him and be sure he doesn't come back here and bother you or any other vampyre."

"Oh, my dear, please do not worry about a human man being a bother. That's nothing new. That's what human men seem to do best—bother their betters."

Dream Zoey didn't appear to know what to say to that, and about then Neferet picked up her pace, so both of us had to hurry to keep up with her as she strode across the lawn, heading straight to the trapdoor in the east wall.

"The east wall. That figures. Horrible stuff always happens there," I mumbled.

But Dream Zoey couldn't hear me, so we followed Neferet to the trapdoor, which she tripped by pressing the stone stamped **1926**, the year the wall was built. I floated through the opening behind them out to the area just outside the wall. If the sun hadn't set yet, it sure seemed like it had, because it was so dark under the arms of the giant old oaks framing the wall that we were all cast in shadow.

"John?" Dream Zoey called, looking around the dark, empty area. "It's me. Zoey. What did you need to tell me?"

Dream me was searching the area, hands on hips, obviously exasperated. But my attention wasn't on Dream Zoey. It was on Neferet. The High Priestess had stayed close to the wall, where I noticed a wooden fencepost had been stuck into the ground—you know, like something a rancher would use to string barbed-wire on.

But there were no barbed-wire fences in midtown Tulsa. What the hell was going on?

Neferet went to the fencepost and opened a big duffel bag that was lying behind it—*and unsheathed a long, dangerous-looking sword.*

I understood in a flash. The fencepost was way too much like the one I'd found Professor Nolan staked to, without her head.

"Zoey! Get the *hell* out of here!" I yelled at my clueless dream-self, but that Z did nothing but peer around looking for her annoying stepfather.

Soundlessly, Neferet approached her from behind, carrying the sword with two hands, looking like a samurai assassin.

"Ohmygoddess, turn around!"

Dream Zoey didn't hear me, but she did turn as she said, "Neferet, I think he took off. I'm really sorry this was such a waste of your time and you had to—" Her words cut off as she saw Neferet's sword.

"Oh, my dear, there is *absolutely* no need to apologize. And things have gone *exactly* as I planned. When they find you they will believe this was the work of humans—the People of Faith in particular. I will have my war." Neferet's smile was feral—a victorious baring of her teeth. "And you will never have to be bothered by your ridiculous stepfather again. I consider it a win for both of us."

Dream Zoey's eyes looked glassy with shock, and she kept shaking her head back and forth, back and forth. In a little girl's voice she repeated over and over, "No, I don't understand … I don't understand … I don't—"

I screamed as Neferet whirled around in an arc that was as graceful as it was deadly, and with one single strike she severed Dream Zoey's head from her body. Blood sprayed everywhere as the body collapsed, twitching spasmodically.

*So much blood! There's so much blood!*

I couldn't stop screaming. I wanted to close my eyes. I wanted to wake up. But I was frozen in place, hovering over my dream-self as Neferet wiped her sword on the ground and then returned to the duffel bag to pull out rope and a rough, homemade plaque that had scrawled on it: **THOU SHALT NOT SUFFER A WITCH TO LIVE! EXODUS 22:18**.

I recognized the Bible quote. It had been the same one found on Professor Nolan's crucified, headless body.

And then I heard her. Heard *me*. My gaze went from Neferet to the severed head that had rolled to land in a bloody pool beneath me, face up. As I stared in horror at it, the eyes opened suddenly and my own voice blasted inside my head.

*You have to help Kevin stop her—nothing else matters!*

From behind me someone grabbed my shoulder, and I screamed so loud it felt like my voice was tearing …

"Z! It's just me! It's okay!"

Still screaming, I sat up, smacking into Stark and almost breaking his nose. Persephone snorted and laid her ears back, as if looking for something to attack.

"Sssh, all is well, sweet mare." Lenobia was suddenly there too, soothing Persephone while she sent me worried looks.

"Stark?" I glanced frantically around us, my heart beating so hard and fast I could feel it in my temples. *I'm in the stall with Persephone. It was just a dream. It wasn't real.*

"Hey, yeah, of course it's me. What the hell's going on? I felt your fear like a branding iron. What happened?"

I opened my mouth to tell him about the dream—and I couldn't. Because I realized I was wrong. It hadn't been *just a dream.* It was a message. A message I had to, for now, keep to myself.

"Stark!" I let him pull me into his strong, safe arms. "I'm so sorry." I turned my head so I could see Lenobia. Persephone had stood, and she was pressed against the horse mistress, looking frightened and worried. "Oh, no! I scared Persephone too!" Stark helped me to my feet and I went to the mare, petting and kissing her. "I'm so, so sorry, pretty girl. I'm okay. Everything is okay."

"No. It's not. I could feel how terrified you were. What. The. Hell. Happened?" Stark asked.

I attempted a laugh, which came out more as a sob. "This is really embarrassing. It was just a dream."

"But often your dreams are more than just images from your imagination," said Lenobia, not unkindly. "Last time a dream woke you, it was Kalona."

"Only it wasn't *really* Kalona," Stark added. "So what was it?"

I wiped sweat from my face. "You guys, I really am sorry. It wasn't anything like the Kalona/not-Kalona dream. It was spiders."

"Spiders?" Lenobia said.

I nodded and shivered. "Spiders."

Stark sighed and pulled me back into his arms. "She's terrified of spiders," he explained to Lenobia.

"In my dream I fell into a pool of them. It was awful," I lied—feeling pool-of-spiders-awful about it.

"Well, that's a relief," said Lenobia. "But, Zoey, if spiders frighten you that much, you really should look into hypnotherapy. One of the High Priestesses at the St. Louis House of Night is a specialist in it. I'm sure she could help you."

"Thanks, I'll keep that in mind. I'm usually not bothered by my spider phobia much."

"But you've been stressed and not sleeping," said Stark. "So, maybe you could use some therapy."

"Yeah, maybe. If I have another dream like that, definitely."

Stark kissed my forehead. "Hey, would some *psaghetti madness* make you feel better? You slept through lunch, so it's almost dinnertime."

I didn't show how shocked I was to find out I'd slept for *hours* instead of twenty minutes or so. Instead I nodded and tried to appear enthusiastic. "Psaghetti *always* makes me feel better."

"That's what I thought," said Stark, taking my hand. "It's been a long day for me too. Let's go eat."

"Sounds good." I kissed Persephone one more time and smiled sheepishly at Lenobia as we left the stall. "Sorry about scaring you. I really do feel stupid about that."

Lenobia was looking at me with her sharp, gray eyes. "You are forgiven," she said. "And, High Priestess, if you need to talk, please remember I am here for you."

"Thank you! I'll remember." I closed the stall door. Hand in hand, Stark and I left the stables, heading to the dining hall.

*I'll talk about it, but only when I've decided exactly what I'm going to do and how I'm going to do it.* Truth be told, I already had an idea. I glanced at Stark, knowing he would be my biggest obstacle. He was going to be mad. Real mad.

*Ah, hell . . .*

# 5

# *Other Kevin*

"You look cold, G-ma. Next time I stop to move one of those logs from the path I'll get you a blanket from that box behind us. I don't want you getting sick."

The old woman waved away her grandson's worry. "U-we-tsi, I still cleanse myself in the stream that runs behind my house. It is always cold. I am fine. And we're almost to the top of the ridge. I believe next time we stop, we won't be alone."

"What is this land?" Kevin peered around them, looking through the darkness at the wilds of an Oklahoma ridge filled with old-growth oaks, waist-tall grasses, and lots and lots of sandstone boulders.

Grandma gestured at the rough dirt path the sturdy Polaris had been bumping along. "These are old oil trails—and I do mean *old*. They were established right around 1901 and, lucky for us, they dried up in 1902, well before they thought to tame all of this, or at the very least widen these paths and pave them. Tina's people on her mother's side were leaders of the Creek Nation, and the ownership of this huge section of land passed to her. She's been protecting it for decades."

"So, the electric fence happened before the war started?"

"No. That was an addition she made this past year—quietly, using only those of us who are allied with the Resistance. She knows it won't stop an attack by the Red Army, but it certainly dissuades random snoopers and poachers."

"I'll bet this is really pretty during the day. It'd be easy to imagine we were living a hundred years ago."

"It would, indeed."

"It'd be more fun imagining if there weren't so many spiders, though. With no windshield or top to this thing, we're like spider magnets." Kevin grimaced as he raised the thick stick he'd broken off at their first stop, waving it in front of him and G-ma, trying to let it snag spiderwebs before their faces did.

"Spiders eat ticks and mosquitoes, u-we-tsi. They are merely a nuisance for us." Her brows lifted. "Unless, like Zoeybird, you're afraid of them?"

"G-ma, my manliness says that it's better if I don't answer that question."

Kevin drove on enjoying the sound of his grandma's sweet laughter. Soon, though, he found that he had no choice but to let the spiderwebs decorate his face as he had to keep both hands on the wheel and concentrate so the Polaris wouldn't tip over when the way grew more and more treacherous. His headlights caught a huge tree, fallen like a sleeping giant over the path, and he slowed down to a crawl.

"That must be the final barricade," he said.

"Ready yourself, u-we-tsi. Drive directly up to the tree and then stop. Cut the motor immediately."

Kevin swallowed his nerves and did as she told him to do. He drove to the huge felled tree, put the vehicle in park, and cut the engine. And as he did so, his little old grandma totally shocked him by climbing lithely up to stand on the bench seat of the Polaris, so close to him her leg pressed against his arm. She poked her head up through the roll bars, drew a big breath, and then shouted.

44

"I'm trying to harvest mustard plants by the light of the moon. That's when they are most potent!"

"Is that true, G-ma?"

"Of course not. It's my code phrase. Now, shush."

There was a sound like the rustling of wind through tall grass and from the huge oaks surrounding them, half a dozen blue vampyres dropped—swords held up at the ready as they formed a tightening circle around the Polaris.

A short, powerfully built vampyre whose face held an intricate tattoo of two dragons roaring fire stepped to within a few feet of Kevin. He held a longsword with both hands and his attention was centered on Kevin. "Red vampyre—set Sylvia Redbird free. She does not deserve to lose her life along with you tonight."

Sylvia stepped carefully across Kevin, so that she perched between her grandson and the blue vampyre's sword.

"Merry meet, Dragon."

Dragon Lankford's eyes narrowed, and still he didn't speak directly to the old woman, but continued to command Kevin. "Free her."

Slowly, carefully, Kevin lifted his hands from the steering wheel, holding them up, palms out. "My grandma is completely free."

"Sylvia, come to me," said Dragon.

"Only if you give me your word you will hear me out before you behead my grandson."

Dragon's gaze flicked to the old woman. "Your grandson?"

"Yes, my friend. This is Kevin. He comes in peace as your ally, just as I do."

Hard and flat, Dragon's gaze went back to Kevin. "Then I am sorry for the pain his death will cause you."

"Dragon, you must listen to me. If you don't, if you slaughter without thought, how are you different than Neferet and her army of red monsters?"

Dragon Lankford paused long enough to glance sadly at Sylvia again. "I do not blame you for leading him here. You are clearly under his influence. You will forgive me when you are yourself once more."

Kevin's sight, which was preternaturally sharp, caught the cues an instant before Dragon struck. All Kevin could imagine was what that razor-like longsword could do to his little old grandma. He moved with blurring speed as Dragon lunged, grabbing his spider stick and deflecting the sword while he hurled himself in front of her. Knocked to the side, the blow that was meant to sever his head from his neck streaked across his back from shoulder to shoulder.

At first, he didn't feel any pain—just a tug and the sudden heat of his blood gushing down his back.

Grandma Redbird screamed and fell forward across Kevin's body, blocking Dragon's next, fatal blow.

"Sylvia! Move away from him!" Dragon ordered.

"Smell his blood!" shouted Sylvia. "Smell it, Dragon! His isn't like the rest of the red vampyres!" Pressed against her grandson's bleeding body, Sylvia's anger was almost palpable. "You will have to kill me to get to him!"

"Bryan, wait."

Through a haze of shock, Kevin watched a woman step to the Swordmaster's side and gently touch his arm. Her beauty was ethereal, making her look like one of the ancient fey. Kevin thought her long blond hair seemed to hold a light of its own. And a huge raven perched serenely on her shoulder.

"My love, our friend Sylvia is correct. This boy's blood does not smell of death."

That had Dragon's sword wavering. The Warrior drew a deep breath, and his eyes widened. He moved forward, easily plucking Grandma Redbird away from Kevin and depositing her on the side of the path near the raven woman, before Dragon pressed the sword against Kevin's neck.

"Is this dark magick? Has the Red Army learned to cloak their scent?" Dragon demanded.

"No," Kevin gasped, trying to speak through the pain blazing across his back. "Not dark magick—love. Nyx interceded and returned my humanity. Please don't hurt my grandma."

And then the ethereal beauty was there. Easily brushing aside the killer sword, she touched Kevin's face, smiling sweetly at him, and he realized who the beauty must be—Anastasia, Dragon Lankford's mate. "Bryan, look beyond your anger and *see* this boy."

Dragon smoothly sheathed the longsword in the scabbard strapped across his back. Then he stepped up to within a hand's distance of Kevin, who was trying his best not to slump over the steering wheel. The Warrior sniffed at him and studied his Mark.

"What are you?" he finally said.

"A vampyre boy you almost killed," said Sylvia Redbird as she pushed past Dragon. "This wound needs to be bandaged. He's losing too much blood."

"We will tend to him. Can you walk?" the beauty asked Kevin.

Dragon spoke before Kevin could make his voice work. "No, Anastasia. Different or not, he is still a red vampyre, and therefore our enemy. I need to make an end of him."

"My love, we must not lose our ability to show mercy or, as Sylvia so succinctly said, there will be no difference between us and Neferet's monsters. Trust me. I have a feeling about this boy."

Dragon looked at his mate for a long moment before nodding. It was a curt nod, but it was still a nod. "We will tend him and hear his story. We are not monsters."

Anastasia kissed Dragon's cheek as the raven on her shoulder watched Kevin with dark, intelligent eyes. "Of course we are not." She turned back to Kevin, repeating, "Can you walk?"

"Yeah. I think so." He started to slide his legs around and get out of the Polaris. Before he could stop himself, Kevin gasped at the flood of pain. Bright specks of light blossomed in his vision. He would have fallen had Anastasia not caught him. "I'm—I'm s-sorry," he said through chattering teeth.

"Bryan! This boy is wounded badly," said the beauty while her raven took flight, squawking indignantly.

"There are blood and blankets in the container with the rest of the supplies Tina sent." Grandma Redbird hurried to the carry-all in the rear of the Polaris, returning to Kevin's side with two rolled up blankets and an armful of blood baggies. She rolled out a blanket onto the path in the space between the Polaris and the fallen tree, and tossed the second blanket at Dragon. "Use that sword for something besides hurting children. Cut this into strips."

Kevin thought he heard Dragon mutter, "Yes, ma'am," but it was hard to tell through the ringing in his ears.

"U-we-tsi, Anastasia and I are going to help you lay down on that blanket. Then we're going to bandage that cut. But first drink a couple of these. They'll help."

"A-Anastasia?" Kevin stuttered. "Y-you are Dragon's mate, r-right? M-my sister told me to f-find you. She d-d-didn't say anything about you having a bird, though." His hands were shaking too badly to hold the baggie, so G-ma held it to his lips as he drank first one, then a second and a third.

"Yes, of course I am Dragon's mate, and Tatsuwa isn't a bird. He's a raven. If he hears you calling him a bird he'll never forgive you." Anastasia spoke to Kevin in a calm, soothing voice. "Okay, let's move him." She sent her mate a pointed look, and the next thing Kevin knew a wash of pain and surprise threatened to drown him as the compact Warrior pulled him from the vehicle as if he weighed no more than a toddler, and carried him to the blanket, plopping him down on it, face-first.

Determined not to cry out, Kevin bit a bloody hole in his cheek as his grandma and Anastasia pressed strips of blanket against the weeping wound and then helped him sit so they could tie the bandages into place around his chest and upper arms.

"I feel weird," Kevin said. "Kinda like I'm floating."

"The cut is long and deep, but you will recover," said Anastasia. "I will sew it closed as soon as we get you back with us."

"You're really pretty," Kevin blurted.

"Hrumph," said Dragon from where he stood close beside his wife, still watching Kevin warily.

"Thank you. And you are being a very good patient," said Anastasia, ignoring her mate.

"There. That is as good as we can do here," said Grandma Redbird. "I don't think he should try to walk. The bleeding hasn't actually stopped. The more he moves the worse it's going to be."

"Agreed." Anastasia looked up at her mate and raised one arched blond brow. "Bryan?"

Dragon Bryan Lankford sighed. "Johnny B and Erik—get the rest of the supplies from the Polaris."

"Erik?" Kevin turned his head so that he could see the tall, young vampyre. "Erik Night?"

Erik glanced his way. "Yeah, I'm Erik Night."

"I loved you as Superman! But, uh, I thought you'd died. That's the rumor in the Red Army."

Erik snorted. "The only thing that's dead about me is my acting career—killed by Neferet's bullshit."

"Hey! That's enough chitchat. You two get the supplies like I said." Dragon sent Kevin a dark look before turning to Grandma Redbird. "Sylvia, I assume you are coming with your grandson and not returning to Tina's ranch tonight?"

"You assume correctly."

Dragon sighed again. "Drew, hide the Polaris. The rest of you spread out down the ridge and be sure the Red Army isn't following him. And I mean way down the ridge. Cover all the paths that lead from Lone Star Road especially." He raised his voice and called, "Erik! On second thought, let Johnny B unload the supplies. You cut down the side of the ridge that faces Tina's place and be sure she doesn't light a warning fire."

"Will do!"

"No one's following me. They don't know I'm here," Kevin said.

"It'd be best if you don't speak," Dragon told him.

"It doesn't hurt more or less if I speak," Kevin said, attempting to smile at the scowling vampyre.

"I meant best for me." In one movement Dragon bent and hooked his arms around Kevin, lifting him in a fireman's carry and draping him over his broad back. Then the Warrior turned to his mate. "I'll follow you."

"Of course you will, my love," Anastasia said.

The last thing Kevin heard before he slipped into blissful unconsciousness was Anastasia Lankford's musical laughter and her raven's call as he circled above them.

# 6

# *Other Kevin*

Kevin regained consciousness to the sound of an argument.

"He can't climb up to any of the hunters' blinds. We need to take him to the cave," Anastasia was saying.

"I'm not comfortable with that," Dragon retorted. "If he knows we're digging out a cave, then there's a chance the Red Army will know it too."

"My love, the boy already knows the way here. He knows Tina is an ally. If he betrays us it will be like Keystone Park all over again, and we will never be able to return here," said Anastasia.

"Kevin will not betray you," his grandma said. "Dragon Lankford, you can smell that he is not like the others. He does not act like the others. There is an explanation for what has happened to him, but that explanation will not matter if my grandson dies of the wound you inflicted upon him."

It took several tries, but eventually Kevin made his voice work and, even though he hardly spoke above a whisper, his face was near Dragon's ear and the Swordmaster had no trouble hearing him. "Please put me down."

"Kevin? Are you back with us?" Grandma Redbird reached up to wipe Kevin's sweat-filled hair from his eyes.

"P-please. I'd rather bleed to death than be carried any farther."

"Bryan Lankford, carry that boy to the cave. Now."

Kevin felt Dragon's sigh, but the powerful Warrior did as his mate commanded. He followed a narrow path from what Kevin could make out was a flat, grassy area at the top of the ridge, down and around several enormous sandstone boulders, finally coming to a narrow cliff-side opening. Wan, flickering light from within cast dancing shadows against the rocks as Dragon paused while Anastasia slipped inside. Moments later, three hooded figures scurried out. They didn't look up or around, but kept their heads tucked down, hiding their faces as they eased past Dragon, Kevin, and Grandma Redbird.

"Okay, bring the boy inside," Anastasia's voice drifted to them.

Dragon turned sideways so that he and his burden could fit within. He unceremoniously dumped Kevin on the rocky floor of the small cave, and Kevin's world went temporarily gray with bright spots.

"You could have been gentler," admonished Anastasia.

"I could have killed him and saved all of us the trouble he's going to bring," retorted Dragon.

"My grandson brings hope, not trouble, Dragon Lankford," said Grandma Redbird firmly.

"Sylvia, forgive me for saying this, but of course that is what you would think. He is your family. The great loyalty you show for him is admirable, whether it is justified or not," said Dragon.

As Kevin's vision cleared he saw his grandma face down the Swordmaster. Hands on her slim hips, her wild silver-streaked hair flying around her shoulders, he'd never heard her sound so angry.

"Kevin was Marked more than one year ago. He Changed shortly after that. Have I ever even mentioned him to you?"

"No, but—"

"No! I have not," she interrupted. "And I have not because I would not, *could not* put the Resistance in danger, and yet here I am. Suddenly bringing my grandson to you—a grandson who is clearly a red vampyre, but who smells no different than you and who acts perfectly rational."

"Sylvia, since the murders of Lenobia and Travis, the safety of the Resistance is my job. There have been so many deaths, and if there is even a chance of your grandson compromising us, then we must take every precaution. Do you think it gives me pleasure to behead a boy? It is no fault of his that he was Marked red. I'm no monster, Sylvia Redbird."

"Of course you aren't, my love." Anastasia carried an oil lantern to Kevin and placed it in a niche in the rock near them before dropping a large leather satchel beside him. She opened it and began searching through it as she spoke. "But Sylvia does have a point. She has been working with us for many months and never once attempted to bring her grandson here."

"Because it wouldn't have been safe to bring me here before it happened," Kevin forced himself to speak. "No matter how hard I tried to hold on to my humanity."

"Don't speak yet. Let me get this wound stitched," Anastasia said as she unwound the makeshift bandages. "Sylvia, there are several bottles of clean water there in the rear of the cave. Would you bring them to me, please?"

Sylvia hurried to the back of the little cave, returning with a couple liter bottles of fresh water, which she handed to Anastasia. "What can I do to help?"

Anastasia passed her a wad of gauze. "Dab the blood away as I stitch so that I can see what I'm doing." She held up a long, hooked needle that was threaded with dark suture material. "Kevin, I'm afraid this is going to be quite unpleasant for the both of us—though for you more than me."

"It's okay. It's not as bad as feeling my humanity slipping away from me."

"What happened to you? What changed you?" Dragon suddenly demanded.

Anastasia's eyes flashed as she looked up at her mate, who was standing near the entrance to the cave, arms folded, a dark expression shadowing his handsome face.

"You may question him after I sew him up."

"I'd rather talk. It'll take my mind off it," Kevin said.

"Very well. I'm going to begin. First I'll pour alcohol over the wound. It will be very painful."

"I'm ready. Okay, so, what happened to me? Well, I—!" Kevin's words broke off in a terrible gasp. It felt like Anastasia was pouring liquid fire on his back and he had to struggle to stay conscious.

"Breathe, u-we-tsi. Breathe. Deeply, in and out, in and out. This will pass," Grandma soothed as she blotted his back.

Kevin fisted his hands and drew several long breaths with his g-ma.

"And now I will begin the sewing. The good news is that this is a long, straight wound. You'll have a scar, but it should heal well."

"It beats losing my head," Kevin managed through gritted teeth.

When she started sewing he thought he was going to pass out—wished he would pass out, but when he didn't, Kevin turned his concentration to his story and tried to pretend he was outside his body, standing beside Dragon, looking out at the cold winter night as he spoke.

"Three nights ago, I was part of a group of red vampyre soldiers and fledgling trainees who were pulled from our quarters in the tunnels under the depot and dropped into an alternative world." Kevin had to pause and draw several breaths as the pain in his back threatened to overwhelm him.

"What do you mean by alternative world?" Dragon said.

"That world is just like this one, only Neferet isn't in charge there. My sister is."

Anastasia's busy hands paused. "Zoey?"

"You knew my sister?"

"I did. She was a lovely young woman. She was only in my Spells and Rituals class a few weeks before she was killed, but she already showed promise with spellwork. You remember her, do you not, Bryan?"

"I remember that her death was the official beginning of Neferet's war," Dragon said.

"Neferet killed her," Kevin said.

"How do you know that?" Dragon asked sharply.

"Because in the other House of Night world, Neferet tried to start a war with humans the same way—by framing humans for vampyre deaths she was actually responsible for."

"And your dead sister told you that?" Dragon said.

"No, my alive sister told me that—at the Tulsa House of Night where she is one of several powerful High Priestesses who run everything. Zo and her group defeated Neferet and stopped the war from happening."

"Boy, you just made your first mistake. Their number is few, but we do have spies in the Red Army camp. I can check with them about this disappearance yarn you're spinning."

"Good," Kevin said between gritted teeth as Anastasia hooked the needle through another piece of his torn flesh. "I want you to. Have your people ask what happened to General Dominick and his soldiers."

"I will. You may count on that."

"Good," Kevin repeated.

"But until then, let's say I believe you. How did being pulled into another version of our world restore your humanity?"

"It was something Nyx did after she gifted Aphrodite with the ability to grant second chances."

"Aphrodite?" Dragon laced the name with sarcasm. "You mean the blue priestess who has death visions?"

"That's her. Only in that world she's a Prophetess of Nyx who is as powerful as she is beautiful."

Dragon scoffed. "Well, in *this* world she's practically useless, unless you're so besotted by her beauty that you can overlook her selfish indulgences and petty greed."

"But even here she's a Prophetess," Kevin said.

"She's a Prophetess who has visions she can rarely interpret. Even before Anastasia and I fled to join the Resistance there were rumblings that Neferet was displeased with her."

"And why wouldn't she be?" Anastasia said as she continued to sew sutures along Kevin's back. "I loathe everything Neferet stands for, but Aphrodite is a terrible Prophetess. She uses her beauty and her Goddess-given gift to manipulate. I truly believe she withholds information from her visions unless she believes she can gain from them. I don't understand why Neferet doesn't rid herself of the creature."

"I do. Aphrodite is a master at knowing how far she can push Neferet. When she's pushed too far, Aphrodite simply has a vision that is suddenly clear enough to interpret, and that *coincidental* vision is also of high value to Neferet," Dragon said.

"She's different in the other world," Kevin insisted. "She sacrificed her humanity to save the first red fledglings. And since then, in that world, *every red fledgling and vampyre has the ability to maintain their humanity.* All because of Aphrodite."

"And because of that difference, Kevin believes he can reach the Aphrodite who is in this world and convince her to make the same sacrifice," Grandma Redbird added.

There was a long silence during which Kevin tried to think through the blazing pain in his back for something more—something that would convince Dragon that he was telling the truth.

When Dragon spoke again, Kevin heard the change in his voice. It was only slight, but some of the sarcasm and anger seemed to be missing. "What makes you think Aphrodite is reachable? The Prophetess you describe has little in common with the one in our world."

"Because even in another world, who we are at our core seems not to change too much. The only difference is that we have been through alternative life experiences, which have the power to change our personalities and our reactions," Kevin said. "Zoey told me to find you and Anastasia in this world. She said you would help me defeat Neferet because you helped her in that world."

"Are Bryan and I mated in that world too?"

Kevin considered not telling her, but he rejected that thought quickly. The truth was one of the few strengths he had, and he wasn't about to start lying and messing that up.

"You were," he told Anastasia.

"Were?" Dragon said.

"You were killed. I'm not sure how. Zoey didn't have time to tell me that. Only that you died bravely saving others."

"We both are dead?" Anastasia's voice sounded shaky.

"Yes. I'm sorry," Kevin said.

Anastasia's bloody hand rested gently on his shoulder for a moment. "Don't be. If my Bryan perished, I would not wish to live without him."

"And I would not draw breath in a world without you, my love," Dragon said.

From the corner of his eye, Kevin saw Anastasia turn and look up at her mate. "And it is your capacity to love that makes you more than your sword—more than a dragon. Think of it, Bryan. If it is true—if Kevin can reach Aphrodite and convince her to repeat whatever it was she did in that other world—*Neferet's war would be drastically changed.*"

"Yeah," Kevin said. "She wouldn't have an army of mindless weapons. She would only have the blue officers and the Sons of Erebus Warriors, and how many of them would stay faithful to her and fight for her if they realized Nyx didn't bless this war?"

"She would lose power, but perhaps not enough to stop the war," Dragon said thoughtfully. "She has been careful to only put Warriors in key positions of power who seek more—more land, more riches, more of everything."

"But at least we'd have a fighting chance then," Kevin insisted. "Dragon, I saw what happens when red vampyres and fledglings have their humanity restored, and I promise you, none of them will ever fight again."

"Where are they, these other changed red vampyres and fledglings?" Dragon asked.

"Still in the other world. Zoey would have had to force them to come back here, and she refused to do that. It was a terrible shock when they returned to themselves and realized what they had done. Several of them committed suicide before we could stop them."

"And how about you? Why weren't you devastated and suicidal?" the Swordmaster asked.

"Because I was different from the moment I was Marked. I held on to more of my humanity than anyone knew, and because of that I made sure that I didn't—"

Suddenly from outside the cave came the warning cries of a raven, immediately followed by a flurry of activity. The bird flew frantically to Anastasia as Erik Night rushed to Dragon.

*"Danger! Danger! Danger!"* the raven shrieked as he landed on Anastasia's shoulder.

"Tina's lit a warning fire!" Erik told Dragon.

Kevin was too busy staring at the raven and wondering if normal ravens could actually speak or if this one was magickal, when Dragon whirled around, staring at him.

"You traitorous little bastard!" Dragon hurled the words at Kevin.

"No! It's not me! It couldn't be me. I—I didn't even go to the barracks yesterday. I went straight to Grandma Redbird's farm when I got back."

Another blue vampyre rushed into the cave. Between panting breaths, he announced, "Soldiers of the Red Army are coming up the ridge!"

Dragon Lankford strode to Kevin and grabbed his arm in a viselike grip, lifting him to his feet and dragging him to the mouth of the cave.

"Before I kill you, you're going to tell me how many soldiers you led here!"

7

*Other Stark*

"Lieutenant Dallas, explain to me again why the hell we're out here in the middle of nowhere on a cold-ass winter's night when I could be in my quarters with a roaring fire, worshipping my current priestess flavor of the month?"

The slight young vampyre rushed up to Stark. His adult blue Mark looked like lightning bolts, which made sense because of his weird affinity for electricity, but Stark thought it looked ridiculous on his ferret-like face.

"Well, General, like I told Artus, today our security sweeps were in Sapulpa and Sand Springs. At the Reasor's grocery at the corner of Taft and Hickory here in Sapulpa, the manager reported that he was sure he saw Erik Night in a group of blue vamps who were lurking around the parking lot."

"Well, Night did join the Resistance a few months ago, but why are we *here* if he was spotted in town?"

"'Cause I did some digging with a lieutenant of the Red Army, and he was able to *encourage*," Dallas enunciated the word with malicious glee, "some of the locals to admit that they've been noticin' strange lights and such comin' from this here ridge. Most of the local yokels think it's haunted—talked some nonsense about it belonging to the Creek Tribe for generations. Said the ghosts even chased oil drillers out in the early nineteen hundreds, but I don't believe that crap." They were standing on the side of a road named Lone Star that meandered along the ridge. Dallas pointed at eight strands of thick wire that seemed to frame the entire wild acreage that made up the area called Polecat Ridge. "So, I poked around and found this."

"A fence? There's farmland all over here that's fenced in. Why is this an issue?" Stark said.

"'Cause this isn't farmland. The ridge has gone wild. No one's done anything with it since early last century. So why's it protected by high-voltage wire?"

"That's hot?" Stark took a step closer to the wire and did pick up a faint hum and something that felt different in the air.

"Very. I tried to talk to the old woman who owns the ridge, but she wasn't very helpful—and she's protected by Neferet's directive because she also owns the best alfalfa fields in the entire state—so I couldn't be as *persuasive* as I wanted to be."

"She had to give you an answer, though."

"Yes, sir. And she did. She told me that she breeds a special kind of deer—one that Neferet also loves."

"White-tail deer." Stark nodded. "Neferet likes venison. A lot. I didn't realize this was her supplier."

"Yeah, it's that same old Tina woman who owns this ridge and the fields all around here. Anyway, she said she breeds special deer and lets 'em roam free on the ridge because they're healthier that way, so their meat is better. That's why she ran high-voltage wire all around her property—to keep the deer in and as many predators out as possible."

"I guess that makes sense. Did you ask her about activity on her ridge?"

"Yes, sir. Got nothing from her. She said it's quiet out here, which is why she lives here, *away* from people. She also said she polices her own ridge, keeping poachers out, and that she doesn't need or want our help. Then she shut her gate in my face."

"Not surprising," Stark muttered. And it wasn't. Since Neferet's war humans had suffered. Not that he was overly concerned with humans. The only thing Stark was overly concerned with was his own skin—life was easier that way—especially these days. But humans hiding behind closed doors and showing nothing but fear and/or loathing for vampyres didn't help the fight against the damnable, pain-in-the-ass Resistance.

"So, when I reported everything to Artus he said the ridge needed to be checked out—and that's why we're out here."

"All right, well, did the old woman turn off the juice to that fence?" Stark asked, keeping a healthy distance from the thick wires.

"No, but we don't need her to do that. I can get us in there with no problemo."

"Well, get it done," said Stark.

He turned from Dallas to motion to the first of the five Humvees parked behind his lead vehicle. The driver obeyed immediately, and red vampyre soldiers and their officers in charge began unloading. Stark made a hold motion, which was passed down the line, but he needn't have had the soldiers pause. Dallas had gone to the fence and pressed his hand to the post closest to him. The young vampyre's eyes were closed, and the expression on his face almost looked like he was experiencing pleasure—which wouldn't have surprised Stark. He'd always thought Dallas was a strange one.

When Dallas lifted his head a moment later and looked back at Stark, his eyes were glowing with a bizarre yellow light.

"Have the soldiers climb over the fence here." Dallas kept both of his hands on the post, jerking his chin to the left of him. "Tell them to hurry. She's got a lot of volts going through here. I can only hold them for a few minutes."

"You heard the lieutenant, get the men moving!" Stark shouted.

Stark stood back and watched the red vamps crawling over the fence. *They look like fucking ravenous roaches.* Stark didn't let himself shiver, even though it felt as if bugs were crawling over his own skin. *The Red Army is necessary*, he reminded himself sternly. Plus, it wasn't like they could be offended. They didn't give a damn about how disgusting they were; all they gave a damn about was their insatiable hunger.

"Your turn, General." Dallas' words pulled Stark out of his thoughts, and he quickly made his way over the fence. "Okay, let's spread out and form a loose line, then we'll move that line up the ridge."

They'd been walking for about fifteen minutes, pushing their way through winter-brown undergrowth and forest debris before they found a rough dirt path barely wide enough for an ATV, though it was obvious it had been used recently.

"This doesn't look good," Stark said. "Lieutenant, did you see any ATVs on the old woman's property?"

"Yes, sir. Saw a couple of those fancy things that look like souped-up golf carts. She drove one down to the gate to talk to me."

"Polaris," Stark said, studying the tracks.

"Pardon, sir?"

Stark looked up at Dallas. "That's the name of the vehicles. And these tracks look like they were made by one. Might not be as bad as I thought. The old woman could actually just be checking for poachers. But let's follow this trail up a ways and be sure."

"Yes, sir!"

After about thirty more minutes of walking and there was a shout from Stark's right. "Incoming!"

Stark pulled his ever-present bow from the sling across his back and nocked an arrow. Six deer, thoroughly spooked and wide-eyed, bounded past them, causing the red soldiers to mill uncertainly as they stared after the moving venison, obviously considering whether they should chase down this prey or wait for more delicious and slower moving two-legged dinner.

Stark frowned in disgust. "Dallas! Get those soldiers under control. No one kills a deer without Neferet's permission. Be sure those eating machines understand that."

"Yes, sir!" Dallas sprinted back down the path.

Stark could hear him yelling at the Red Army lieutenants, and he was, for the second time that night, annoyed as hell that General Dominick and his squad of soldiers had seemed to suddenly disappear a few days ago. Dominick was widely acknowledged as the most ruthless and intelligent of the red generals, which meant his soldiers were always the most disciplined.

"Fucking undependable Red Army," Stark muttered. He made a mental note to try to get Neferet to consider phasing as many of them out as possible in the day-to-day running of the war, and only use them during major altercations with human armies or the Resistance. "They're a bigger liability than they're worth." Not to mention that he thought it was disgusting that the bite of any fledging or vampyre Marked red was poisonous to humans—always killing them, and always causing them to rise within three days as grotesque, zombielike things whose bite was also contagious. "And they fucking smell awful."

"Sir, the soldiers are under control," Dallas said, panting, as he rushed up to Stark.

Stark grunted. "Then let's get moving again. Crawling around this ridge is not the way I wanted to spend my evening."

The line of soldiers kept moving forward, snaking their way around as they followed what could barely be called dirt roads. Soon the trail took a sharp turn to the right, and then headed almost straight up. Stark sighed and bent to the task, not liking that the air felt colder and damper. He tried to remember if ice or snow had been forecast. He checked his phone and cursed softly under his breath.

*Of course there's no damn service out here in the middle of nowhere.*

Suddenly, overhead, a single raven began circling and shrieking, as if it was pissed that they were on his ridge.

"Let's pick up the pace," Stark told Dallas. "Go back down the line and tell them to keep up with me."

General Stark didn't wait for an answer. Pumping his arms, he began to jog up the red dirt trail, wishing he was just about anywhere but there.

(

## Other Kevin

Dragon Lankford grabbed Kevin's arm and pulled him roughly to his feet, dragging him to the lip of the small cave. His longsword was drawn and he stood in front of Kevin, holding the pointed razor tip of the weapon against his throat.

"How many of them are there?" Dragon demanded.

Grandma Redbird tried to rush to his side, but Anastasia snagged her wrist, not allowing her to go to him.

"No, my friend. This has gone beyond your good will. Dragon must deal with your grandson now."

"How many?" Dragon repeated, and the sword drew a tiny bead of blood from Kevin's neck.

"Kill me. Cut off my head. Do any damn thing you want, but it won't change my answer *because I am telling you the truth.* I don't know what's going on out there. I don't know how they found your ridge, but it has nothing to do with me."

"So, it's just a coincidence that a lieutenant in the Red Army shows up here, and the same night so do soldiers of the Red Army?" Dragon's voice was filled with barely controlled rage. "Do you know how many innocents are with us? Dozens! They're scattered all around us in deer blinds. Humans *and* blue fledglings—just children. All looking for safety and freedom, and tonight they will lose their lives. Because of you!"

"No!" Grandma Redbird shouted. "Kevin has been with me.

He's telling you the truth! I swear it to you on my own life."

Dragon spoke only to Kevin. "She'll die tonight too. Horribly. And if they leave enough of her, she'll rise in three days a ravenous, brainless eating machine. Your soul must be completely filled with Darkness to do such a thing as this."

Kevin turned his head away, unable to look at his grandma. "I'm so sorry, G-ma. I should never have let you bring me here. I knew it was too dangerous. I should've spied on Neferet like you told me to and let you report to the Resistance for me. I'm so, so sorry."

"They're coming up the west trail!" A blue vampyre Kevin didn't recognize scrambled up the last few feet of the ridge to them.

"Bank all of the fires!" Dragon turned his head to look at his mate. "My love, lead the innocents down the back side of the ridge. They might not have us surrounded." His hard gaze found Kevin again. "The rest of us will remain here and buy you time to escape."

"No. I won't leave you." Anastasia spoke quietly but firmly. "Sylvia is accustomed to the Oklahoma wilds. She can lead the innocents. I will remain with my mate. I can wield a sword too, and I prefer to die by your side."

Kevin saw the pain flash through Dragon Lankford's eyes and the despair that curved his shoulders, and he couldn't bear it.

*What the hell would Zoey do?*

He knew what she wouldn't do. Zoey Redbird—the High Priestess who ruled the Tulsa House of Night with strength and honesty—would *not* give up.

"My mate's blood will be on your hands." Dragon ground the words from between clenched teeth. "And after I kill you, what kind of welcome do you think Nyx will have for you? Well, one good thing about dying. I'll be there, in the Goddess' Grove, to witness Nyx's punishment." As Dragon spoke, he pressed the longsword harder against Kevin's neck.

Kevin reacted automatically. He lurched back, shouting, "I would do anything to make this right!" His wounded back screamed as it collided with the rocky wall of the cave, ripping apart the few stitches Anastasia had already sewn. Kevin tripped and fell as his blood spattered the rocks and flowed down his back.

Instantly, there was a change in the air so great that it penetrated Dragon's rage. He froze, sword above his head, ready to strike a killing blow.

Later, Kevin thought that it was similar to how the air felt around the tear between his world and Zo's, but at that moment all he could do was stare in open-mouthed wonder as ethereal beings began to materialize around him. Some lifted from the cave's sandstones. Some descended from the sky, like feathers floating to ground. Still more seemed to emerge from within the gnarled bark of the old oaks perched precariously on the steep ridge around them.

They differed greatly from one another. A bunch of them looked like a cross between fallen leaves and butterflies, and then the wind blew a small gust and they changed form and suddenly they were beautiful, winged women. A few of them reminded Kevin of hummingbirds, only they had the delicate heads of impossibly beautiful women and handsome men. Some looked like Fourth of July sparklers, only smaller and see-through. Several of them were in the form of fireflies—big, beautiful fireflies that should not be flitting around in the middle of winter. And more of them appeared to be mermaids and glittering jellyfish.

They were all descending upon Kevin.

*"Old Magick! Old Magick!"* croaked the raven from his perch on Anastasia's shoulder.

The beautiful priestess was suddenly crouching beside Kevin, studying the creatures with awed curiosity. "Yes, Tatsuwa! These sprites *are* Old Magick. I never thought to see even one, as Old Magick has almost disappeared from the world."

A butterfly winged figure of a voluptuous woman about the size of his hand, and naked except for a dress made of glitter, fluttered up to Kevin, giving him a beseeching look.

"W-what do they want?" Kevin stuttered.

"You conjured them. Ask them," she said.

"Um, what do you want?" Kevin tentatively asked the floating sprite.

> *"We heard your call*
> *Your blood is true.*
> *What is it you wish*
> *That we shall do?"*

Kevin didn't hesitate. "Hide us! Don't let the vampyres coming up the ridge find any of us who are already up here." He paused and then added, "Please."

> *"If we do this for you*
> *For us what shall you do?"*

Kevin opened his mouth to answer, but Anastasia's hand on his arm stopped him. Urgently, she whispered, "Be careful. Old Magick is powerful. It is also never free."

"What do you think they want?" Kevin whispered back.

"Sprites are tied to the four physical elements—air, fire, water, and earth. It should be easy enough for them to cloak this ridge. Offer them your blood, but only as much as you've already shed."

Kevin cleared his throat and then replied to the glittering sprite. "I'll pay you with my blood, but only the blood I've already spilled. Is that enough to keep us safe?"

The sprite spun in the air and was joined by one each of the different creatures. Kevin could hear that they were speaking, but the words were strange. Not like a different language, but like a different way of thinking and forming sounds.

Then she fluttered back to hover above him again.

*"We accept your price tonight*
*As your blood is strong with Light.*
*We seal this deal with thee*
*So we have spoken—so mote it be!"*

With Tatsuwa squawking a complaint, Anastasia backed quickly out of the way, joining Dragon where he stood a few feet from Kevin, his sword still unsheathed, as the sprites covered the young red vampyre. At first Kevin flinched, expecting them to cause him even more pain than he'd already endured that night, but their touch was oddly soothing, like cool rain falling on a forest blaze. The sprites also covered the rocky wall of the cave, the dirt floor around him, even the tip of Dragon's blade—anywhere any of his blood had spattered. As they drank, their bodies blazed with light and color, and they made excited chirping and clicking sounds that actually had Kevin's lips turning up.

Then, just as quickly as they'd appeared, they were gone.

And the night around them changed utterly.

(

## Other Stark

It began innocently enough. Stark felt the direction of the cold night breeze shift and sharpen. He was sweating from the climb up the ridge, so his damp face instantly registered the change and he shivered, increasing his pace.

And then the night sky began belching ice.

Stark slid on a rock, suddenly slick with ice as black as the forest around them, and he had to windmill his arms to keep from falling. He tucked his head against the frigid rain and slowed his pace.

The mist began then, rolling from low spots around them, lifting from the bowels of the ridge. Behind him, someone cried out sharply, and a few moments later Dallas was panting beside him.

"Sir, the men are losing their footing. One of the soldiers just fell and smashed his head against a rock."

Stark stumbled to a halt. "The weather's turned. I should've checked before I left the House of Night."

"Sir, I did," Dallas said, wiping his face with the back of his sodden sleeve. "It was supposed to be clear and cold."

"So much for listening to Travis Meyer and the News on Six," Stark grumbled. "Well, tell the red officers to get their soldiers back to the Humvees. You and I will go ahead and scout up to the top of the ridge so that I'm sure—"

A cluster of impossibly large fireflies flitted from a bank of mist, darting around in the icy rain as if they were kids playing in a sprinkler. Stark stared at them through the ice and rain and mist as their insectile bodies shifted from bugs to naked women, and then back to bugs.

Stark felt his blood go as cold as the falling ice.

"Old Magick," he said softly.

"What was that, sir?" Then the glowing insects caught Dallas' vision. "Hey, fireflies! That's weird as shit."

"Not fireflies. Sprites. Back away, Dallas. Tell the soldiers we're getting out of here. Now!"

Dallas gave him a confused look but hurried to do as he was ordered. Stark paused only an instant before he followed him back down the path.

The sprites were truly spectacular—as beautiful as they'd been described in the ancient tomes his Spells and Rituals professor had insisted his advanced classes read, cover to cover. Stark had immersed himself in the Spells and Rituals class, mostly because he loved reading. The entire last half of the most advanced textbook used in the class had been devoted to Old Magick, and elemental sprites in particular.

Stark searched his memory as he backed slowly away from the glittering cloud of creatures. Sprites were powerful, but as capricious as the Old Magick that formed them—in other words, they could aid you one moment and turn on you the next.

*What had Dallas said about this ridge? It was ancient Creek Nation land.*

"That figures," he muttered to himself as he continued to back down the path, unwilling to look away from the sprites. They must have been protectors of the land, allied with the Creek Nation when they lived here, and they don't understand the world has changed, moved on. They're still protecting the land.

He joined the retreating line, ordering the soldiers to move as quickly as possible to get off this land. Dallas hurried ahead of them, holding the electricity at bay long enough for the group to cross over it again. By the time Stark had gotten back in the Humvee and Dallas turned their lead vehicle around to head to Tulsa, the road was almost impassable with ice.

"Sir, what the hell was that up there?" Dallas asked.

"The assurance that no Resistance members are sneaking around on that ridge. Old Magick that protective doesn't allow trespassers. That human woman, Tina, she owns this whole ridge?"

"Yes, sir."

"She must have Creek blood. That's why the sprites let her putter around up there, pretending to look for poachers." Stark snorted. "Poachers, hell! I'd hate to see what Old Magick would do to anyone trespassing on this land."

"Well, at least we know the locals weren't lying," Dallas said. "Don't know hardly nothin' 'bout Old Magick, but I saw them bugs. They glowed like lights. Must've been what people were talkin' 'bout seeing up there."

"Has to be." Stark hesitated. "Is that all you saw? Just big lightning bugs?"

"Yeah, isn't that weird enough?"

"Yes, it is," Stark said, wondering why he felt relieved that Dallas hadn't seen the sprites shifting to semihuman form.

"Well, it don't look like we need to worry 'bout policing that ridge. Good thing. Too many damn brambles and rocks and crap for my taste. Plus I hate the country. I'm a city guy."

"Lieutenant, I want you to keep your mouth shut about what we saw up there. The last thing we need are a bunch of idiot fledglings thinking that it'd be an adventure to check out Old Magick."

"Whatever you say, sir, but they didn't look dangerous. They looked like abnormally big fireflies, which are pretty damn cute."

"Dallas, just one of those cute little bugs has the ability to devour you whole—and I mean *all of you*. Sprites can drain souls as easily as they drain blood."

"Nyx's tits! Are you kidding with that?"

Stark gave him a hard look. "Do I look like I'm kidding you, Lieutenant? And don't ever use the Goddess' name like that around me again."

"Yes, sir. I'm sorry, sir."

"Just shut up and drive."

The lieutenant did as he was told, leaving his general to stare out at the night.

*Old Magick is supposed to be almost gone from the world. The textbooks said it can only be found on the Isle of Skye, and no one's been allowed to enter that island for centuries.* Stark didn't wonder what the sprites were doing there. The fact that it was Native American land that they were still protecting made sense.

But that didn't explain why they were awake and active enough to be seen by local humans.

*Could it have something to do with Neferet's war?*

A shiver of foreboding skittered down Stark's spine, colder than the ice that had stopped falling as soon as they turned off Lone Star Road.

Stark was pretty sure he knew the answer to his question. What he didn't know was if it was a good or bad thing that the sprites were stirring. He also didn't know what the hell to do with his discovery.

His duty was to report it to Neferet. But Stark was a sworn Son of Erebus Warrior before he'd become Neferet's general, and his first allegiance was to the Goddess Nyx.

The secret truth that Stark kept buried deep within him was that he didn't trust Neferet, and he didn't agree with her war.

Sure, he'd been part of a very large, very vocal group of blue vampyres who had been demanding better treatment from humans. He'd been sick of the separate-but-equal bullshit human politicians had been shoveling at them for too damn long. He'd even supported the beginning of Neferet's war, but after a few months it was obvious that Neferet never intended to create a world order where all were equal. Neferet wanted to rule and to subjugate all humans.

Stark wasn't a red vampyre. He had morals. He retained his humanity. And he wasn't a killer. He was a Warrior, sworn to protect the High Priestess gifted with the leadership of the vampyre nation by Nyx.

But what if the rumors were true? What if Neferet no longer followed Nyx, and the Goddess had truly turned from her High Priestess?

"I have been praying to Nyx for a sign …" Stark murmured to his reflection in the darkly tinted window.

"Sir? Did you say something?"

"Just talking to myself," Stark said. He closed his mouth, but his whirring mind didn't stop.

*I've been praying for a sign that Neferet is doing the Goddess' will. Is this it? Or is the appearance of Old Magick a sign of the opposite?*

Stark rubbed his forehead, hating the headache that was building there. Until he knew for sure that Neferet had forsaken Nyx, he would do his duty. He would protect his High Priestess.

But he would also keep his mind and his eyes open, and at least for now he would tell no one the magickal details about what happened on the ridge that night.

# 8

# *Other Kevin*

"They've retreated! Every one of them!" A tall, blond blue vampyre rushed into the small cave, brushing icy rain from an adult tattoo of Celtic knots as he ran to Dragon.

"Cole, are you certain?" Dragon said.

"Absolutely. It's a mess out there, but I saw what happened. It was right by our first checkpoint. A whole bunch of things that look like fireflies appeared out of the mist in front of General Stark. He immediately ordered a retreat. I couldn't get close enough to make out everything he was saying, but I did hear the words *Old Magick*, and I could see that he looked scared. Real scared."

"Oh, thank the Goddess!" Grandma Redbird collapsed to the rough stone floor of the cave.

"G-ma! Are you okay?" Kevin tried to go to her, but his legs refused to work, and he couldn't do much more than lean painfully against the side of the cave.

"Sylvia?" Anastasia started to go from Kevin's side to the old woman, but Grandma Redbird raised a hand to stop her.

"I am quite well. I just needed to sit. I believe my rush of adrenaline has left me. Please tend to my grandson and do not worry yourself about me." She wrapped her arms around herself and shivered.

"My love, do you think we can relight at least a few of the fires?" Anastasia asked Dragon.

The Swordmaster stared out at the ice and mist that shrouded the ridge. "Yes. If they return it won't be tonight. The roads won't be passable and the mist is excellent cover for the fires. Light the one in the rear of the cave. Cole, go to the hunters' blinds and tell them it's safe to keep the fires going as long as the ice and mist last." Cole disappeared into the night. Dragon faced Kevin. "It worked. Your sprites saved us."

Kevin shrugged, and then grimaced in pain. "They're not really *my* sprites. They just like my blood."

"Because it holds the power of our ancestors, who were once as much a part of this land as these rocks," said Sylvia Redbird. "And because it is good, honest blood—not tainted by lies and hatred. Do you believe now, Dragon Lankford?"

"I believe your grandson saved us. But there is still the question of how the Red Army knew we were here, and why they came here the same night as Kevin."

"I can't answer either of those questions right now," Kevin said. "Not from here. But I can get answers for all of us from inside the House of Night."

"You expect me to let you go?"

"No. I expect you to let me join you. I want to be part of the Resistance. I want to spy for you—for us."

"Impossible!" Dragon said.

"Why is that impossible, Bryan?" Anastasia crouched beside Kevin again, reexamining his back while her raven found a perch on the craggy wall of the cave. Kevin thought his black eyes seemed as judgy as Dragon's.

"He's a red vampyre! He can't be part of the Resistance. We're fighting his kind."

"You're not fighting *my* kind," Kevin said. "There are no more of *my* kind in this world, and that's why I'm the perfect spy. No one at the House of Night will pay any attention to a Red Army lieutenant. They don't give a crap about us except as expendables. I can go anywhere—listen to anyone—and they'll barely notice."

"You could also rise to the rank of general in the Red Army and have a squadron of men follow your orders. Why would you choose to put yourself in harm's way instead?" Dragon asked.

"Because I *am* a decent person!" Kevin blurted. "Sheesh, what's wrong with you? Anyone who isn't a monster or a greedy ass would do the same."

"That simply is not true, Kevin." Anastasia rested a soft hand on his shoulder. "There are many people we'd all call decent—vampyres and humans alike—who aren't willing to do more than sit on the sidelines and shake their heads at the state of the world."

"Well, I think if you're a decent person and you don't stand up against monsters, then you're worse than one of them," Kevin said. He turned his head and met Anastasia's distinctive blue eyes. "You can go ahead and start sewing again. I'm as ready as I'm ever going to be."

She smiled kindly at him. "That won't be necessary. Not after Old Magick did its work." Anastasia nodded at the back of his shoulder.

Kevin reached carefully behind his back to find a tender, raised scar and smooth skin where just minutes before there'd been a deep, bloody slash. "But that's impossible!"

"Apparently not. When the sprites drank from you, they also touched you—all along your wound—and their touch healed you. Although, not completely. You'll be weak and stiff and sore for a while, and you'll have a long, nasty scar. But you no longer have need of my sewing skills."

Grandma Redbird shuffled to Kevin, bending to peer at his naked back. "That is remarkable! U-we-tsi, the sprites truly did close your wound."

"Huh," was all Kevin could think to say.

"Does that tell you anything about his character?" Dragon asked his mate.

"Only that the sprites like him, and as they are neutral—neither good nor evil, that does not tell us much," Anastasia said. Then she stood and took her mate's sword-callused hands in her own. "Bryan, I believe we know about Kevin's character already. He most definitely is not like the other red vampyres. We should trust him." Dragon opened his mouth, obviously protesting, but Anastasia's words silenced him. "He is different. His humanity is intact. And he can wield Old Magick. Not even Neferet can do that."

"Yet," Kevin said.

Dragon turned to him. "Explain that *yet*."

"In my sister's world, they did defeat Neferet, but they didn't kill her because she'd become immortal."

Anastasia gasped in shock. "She learned to wield Old Magick!"

"G-ma, do you have the journal?"

She nodded weakly and motioned to where the supplies from the Polaris had been piled in the rear of the little cave. "I do. It is in the basket I packed with cookies."

"I brought a copy of a journal Neferet wrote when she was still a human. It's from my sister's world, but in it there's proof that Old Magick had been influencing Neferet since she was a kid."

"And just because the journal was written by another version of her does not mean it holds no relevance for us," Grandma said. "As Kevin already explained, who we are in each world remains essentially the same. It is only our experiences that change us. I will give you the journal. Have copies made of it. Pass them around. We must all read it to have as much knowledge as possible about ways to combat Neferet's evil."

"Agreed. We need all the help we can get, especially if that help comes in the form of a young vampyre who brings us knowledge and can also wield Old Magick," said Anastasia.

Dragon blew out a long breath and went to Kevin, crouching

beside him, as had his mate. "I don't like being put in a position where I must trust an enemy."

"I'm not your enemy."

"Prove it."

"I just tried to," Kevin said. "And I'll keep trying to prove it to you. I'll go to the House of Night and spy for you. I'll tell you everything I learn. I'll help in any way I can."

"My grandson speaks the truth, Dragon. You will see," said Sylvia Redbird, through teeth that chattered with cold.

"G-ma, you need to move to the back of the cave where the fire is."

"I'm fine here. It's much too smoky back there."

"Boy, if you want to do something to get in my good graces, figure out a way Old Magick can help us make this cave habitable." Dragon spoke softly, more to the night than to Kevin, as he stood, staring out at the freezing rain and mist.

Kevin looked from his g-ma to Anastasia. "Do you think I could actually do that? Get the sprites to help make this cave bigger and better?"

"Of course," Anastasia said without a pause. "As I said when they appeared, sprites are always tied to the elements, and earth is one of the elements. It would not be a stretch to imagine earth sprites fashioning a cave from the bosom of this ridge."

"Cool! I'll just call them or something and ask if they—"

"Remember, Kevin, you must never use Old Magick flippantly," Anastasia interrupted. "It is one of the most powerful magicks in the world—and one of the most unpredictable."

"But the sprites did exactly what I asked them to do," Kevin said.

"Oh, they always keep their word—as long as they are paid. The problem comes with the payment," Anastasia said.

"Please explain," said Grandma Redbird.

"It is simple *and* complicated. Simple because the sprites agree to a payment for a service. When it's something like they just did—a specific task for a specific service—all is usually well. It's when the payment isn't rendered immediately that you can get into trouble, and by trouble I mean soul-deep, often deadly trouble."

"If I understand what you're saying, then Kevin should only agree to a payment that is immediate and very specific, correct?" Grandma Redbird asked.

"Well, yes and no. He can still have problems. That's more of the complicated part of the process. The ancient texts warn that using such power is dangerous and can hurt the vampyre wielding it."

"But I already have an affinity for the five elements. So does my sister in the other world I just visited. She's a good High Priestess—really good. She defeated Neferet there. I really don't think she's been hurt by it."

"Elemental affinities are gifted by Nyx, and thus they are not Old Magick. It is impressive that you have such affinities. That, mixed with your Cherokee blood, is probably why the sprites heard your call," Anastasia said. "And as to what the texts meant by being hurt by wielding the power—I am sorry to say I simply don't have enough knowledge to explain further. I have never known Old Magick before, or anyone who could call it. All I know is what I have read in ancient texts."

"Well, I'm willing to take the chance and use it—at least one more time. You think they'll hear me again?"

She hiked her shoulders. "I cannot answer that, Kevin. Nor can I answer if you *should* call to them again. I do not know the nature of your soul. I do not know how susceptible to Darkness you are."

"I do," said Grandma Redbird. "His soul is good. Truly good. He is not prone to Darkness or hatred or evil. Even before Nyx restored his humanity in that other world, he fought the hunger and the mindlessness of what so many of us are calling the Red Curse. U-we-tsi, I believe you can help us set the balance of Light and Darkness to right because you *can* wield Old Magick. But do not forget Anastasia's words. Remember—the payment must be specific and immediately given."

"I'll remember. I promise. But, um, do you think I have enough blood right now for that?"

"No, you do not," Anastasia said.

"I have an idea for an alternative payment." G-ma's hand reached up to rest over the small bag that made a mound under her shirt.

"Wait, no. You can't give up your medicine bag," Kevin said.

"I can and I will. *Both* of my medicine bags."

Kevin pressed his own hand against the replica that rested in the middle of his chest. "I dunno, G-ma. Is it a good idea to give away your power like that?"

"Oh, u-we-tsi, a medicine bag holds no power on its own. It only symbolizes the power of its maker. And I shall simply make another, just as the other Sylvia Redbird has probably already done in Zoey's world." She pulled the beaded bag from beneath her shirt and lifted its leather thong over her head, handing it to Kevin. "Summon your sprites."

Kevin took the medicine bag after squeezing his g-ma's cold hand. Then he looked up at Dragon. "Help me stand?"

The powerful Warrior took Kevin's elbow, lifting him to his feet. Kevin stood, swaying slightly as bright spots glittered in his vision, but he settled quickly. His back was stiff and hurt all the way from one shoulder to the other, but his dizziness passed. He couldn't run a marathon, but he was pretty sure he wasn't going to fall over. Again.

Then he realized he had no clue about his next move.

"Um, Anastasia, how do I call them?"

"When they came to you before it was when you'd torn open your wound, so it was bleeding pretty heavily, and you'd just said something about wanting to make this right."

"So, do you think I should cut myself again and then call them?"

"Are they not still here?" Grandma gestured out at the icy night. "Can you not simply ask them to return to you?"

Kevin looked questioningly at Anastasia, who shrugged and nodded.

He cracked his knuckles and shook out his hands as he moved

closer to the mouth of the cave. Kevin cleared his throat, drew a deep breath, and opened his mouth to shout Goddess-only-knew-what, but he hesitated. *Maybe I should think before I speak—or more specifically, pray.* Kevin closed his mouth. Closed his eyes. And bowed his head.

*Please help me, Nyx. I'm way out of my league here—and not just with the sprites. I want to help the Resistance, but I'm just a kid. I'm not even as old as Zo. I promise I'll try to do the right thing and follow the path you want me on. Could you give me a little help to keep me walking the path?*

Kevin raised his head and stared out at the ice and mist magick that had kept Stark away.

"Water sprites protected us with ice and mist ..." he murmured to himself, thinking aloud. "And sprites are tied to the elements." Kevin thought hard. And then he sucked in a giant breath. "Earth sprites!" Grinning, he turned to catch the confused looks Anastasia, Dragon, and his g-ma were throwing him. "I think I've got it!" He faced the night again, and, with more confidence than he felt, spoke in a loud, clear voice. "Sprites of air, fire, water, and earth, I am Kevin ..." He hesitated, and then knew exactly what he needed to say and how he needed to say it. "I am Kevin Redbird, and with my Goddess-given affinity and by the right of my blood—the same blood that once beat strong through those who were protectors of the land—I call to you, especially those of you who are earth elementals! Sprites already playing out there on the ridge, please come to me!"

It was as if the night inhaled, held its breath, and then, with its exhale, released magick. Anastasia and Grandma Redbird gasped as a cloud of sprites, shifting form from firefly to winged fey, flew up from lower on the ridge. They hovered before the cave, lighting the icy night so that Kevin could clearly see the huge boulders that dotted the craggy area around them begin to shimmer. Then figures emerged, as if they'd been curled within the rocks sleeping, awaiting Kevin's summons. They were larger than the firefly sprites—about the size of toddlers. The rock sprites were unbelievably beautiful.

They didn't appear to have genders. The skin of their bodies looked exactly like the tiny compacted veins of quartz that marbled the Oklahoma sandstone from which they emerged—they glistened as if lit from within—and Kevin realized they were what he'd at first mistaken for sprites that seemed to be Fourth of July sparklers. Their delicate feet didn't touch the earth as they drifted toward him.

"*Old Magick*!" squawked Anastasia's raven as he took flight from the cave.

Movement to his right and left drew Kevin's attention and he watched the gnarled bark of the old, winter-bare oaks waver, like heat waves lifting from an Oklahoma blacktop road during the summer. From within the trees, sprites materialized. Kevin had to check that his mouth hadn't flopped open (one glance at Dragon showed him that the Warrior was wide-eyed *and* opened-mouthed). The tree sprites were the most exquisite things he'd seen since he'd been introduced to Aphrodite in Zo's world. They were all female. Their skin was as earthy brown as tree bark, but instead of being gnarled and ancient, it looked like velvet. Their hair drifted around each of them, falling well past their waists, in all the shades of leaves: spring's bright, new lime; summer's strong, steady jade; and fall's russet, fuchsia, and gold. They were as unique as the trees from which each of them emerged. At first Kevin thought their bodies were covered in tattoos, but as they moved gracefully closer to him, he realized that they were actually covered in a myriad of different forest plants—ferns, mushrooms, flowers, and moss—instead of clothes.

The different types of elemental sprites formed a semi-circle around the mouth of the cave where they waited silently in the still-falling freezing rain. The light from the firefly sprites caught the ice as it had already begun to cover the ridge, making their small area glisten, diamond-like.

"Hello," Kevin said, hoping the huge smile he couldn't stop his face from making wasn't inappropriate. "Um, thank you for coming."

A tree sprite stepped forward. She was taller than the others, and her hair was the orange, red, and gold of a mighty oak in the fall. Her body was supple and curvaceous, and barely covered by the delicate fronds of a maidenhair fern.

*"Redbird Boy, we did not expect you to repeat your call, especially when our children are still about your business."*

Her voice was unexpected—pleasing and sweet, like the shade of an old oak on a hot Oklahoma day, but also filled with a strength that had the bare branches of all of the nearby trees shivering in response.

"I apologize. I don't mean to bother you," Kevin said quickly.

*"You misunderstand. I do not complain. I only wish to show my surprise. We have not been awakened in many ages. The children have enjoyed themselves this night."* She lifted one hand, palm up, cupping the ice so that it coated her dusky skin, turning it from velvet to smoky quartz crystal. *"Though water might have been over exuberant."* She shook the ice from her hand and arm, and it rained around her, sparkling in the wan moonlight. *"And they did so appreciate the taste of Native blood, diluted though it may be."*

Kevin heard his g-ma's derisive *hurmp* behind him, but he kept his attention focused on the sprite.

"Your children saved us tonight," he said. "Please thank them for me."

The sprite cocked her head, birdlike, studying him. *"You have already thanked them, Redbird Boy, with your blood. You needn't have called us for that."*

"That's not the only reason I called you. I was hoping you could help me again."

Her eyes, dark and almond-shaped, sparkled with what Kevin decided was a mischievous light. *"What further service do you require, and what payment do you propose, Redbird Boy?"*

"Two things," Kevin said. "One, we really need this cave to be bigger and better. You know, so, about …" He hesitated and glanced at Dragon, then whispered softly to the Warrior. "About how many people need to fit in there?"

Dragon just stared at him, still open-mouthed, but Anastasia stepped forward quickly. "It would be lovely if the cave could hold one hundred of us."

Kevin thought that sounded like an awful lot to ask, but he turned his attention back to the tree sprite and spoke with way more confidence than he felt. "It would be great if it were big enough to hold about one hundred people."

The sprite didn't so much as blink at the number. *"And the second service you require?"*

"What your children did for us tonight—hiding us from the Red and Blue Armies—well, um, could you keep doing that? Please?" When she didn't respond, he added, "We have our own children and other innocents who need a safe place, and this ridge would be perfect if the cave were bigger. I promise we'll respect the ridge. We won't build anything else on it, and we'll totally pick up after ourselves."

*"Ah, I see. You request permanent sanctuary."*

Behind him, Anastasia whispered urgently. "Stop, Kevin. You're asking too much."

Kevin ignored her. He'd already thought about whether he was pushing his luck with the sprites, but he rationalized that he had two gifts to offer—so he might as well ask for two services.

"Yes. I'm requesting sanctuary—in the form of a new cave, and your protection—but not permanently. I only request it until we restore the balance of Light and Darkness in this world—then we will no longer need to hide."

*"And what do you offer as payment for these services?"*

Kevin quickly lifted the medicine bag from around his neck, and then held it and its twin out to the sprite. She moved forward—not exactly floating, but her bare feet didn't stir the ground over which they strode. She came so close to Kevin that he could smell her—she was all the scents of autumn: the cinnamon of falling leaves, the sharp freshness of the first cool day of fall after a long, hot summer, the richness of thick roots reaching far down into fertile earth. Realizing he was staring, he mentally shook himself as she took the bags from him.

The sprite lifted them to her face, sniffed them, and then her tongue flicked out, tasting each of them. She blinked in surprise.

*"These are from two different worlds."*

"They are," he said. "Two different world payments for two different services."

*"Your payment is more interesting than powerful. Let us see if interesting is enough."*

The tree sprite turned her back to him, facing the others who had gathered at his call in a loose semicircle around the front of the cave. She spoke quickly to them using the strange language that was more music than words.

In response one sprite stepped forward from each of the different groups, speaking a series of very similar-sounding whistles and clicks. When they'd all had their turn, the tree sprite bowed her head slightly before turning back to Kevin. When she spoke her voice fell into a sing-song rhythm that reminded him of the voices he'd heard when the other sprites accepted his blood earlier, only this time the power in this sprite's voice pressed over his skin like the threat of a thunderstorm.

> *"We accept this payment—this magick*
> *from worlds numbered two*
> *Formed from ancient wisdom and given*
> *with love to you*
> *In return—*
> *Earth shall be moved*
> *Air shall listen*
> *Water shall watch*
> *And fire shall warm and protect*
> *But heed my command, Redbird Boy*

*Not one living tree shall you destroy*
*Or our deal will forever be void*
*I seal this bargain between thee and me*
*So I have spoken—so mote it be!"*

Then the tree sprite opened her mouth impossibly wide, giving Kevin a disconcerting view of white, pointed teeth, and she swallowed one of the bags whole. Next, with a movement so quick that for Kevin it was only a blur, she tossed the second bag in the air, where it exploded. Pieces of it began drifting down with the frozen rain, and time slowed as the sprites began flitting about, feeding on the remnants of Grandma Redbird's medicine bag like a swarm of beautiful but deadly piranhas. All the while they chirped and whistled and sang a wordless but joy-filled song.

Time sped up again and the tree sprite looked past Kevin to where Grandma Redbird stood within the lip of the cave.

*"Wise Woman, your essence is delicious. You wield your own type of earth power. I would come to you once, should you ever have need of me."*

Grandma Redbird bowed her head in respectful acknowledgment to the sprite before responding. "Should I ever have a need so great that I am willing to pay your price, I shall call you, lovely tree sprite."

*"You and this child of your blood may call me Oak."*

This time when his g-ma's head bowed, Kevin mimicked her. "Thank you, Oak," he said.

*"You have already thanked me. And your payment was delicious. Now, your people should leave the cave while we work."*

Dragon and Grandma Redbird left the cave with Kevin, but Anastasia paused at the mouth of it to call within.

"Shadowfax, Guinevere! Come on, you two. I know it's cold and wet out here, but you must leave the cave.

From deep inside, two cats emerged—a huge, disgruntled-looking Maine coon and a delicate, cream-colored cat Kevin was pretty sure was a Siamese. Both tucked their ears against their heads as they padded to Dragon to jump up into his arms.

"I've got them. Now, move back with us, Anastasia."

Dragon's mate joined them, and Kevin put his arm around his g-ma, trying to protect her as best he could from the bone-chilling rain, but he was still weak, and he found himself staggering unless he leaned heavily on her. Suddenly Dragon passed the two cats to his mate, and then he was beside Kevin, grabbing his other arm, steadying him enough so that he could climb up between two boulders, which almost shielded them from the wet. With Dragon on one side of him and his grandma on the other, Kevin watched as in less time than it had taken to run the Red Army from the ridge, the sprites worked a miracle, and then, without another word, they dissolved back into the trees and rocks and the dark, frigid night.

# 9

## *Zoey*

"It's only been a few days since Kevin left, but it feels like months. Please, Nyx, watch over him and don't let him get into too much trouble." I lit the purple candle and then placed it at the feet of the exquisite statue of Nyx that stood as the focal point of the courtyard between the school buildings and the Goddess' temple. It flickered there, adding its happy little light to the other votive offerings, each representing a prayer that had been lifted to our Goddess. Then I stepped back to sit on the carved stone bench beside my BFF, Stevie Rae.

"Yes, Nyx, please keep an eye on Z's brother in the Other World," Stevie Rae said. "And I know what ya mean, Z. It's this weather. Two days ago we were buried in snow, and today it was almost sixty degrees. That makes it seem like lots more time has passed. Hey, you know what's even weirder than Oklahoma weather?"

"Nope, 'cause OK weather is the weirdest."

"I know, right? But the even weirder thing is that I missed it. A lot. I mean, Chicago weather can be super cray too. But not Okie cray. I missed the ice and wind and how thunderstorms sweep in across the land like a stampede from above."

"Uh-huh," I replied automatically, my eyes trapped by the way the candlelight played across the marble skin of Nyx while my mind was far away … a world away, actually.

"You'd be surprised what all you miss when you've left your home."

"Yep." My gaze went from the statue up to the perfectly clear, starlit night.

"Like goathead thistles. You know, the kind that hurt as bad to pull 'em out of your skin as they did goin' in."

"Uh-huh."

"Oh, and ticks. I missed them *a bunch*."

"Yeah, I hear ya."

"Um, Z. No, you don't."

"Right."

"Zoey Redbird, stop gatherin' wool in that head of yours!"

Stevie Rae shoved my shoulder with hers. Hard.

"Hey! What's that for?"

"Z, seriously? What'd I just say?"

I chewed my cheek. "Um, something about wool? Which doesn't make much sense. Are you okay? I was serious when I said you and Rephaim don't have to go back to Chicago. You wouldn't have had to stay there this past year if I'd known you were miserable."

Stevie Rae turned to face me on the bench. "Zoey, you trust me, don't you?"

"Of course I trust you."

"Then please tell me what's wrong."

I sighed. "There's nothing—"

Stevie Rae's hand shot up, palm out like a stop sign. "Nope. Tell that to someone else. I know it's a lie and after all we've been through, it's just insultin'."

"Hey, you know I'd never insult you on purpose," I said, feeling like crap that I'd made my bestie feel like crap.

"Then tell me what's wrong."

I sighed. "I'm worried about Kevin. Well, Other Kevin. Not the

Kevin over here. He and I are actually going to meet at Andolini's for pizza before his winter break is over."

"Is that it?"

"Well, yeah. Pretty much. I mean, we still don't know what caused the roses to turn all black and disgusting before Aphrodite's vision, but if it was Neferet I'd expect her to do more. Anything more. And the Warriors guarding the grotto say nothing's so much as stirred there."

"The roses went back to normal."

"What? They did? How do you know that?"

Stevie Rae grinned. "The rose garden is another of the zillion things I missed about Tulsa. Rephaim surprised me last night and we went on a walk through the gardens after we had dinner at the Wild Fork. It's when he gave me this." She tapped the silver necklace twinkling around her neck. Hanging from the sparkling chain was the perfect replica of the state of Oklahoma as a little charm.

"Aww, that's pretty. I didn't even notice it. Sorry about that."

"Z, there's a lot you haven't been noticing for the past few days. I … I wish you'd let me help."

"There's nothing you can do. I just have to figure out a way to stop worrying about Kevin." *And thinking about Neferet—the Neferet who's over there, in charge, and probably slaughtering zillions of innocents like she slaughtered Other Zoey!* But I didn't let my mouth speak those words aloud. If I did I was afraid I wouldn't stop—wouldn't stop talking about Neferet—wouldn't stop knowing I needed to help Kevin.

And then there was Heath. Alive Heath. Other Heath, who was mourning that Other Zoey I'd watched Neferet murder.

"Just Kevin?" Stevie Rae said.

"Yes. No."

"Uh, Z, which is it?"

"No," I said miserably. "There's also stupid Neferet and whatever fresh hell she's plotting. Plus, well, Heath." Then I forced myself to hurry on. "And my mom. She's alive over there too. And there's another Grandma Redbird. Can you imagine how hard she took my death?"

"Z! There you is!" Kramisha clattered up on a bright-red pair of knee-high stiletto boots. "Move over, Stevie Rae. I got lots more junk in my trunk than you skinny white girls." She hip-bumped Stevie Rae, who slid over next to me, and we scooted to make room for Kramisha.

"Hey, I'm not white. Or at least I'm not one hundred percent white," I said.

"Sorry. Forgot you got you some brown in there, Z. Your butt's still skinny, though."

"I like your new boots," Stevie Rae said. "They're the exact color of your wig. How do you do that?"

"Talent. Pure talent. And, girl, these ain't new boots. But this catsuit is. What do ya think? Meow!" She pretend-hissed at Stevie Rae, who giggled.

"Kramisha, I love you! And I missed you like I missed T-Town," said Stevie Rae.

"You gonna love me even more in just a sec. Z, I want to go to Chicago."

"Huh?" I said. "But you've barely started the redo on the Depot Restaurant."

"Look, we all know Damien and Other Jack can do a better job with this redo than me. Z, *they gay*. And they called in more gays."

I rolled my eyes. "Kramisha, that's a terrible stereotype."

"Tell me it ain't true and I'll shut my face." She paused, and when I didn't say anything because, well, Damien and Other Jack and Toby, the OKEQ director, *were* all super awesome at interior design, she continued. "Where was I? Oh, yeah." Kramisha turned to Stevie Rae. "Do you wanna go back to Chicago?"

"Well, um, not really, not permanently, but Z and I already talked about me returning to Tulsa for good as soon as I get things settled at the Chicago House of Night."

"Settled meaning pick your replacement?" Kramisha asked.

"Yeah, I guess. Right, Z?"

"Sure. Unless you already have someone in mind, like Damien did," I said.

"I wish I did, but I don't. There're a few High Priestesses who have potential, but no one who stands out," said Stevie Rae.

"I'll do that," Kramisha said.

"Do what? You're confusing the crap outta me, Kramisha. Just tell me the bottom line," I said.

"Fine. The bottom line is I can't go back to that depot. Not now. I need me some time. I … I still hear them screaming." Kramisha paused and brushed a few bright red strands of hair from her face with a trembling hand. "Stevie Rae's a red vamp High Priestess. She and Rephaim fit good at the depot. The fledglings like them, which I think is kinda weird, 'cause he's a bird part of the time, but whatever. I don't like to judge." She shrugged. "And you know I can organize the shit outta stuff. I'll go to Chicago and get it organized and settled, and when that's done maybe the screaming I hear at night will be done too, and I can come home for good," Kramisha finished in a rush.

"I didn't know," I said softly, reaching across Stevie Rae to take Kramisha's hand. "Kramisha, I'm so sorry."

"You been distracted. No one holds it against you, Z. Other Kevin was only here for a little while, but everyone who met your little bro liked him. A lot."

I shook my head. "No, I'm your High Priestess, and I'm doing a bad job of it."

"You'll be back to yourself soon, like me. We just need time and some rest."

"You won't get much rest if you go to Chicago. That House of Night is crazy busy," Stevie Rae said. "And they don't even have an equestrian program. I've been talkin' to Lenobia 'bout—"

"I knows all about that. Me and Lenobia, we've been talkin' too," Kramisha said.

"She wants to go to Chicago with you?" I asked, not sure

whether I should feel surprised, pissed, or relieved that there obviously was a bunch going on around me that I was clueless about.

"Just long enough to get the horse stuff settled. What do ya think, High Priestess?"

*What do I think?* I stared at the statue of Nyx. *I think I need to figure out a way to help Kevin without totally messing up my own life.* But what I said aloud was, "I think you're highly capable. You and Lenobia will do a great job, as long as Stevie Rae doesn't mind you taking over for her immediately."

"Does that mean Rephaim and I get to stay here and not leave at all?"

"That's what it means," I said.

"Then I do not mind one tiny little bit! Kramisha, you just made me happier than a buzzard on a meat wagon!" Stevie Rae threw her arms around Kramisha, who grunted, briefly hugged her back, and then pulled away, straightening her wig.

"Watch the hair. I know it don't look like it, but all this glamour can mess up fast if the hair goes wrong."

I'd opened my mouth to ask Kramisha how soon she'd be ready to leave, when the first feeling hit me. It started in the middle of my chest—just a small building of heat—but not small enough that it went unnoticed. The feeling pulsed and spread, a little like I'd just sprinted up stadium stairs on a hot day (which I absolutely would *not* do unless someone was chasing me).

I coughed. Wiped my suddenly sweaty face. Cleared my throat. Coughed again.

My hand lifted as if I had no control over it, finding the center of my chest. My palm pressed against my skin.

There was nothing there. No heat. Nothing.

But I swear I'd felt something. Something hot and strong and strangely familiar.

"Zoey! Can you hear me?"

I looked up to see Stevie Rae standing over me with Kramisha

92

at her side. I was still sitting on the bench, but they'd moved and were hovering, obviously worried.

"Yeah. I can hear you. I'm—I'm okay. I think."

"What happened? You froze—with your hand pressed to your chest almost like you was clutching your pearls—'cept you don't have no pearls on," said Kramisha.

"I don't know. It was a weird feeling. It's gone now."

The sound of running feet came from behind us and Stark was suddenly there, crouching before me, his hands on my knees as he peered up into my face. "Zoey! What is it?"

"Did you feel it too?"

"Heat? And something else. Something I couldn't place." He touched my face, brushing my hair from my damp cheek. "Z, is your breathing okay? Does your chest hurt?"

"No, not at all. There was never any pain. Just heat and … a strangeness." I was relieved and afraid at the same time. If Stark had felt it, I hadn't imagined it. But also, if Stark had felt it, whatever had happened was real—and that might be *real* bad news.

"I think we should take Z to the infirmary so she can get checked out," said Stevie Rae. Rephaim must have been with Stark because he too was suddenly there, holding Stevie Rae's hand and studying me with birdlike concentration.

"Infirmary? What the hell's going on? Z, did you hurt yourself?"

I looked from Rephaim to see Aphrodite standing beside Darius (Goddess, had they *all* been in the Field House with Stark?). Her hands were on her hips and she was giving me a narrow-eyed glare that she probably meant as concern but was actually coming off as OMG-what-now-you're-bothering-me instead.

"I don't need to go to the infirmary. I'm fine. Really," I insisted.

"And it wasn't something Z did to herself," Stark said. "It was something that happened *to* her."

"That don't make no sense," said Kramisha.

"Or, said correctly, that doesn't make any sense.

Grammar—incorrect. Sentiment—correct," Aphrodite quipped.

"It does make sense," I said quickly, before Kramisha could verbally skewer Aphrodite. "Stark means there's nothing wrong with me. That whatever he and I felt, it was something happening outside me. And it was more strange than scary."

"Hey, what's going on out here?" Damien said as he and Other Jack joined their group. They were each carrying perfect white pillar candles that they were obviously intending to light at the feet of Nyx. "Z, are you okay?"

I sighed. Sometimes it was seriously like I had zero privacy. "I'm fine. It was nothing."

"Don't say that." Stark spoke earnestly as he sat beside me, putting his arm protectively around me. "You feel fine now—*we* feel fine—but it wasn't nothing. Something happened. Something that touched you or me or both of us."

It was Damien's turn to crouch before me. "Tell me what it felt like."

I described the sudden heat to him and watched Damien get paler and paler as Stark nodded in agreement with my description, but before Damien could say anything Aphrodite spoke up.

"Oh, for shit's sake, morons! It's obvious what it is."

"Aphrodite, it's super offensive to call us morons," said Stevie Rae.

"Bumpkin, this is just a guess, but before I joined this little impromptu group I'd bet you made at least one awful comparison that either had to do with your mama or with ticks. Am I right?"

"Almost," Kramisha said. "It had to do with a buzzard on a meat wagon, which is nasty." She glanced at Stevie Rae and sent her an apologetic smile. "I's just tellin' the truth."

"Right," said Aphrodite. "And that's offensive, but you're going to keep on with the bumpkin analogies, and as long as you do I'm going to call a moron a moron when I see you guys acting moronic."

"Oh, my Goddess, stop bickering!" I felt like my head might explode. "Aphrodite, did you actually have a point?"

"Of course," she said. "It's Old Magick. And that slapping sound you metaphorically hear is all of you face-palming as you realize I'm right."

"She *is* right," Damien said as he stood and took Other Jack's hand again. "It's what I was thinking too."

I just sat, unable to say anything because I was remembering … the time I spent on the Isle of Skye … the talisman of Skye marble that I brought back to Tulsa … the heat and power of that magick … and how it almost engulfed me and turned me into someone too similar to Neferet to be allowed to live.

"Z?"

I could feel Stark's worry, and I let it pull me out of my head.

"Aphrodite and Damien are right," I said. "I didn't realize it at first because it was only a distant echo of how Old Magick actually feels to wield."

"So, that must mean someone is usin' Old Magick again," Stevie Rae said.

"And that's bad," Rephaim said.

"Real bad," Kramisha said.

"You should call Queen Sgiach," Aphrodite said. "She's the Old Magick expert."

"I'd love to," I said. "But she's in mourning, which means she's cut herself off from the outside world. I know. I've been checking on her once a week, and this week's checkup was yesterday. She's still totally off-line and her phone just rings and rings and rings."

"She's *still* not taking calls? What's it been now, almost a year since the White Bull attacked Skye the same night Neferet attacked us here? You'd think she'd at least check her Facebook," Aphrodite said.

I looked up at her. She was my friend, a powerful Prophetess of Nyx, and with her new red and blue Mark, an adult vampyre—but she could still sound like a selfish brat. "She and Seoras were mated for centuries. I think a year of mourning isn't much in comparison. Would you have moved on already had Darius been killed that night?"

Aphrodite paled and leaned into Darius. "No. No, I would not. You're right, Z. I apologize for sounding like a moron."

"Aphrodite, you know Damien could help you increase your vocabulary so that you don't have to use words like—" Stevie Rae began a new admonishment when the second wave of feeling hit me.

I gasped and hugged myself, wrapping my arms around my torso while Stark held me close.

"It's okay, Z. It's okay. We're okay. This'll pass." Stark murmured reassurances.

"What is it? What's happening?" Aphrodite moved closer to me, shoulder to shoulder with Damien.

"Are you in pain?" Damien asked.

"N-no," I said in a voice that wavered. "Just feels like … like …"

"Like someone just walked over her grave," Stark finished for me.

"S-someone who uses Old Magick," I added, and Stark nodded in agreement. As my Oathbound Warrior, Stark shared my feelings. The High Priestess–Warrior bond was set up that way so that our protectors would always know when we needed them, but there were times, like now, that I wished I could flip a switch and not put him through the strangeness that was too often me.

"It's fading," Stark said.

I breathed a long, relieved sigh. "Yeah. It's gone."

"Z, where's it comin' from?" asked Stevie Rae.

"I have no clue," I said. "Stark, could you tell anything?"

He shook his head. "No, I don't think I'm getting the actual feeling, but just an echo of what you're experiencing."

"Well, it's attached to you," Damien said. "Whether that means the magick itself, or the person wielding it."

"What if Sgiach has called Old Magick? Is that what you could be feeling? You two got pretty close," said Stevie Rae.

"I don't think that's it," I said. "Queen Sgiach is the guardian of Old Magick, and I know it stirs on her island pretty often, but unless I'm there with her, I've never felt it."

"She used it in the battle against the White Bull the night we entombed Neferet," Damien said. "You didn't feel it then, did you?"

I shook my head. "Nope."

"Shit! Could it be Neferet?" Aphrodite said.

I suddenly felt chilled. "I don't know."

"Well, find out!" Aphrodite said.

I frowned at her. "You're the prophetess. How about *you* find out?"

She shook back her long, blond hair. "It doesn't work that way and you know it."

"Plus, you don't need no prophetess. You just need you a High Priestess who can invoke Old Magick. Know anyone like that, Z?" Kramisha asked, sending me a pointed look.

I metaphorically slapped myself on my forehead. "I may be a moron."

"Z!" Stevie Rae sucked air.

I waved away what was probably going to be a lecture on political correctness while Aphrodite snort-laughed. "Sorry. I was just kidding. Mostly. I'm the High Priestess that Kramisha's talking about."

"I don't like you messing with Old Magick," Stark said.

"I'm not going to mess with it," I said. "I'm just going to give it a quick call, that's all."

"That's *never* all where Old Magick is concerned," Stark said darkly.

I sighed and silently agreed with him.

"Should we go to Skye? Even though she's in mourning, I can't believe Queen Sgiach wouldn't let you back on her island."

"That's awful far away," Stevie Rae said. "There's gotta be an easier way. Or at least a closer way."

"I know a closer way," Rephaim said.

Everyone's attention turned to the tall, handsome young Cherokee.

"Okay, I'm listening," I said.

"There is Old Magick here. On these very school grounds," he said softly, but earnestly. "I know because I came from it."

I sat up straighter as what Rephaim said settled into my mind. My gaze drifted across the school grounds eastward, where in the distance I could barely make out the dark silhouette of a huge, broken oak.

"Rephaim is right. There is a closer way, but I'm not sure how much easier it's going to be," I said.

Stark's gaze followed mine, and I heard him mutter under his breath, "Ah, hell."

# 10

## *Zoey*

"I'm not real sure this is a good idea," Stevie Rae said.

"I'm real sure it's *not*," Stark said.

"Zoey, shouldn't you circle before trying to call Old Magick?" Rephaim asked. "Shaylin's still here, isn't she? I could go get her. And I saw Shaunee heading to the Drama classroom with Erik. I could let her know you need her here too."

"Wow! This is definitely not how this tree looks in my old world," said Other Jack.

"Okay, listen up." I turned my back to the ruined oak to face my friends. "I'm not going to circle. I want to keep this short and simple—and not focus too much energy on Old Magick." I turned to Rephaim. "Thank you for reminding me that this is here. I'd like you and Stevie Rae to stay." My gaze went from him to take in Aphrodite and Stark. "But I want everyone else except Stark and Aphrodite to leave. My gut is telling me not to make a big show of calling on Old Magick, and the more people here with me, the bigger the show. I'd do this alone, but I know my Warrior well enough to know that's not possible."

"Damn right," Stark said, looking very Warrior-ish and totally badass as he glared over my shoulder at the ruined tree I hadn't even actually looked at yet.

"And Aphrodite is, well …" My words faded as I realized I wasn't entirely sure how to describe what Aphrodite had become.

"Weirdly attached to Nyx and powerful?" Stevie Rae offered.

"How about awesomely attached to Nyx and powerful?" Aphrodite said, narrowing her eyes at Stevie Rae.

"Both," I said.

"And I'm going to use my High Priestess rank and stay right here with Z," said Stevie Rae.

"I stay with Stevie Rae," added Rephaim.

"Which is exactly what I expected," I said.

"What can the rest of us do?" Damien asked, threading his fingers with Other Jack's.

"Thank you for understanding," I said. "Could you and Jack make sure all the students stay inside?"

"Of course," Damien said. "It's the middle of second hour. We'll send each professor an emergency email. No one should be going anywhere for a good thirty minutes or so."

"And if they do, Damien and I will shoo 'em right back to class," said Other Jack, dimpling at me.

"But are you absolutely sure you don't want me to stay?" Damien asked. "I could take notes about what happens."

"Actually, what would help even more than that would be if you'd pull those books on Old Magick from the restricted section of the Media Center, and mark anything you think I should read."

"I can do that, Z."

"May I help too?" Other Jack asked, looking at me with big, anxious eyes. "I mean as soon as we let the professors know not to allow fledglings out of class."

"Of course," I said. "I'd appreciate that."

Other Jack did a happy little skip step that made me smile as he and Damien hurried away hand in hand.

"Well, I for one don't need to see no Old Magick spirits or any other mess like that," Kramisha said. "I need to pack. Z, if a poem come to me, I'll text it to you. Sound good?"

"Yep," I said, secretly hoping there would be no crazy prophetic poem texted to me in Kramisha's bright purple font.

"High Priestess, I would prefer to remain with Aphrodite."

My eyes met Darius' serious gaze. I sighed, but nodded. "Yeah, I get that. You can stay." Darius bowed to me respectfully, fist over his heart.

"Okay, Z. Meet us in the dining hall after? It's almost lunch time, and I'm getting hangry," Kramisha said.

"Yep, will do. I won't be long." I hoped if I said it, I could make it true.

As my friends headed back to the main school building, I finally turned my attention to the ruined tree.

It looked awful. As I studied it I realized I should have had it cleaned up months ago. It was a creepy eyesore. I knew students avoided the east wall because of it, and I suppose part of the reason I'd ignored doing anything about it was because it discouraged fledglings from using the trapdoor hidden in the wall behind it to sneak off campus. But then again, I was now the High Priestess of this House of Night. Like I'd know if fledglings were sneaking off campus?

Probably not.

"Z? You okay?" Stark asked.

I nodded. "Yeah, just thinking about having this mess cleaned up."

"Don't. Leave it like this," Aphrodite said. "If you want to do something, smudge it and add a salt circle of protection. But leave it."

I turned to her. "Why?"

She gestured at the leafless, malevolent ruin of a tree and the broken hole in the earth from which Kalona and his Raven Mockers had exploded what seemed like so, so long ago. "I could be wrong, but it seems to me that this mess is a visible lesson in what happens when you screw around with powers that are better left undisturbed."

My eyes focused on the clawlike black branches that refused to grow leaves. "You have a point."

"I always have a point. So, are you going to call Old Magick, or what?"

I wished I could choose the *or what*, but knew I couldn't. "Does someone have a knife?"

Together Darius and Stark pulled dangerous-looking daggers from Goddess-only-knew where on their well-armed bodies. I held my hand out, palm up, and told Stark, "Cut me."

He frowned. "How about I cut me and you use my blood?"

"James Stark, I am your High Priestess and your Queen. I said cut me. *So cut me.*"

He was still frowning, but this time he did as I asked, swiftly slicing a shallow cut across the meaty part of my palm. His dagger was so sharp I didn't even feel any pain. I fisted my hand, pumping it slightly to encourage my blood to well in my palm.

"Aphrodite and Darius, please stand on my left. Stark, Stevie Rae, and Rephaim, stay here on my right. I'm going to walk to the tree. Let me get a little ahead of you. Don't do anything as long as I'm still making sense, but if something too weird happens—"

"If weird shit happens I'm going to carry you out of here," Stark said.

"No," I said sharply. "Weird is going to happen. It's Old Magick. Don't do anything unless I stop communicating with you—or I get pulled into the, uh, tree." I paused, forcing myself not to shudder as I remembered the last time Old Magick had touched me here … the last time I'd almost lost myself. I met Stark's worried gaze and my voice softened. "You'll know if this goes wrong. You'll feel it. Just don't do anything *unless* it goes wrong. Okay?"

"Okay," he said reluctantly.

"I love you, and I'm sorry this is stressing you out," I said.

Stark's shoulders relaxed just a little. "I love you too, Z, and stress is part of a Warrior's job."

I tiptoed to kiss him, and then faced the tree. I held my fisted hand up before me, and then drew three deep, even breaths, centering myself. And hesitated.

"Well, hell. I'm not sure who I should call to," I said.

"You told me you liked the elemental sprites that came to your call on Skye," Stark said.

"Yeah, but that was different," I said.

"Not really. Stop worryin' so much that it's Old Magick. Think of it in simpler terms. It's a messed up old tree. So, call to the earth sprites," Stevie Rae said. "That's what I'd do."

"Yeah, you're right. Earth sprites. That sounds good," I said nervously.

"And stop being so damn jittery. They're just elementals. You have an affinity for all the elements. Imagine you're calling earth to a circle," Aphrodite said.

"That's actually a good idea," I said.

"Of course it is. I'm full of good ideas," she said, tossing back her mane of blond hair and waggling her perfectly arched brows at me.

"How 'bout I help?" Stevie Rae moved to my side. "I don't know much about Old Magick, but I am earth. Let's call together. Like we do when we circle."

"Okay, that makes sense. Stevie Rae, you start, and I'll use my blood like I'm lighting an earth candle."

"Easy-peasy!" Stevie Rae cleared her throat and spoke to the ruined tree. "I am Stevie Rae, Red Vampyre High Priestess to Nyx, who has gifted me with an affinity for earth. With the power the Goddess granted me, I would like to call the ancient sprites of earth." Then she nodded and took half a step back, allowing me to lead the final call.

I held my hand up again, took a deep breath, and said, "Earth sprites—Old Magick spirits of trees—I am Zoey Redbird, High Priestess in the service of Nyx, and I wield Old Magick. With the ancient power in my blood, I call to you and ask you to appear to me." Then, like I was tossing a handful of water away from me, I flung my blood onto the gnarled, broken bark.

Nothing happened for a moment, and I felt my heart sink into my gut. Was I really going to have to fly to Skye and try to pull Sgiach out of her mourning? Could that even be done? Or maybe I should try to talk to the Vampyre High Council—the European one—the one that wasn't particularly pleased my friends and I had taken over their leadership of North America …

"Uh, Z. Wake up. Someone's here," Aphrodite whispered.

I mentally shook myself and stared at the figure emerging from the center of the splintered tree. She was obviously a tree sprite. Tall and graceful, her skin was dark—the color of bark at midnight—but there was nothing rough about it. Instead her skin looked unbelievably soft and smooth—and there was a lot of it visible, because the things she wore that resembled clothing were the delicate fronds of a fern, though the more I looked the more I realized the fern appeared to be applied to her skin, like body paint, or even a tattoo. She blinked at me with large, beautiful dark eyes.

"Hello," I said. "Thank you for answering my call."

The sprite tilted her head to the side in a birdlike movement, making her spectacular hair, which was all the colors of autumn leaves, ripple like it moved in a wind that only touched the sprite.

I was trying to figure out how I could coax her to talk to me, when the sprite inhaled deeply, and then her big, dark eyes grew even larger. "Another Redbird? This has been such an interesting night."

She stepped from the center of the shattered tree, giving it a sorrowful look as she let her hand trail across the broken bark. She didn't actually float, but her bare feet made no sound and stirred none of the winter-brown grass over which she strode. The sprite halted in front of me, leaned forward, and sniffed at me.

*You are, indeed, a Redbird Girl.*

"How do you know my name?" I blurted.

*"I just left others of your blood. A young man and a woman."* The sprite's musical voice hesitated before continuing. *"But they are not in this world. How odd."*

"Wait, are you talking about my brother, Kevin?"

*"The Redbird Boy—yes, I believe Kevin is what he is called."*

"Who was the woman? Z, I thought you were, um, dead over there," whispered Stevie Rae.

The sprite turned her attention to Stevie Rae, who smiled nervously and waved at her, saying, "Hey there! I'm Stevie Rae. Nice to meet ya."

*"I do not know you, though I do feel the strength of your bond with the earth. As a tree sprite, I appreciate that. You may call me Oak."*

"Thank you, Oak." Stevie Rae bowed respectfully.

Then Oak began sniffing the air again, and as she did so she moved closer to Rephaim, who stood so still I didn't think he was even breathing.

*"What are you? I smell Old Magick in your bones, but it has been changed."*

"I am Rephaim. Son of Kalona. I was a Raven Mocker."

*"So, not human. Not raven. But something changed to meld the two together."*

"Changed by Nyx." I spoke up, feeling the need to gain some kind of control over the conversation. "Rephaim earned the forgiveness of the Goddess, so she granted him the body of a boy."

"But only from sunset to sunrise," Rephaim continued for me. "While the sun is in the sky, I am a raven."

The sprite continued to stare at Rephaim, sniffing the air around him cautiously. *"It is in atonement for dark acts you once committed that the Goddess allows the raven to take your body."*

Rephaim lifted his chin. "Yes. Nyx is just. My past is not something I view with pride."

"Except for the past year," Stevie Rae said, taking Rephaim's hand. "He chose Light, and Nyx forgave him."

"So, Oak, you're not from this world?" Aphrodite said.

Oak's head swiveled, owl-like, to peer at Aphrodite. *"I do not know you, Prophetess."*

"Yet you call me Prophetess."

The sprite nodded her head, causing her long, multicolored hair to shimmer around her with a sound like wind sloughing through autumn leaves. *"Old Magick easily recognizes a Prophetess of Nyx. There was a time, long past, when we stood beside Nyx's prophetesses, doing the Goddess' bidding. Sadly, that time is no more, but we remember,"* Oak said cryptically before she glanced at Darius. *"I do not know you, either, Warrior."* Then her gaze found Stark. *"You, I recognize. The Redbird Boy asked for sanctuary from you and your army—though your Mark was blue, not red."*

"You *are* from the Other World!" Stark said. "You know Kevin Redbird there, right? But who's the other Redbird woman?" Stark turned to me. "Could your sister have been Marked in the Other World without Kevin knowing about it?"

I started to open my mouth, but Oak's voice interrupted.

*"So many questions, but I have been offered no payment."* Oak turned her head and gazed somberly at the broken tree from which she'd materialized. *"And I have been called forth through a place that has been tainted by Darkness and destruction."*

"I'm responsible for your call. I apologize. I do have questions to ask you, but I also have your payment." I opened my hand, showing Oak the bloody wound that still wept there.

Oak sniffed delicately at my palm. She licked her bow-shaped lips—reminding me weirdly of how I look whenever it's psaghetti madness night in the dining hall. But then she surprised me by turning her attention from my blood to meet my gaze.

*"You offer an acceptable payment, but I would rather have something else."*

"What payment do you want?" I felt the urge to hold my breath as I waited for her response.

Oak turned her head to look over her shoulder at the ruined tree.

"*The payment I want for the information you seek is that you cleanse the abomination that happened here and restore this place to balance.*"

I blinked in surprise, but said, "I can do that."

Her head swiveled back to me and her voice turned rhythmic, like she was reciting a beautiful poem.

> "*I accept the payment of balance restored to this tree*
> *High Priestess—you have promised this to me*
> *I agree to give information to you*
> *I agree to speak only that which is true*
> *Ask then, Girl Redbird*
> *But listen well, so that my words are truly heard*
> *And if you renege on payment promised today*
> *Know that there are other ways to pay and pay and pay …*"

Oak didn't toss blood into the air or make any other kind of dramatic flourish, but the instant she was done speaking the binding spell, the air around her shimmered like someone had blown glitter across the schoolyard. I tried not to think about the other ways Old Magick could make me pay and asked my first question.

"Do you know my brother, Kevin?"

"*I do. He is much like you.*"

"So, you're from another world?"

"*To the ancient fey all worlds are one. We pay little attention to the veils that separate them.*"

"The other Redbird woman you mentioned. Can you tell me who she is?"

"*Yes, Redbird Girl. She is a Wise Woman—one of your blood. She is exquisite. I did so enjoy her medicine bags. They were not powerful payment for our services, but they were tasty.*"

"She's talkin' 'bout Grandma Redbird!" Stevie Rae said.

I nodded in agreement. "She's also talking about medicine bags—plural. Oak, the Wise Woman you're talking about must be my grandma. Are she and Kevin wielding Old Magick in that Other World?"

*"The Wise Woman did not wield Old Magick, though out of respect for her ancient blood, I would answer if she called and needed my assistance. It was the Redbird Boy. He required our aid."* Oak's dark eyes flicked to Stark. *"He needed protection against a Warrior much like yours."*

"Kevin must be working with the Resistance," Stark said.

"Where were Kevin and my grandma when they used Old Magick?" I asked.

*"On a ridge not far from here. That is where their people gather and hide from those who hunt them."*

"That's it. Other Kevin joined the Resistance," Darius said.

"And you really didn't see me anywhere?" Aphrodite asked the sprite.

Oak gazed at her. *"No. You were not one of the Redbird Boy's people."*

"Well, shit," Aphrodite said.

"Why does that make such a difference?" Rephaim asked Aphrodite.

Stevie Rae answered for her. "Because Aphrodite is the reason red fledglings and red vampyres in our world can choose to maintain their humanity. Without her, we'd all be monsters like poor Other Jack used to be."

What Stevie Rae said nudged my memory, and I suddenly had another question for the sprite. "Oak, you really are formed from Old Magick, right?"

It almost seemed that the sprite struggled against laughter. *"Of course, Redbird Girl. What else would I be?"*

"Well, I don't know, but I'm confused. I thought Old Magick didn't take sides in the struggle between Light and Darkness. Yet here you are, telling me you protected my brother and his people against the Red Army, and the payment you want is for me to basically cleanse the Darkness from this tree. That sounds like you're taking sides—not that I mind. I'm glad you're choosing Light. I just wonder why."

*"You are partially correct, Redbird Girl. Old Magick does not choose sides as we see the many layers that make up Light and Darkness, and we understand deeply that no one is completely good, nor completely evil. I granted your brother sanctuary because I accepted his payment, not because I sided with him against Darkness. As to this tree—elemental sprites are not neutral when an abomination is committed against nature. And this tree—this place of elemental power—has indeed been desecrated, which is an abomination against nature. It must be set to right."*

"That's understandable, Z," Stark said. "She sounds a lot like Sgiach did when we first got to her island. She wouldn't leave the island to fight Darkness, but when it trespassed on her island, she fought against it."

*"Ah, Queen Sgiach. We are saddened by the loss of her Warrior."*

"You know her!" I said.

*"Yes. For centuries."*

"How is she?"

*"In deep mourning."* And then Oak closed her mouth, making it clear she was done speaking about Queen Sgiach, the Great Taker of Heads.

"Okay, so, how's my brother doing in the Other World?" I asked.

*"His wound heals. We have granted his people sanctuary on the ridge. He wields Old Magick well."*

"His wound?" My question came out as a squeak.

*"It heals,"* Oak repeated, like she thought I might be slow.

I wanted to ask more about Kevin getting hurt, but Aphrodite snagged my wrist and spoke urgently to me. "Kevin is wielding Old Magick. That's what you felt."

"Yeah, I know."

"Z," she looked exasperated. "Remember what it's like to wield Old Magick."

And I realized what Aphrodite was saying. Kevin was in trouble, and he probably didn't know it.

"Oak, can you get a message to Kevin for me?"

*"Your payment was for information. Not for messaging."*

I looked down at my hand. The wound had begun to clot, but I knew I could dig it open again with my fingernails. "Blood. I'll pay you with my blood to take a message to my brother."

*"No, Priestess. You misjudge me. I am not your messenger. I have no allegiance to you at all. You offered a payment for information. I gave you that information. Now you must complete what you owe me. Do that, then perhaps ask me for another task. Just be sure the payment you offer is enticing . . ."* And without a sound, Oak turned her back on us, and in a *poof* of fog she disappeared into the middle of the fallen tree.

# 11

# *Other Kevin*

Rainwater dripped down the curved rock ceiling of the cave and pooled into mud and sludge around Kevin's feet. He wiped his sleeve across his face and sneezed violently.

"I think I prefer the ice to this drizzly, foggy crap. Much more of this and it'll be an early Oklahoma spring and the trifecta of natural pains in the ass that go with it: rain-wrapped tornados, ragweed, and ticks," Kevin muttered to himself.

"Hey, chin up! It could be way worse. Hell, it would be way worse if you hadn't come along. At least we're safe, warm, and relatively dry here."

Kevin smiled wryly at the short but powerfully built vampyre who seemed to materialize suddenly beside him. "Dude, could you be less soundless? Your creeping isn't good for my nerves."

"There's nothing wrong with your nerves, sweet Kevin. But Dragon shouldn't tease you by creeping around like a sprite." The lovely woman with the veil of long, silver-streaked blond hair touched Kevin's shoulder gently, though the warmth of her look was for Dragon and Dragon alone. "Especially with the number of sprites we have around here. They could get jealous."

Dragon Lankford held up his hands in surrender. "Anastasia, my love, do not let it be said that I disparaged the sprites." He paused and then asked Kevin, "How are they?"

"The sprites?" Kevin said, wiping more rainwater from his face as he turned from the mouth of the much larger, much improved cave.

"Yes, the sprites. You remember them, right?"

"Oh, Bryan, leave the boy alone. They're *his* sprites. Of course he remembers them. We all remember them, and we're thankful for them." Anastasia Lankford admonished her mate, though she did so as she slid her arm around his waist intimately and rested her head briefly on his shoulder, which Kevin thought totally took the sting from her words. After all, what guy *wouldn't* take a scolding from the beautiful priestess if she were also resting her smooth cheek on his shoulder?

Into the growing silence, Dragon Lankford snapped his fingers a couple of times in front of Kevin's face, making him blink and jerk back—and realize he'd been sitting there staring at Anastasia like a lovesick schoolboy.

*Man, I need a girlfriend.* Kevin sighed internally and shook himself. "Sorry. I was thinking."

"I could see that," Dragon gave him a half-amused look.

Kev returned the look with his own grin. "I was actually thinking about more than the beauty of your mate."

"Why, thank you, sweet Kevin." The corners of Anastasia's eyes crinkled endearingly.

Dragon cleared his throat. "What was the *more* you were thinking about?"

"That I really have to go." Kevin held up his hand as Anastasia started to protest. "No, it's been three days. The roads are clear. The Red Army hasn't been back." Kevin paused and gestured at what used to be the rear of a tiny cave, but was now a smoothly arched entrance to a cave-and-tunnel system that snaked, labyrinthine, well back into the rocky ridge. Even from where he and the

112

Lankfords stood, they could see people—blue fledglings, vampyres, and humans—hurrying around, preparing dinner, mending torn clothing, simmering herbs for tea, and other homey tasks. Cats padded around, getting underfoot, but also keeping the mouse and mole population down. And from somewhere farther down in the cave, the scent of chili lifted, making Kevin's mouth water. "This setup works. The cave is warm and dry and well ventilated, and the sprites are keeping the ridge fogged in. It's time for me to leave."

"I agree." Grandma Redbird made her way to the entrance of the cave from deeper in its newly completed interior. "It's so lovely and warm back in there! I do not know how the sprites did it, but the ventilation system is a miracle. There's next to no smoke— anywhere. Oh, but where was I … Ah, yes. Kevin, I am in agreement with you. If you wait much longer to return to the House of Night, your reappearance is going to create undo suspicion."

"But won't it already?" Anastasia said. "According to what Kevin has told us, he and an entire group of Red Army fledglings and soldiers *and* a red general all disappeared. How are you going to explain where you've been? Where they've been?"

Kevin blew out a long breath. "I've been thinking about that and I have an idea. I'm going to lie."

Dragon barked a laugh. "Obviously!"

"What do you mean by that, u-we-tsi?"

"Well, if anyone asks me about the rest of my group, I'll say I don't know anything about it because my general—the one who is dead back in my sister's world—sent me on a reconnaissance mission several days ago. And I went. I didn't find much of anything. But I did get lost."

"Lost?" Dragon snorted.

"Oh, they'll believe it. And they won't question me anymore about the general, either. Think about how most red vampyres act. Even the officers aren't much more than eating machines. General Dominick was my superior officer, but even he was basically a mean, angry jerk who controlled his soldiers with intimidation and fear. For a red vampyre he was considered smart, but he really didn't think about much except who we could attack next." Kevin shook his head in disgust. "Believe me, I know all about this. I've been hiding among the Red Army for almost a year, and not one of them ever suspected that I was different."

"But, Kevin, you *smell* different now," Anastasia pointed out.

"That's the last part that I've been trying to figure out. I'm almost sure no blue vampyre is going to pay enough attention to me to notice that I don't stink."

"But almost is not good enough, u-we-tsi."

"The red vampyres will notice, won't they?" Anastasia asked gently.

"I think they might. Well, not the regular soldiers, but someone like one of the red generals—I'm pretty sure he would."

"What can Kevin do about that?" Dragon asked.

"Well, I can consider casting a spell over him—something that carries a scent with it," mused Anastasia. "But any priestess who crosses paths with him could easily pick up the spell's energy trail. And if you were anywhere near Neferet she would recognize my spellwork immediately."

"Then that idea is definitely out," Dragon said.

"How about something simpler?" said Grandma Redbird. "Kevin, how strong does this scent need to be?"

Kevin shrugged. "I'm not sure. When I was a red vampyre I didn't really notice the stink."

"It depends on the type of red vampyre," said Dragon. "Soldiers reek like death and mold. With officers, especially higher ranked officers, the smell isn't so bad."

"So, with an officer, which is what Kevin is, the scent isn't much stronger than a woman's perfume?" Grandma asked.

"I suppose that's a good comparison," said Dragon. "If the woman is heavy-handed with her perfume."

"Well, u-we-tsi, this is going to sound vile, but I think you should wear the blood of a red vampyre like you would perfume."

"You want me to spray blood on myself?"

Grandma smiled. "Perhaps smearing some of it on your skin in places that can't be seen would work better."

"Disgusting," Kevin muttered.

"But doable," Anastasia said.

"Yeah, I guess you're right," Kevin said. "Man, I wish I could just give it a try without the stinky blood perfume."

"You cannot," Dragon said. "They discover you and they'll discover us."

"I would never tell them where you are!" Kevin said.

Anastasia put a hand on his shoulder. "Not willingly you wouldn't, but after they starve you and torture you—well, let's just say it's better to be stinky."

"Yeah, you're right. So, I go back to the depot tonight—after I get some red vamp blood. I'm not gonna enjoy that." Kevin shuddered and then cracked his knuckles. "But I'll do whatever I have to. Okay, I do have a plan, but I want your input."

"Of course," Anastasia said, and the four of them moved to the stone benches the sprites had somehow carved out of the wall of the cave. The huge raven that seemed never to be far from the priestess flew into the cave in a flutter of cold air and dark wings, landing on a stone outcropping above Anastasia. "What are you thinking, Kevin?"

"We need Aphrodite."

"Aphrodite?" Dragon grunted.

"Before you complain about it, just think about what I said before. What would happen if there were no more Red Army for Neferet to use as a wartime eating machine?"

Dragon sighed and nodded. "Yes, it is true. Without the Red Army, Neferet would no longer have such an easy time winning the war."

"Exactly," Kevin said.

"Then you must know it is worth the risk," Grandma Redbird said.

"All right. I'll have Johnny B lead you to where we hid the

Polaris." Dragon turned his somber gaze to Grandma Redbird. "Sylvia, I want you to know that you have a place here with us should you choose to stay."

"Thank you, Dragon, but I must return to my farm. I've been granted protection, so I am in no danger, and I can do more good out there than hiding here."

"How do I get messages to you guys here?" Kevin asked. "I'll try to get back here as often as possible, but I'll have to be one hundred percent sure no one's following me. What if I have information you need, but I can't get away?"

"That's easy," said Anastasia, casting her big blue eyes upward at the raven. "I will send Tatsuwa to find you every day. He'll circle around you. If you have a message for us, write it on a strip of paper and give it to him. He'll get it to me. Likewise, if we have a message for you, Tatsuwa will bring it to you."

"Um, how's he going to find me?" Kevin gave the raven a side glance and the big bird croaked at him.

"Oh, you need not worry about that. If you're outside, Tatsuwa will find you. His eyesight is as sharp as his intelligence."

"Anastasia, my dear, I have seen your lovely raven before—he seems to always be close to you—but I have not heard you call him by name until recently. I have been meaning to tell you that I appreciate that you chose our Native word for him," said Grandma Redbird, who moved over to stand close enough to the bird to stroke his shiny black feathers.

"Tatsuwa is Cherokee for raven?" Anastasia sounded surprised.

"It is," said Grandma Redbird. "If you did not know that, how did you name him?"

Anastasia's brilliant smile lit up the cave as she gazed lovingly up at the bird. "I did not name him. He told me his name, didn't you, Tatsuwa?"

*"Tatsuwa!"* the raven said as clearly as the priestess he'd chosen as his own.

"Sometimes I think the two of them are closer than we are," muttered Dragon.

*"Jealous!"* croaked Tatsuwa.

Anastasia laughed musically. "Oh, Tatsuwa, stop teasing Bryan." The bird hopped down from his perch and waddled to Anastasia, snuggling against her side while she used one long, slender finger to stroke the downy feathers above his beak.

"How many words does he know?" asked Kevin, totally intrigued by the strange black bird.

"Oh, Tatsuwa doesn't just mimic words. He speaks," said Anastasia. She kissed the big bird on top of his head, and Kevin could swear he heard the creature purr.

"A ta-tsu-wa is a powerful ally," said Grandma Redbird. "When they bond—they bond for life."

"If only I'd known that when I found him, freezing and almost completely featherless last winter," Dragon grumbled.

"Oh, Bryan, you would never have let him suffer and die," said his beautiful mate. "Tatsuwa and I thank you for your good heart."

*"Thank you, Bryan,"* said the bird, sounding disconcertingly like Anastasia.

"I draw the line with him sleeping with us," said Dragon.

"My love, you know he prefers his nest."

"Made from your hair."

"Seriously?" Kevin asked Anastasia.

"It's only partially made from my hair. The rest is from one of my old sweaters. And he doesn't pull the hair from my head. He's great at cleaning out my brushes." The priestess' eyes sparkled as she kissed the top of the raven's sleek black head again.

"Hurmph," Dragon grunted. Then his sardonic gaze went to Kevin. "But what all that means is the bird is freakishly smart and will do whatever Anastasia asks of him."

"Okay, well, I guess he'll be my cell phone then. It's weird, but not as weird as the fact that he sleeps in a nest made of your mate's hair." Kevin stood and stretched, grimacing only a little at the tightness of his healing wound. "Are you ready, G-ma?"

"Absolutely." Grandma Redbird stood and gave the raven another long stroke before embracing Anastasia and then her mate. "Thank you for trusting me."

"And me." Kevin held his hand out to Anastasia, who smiled sweetly before hugging him and kissing his cheek.

"You are as easy to trust as your grandmother," said the priestess.

"Well, once we got over that red Mark of yours." Dragon pulled Kevin into a back-clapping embrace as well. "Stay safe, Kevin Redbird. You may be our only hope at stopping this war without surrendering and dooming our world to Darkness."

"Hey, no pressure, right?" Kevin forced himself not to crack his knuckles. As he and his g-ma followed Johnny B from the mouth of the cave, Tatsuwa flew past them and Kevin heard the bird calling on the wind, *"Redbird Boy … Redbird Boy … Redbird Boy … "*

## 12

# *Other Kevin*

"U-we-tsi, are you quite sure about this?" Grandma Redbird asked as she leaned over her seat, searching through a big basket that took up most of the back seat of her car. She'd parked in one of the rear spaces in the darkest part of Utica Square's rear parking lot.

"No, but I'm sure you can't drive me onto the school grounds. You're under Neferet's protection, but no rational human would ever get in a car with a red vampyre unless they were about to be lunch."

"Ah, here it is! I knew I had one of these back there. Put this on. It has a hood and it should be big enough to tug down to cover your face." G-ma handed him an old, dark hoodie that smelled vaguely of lavender, which he slipped over his head. Then she opened the basket again and pulled out a leather satchel that had a thick shoulder strap. "Here, take this as well. I packed a few things for you I thought you might need. And, no, I didn't mean that I should drive you there. I understand that's impossible and you can easily walk to the House of Night from here. I am worried about your blood perfume." Grandma Redbird's nose wrinkled as she said the last two words.

Kevin laughed, slung the satchel over his shoulder, and hugged her. "You don't need to worry about that. I have it all figured out."

"I know it's something you must do, but it makes me very uncomfortable to think about you killing a red fledgling or vampyre."

"G-ma, I'm not going to kill anyone."

"So, you're just going to cut a red vampyre to get the blood you need?"

"G-ma, I have a better idea than that. I'm going to visit the school's morgue."

Grandma Redbird hugged him tightly. "Oh, u-we-tsi, I am so happy to hear that!" Then they both giggled like schoolgirls at the ridiculousness of being happy about visiting a morgue.

Finally, Kevin gave her a kiss on her soft cheek. "Promise me you won't do anything that could get you hurt."

She took his face in her hands and smiled lovingly into his eyes. "I cannot promise that, but I can promise that I will be wise and think before I act."

"I guess that'll have to be promise enough."

"I guess it will." Grandma kissed him. "Go under the protection of the Great Goddess, u-we-tsi, and always remember how proud I am of you."

Kevin hated leaving his g-ma. He had to force himself not to immediately begin imagining hordes of insatiable red vampyres descending on her farm to devour her for working with the Resistance.

*G-ma is under Neferet's protection.*

*No one in the Red or Blue Army knows she's part of the Resistance.*

*I really need to chill the hell out.*

Thoughts about his g-ma and the Resistance swirled around and around in Kevin's head as he cut across Twenty-Second Street and headed down Yorktown Avenue and the east side of the House of Night.

It was late—only a couple of hours from sunrise—but he wasn't worried. His visit with Zo had given him insight into the House of Night, and he knew where he could hide safely from the sun, and from curious vampyres. *If* the two worlds were really more similar than they were different. If this House of Night *hadn't* been built like Zo's ...

Kevin shook his head. *No reason to get all negative unless I have to.* If all else failed, he could always play stupid and be just another red vampyre who'd missed the predawn bus to the depot tunnels. Hopefully the blue vamps would let him stay in one of the darkened dorm rooms and not toss him out on the street to fry.

The stone wall that surrounded the House of Night loomed suddenly on his right, looking austere and intimidating and basically nothing like the well-lit, welcoming House of Night over which his sister presided.

For an instant, a deep yearning gripped him, and Kevin wished more than anything that he could run back to Woodward Park and figure out a way to reopen the doorway between worlds and slip back through—never to return.

"But what if I did that? What would happen to G-ma over here? She'd never stop worrying about me, and she'd never stop mourning the loss of Zo *and* me," he said to himself. And then there was Dragon and Anastasia and the rest of the Resistance. They'd believe he'd been caught and killed, or that he'd lied to them. They'd probably abandon the cave on the ridge, which would be really awful. No, Kevin couldn't leave. No matter how much he wished he could.

Streetlights meant to look like they were from the early 1900s, complete with flickering gas, cast moving shadows along the huge wall. Kevin cut across Yorktown to join them as his preternaturally sharp vision began searching the stones, looking for the old, rectangular one that was stamped with a **1926**—the year the wall surrounding the school had been completed. He cracked his knuckles nervously as he searched, not even sure if it was there. Zo had told him about it—that there was one particular brick on the east wall of the school that was actually a spring-loaded trapdoor system. The brick on the school side didn't look much different than the others, but she said the one on the outside of the wall was marked, and it was through that trapdoor that fledglings had been sneaking on and off campus for almost a century.

At least it was in *her* world.

This was the first test—the first time he'd know just how similar the worlds were in their structure.

When his eyes caught the **1926** stamp he felt a thrill of relief. The brick was at his eye level. He drew a deep breath and pressed it.

There was a faint click as some mechanism unlatched and then the wall seemed to sigh as a gap, just big enough for him to squeeze through, appeared in the otherwise perfect-looking brickwork.

Once inside he pushed the brick again and the door closed. Then Kevin paused. He crouched against the wall, wishing the predawn darkness had been less clear and instead foggy or rainy or even icy, but as his gaze swept the school grounds he began to relax. This wasn't his sister's House of Night. There were no human kids mixing with fledglings, blue and red, playing on the grounds. All Kevin saw was a meticulously manicured lawn, a few slinking cats, and Sons of Erebus Warriors standing guard at each of the doors to the main building.

Kevin was definitely going to avoid the main building.

Staying close enough to the wall that he blended with the flickering gaslight shadows, Kevin kicked into a swift jog. He followed the wall all the way around until he passed Nyx's Temple. As he did he sent it a longing look. He'd never forget the sense of love and acceptance he'd felt with Zoey and her friends inside the Goddess' Temple. It looked almost exactly like this temple, though there didn't seem to be nearly as many candles glowing through the paned windows, and he didn't catch even the smallest scent of vanilla or lavender.

*It's Neferet. She's not honoring the Goddess like Zo does.*

That thought made Kevin angry and heartsick.

Just beyond Nyx's Temple, the wall began to curve to the right, where it would run parallel to Utica Street, and not long after that Kevin caught sight of the solitary building he sought, built of the same stone as the wall and the rest of the House of Night. But this building was different.

Not that it looked that much different. It was small—really a miniature version of Nyx's Temple. It had a Japanese-style meditation garden situated adjacent to it that was framed on three sides by a mausoleum, which held the ashen remains of blue fledglings who had rejected the Change.

"And just blue fledglings," Kevin muttered softly to himself. "Red fledglings get dropped off at the morgue, burned, and then their ashes are thrown away. Literally. Like garbage, they're collected with the rest of the school's trash every week. I hope today wasn't trash day."

Kevin approached the mausoleum. He'd have to make his way through the meditation garden to enter the morgue itself, but he didn't anticipate any problem with that. The morgue wasn't exactly a hot spot of House of Night activity. Actually, hardly anyone ever went there, as Neferet encouraged fledglings not to "mourn those who were found unworthy."

The sand of the meditation garden gave silently under Kevin's feet, and even though the area appeared deserted, he was glad for the decorated wooden screens that partitioned off sections of the garden, creating private alcoves of shadow.

He could see the arched wooden door that was the entrance to the morgue not far from him, and Kevin had almost allowed some of the tension to leave his shoulders when movement caught the corner of his eye.

In the middle of the meditation garden there was a beautiful statue of Nyx. This particular statue portrayed Nyx as the compassionate goddess Kwan Yin. She was fashioned of dreamy white onyx, sitting cross-legged on a lotus flower, and was lit from within by the only light in the serene garden.

In front of the statue was a simple wooden bench, much like the benches within each of the meditation alcoves, except larger. On the bench there sat a solitary figure, face upturned, staring at the Goddess.

*Shit! A priestess!*

Kevin quickly and silently ducked into the nearest meditation alcove. He studied the woman sitting on the bench, trying to get a clear view of her face, and thinking that she seemed familiar, when someone else rushed into the garden from the opposite direction, as if she were coming from the main school building. She strode up to the bench, making a big show of looking down at the priestess who was sitting there by herself. Kevin pressed himself into the corner of his alcove and prayed that neither woman would discover him there.

"There you are! One of the Warriors said he saw you heading this way, but I was sure he was mistaken. I even said so. I said, 'Why would the lovely Aphrodite want to spend time in the morgue garden?' But as I couldn't find you elsewhere, and as you refused to answer your phone, I decided to come here looking for you."

Kevin felt a jolt of electric shock. *That's Aphrodite!* And then his mind caught up with his shock as he recognized the voice of the second priestess.

Aphrodite's sigh carried across the sand to Kevin. "Hello, Neferet. To answer your question, I come here often because hardly anyone else does. I like to have time to think. Alone. Which is why my phone is off."

"My dear, that would be acceptable if you were any other priestess, but you are not. You are my Prophetess."

"It's not like I'm having a vision."

Kevin's lips turned up at Aphrodite's sarcastic, sexy voice. He'd rarely seen Neferet up close. He'd never spoken to her. But he had witnessed how other vampyres treated her—with respect and a very healthy dose of fear. Not Aphrodite. Aphrodite spoke to her as if they were peers, and she was annoyed at being interrupted.

"Not at this moment you're not, but you had one earlier this afternoon."

Aphrodite stood and faced the taller High Priestess. "You have spies watching me?"

"Spies? No. Only the faithful fulfilling their duty to inform me about anything I would consider important, and my Prophetess having a vision and then hiding from me is definitely important."

Aphrodite tossed back her mane of hair, which caught the slight light from the image of the Goddess and shined like newly spun gold. "Oh, for shit's sake! I'm not hiding. I seriously thought coming to the morgue would help. I've been seeing nothing but death in my visions. Today's was no different. You want to know what I saw? Blue fledglings and vampyres being slaughtered in a field by a disgusting horde of red vampyres. Actually, the one thing I can tell you specifically, besides who was slaughtering whom, is that it was a field of winter wheat that had just been cut. It smelled really good. Until the stink of red vampyres took over. Nothing else was very clear. Just death, blood, slaughter, and panic in a field overrun by red soldiers."

"What field? Where?" Neferet snapped.

"I don't know! Neferet, I keep trying to get you to understand that I *always* experience my visions from the point of view of someone who is dying—usually horribly. That's why it's so hard to understand them. So, because my Goddess-be-damned visions are so full of death, it made sense that I might find an answer near the morgue. Like I *want* to hang out here? Get real. This place is not my style."

"Oh, so you want to *get real?*" Neferet said in a low voice. Kevin felt his soul shiver as Neferet glided closer to Aphrodite, causing the younger vampyre to step back into the sands of the garden. "What's *real* is that there is a Resistance movement of *my own people* fighting against me. What's *real* is that every day blue fledglings, blue vampyres, and even loathsome, weak *humans* desert me. They *leave*! As if I don't know what's best for them? As if I'm not their High Priestess!"

"Well, you're really not High Priestess of any humans," Aphrodite said.

Quick as an adder, Neferet struck Aphrodite. The slap echoed from across the serene space, and Kevin cringed in sympathy.

"Never tell me what I am or am not! All I want you to tell me is how to bring about the end of the Resistance. If you cannot do that, you are of less use to me than a rabid, newly Changed red vampyre. At least they fight for me. Remind me, my dear, what is it *you* do for me?"

"I am your Prophetess."

"Really? Your visions have become nothing but muddled nonsense."

"But I can only see what Nyx allows me to—"

"Perhaps you would do better if you groveled less to Nyx and spent more time serving your High Priestess!" Neferet interrupted.

"Neferet, I am a Prophetess of Nyx. My power comes from the Goddess. If I don't, as you say, *grovel*, then I don't get visions."

"Then maybe you should look elsewhere for power, my dear. Or would you rather I send you out with the Red Army when they next engage our enemies? Better yet, a few of my generals have suggested I should be more visible to my red soldiers." Neferet paused and Kevin watched her shudder in disgust. "But I simply cannot abide their scent and their stupidity. They're really nothing but rabid animals. Maybe *you* are my answer to the generals' request. Perhaps you should move your things to the depot and become *their* Prophetess. You could even go to war with them. Seeing *real* death instead of your convoluted visions could be an enlightening experience for you! You might get used to it and start being able to *think* during your visions."

Kevin was appalled at Neferet's words. The depot and the tunnels beneath were little more than holding cells for the Red Army and newly Marked red fledglings. It reeked down there—Kevin had even been disgusted by it. And it was filthy—truly disgusting, with the decomposing remains of humans the army fed on strewn about like giant, broken dolls. The red fledglings and vampyres housed there were not far removed from animals. Kevin hated to even imagine what being forced to live with them would do to Aphrodite.

"I'll go wherever you send me, but I promise you that being surrounded by the Red Army will not help my visions." Aphrodite tried to sound strong, as if she didn't particularly care where Neferet sent her, but Kevin could hear her panic, thinly veiled by nonchalance.

"You need to figure out what *will* help your visions! If you don't start giving me some information I can use, you're going to lose your opulent chambers, your room service, and your bottomless supply of champagne and virile blue vampyres with which to dally. All that—*all of this*," Neferet made an angry gesture that took in the serene garden, the school grounds, and the tidy little morgue, "will be replaced by damp, fetid tunnels and death, as I am beginning to believe that your *gifts* are only meaningful to the dead. So, the next we speak I will expect you to have *remembered* more details about your last vision—or pack your Louis Vuitton bag and get ready to move." In a swirl of her long, silk gown, Neferet turned her back on Aphrodite and strode away, leaving her Prophetess standing alone in the moonlit sands of the meditation garden.

Kevin remained there, silently watching Aphrodite. As soon as Neferet was gone, the young Prophetess' shoulders slumped. She rubbed the side of her face where she'd been struck, and Kevin was almost certain he heard her breath catch in a sob.

And then she did something Kevin absolutely did not expect. Aphrodite didn't leave. She didn't head back to the warmth and opulence of her chambers in the main House of Night building. Instead, she turned, and for an instant he thought she was heading to his alcove. His mind whirred, frantically testing and discarding lies he could say, excuses he could use for being there.

But she stopped and slumped on the bench she'd been sitting on before Neferet had interrupted her. With a sigh that sounded like it'd originated in the depths of her soul, she slipped off a sparkly, very uncomfortable-looking high-heeled shoe from her right foot and began drawing little designs in the sand with what he could clearly see were her toes painted a bright pink.

"Nyx, she's so horrible!" Aphrodite said to the statue. "Maybe I should tell her she's looking old. She's not, of course—the *bitch*, but if I start asking if she's getting enough sleep and mention crow's feet and sagging boobs—just in general—*not* about her specifically, she's so fucking paranoid that she might focus more on her mirror than on me." She blew out another long, defeated sigh. "I don't want to tell her everything I see. I … I can't bear knowing that I am the cause of more deaths. Lenobia and Travis and all those horses …" Aphrodite's voice trailed away on a sob. Then she angrily wiped at her eyes and stared up at the Goddess. "Nyx, she's your High Priestess, but I just don't get it. She's *awful*. I hate her more than I hate those horrible cheap department stores where everything's on sale and the peasants who shop there have to paw through racks and racks of tacky crap without the benefit of dressing rooms with crystal chandeliers and flutes of champagne." She shuddered delicately.

Caught completely off guard by the very bizarre, very Aphrodite-like comparison, Kevin snorted a laugh.

Aphrodite's demeanor shifted instantly. Her spine went straight. She tossed back her hair. Her blue eyes narrowed as her gaze swept the meditation garden.

"Who the hell is here?"

Kevin froze. Then, remembering the sweatshirt G-ma had given him, he pulled the hoodie up over his head, and tugged and tugged—hoping like hell that it and the shadows would be enough to cover his red tattoo.

Aphrodite stood, slipping her arched foot back into her sparkly shoe. She took a few steps further into the meditation garden—directly toward Kevin's alcove.

"I said, who the hell is here?"

"S-sorry. I didn't really mean to disturb you," he stuttered, thinking it was smarter to admit to his presence than it was to be discovered creeping in the shadows.

She marched to his meditation alcove and stopped in front of it, hands on hips.

"What? What the fuck do you want from me? To know the

future? To know the Goddess? To know *me*?" she scoffed, and her beautiful face twisted into something mean and spite-filled. "Well, you're out of luck. I can't help you with any of those things."

"I-I'm not here because I want anything from you!" Kevin blurted honestly. His mind was speeding around like a bumper car at the Rooster Days Festival, smacking against ideas and bouncing off as he rejected them.

"Oh, sure you don't. *Everyone* wants something from me." Kevin saw a flash of raw emotion, bitter and pain-filled, cross her face. "How long have you been here?"

He opened his mouth to try to answer, but she didn't give him a chance to speak.

"Are you one of hers? Did she put you here to spy on me? If so, listen and listen well—*I do not give one solitary shit if you tell her what I said.* I will lie. I will tell her I sat and prayed to Nyx and *you* interrupted me when I was just getting a response from the Goddess. She'll believe me because no matter how much she likes to fuck men, Neferet doesn't actually *like* men. And she never, ever trusts them. So, whoever you are, if you tell on me to her, Neferet will end up believing me and loathing you, because she needs little excuse to loathe any man."

Kevin was astounded by the depth of cruelty in her voice. The beautiful, sad Prophetess who had, just seconds ago, been sitting morosely on a rock talking to her Goddess, had turned into someone awful.

Slowly, distinctly, Kevin said, "Oh, I believe you. You obviously know what you're talking about. You sound just like her."

Aphrodite jerked back as if he'd struck her other cheek.

"Who the hell are you?"

Kevin pressed himself back, wishing he could become a shadow. "I'm no one. Neferet didn't send me here. I had no idea she'd be here. I had no idea you'd be here."

"Then what the hell do you want?" Aphrodite asked again.

She looked so cold, so unlike *his* Aphrodite, that Kevin's anger began to simmer along with his fear. If she screamed or cried out, a Son of Erebus Warrior would surely hear her. He'd be hauled out of the gardens for disturbing Neferet's Prophetess and become the center of attention—*without any stinky blood perfume.*

He'd be discovered as different, and that would suck on many levels. So he hardened his voice and fueled his anger with fear.

"Hey, I already told you. I don't want *anything* from you. I don't even want to be here—at this awful place of death in this awful fucking world!"

He could see that his words took her aback. There was a long silence while she stared at the sitting shadow that was Kevin. When she spoke, her voice had lost its bitter edge, and her simple question surprised him.

"Did you lose someone you loved?"

The question settled over Kevin, bringing with it images of a lost world ... a missed life ... Zoey, laughing with her Nerd Herd. Grandma Redbird, gifting him with a medicine bag and trying not to cry as she told him goodbye. The other Aphrodite, smiling at him as her eyes sparkled like gemstones with humor and her special, snarky brand of intelligence. Damien and Jack, holding hands and looking so, so happy and in love, and red and blue fledglings playing peacefully in the snow, surrounded by cats and love. Always love.

"Yes." His voice broke and he had to clear his throat before he continued. "Yes. I lost my whole world."

Her face changed again then. It softened, and one tear slid down her smooth cheek, and Kevin thought he'd never seen anyone look sadder or more beautiful.

"Yeah, me too. I lost myself. Same damn thing."

Then she turned and left the meditation garden without another word or glance his way.

# 13

# *Other Kevin*

Kevin made his decision quickly. He could leave—fast. He could run away, back to Utica Square, call G-ma, and return to the ridge. Or he could get his butt up off the bench he felt practically adhered to and go in the morgue and harvest some stinking red vampyre blood to camouflage his smell and get on with the job he'd set out to do.

He knew what Zoey would do.

Kevin moved as quickly and silently as possible. His gaze swept the area as his ears strained to listen for even the smallest sound of anyone approaching while he walked across the meditation garden to the door to the morgue. When he got there, he didn't pause. Kevin opened the door and ducked within.

He'd been to the morgue once before. It'd been with General Dominick right before he'd been promoted to lieutenant. They'd had a skirmish with a group of humans who had formed a militia unit east of Broken Arrow in the middle of some state-owned lands that had once been a Boy Scout camp but was now a mess of deserted trails and overgrown woods. The humans had refused to give up. Neferet sent in her Red Army.

It had been a brutal massacre. Every human was killed. The Red Army lost a dozen soldiers. The general had asked for volunteers to bring the bodies of the fallen red vampyres back to the House of Night, and Kevin had immediately stepped up, thinking that driving a military truck piled with dead vamps was a lot better than staying and joining in with the rest of the army as they tore the humans apart and devoured them. General Dominick had been impressed with Kevin's ability to handle the job and immediately gave him a field promotion.

So, Kevin knew exactly where he was going—though he wasn't eager to get there.

He followed the entry hallway all the way to the end, ignoring the doors to his left and right. They were full of blue vampyres that had died or been killed in battle and blue fledglings that had rejected the Change. There wouldn't be any red vampyres in any of those rooms, as Neferet made sure to keep her Red and Blue Armies segregated, even in death.

There were no markings on any of the doors, except the very last one at the end of the hallway. That door was marked clearly with a large red X. Kevin didn't hesitate. He opened the door and slipped inside the dark room.

The smell was the first thing that hit him. The room was cold, kept that way so that the bodies wouldn't decompose too much before they could be burned and then discarded like trash. There was little in the room except metal tables and metal cabinets lining one wall. He quickly counted ten tables. Only one of them was occupied. Averting his eyes from that table, Kevin hurried to the wall of cabinets and began searching through the medical supplies.

It took little time to find a glass jar with a lid.

Kevin took the jar and went to the occupied table. A body lay there, covered by a bloody sheet.

*Just do it. Just get it over with.*

Kevin lifted the sheet from the body and sighed sadly.

"Damn, dude, that musta hurt." The cause of death of the young red vampyre that lay there was obvious. Something had smashed into his head. The whole right half of his face, from his cheekbone up, was a mess. Kevin wanted to avert his eyes. He didn't want to look at the guy's face, but he couldn't seem to stop himself.

The dead vampyre had been so young! His face, frozen in death, was hideous on the wounded side, but the rest of it didn't even look like he was eighteen. "You can't have been Changed for very long." He spoke quietly to the corpse. "Me either. I remember Changing so well. I remember how scared I was, knowing that my humanity was slipping away from me. I still don't know what's worse. Totally losing your humanity and turning into an eating machine or hanging on and understanding just how much of a monster you're becoming." Kevin rested his hand on the kid's cold, lifeless shoulder. "I'm sorry. I'm going to try my best to stop anyone else from becoming a monster, but I need your help. This isn't gonna be pleasant, and I'm real glad you can't feel anything, but I'm still sorry I have to do this to you. Okay, well, I'm going to get it over with, then I'll cover you back up."

First, Kevin lifted the dead vamp's arm, turning it so that he could get to the underside of the forearm. "Again, dude, sorry." Then, he pressed the nail of his index finger hard against the flaccid skin, drawing it slowly along the major artery from wrist to elbow. The skin split easily under Kevin's preternaturally sharp fingernail, and he worked quickly, squeezing and pressing to coax the settled and congealed blood into the glass jar.

The smell was awful—worse even than living red vampyres, which was pretty damn terrible. But Kevin kept at it, moving from one arm to another, and then finally rolled the body on its side to expose more settled blood. It was slow working. The blood was sticky and clotted, and utterly disgusting to milk from the dead body. Eventually, Kevin found himself having to stick his fingers in the slash wounds he was making and scoop the gooey stuff out. Bottle filled, he finally screwed the lid on before going to the sink.

Carefully, Kevin lifted his sweatshirt and the T-shirt he had on under it. With a grimace of disgust, he rubbed a line of foul-smelling bloody goo on his belly, just above the waist of his jeans. He also pushed up his sleeves, rubbing more blood into each of his elbow creases. Satisfied that he would pass a red vampyre sniff test, he washed his hands, the jar, and then grabbed a bunch of paper towels from the metal dispenser positioned over the sink. Kevin wet half of the paper towels and then went back to the body.

"I'm never eating anything that looks like strawberry Jell-O again. Ever," Kevin told the corpse. "I won't leave you like this. Not that anyone would notice. They're gonna wheel you into the crematorium probably without even looking at you. But still—it isn't right to leave you like this."

Kevin cleaned the blood from the body, repositioning his clothes, and even wiping down the table. When the dead vampyre looked semitidy, Kevin again put his hand on the dead kid's shoulder.

"Thank you. Your blood will make it so that I don't get caught—so they don't know I'm different. I'm going to change things here. I give you my word. I'm going to be part of a miracle. I know it can happen because I've seen it. I've felt it. And now I live it. I'm going to make sure red vampyres aren't monsters anymore. I promise." Kevin bowed his head and whispered to his Goddess, "Thank you, Nyx. Please welcome this kid to your grove. He didn't ask for this. No matter who he was when he was human, good or bad, he didn't deserve this." Then, slowly, Kevin pulled the bloody sheet back up over the young red vampyre's body.

Kevin slipped the jar inside the satchel's internal pouch—well away from his g-ma's delicious cookies. Then he slid the strap over his shoulder again and went to the door, opening it just enough to peer into the hallway, breathing a sigh of relief when he saw it was deserted.

Not wasting another second, Kevin rushed down the hallway and out the door. He slipped around the side of the morgue that faced the rest of the school grounds and studied the area.

A familiar feeling of terrible unease crawled up his spine as he realized that instead of a black sky, the world around him had begun to shift to gray and pink.

*Dawn!* Kevin wanted to kick himself. *Of course I feel uneasy. In fifteen minutes the sun is going to rise and fry my ass!*

He didn't have any time to waste. Pulling his hoodie down to cover most of his face, Kevin strode quickly and with confidence across the schoolyard.

He saw no fledglings, and the only vampyres he noticed were Sons of Erebus Warriors as the day shift began relieving the night guards. Kevin cut across campus to the back entrance to the Field House and the abandoned equestrian center, and kept his face turned away as he walked past two Warriors who were discussing the officers' briefing that Neferet had announced they needed to attend in the auditorium at 2000 hours the next day.

It took everything in him not to give a big fist pump and yell *Yes!* An officers' brief was *exactly* what he needed—and what Dragon needed to hear about!

Once Kevin was inside the Field House he followed the hallway, taking a couple turns until he came to an indistinct door that he desperately hoped led to the basement, just like it did in Zo's world. He tried the door handle, *and it was locked!*

"Dammit!" Kevin breathed the word. "Now what the hell am I supposed to do?"

If someone saw him during daylight hours he'd get caught. Red vampyres were *never* at the House of Night after dawn. He couldn't even feign ignorance and say he was lost. No one would believe him. From the moment a fledgling was Marked red and brought to the House of Night, it was drilled into him that he *must* be in the tunnels before sunrise. The only exception was if the red vampyre was on a Red Army mission.

Kevin's mind thought of and rejected one idea after another. He was simply out of time. He had to hide in the basement.

He needed help.

"Damn, if only I could slip through that keyhole like air ..." Kevin muttered to himself as he cracked his knuckles and wished that he knew this House of Night like he knew the tunnels. Then he'd know where he could hide and be safe until—

An idea hit him! He didn't have time to wonder if he was making a mistake. He didn't have time to second-guess himself. He only had time to close his eyes and take several deep, grounding breaths, and then he opened his eyes, faced east, and made the call.

"Old Magick sprites of air, I am Kevin Redbird, and with the power in my blood, and the power Nyx has gifted me with, I call you to me!"

His answer came disconcertingly fast, as before him several glowing firefly-like fey suddenly popped into view, hovering at his eye level, bringing with them the skin-crawling sensation Kevin had every time he invoked Old Magick.

*"Redbird Boy! You call us again! And we come! We come!"* They flitted about, changing places as their little bodies shifted from insect to glowing, winged women, and back to insect.

"Thanks a bunch! Okay, I only need one thing, but I need it real fast." He pointed at the keyhole in the door. "Could you go through there and unlock this door? I need to get inside there—now."

*"We can do that,"* said one flitting fey.

*"But what payment? What payment?"* trilled another.

Kevin opened his mouth to tell the fey that he'd pay with more of his blood, but one giggling sprite, who showed too many sharp teeth as she laughed, interrupted before he could speak.

*"No blood this time! We want something special!"*

*"Yes,"* the first fey agreed. *"Special!"*

Kevin wanted to rip the hair from his head in frustration and wondered briefly if the sprites would consider his hair a *special* payment. Thankfully, he had another idea. He reached inside his g-ma's satchel and pulled out a fragrant, homemade lavender chocolate-chip cookie. Holding it up he grinned at the sprites.

"Well, this cookie is about as special as it gets. It was made by my grandmother—the Wise Woman who was on the ridge with me. You know, you guys ate one of her medicine bags."

"*Ooooooh!*" The sprites glowed even brighter as they hovered in the air around the cookie. Then, together, so that their voices echoed eerily from the stone walls around him, the fey spoke rhythmically.

> *"A special payment we do see*
> *One offered by thee and accepted by me.*
> *Our deal is sealed—so mote it be!"*

The flock of Old Magick air sprites descended like locusts on the cookie. Kevin yelped and he let it loose as they devoured every crumb. Then, with no hesitation, the glowing sprites dived down, flowing through the door's keyhole, under the door, and through the crack at the doorjamb.

Kevin stood there, wondering what would happen next, when he heard the deadbolt turn. He grabbed the door handle and pushed. It swung open easily. He closed it behind him, and when he turned to navigate his way down the steep basement stairs, a single sprite appeared, floating by his head.

"Thank you," Kevin said. "You helped me out a lot."

"*We like your call, Redbird Boy. We like your payment. Call when you have need of us, but do not forget that we like special payment … special, special payment …*" As the sprite spoke, her appearance continued to shift—from a big firefly, to a beautiful, winged woman, to something with more arms and legs than she should have had and a mouth that seemed to grow and grow and grow until her face appeared to split in half.

And then, in a flash of light, the sprite was gone, leaving Kevin with a terrible feeling of unease.

(

## *Zoey*

"Z? You in here?" Stark called as he entered our bedchamber. "I got your text to meet you."

"You're early!" I yelled from the bathroom. "Don't move!"

"Huh?"

"I said don't move! Stay by the door. Shut your eyes!"

"Shut my eyes?"

I heard the confused amusement in his voice, but I seriously didn't want him to spoil my surprise. "If you don't want to shut your eyes then turn around."

"Okay! Okay! I'm shutting my eyes. Uh, Z. What are you doing?"

What was I doing? I was trying to make up for worrying the crap out of my Warrior *and* be romantic. "Hang on. You'll see in a sec!"

"I didn't even think you'd be back here until after sunrise. Weren't you at the depot with Damien and Kramisha?"

"Yeah!" I yelled through the bathroom door. "Well, for a while I was, but Aphrodite decided to get in on the redecorating, and I had to leave."

"Too much bickering?"

"Totally," I said. "Okay, I'm coming out. Keep your eyes shut until I tell you to open them, 'kay?"

"Whatever you say, my Queen."

I could hear the smile in his voice, which made me grin in response, and I gave myself one last check in the mirror. I don't wear much makeup. Actually, I have an issue with makeup. I hate that society says we have to wear it to "look our best." Look our best? With crap slathered all over our faces, hiding everything about us that's really us? Um, no. I'm with the fab Alicia Keys—I don't want to cover up my face … my mind … my soul … nothing. So, I fluffed my hair and smiled at my freshly washed face. *Ready!*

I peeked my head out of the bathroom. No Stark. On bare feet I padded through our bedroom area, straightening the picnic blanket I'd spread out on the floor, and fluffing the cushions that I'd arranged perfectly for us to sit on.

"Z?"

"Keep your eyes closed!" I hurried through our bedroom to the sitting area, and smiled when I saw my Warrior, still standing in front of the door with his eyes closed. I went to him and took his hand.

"Can I open them now?"

"Nope, not till I say, but follow me."

"I'm gonna run into something."

"Don't be a baby. I've got you." I led him slowly around the coffee table and other obstacles, finally situating him beside the picnic blanket. "Okay, hang on just one more sec." I left him standing there and hurried around to the other side of the blanket, clicking on the remote to the big TV that was mounted on the wall, checking to be sure it was muted. Then I nervously fluffed my hair again, before saying, "Okay, you can open your eyes now!"

He did, and his lips quirked up in that sexy half-smile I loved so much.

"Z! You're practically naked!"

I could feel my cheeks flushing, but I grinned at him. "No, I have on one of your T-shirts."

"Yeah, my old, holey T-shirt that's totally see-through. Damn, Z! It never looked like that on me!"

"Heehees!" I giggled. "So, are you hungry?"

"For you! Hell yes!"

"No, silly. Well, yes, silly, but first how about we eat?" I pointed down at my picnic dinner.

His gaze reluctantly left my body to check out the blanket. "Z, is that nachos? With *everything* on them?"

"Yep, it totally is. I even added jalapeños. Lots and lots of them, because even though I think they are the peppers from hell sent to burn mouths into submission, you like them." I sat on one of the cushions and patted the one beside me, motioning for Stark to join me.

"Nachos are my favorite," he said as he sat.

"I know."

He lifted an icy glass, sniffed, and then took a big gulp before he gushed, "And Dr. Pepper! You got me Dr. Pepper!"

"I know how much you heart it, even though I totally disagree with you because it's—"

"*An abomination of brown pop*," he finished the sentence for me.

"Yes, indeedy, it is."

He reached for a nacho and his gaze lifted to the TV screen. "Holy crap, Z! *Game of Thrones*? You're going to actually watch an episode with me?"

"I'm going to watch as many episodes as you want."

"But you hate *Game of Thrones*."

"No, I don't hate it. I don't watch it because Cersei reminds me too much of Neferet's craziness, but it's not always about me, so let's watch it."

Stark stared at me. "What have you done with my Zoey?"

I bumped his shoulder. "Oh, stop."

"Seriously, am I in trouble?"

"Of course not!"

"Ah, crap." He put the nacho down and turned me so that I had to look into his eyes. "What have *you* done?"

I sighed. "I've been acting like a selfish bitch since Kevin left, and I'm sorry. Really sorry, Stark. I know you've been worried, and this is my way of apologizing."

"Hey, it's understandable that you've been preoccupied, especially knowing Kev is using Old Magick."

"Understandable, yeah. But it's pretty immature of me to

be so distracted that you have to be stressed about me, and my High Priestesses have to pick up the slack for me. I'm going to do better, I promise."

Stark touched my cheek gently. "You always do better, Z. I knew you'd come around."

"Do you understand how much I love you?" I blurted.

"Yeah, but it's good to hear you say it." He devoured a nacho that was covered in gooey cheese and jalapeños, licking the extra cheese from his fingertips as he swallowed.

"You're the best. You are always here for me, but you also give me space to deal with my stuff on my own. That means a lot to me, especially because I know you can feel how distracted I am."

"I don't think you're distracted right now." He bent and touched his lips to mine.

I smiled. "No, you have one hundred percent of my attention right now. And I know the sun's rising soon, but if you can stay awake a while, I promise as long as you're conscious you'll have one hundred percent of me." I wrapped my arms around his broad shoulders and pulled him to me. Our lips met again and the kiss became deep and hot. I loved the way he tasted, the minty gum he chewed, the gross sweetness of Dr. Pepper—which suddenly wasn't gross at all—and the saltiness of nachos.

As he pressed me back against the cushions, his lips traveled down my neck, kissing and taking teasing nips at my skin, which had me gasping and goose bumping.

"How about we don't go to sleep?" His voice was low, and his breath was warm and sexy against my skin. "How about I kiss every inch of you, then we eat nachos and watch *Game of Thrones*, and then I kiss every inch of you again."

His tongue flicked out as he began finding the holes in his old T-shirt, kissing my breasts through them.

"But you have to teach tomorrow." I sounded breathless, like I'd just sprinted up several flights of stairs.

"Tomorrow is fencing, not archery. Damien can sub for me. He's a better fencer anyway."

Slowly, he started pulling the T-shirt up over my head.

"Damn, Z! You really *don't* have anything on except my shirt."

"Surprise!" I said.

And my chest bloomed with heat as my stomach clenched.

"Zoey?" Stark sat up abruptly, pulling my T-shirt down and staring at me. "It's happening again, isn't it?"

Through tears of fear and frustration, I nodded. "Kevin's using Old Magick again," I said brokenly. "And he has no clue how much trouble he's getting himself into."

"Shhh, I know. I know. Come here, my Queen."

Stark pulled me into his arms and held me close as the horribly familiar warmth in my chest faded, leaving only a sickness in my stomach and a realization about what I had to do. Now. I had to stop thinking about it. Stop weighing the consequences. And just … Do. It.

Ah. Hell.

# 14

# *Other Kevin*

Kevin woke abruptly, and for the first few seconds of consciousness he thought he was back in the tunnels below the depot—before he'd been pulled over to Zoey's world—before his humanity had been returned, and the bitter taste of despair flooded his mouth with nausea at the thought of trying to control his hunger and maintain his sanity.

Then he sat up, bumped his head on one of the two wooden crates he'd curled up between, and his memory woke with him. Kevin froze and peered silently around him. Nothing stirred. No one had entered the basement. He checked in with his internal clock—red vampyres always knew the exact time of sunrise and sunset.

"Five twenty-two p.m. Sunset." He spoke to himself out of habit. He'd done a lot of that over the past year since he'd been Marked as a red fledgling and then Changed. It was one way he'd tried to hold onto his sanity during that horrible time, and now it comforted him. He stretched, grimacing only slightly at the stiffness his wound still caused, though he felt pretty good. "Hungry, but good." And then he remembered, and his face broke into a grateful grin. "G-ma's cookies!"

Kevin grabbed the satchel and pulled out several cookies, as he did so his hand bumped something hard. Wondering what else his g-ma had put in there, he looked inside and breathed a long, happy sigh.

He lifted the metal thermos from the bottom of the satchel, opened it, took a sniff, and easily recognized the scent of blood. "She thinks of everything!" He chugged blood from the cold thermos as he ate the cookies. Kevin didn't *have to* have a constant supply of blood. He wouldn't lose his mind and attack someone on the street like a normal red vampyre would after a couple of days without it, but his back still needed to heal and the blood would definitely make him stronger. "Thank you, G-ma," he said between bites of cookies, and felt a rush of homesickness. For the amount of time it took him to finish his breakfast, he let himself wish he could leave this basement and this House of Night, go to his g-ma's house, and stay there with her eating cookies and working the lavender farm while they ignored the messed-up world. When he was done eating, he brushed the crumbs off his shirt and with them he brushed away that selfish, impossible wish.

He checked with his infallible internal clock, noting he had about two hours until the briefing Neferet had called.

"Okay, I have to stay down here at least long enough for the first bus to bring red fledglings and vamps over from the tunnels to train with the Sons of Erebus Warriors. So, how 'bout I look around since I didn't do much more than pass out when I got here?"

He found the light switch to the wall sconces, turning the dark basement into a strange place that almost looked like an underwater graveyard with the flickering gaslight shadows playing over row after row of long, wooden boxes stacked two and three high.

"Well, it's different than Zo's House of Night basement, that's for sure." Zo had told him that there could be a fortune of weapons stashed in the basement, but there were definitely no jeweled swords or ancient, priceless crossbows in sight. There were only wooden boxes. Lots of them.

He tried to open one, but it was nailed shut. He searched around the big, open room, and it didn't take long for him to find a crowbar in a pile of discarded hammers, nails, and other small tools. Working carefully, so he could close the box up again after he inventoried what was inside, Kevin pried the lid off the first box.

At first when he looked inside his mind didn't register what he was seeing. He reached out and touched one of the things, and the truth of what he was looking at had him feeling so hot and dizzy that he staggered back several steps.

"Get your shit together, Kev," he told himself. He cracked his knuckles. Shook out his hands. Ran a hand through his dark hair. And then he went back to the box.

The guns were huge and weird looking. And then he saw that there was a paper packed in the box. On it he read, **EX-41 MULTI-SHOT GRENADE LAUNCHER**.

"This is bad. This is really bad."

He didn't want to look in the other boxes, but he had to—so he opened each of the fifty coffin-like crates. Half of them held more grenade launchers and the ammunition for them. The rest of them held M16 machine guns, a lot more ammo, and a bunch of grenades.

Kevin's mind buzzed at the edge of panic as he memorized everything he saw. He had to warn Dragon. Neferet's armies had taken control of Oklahoma, Texas, Arkansas, and Kansas in a massively coordinated series of surprise attacks in the middle of the night. That control had spread like a forest fire to Louisiana, Missouri, Nebraska, and Iowa. They'd destroyed National Guard armories in each of those states and confiscated military vehicles. Holding with vampyre tradition, they hadn't used modern weapons. The teeth and claws of the Red Army, as well as their ability to control the minds of humans, had been enough to defeat the meager human Resistance.

But Kevin knew that as Neferet kept pushing—kept waging war against humans—she was running into more and more opposition. Humans were erecting barricades along state borders. As Kevin was just a lieutenant in the Red Army, he wasn't privy to the hows and whys of military tactics, but he had heard General Dominick complaining that Neferet was spending too much time negotiating with the governors of each state. He, of course, was for attacking, attacking, attacking.

"Apparently, so is Neferet," Kevin said somberly. "Only she means to attack with modern weapons." And then another thought smacked him. "Holy crap! This can't be the only weapons stash she has! All those armories—crap! Crap! Crap! Sure, the armies burned them, but I'll bet my humanity that they *didn't* burn the weapons they found in them."

He paced back and forth, back and forth. "This changes everything. The Resistance has to act right away! We have to take out Neferet and stop this war before she starts using these weapons. And I need to get a message to Dragon. Now."

Kevin checked his internal clock again. He had about forty-five minutes before Neferet's briefing, which should be enough time for him to walk aimlessly around the school grounds, hoping Anastasia's raven would find him.

He made sure the crates looked undisturbed before he reapplied the disgusting blood perfume. Then he slung G-ma's satchel over his shoulder and went up the stairs two at a time and paused at the door. Deciding the best thing to do would not be to try to sneak around, he held his breath and opened the door, stepping quickly out into the hallway. He'd taken one step when the voice behind him seemed to fill the hall—and freeze his heart.

"Hey! What the hell were you doing down there?"

Kevin turned to see General Stark and one of his lieutenants closing the distance between them. And Stark looked pissed.

"Sorry, sir. I musta taken a wrong turn." Kevin made a big show of snapping to attention and avoiding eye contact.

"That door is supposed to stay locked—Neferet's orders," said Stark.

"Sorry, sir," Kevin repeated, still at attention. "It wasn't locked."

"Dallas, Artus has the keys. Find him and lock that damn door."

"Yeah, will do, General." Stark's lieutenant started to leave, and then he smacked himself on the forehead and turned back. "I just realized I know who this kid is. He's one of General Dominick's lieutenants."

"Dominick? The red general who's missing with an entire squad of red fledglings and soldiers?" Stark said, his sharp eyes skewering Kevin.

"Yes, indeedy, sir," said Dallas.

Stark stepped closer, getting in Kevin's personal space. "Who are you?"

"Lieutenant Heffer, sir!"

"Under whose command?"

"General Dominick, sir!"

"And where is your general, Lieutenant Heffer?"

"I'm sorry, sir?"

Stark sighed audibly. "Red vamps are such a pain in the ass." Stark spoke to Dallas like Kevin wasn't still standing at attention right in front of him, hearing every word.

"Yep, they're pretty stupid. Even the officers." Dallas got up in Kevin's face. "Hey! The general asked you a question, boy! Fucking answer it!"

"I—I don't know where my general is." Kevin focused on sounding like any lieutenant in the Red Army would—subservient and confused.

"When is the last time you saw him?" Stark asked.

"Several days ago, sir. He gave me my orders then, and I have been on that mission since."

Dallas snorted. "Did that mission include breaking into a locked basement?"

"No, Lieutenant! That was a mistake."

"What did you do down there?" Stark asked.

"Nothing. When I saw that I was in the wrong place, I left, sir."

"Where the hell were you supposed to be?" Dallas asked.

"Training. I came back from my mission and then it was time for training. I thought I would see General Dominick at the tunnels tonight and report to him."

"What was your mission, Lieutenant?" Stark said.

"Five days ago, General Dominick sent me to Stroud. He'd heard the Resistance had found hiding places in that area and I was supposed to reconnoiter and then report back to him." Stroud was about halfway between Tulsa and Oklahoma City, and not close enough to Sapulpa to cause Dragon and the Resistance any trouble, so turning Stark's attention there didn't seem like a bad idea to Kev.

"Didn't you think something was weird when you couldn't find your general or the rest of your flight?" said Stark.

"Sir, I just got back. Just now."

"Give me a fucking break. You expect General Stark to believe that it took you five days to check out a little armpit of a town like Stroud?" Dallas scoffed.

"No, Lieutenant. I—I got lost."

"This just keeps getting better and better," Dallas said.

"Explain yourself, Lieutenant." Stark commanded.

Avoiding eye contact Kevin spoke quickly and carefully. "Sir, General Dominick gave me orders to check the Stroud area for Resistance members. I did. I started in the town. I didn't find any evidence of the Resistance there, but I heard rumors that there has been recent unusual activity around the Deep Fork River. Like the general commanded, I sheltered in the town, and on day two I went to the river. I found evidence of campers but nothing specific to the Resistance. When I tried to hike out I realized I was lost. I didn't find a major road until sunset today. Then I confiscated a car and returned immediately to the House of Night."

"Lost for days—what a moron," muttered Dallas.

"And you've had no contact with General Dominick since he gave you your orders?" Stark said.

"No, sir. None."

"Did you think about calling someone on your cell phone when you got lost? Or do you really just not think much?" Dallas sneered at Kevin.

Kevin stifled the urge to punch him in his narrow face. But he showed no sign of any emotion except confusion, and answered immediately. "I did, but had no cell service, Lieutenant."

"Lieutenant Heffer, did General Dominick mention where he and his soldiers were going?" Stark asked.

Kevin let his face show surprise. "Of course, sir. He said he was marching on orders."

"Orders? Whose?" Stark said.

"Sorry, sir, but that's above my need to know."

"Yeah, okay. Where were they headed?" Stark asked.

Then Kevin began leading Stark on a trail of total bullshit in the opposite direction of Sapulpa, the Resistance, and their Old Magick–protected ridge. "He said the state militia was coming up out of New Mexico and crossing Texas by using the Red River. I believe the general was heading to Elmer to set a trap for them."

"The New Mexico militia? That's bullshit. There hasn't been a peep outta any of our neighboring states' militias in months. He's making shit up. It's a waste of time to talk to him. To talk to any of them," Dallas said, shaking his head in disgust.

Stark ignored Dallas. "No, something definitely feels wrong. My gut has been telling me that for weeks. Things are happening that we don't know about. Heffer, I want you to come with me."

"Yes, sir! I'd be honored, sir!"

Dallas rolled his eyes. "General, he stinks."

"They all stink, but this red vamp kid has given us the only intel we've had on a missing general and his soldiers. Go get that key from Artus and then join us in the auditorium for Neferet's briefing."

"Yes, sir," Dallas said before sending Kevin another look of disgust and jogging away.

"Okay, follow me, Lieutenant. And don't get lost."

"Yes, sir!"

Kevin's mind was in turmoil as he followed General Stark. He needed to attend the briefing, but he also had to find a way to get free of Stark and that jackass, Dallas, so that he could go outside and wait for Anastasia's raven to find him. Dragon had to know about the weapons stash. Today.

"Hey, quit lagging!" Stark snapped at Kevin, who had, indeed, begun to lag.

"Yes, sir!" He sped up and was just behind Stark as they left the Field House and entered the hallway that led to the entrance to the school and the auditorium, when a familiar voice, sexy and sarcastic, interrupted his escape planning.

"Hello there, Bow Boy. I'd say it's nice to see you, but we'd both know it's a lie."

Stark paused to greet her as she entered the hallway from the direction of the priestesses' quarters, and Kevin got to study Aphrodite, noticing nuances he hadn't been able to see in the darkness of the morgue gardens.

*She looks tired. Really tired. And thin. Almost frail.* This Aphrodite wore a lot more makeup than the one in Zo's world, and Kevin wondered if that was because she was trying to cover dark circles and stress. *And her mouth is different too. Harder. Like she doesn't ever smile.* It made his heart hurt, and he wanted to put his arms around her and tell her everything was going to be okay. Unbidden, his feet started forward a step when Stark's voice brought him back to reality.

"Since when does it bother you to lie, Aphrodite? And don't call me that."

"Oh, hey, *so sorry.* I tend to forget that you're *General* Bow Boy now. Whoop-de-doo. We've all been so elevated by this war." Her perfectly beautiful nose wrinkled as she glanced behind Stark to Kevin. "Eww. It stinks."

"*He's* also a lieutenant in your High Priestess' army, and he puts his life on the line every time he leaves this House of Night. I don't think how he smells would make a damn bit of difference to you if he was all that was standing between you and a mob of humans."

Aphrodite made a show of looking around the hallway, which was becoming increasingly busy as soldiers, Son of Erebus Warriors, and priestesses began heading toward the auditorium. "Funny, but I don't see *any* humans around."

"Funny? You know what I think is funny? The rumor I've heard that you might be joining the Red Army, so my advice to you is to get used to that smell." Stark jerked his head in Kevin's direction. "Come on, Lieutenant." He bowed mockingly to Aphrodite. "Have a real nice day, Prophetess."

# 15

# *Other Aphrodite*

Aphrodite turned her bitch level up to cover her nervousness. She didn't need to say anything. She simply changed her expression from resting bitch face to active bitch face, and soldiers, Warriors, and even the priestesses parted before her like she carried the plague.

*I carry something worse—Neferet's disdain. And they all know it.*

Aphrodite had hastily decided that her performance would be best played out in the middle of the crowded auditorium, so instead of going on stage to serve as an attractive backdrop to whatever drama Neferet had cooked up for her minions today or joining the other priestesses huddled together in their typically sheeplike manner in seating reserved for them in the rear, Aphrodite made her way down the center of the auditorium, found the seat she wanted in the front row next to the aisle, and glared at the current occupant, who hastily removed himself.

She didn't thank him. She sat. And worried. Aphrodite had never done anything like she was planning. She hadn't meant to—not until Stark, the arrogant douche, had made that crack about her joining the Red Army. So, really, what she was about to do wasn't her fault. It was Neferet's. And, probably, somehow Stark's. But definitely, *definitely* not Aphrodite's fault.

She'd never meant to tell Neferet the rest of the vision. Aphrodite hadn't told Neferet all of the details of any of her visions since the Red Army had slaughtered Lenobia and Travis. And the horses. Aphrodite hated thinking about the dying horses. Hearing their screams in her nightmares was bad enough.

*My fault. That had been my fault. I should've known!* She clenched her hands together over her lap and sat ramrod straight. Anyone who looked at her—and a lot of people were always looking at her—would only see a beautiful, aloof young Prophetess looking confident and calm. They wouldn't see her hands tremble. They wouldn't see her soul shake. They wouldn't see her doubts and fears. That was one positive thing her harpy of a mother had taught her—show only one face in public, and that face should be exquisite and in control at all times, regardless of whether she was actually exquisite *or* in control.

Aphrodite sat very still, breathing slowly and steadily, as she readied herself for what was to come, but in the middle of one of her slow, steady breaths she caught a whiff of death and decay. Annoyed at the disgusting smell, she craned her head around, sniffing delicately, and, sure enough, sitting two rows behind her in an aisle seat just like hers was that young red vampyre Stark had been babysitting. Aphrodite shot Bow Boy an annoyed look. Red vampyres weren't allowed to sit in the floor seats of the auditorium or they'd reek up the place. Only officers from the Red Army were allowed to attend briefings, and then they were supposed to remain in the mezzanine. But there was Stark, all full of himself in his general's uniform of solid black, breaking the rules. Again. And letting some stinky red vamp kid sit right there next to him.

Aphrodite swore to herself that when she was back in Neferet's good graces, she was going to do everything she could to undermine

Stark's influence on the High Priestess. Not because he was particularly dangerous, but because he was particularly annoying.

"Room! Atten … tion!" commanded Artus, the Swordmaster of the Tulsa House of Night.

As the room stood, Aphrodite averted her eyes from Artus. Neferet's Swordmaster wasn't just ugly, old, and scarred. There was something off about him—something that made Aphrodite uncomfortable at a visceral level.

And then Neferet swept onto the stage, commanding the attention of everyone in the packed room. She was wearing a long, formfitting silk dress the color of new blood. Over her left breast in exquisite silver embroidery rested an image of Nyx cupping a crescent moon. The only jewelry she wore was a coronet of diamonds and rubies. One of the rubies dropped like a fat tear from the delicate crown to touch the top of the sapphire crescent moon tattooed in the middle of her forehead.

Aphrodite had to give it to her—Neferet knew how to command the attention of a crowd of males. She looked like a silver-screen goddess come to life, which proved once again one of Aphrodite's biggest disappointments in life—not everything that looks like it's filled with beauty and light on the outside is *actually* filled with beauty or light.

"You may be seated," Neferet said after taking her time to get to her glass podium.

Aphrodite sat and tried not to roll her eyes. Every instant of Neferet's briefing was scripted by her—from what she was wearing to how long she made her soldiers stand to the clear podium, which gave her audience an unhindered view of her flawless body.

Not that Aphrodite could blame her for that. Neferet was beautiful to look at, and as another great beauty, Aphrodite knew how easy it was to manipulate males. *Might as well use what we have!*

Then Neferet launched into her speech, and Aphrodite had no energy to waste on anything except deciding when her own performance should begin.

"I come before you today with grave news. I believe the tide of the war is turning."

There were sounds of pleased agreement from the throng of officers and soldiers present.

"I see my armies misunderstand me, which I find highly upsetting. The tide is *not* turning favorably! *Do none of my officers understand that?*" Her anger-filled voice echoed off the walls, electrifying the room with a charge of power and leaving no doubt about Neferet's level of irritation. Her only answer was the rustle of anxious bodies.

And then one of her generals stood. Aphrodite muffled a sarcastic snort. *Of course Loren Blake would feel the need to say something. Goddess, did that smarmy vamp ever stop talking?*

"High Priestess, may I have permission to speak?"

"Of course, General Blake. I am always willing to consider the wise counsel of my officers."

Blake's smile was too intimate for the venue, but everyone knew Neferet's generals were often also her lovers—and practically every male in the room aspired to be her lover—so, whatever.

"High Priestess, you know I mean no disrespect. I am your loyal servant, but maybe your officers don't understand because what we're seeing in the field is the opposite. The militias of our neighboring states have stopped crossing into our territory. There hasn't been a major human uprising within the area under our control for months. The only real problem we're still having is with the Goddess-be-damned Resistance, and we're working hard on tracking every one of them down and exterminating them. If anything, the tide has turned for us—for the better."

"You may sit, General Blake," Neferet said with a deceptively warm smile. "What you say would seem true to someone with your limited connection to Nyx, which is why our society will never be ruled by males—they cannot possibly be as intimate with the Goddess as are her priestesses. Most especially her one and only High Priestess—*me*. You see, Nyx has shown me otherwise. Our neighboring states and the humans that infest them have, indeed, withdrawn from their attempts to enter our territory and take from us what is ours. But they have not withdrawn in peace. They are plotting together to overthrow us!" Neferet spread out her arms dramatically, causing her perfect breasts to press against the silk of her gown and her nipples to be fully outlined and visible.

Aphrodite thought that move was an excellent touch as it had every male eye in the room traveling to her boobs, and every male mind in the room clouding as blood rushed from their brains to the organ that actually controlled them.

There was movement behind her, and Aphrodite turned her head in time to see Stark stand.

"High Priestess, may I have permission to speak?"

"Merry meet, General Stark. I will hear what you have to say."

"I've been feeling like something is off too. I've been trying to figure it out, and today I discovered some intel from an unusual source. I think it aligns with what Nyx has shown you."

Neferet's smile was the one Aphrodite liked to call her part-honey, part-whore grin, and the Prophetess had to suppress another snort. It looked like Bow Boy would be getting lucky tonight.

"I knew I could count on you, General Stark. Please, share your intel with us."

Then Stark shocked Aphrodite and the entire room by motioning for the stinking red vampyre kid slumped beside him to stand.

The kid jerked in surprise, and then got awkwardly to his feet and stood at a very stiff attention.

"General Stark, why is a young red vampyre soldier here on the floor of my auditorium?" Neferet's voice was contemplative, and she looked more curious than upset.

"Because he is my intel, and he isn't a soldier. He's a lieutenant—Lieutenant Heffer of General Dominick's unit."

The susurrus of the soldiers around her reminded Aphrodite of gossipy old women, and she wondered just who the hell this kid and his general were—and why they had elicited such a reaction from the crowd.

"General Dominick? My Red Army general who is missing?" Neferet said.

Aphrodite blinked in surprise. She hadn't heard about any missing generals, but she also rarely paid attention to what was going on with the animals that made up Neferet's disgusting Red Army. They were all boring. And stinky.

"Yes, High Priestess. General Dominick went missing with an entire squad of his soldiers, and they have yet to be found. Except for this lieutenant, and I believe he might know what happened to his unit." Stark nodded encouragement to the lieutenant, who was standing so stiffly at attention that Aphrodite could practically see the poker sticking up his ass. "I would like to ask your permission for Lieutenant Heffer to give his report to you."

Neferet's emerald eyes studied the red vamp kid who was standing stone still beside Stark. "You say his name is Lieutenant Heffer?"

"Yes, High Priestess," Stark said.

"He looks strangely familiar. General Stark, have you used this red vampyre for intel before?"

Aphrodite wanted to stand up then and call bullshit. No damn way Neferet recognized this red vamp, or any other. Aphrodite had heard the High Priestess comment often about how the Red Army was a fetid, disgusting but necessary evil—one she wanted little to do with. She wouldn't recognize one of those soldiers if he'd passed her in the hall every day for a year.

"No, High Priestess, I have not, but I believe you should hear what he has to say."

"Huh. The familiarity is odd." Neferet shrugged her smooth shoulders. "Very well, why not? The lieutenant may speak."

When the kid didn't say anything, Stark prodded him. "Go on. Tell the High Priestess where your general was heading, and what he told you before he left."

Aphrodite saw the kid swallow—once, twice, three times. When he began to talk he spoke in short, clipped sentences devoid of emotion as he stared straight ahead.

And as he began to talk, Aphrodite's eyes widened in shock.

"High Priestess Neferet, my general had intel that the New Mexico state militia was on the move. He heard they were going to cross Texas and enter Oklahoma by using the Red River. The general was heading to Elmer, Oklahoma, to set a trap for them. That is all the info I have, High Priestess. The rest was above my need to know."

Aphrodite barely heard Neferet's delighted response. She was too busy staring at the kid who had just spoken—the red vampyre lieutenant kid whose voice she absolutely recognized as the same guy who had been in the meditation garden the night before!

Except that kid had talked normally, like a real vampyre and not a stinking, red eating machine.

And then another jolt hit her.

*Last night he didn't stink. I know he didn't. I'm super sensitive to the way those things smell, and I would've noticed.*

Something completely bizarre was going on, which seemed like an excellent time for Aphrodite to begin her performance. She turned back around to face the stage. Neferet was still gushing and glowing about Stark confirming her weird neurosis, so when Aphrodite struggled to her feet, the High Priestess was completely caught off guard and stopped speaking midsentence.

Aphrodite staggered into the aisle. She pressed one hand to her forehead as if she was trying to keep her head from exploding. The other hand she held out toward Neferet beseechingly.

"Neferet!" Aphrodite gasped and swayed like the floor was pitching and rolling. "I see … I see …"

Around her, men began talking nervously.

"Silence! My Prophetess is having a vision!" Neferet moved quickly from behind the podium to the edge of the stage right in front of Aphrodite. "Speak, my Prophetess! Your High Priestess is here and will listen!"

Aphrodite moaned, and then stifled a scream. Clutching her head, she put all of her energy into her voice so that it would carry to the remotest corners of the auditorium.

"I see a field. In it is winter wheat that has been cut into huge round bales. There are blue vampyres there. They are hollowing out the bales and putting fledglings, vampyres, and humans within to sneak them without. They are the Resistance!"

"Where, Aphrodite, my dear? Look around you—where are you?"

"The Red Army is there! They are attacking! They are killing us! They are eating us!" Aphrodite sobbed.

"I know it is difficult, but concentrate! Focus! You are the Goddess' eyes and ears. Tell me where you are!"

"Sapulpa! No! No, no, no! Get them away from us! They're killing us!" Aphrodite swayed and sobbed.

Neferet's voice sliced through Aphrodite's sobs. "Prophetess! In the name of Nyx, focus! Where are you in Sapulpa?"

"I see a street sign! It says Lone Star Road! We are in a field in Sapulpa beside Lone Star Road and we are being killed!" Then Aphrodite drew a deep breath and screamed with everything in her before closing her eyes and faking a spectacular fainting spell.

(

## Other Kevin

Kevin moved on instinct. He lunged forward, reached out, and caught Aphrodite before she hit the ground. Around him the auditorium exploded in noise, but as he cradled Aphrodite in his arms it seemed they were suspended in a little bubble of stillness.

The beautiful Prophetess' eyes fluttered and then opened. And then they widened with shock. She turned her head toward him so that no one else could hear her, and she hissed through her teeth at him. "It was you! Last night in the garden. It was you!"

"Shh, relax. I've got you," Kevin soothed.

"Back the hell off!" she whispered. "Today you stink, even though you definitely didn't last night! And you're fucking pulling my hair!"

His gaze met hers. She wasn't in pain—that was obvious. And she definitely wasn't acting like she'd just fainted. And Kevin realized the truth. "You didn't have a vision!" he whispered.

"I did!" She kept her head turned so that it almost rested on his chest, careful no one else could hear. "Just not today. Who are you to judge? You're not even a real red vampyre!"

"I am! Just not the kind you're used to."

"Sure you are. Does Neferet know about you?"

Instead of answering Kevin shot back at her with his own question. "Does Neferet know about *you*? That you're withholding visions from her?"

"Prove it. If you think anyone will believe a red vampyre over a Prophetess of Nyx, you're as stupid as the rest of your stinking kind." Aphrodite turned in Kevin's arms and screamed in panic as she struggled to get free from him. "Aaaaah! Don't eat me! Get your hands off me! Help!"

"I got her, Lieutenant." Stark was there, moving Kevin aside and helping Aphrodite to her feet.

But she even pulled away from Stark, shaking off his help to stagger toward the stage and Neferet.

"D-did I tell you something of value, High Priestess?" Aphrodite's voice still carried throughout the auditorium, especially as the crowd had shut up and were gawking at her.

Neferet rushed to the edge of the stage and bent to take Aphrodite's hands in her own. "Yes! You did well, my dear! I knew Nyx would send me a sign, and I am truly blessed that she sent me two in one day." The High Priestess dropped one of Aphrodite's hands, but kept the other in hers as she faced the auditorium, making it look like she was raising her Prophetess' arm in a victory salute. "We now know that we must send our soldiers to a Sapulpa field beside Lone Star Road." She turned her brilliant smile on Aphrodite. "Could you tell when the battle will happen?"

"No, Neferet. That is impossible to tell unless there is a clock in my vision, or if I can get a glimpse of the moon, but my visions usually foretell events that take place within just a few days. I also can't tell exactly which field on Lone Star Road is the exact one where the Resistance will be hiding fledglings in the hay bales. My visions are simply too chaotic. High Priestess, I am sorry I cannot be more precise." Kevin watched Aphrodite curtsy gracefully to Neferet with a bowed head. She did look sorry, and very, very beautiful.

Kevin knew what he was watching was complete bullshit—at least on Aphrodite's end. *Her acting skills are impressive. She could even be a bigger star than Erik Night.*

"You did wonderfully. And this is an easy fix." Neferet's smile took in the auditorium filled with soldiers. "Tonight General Stark will lead soldiers and officers from the Red Army to Sapulpa where they will locate the Resistance infestation and wipe out the traitors. My Prophetess, the lovely, Goddess-blessed Aphrodite, will be joining General Stark and my Red Army on this combat mission." Neferet looked down at Aphrodite beatifically. "Surely you will recognize the correct field when you see it, won't you my dear?"

Kevin saw Aphrodite's face blanch a sickening white, and he felt nauseous along with her. Aphrodite staged her vision so that Neferet wouldn't follow through on the threat she made last night and force her to join the Red Army, and still the High Priestess managed to twist a knife in her Prophetess' back. Aphrodite opened and closed her mouth. Kevin could tell she was struggling with her response, and he got it—he understood her turmoil. If she said she couldn't help, Aphrodite would be publicly letting Neferet down—and that was something no one did without serious consequences. Neferet had already decided to send Aphrodite to the Red Army. She just used Aphrodite's vision to make it seem logical instead of spiteful.

"I'll do my best, Neferet," Aphrodite said woodenly.

*And I'll do my best to make sure you're protected,* Kevin added silently.

"Of course you will!" Neferet dropped Aphrodite's hand and threw her arms wide, projecting to the mezzanine level and the officers of the Red Army gathered there. "Red Army officers, are you grateful that my lovely young Prophetess will be joining you?"

"*Yes!*" Their response was more of a roar than a word.

Everyone's eyes turned up to gaze, mostly in disgust, at the clamoring, stinking horde, but Kevin kept his eyes on Aphrodite. She looked absolutely terrified.

As if she felt his gaze, her eyes found his.

*It's okay. I'll protect you.* Kevin mouthed the words.

Aphrodite startled slightly when she understood what he'd said, and then she rolled her eyes at him and fixed her face back into its gorgeous mask of indifference as Neferet continued to speak.

"See, I knew that my Prophetess would raise morale. Officers of my Red and Blue Armies, you will do your best to serve me because by doing so you serve our benevolent Goddess of Night, Nyx. And now, General Stark, please gather the soldiers of your choice. Ready yourselves. And then go to Sapulpa and rid us of the traitors!"

"Yes, High Priestess!" Stark responded, and the auditorium cheered in agreement.

Neferet lifted one hand, and the room went silent. "As for the rest of my generals, I want you to join me in my Council Room and we will further discuss what Stark and I suspect, and how I intend we defeat this new wave of enemies. We will not sit idly by and wait for them to burn us as we sleep. We will meet them and defeat them—*all of them.* Not today. Not tomorrow. But I promise you when we battle this new wave of enemies it will be with more power than any vampyre army has wielded in all of history. We will be victorious!"

The room cheered and whooped, and Kevin thought he might be sick. It was a lie! Everything he'd said about New Mexico and their militia had been a lie! He'd only wanted to turn the army's attention away from the Resistance headquarters, but they were *still* heading to Sapulpa and the fields just below their ridge.

And the power Neferet was talking about—Kevin knew what it had to be. She was going to arm her vampyres with human weapons.

Neferet had to be stopped.

Neferet lifted one graceful hand again, and the room silenced. "I have another announcement that I know my officers will be very excited about. Next weekend OSU and OU are scheduled for the Bedlam showdown. Well, I hate waiting, don't you?" The crowd made noises of agreement. Neferet smiled. "Yes, I knew you'd understand! That is why I insisted the game must take place *this* weekend in *Tulsa,* just down the street at the University of Tulsa's Skelly Field on New Year's Day. Won't that be a lovely celebration? OSU and OU certainly thought so." She paused, and her smile was filled with malice. "Or at least they did after I made them an offer they couldn't refuse, and TU, of course, was ever so pleased to accommodate my little holiday request."

Once again, the auditorium erupted into cheers, though this time some of them were shouting, "Boomer Sooner," and others were making the crazy pistol-firing hand gestures OSU fans made.

*I'd totally forgotten that it's almost New Year's,* Kevin thought. And he could easily imagine the "offer they couldn't refuse." College athletes, and the cheerleaders, band, and fans that went along with them were protected from the hunger of her Red Army as long as they amused vampyres in general, and Neferet in particular. She hadn't made them an offer. She'd made a deadly threat and the universities had responded the only way they could to protect their students.

"Merry meet, merry part, and merry meet again, my loyal priestesses, Warriors, and soldiers, and may Nyx's blessings be with you all!" Neferet closed the briefing to an uproar of cheers.

Kevin saw Aphrodite hurry to the stairs that led to the stage and follow Neferet, though the Prophetess should have known better. Once Neferet gave a command, she always followed through—no matter the consequences. Every officer in both armies knew that the only thing greater than Neferet's ego was her pride.

"Lieutenant, you might as well come with me since you don't have a unit anymore."

Kevin turned to see General Stark studying him with an unreadable expression on his face.

He snapped to attention. "Yes, sir! I'd be honored, sir!"

"Don't just stand there gawking at Aphrodite. Follow me."

Kevin trailed Stark as he wove his way out of the crowded auditorium. When they reached the hall, Lieutenant Dallas was there, waiting.

"Yo, General. *That* was some weird shit you just did in there."

"Dallas, try not to speak for a while. I need to think. And while I'm thinking, gather a flight of red vamps and their officers. I'm going to requisition enough trucks for a convoy to Sapulpa. Tell the officers we leave at 2200 hours—sharp." Stark glanced at Kevin. "Oh, and he's coming with us too."

"You mean he's going to join the flight of red vamps that'll be fighting tonight?"

"No, I mean he's coming with us. With me. In my vehicle."

"Nyx's tits, General! He can put some words together, but he's still just an eating machine. Are you sure you want him to ride with us? He's gonna stink up the Hummer."

For once Kevin didn't want to hit Dallas. Not because he liked the guy. He didn't. But because Stark had just given him more hope than he'd had since G-ma Redbird had dropped him off the day before.

"Lieutenant, are you questioning my order?"

Dallas backed down fast. "Hell, no, sir. Just double checking that I heard it right."

"You heard it right. Oh, and apparently Aphrodite will be

joining us too. So, be sure you get that Hummer that has the heating problem for our lead vehicle." Stark winked at Dallas.

"Oooh, I get it now!" Dallas chuckled. "You want to piss off Aphrodite. I think I know who she's gonna be sitting by too, right?"

"Lieutenant Dallas, did I ask you to think?" Stark said.

"No, sir, you did not."

"Then follow my orders. Now."

"No problemo. Whatever you say, General." Dallas gave Kevin a contemptuous look. "You might as well come with me. Just stay downwind."

"Um, excuse me, General Stark, sir," Kevin began.

"Yeah, what is it?"

"Sir, I apologize, but I need to feed before we leave," he blurted.

"Of course he does. Such a pain in the ass," Dallas muttered.

Stark sent Dallas a hard look, but told Kevin, "You have time. Do what you need to do, and then join the head of the convoy at 2200 hours."

"Yes, sir!"

Kevin hurried away—heading in the general direction of the small, dingy room the House of Night called the Red Cafeteria. It was really just a crappy old storage room that had been converted into a place where drugged humans waited to be used as meals. But as soon as he was out of eyesight of Stark and Dallas, he changed direction, pulled the hoodie up over his head, and slipped quickly out the nearest door.

He didn't pause. He walked fast—like he knew exactly where he was going. And he did. He knew what he had to do. Under the hoodie he kept glancing up at the sky.

"Come on! Come on! Bird, where are you? Give me a break, will ya, and don't make me do this."

Kevin kept moving, heading east out on the school grounds. He avoided the better-lit parts of the big, grassy area and tried to stay visible from above as he moved from tree to tree, keeping his gaze upward.

When he reached the east wall and the hidden trapdoor, he huddled in the shadows beside it while his gaze swept the school-yard. There were vampyres and fledglings visible, but they were all off in the distance, and all hurrying around—no doubt getting ready to gleefully slaughter some innocent people. He looked up at the sky again. Nothing. No damn bird.

"Shit!"

Feeling heavy with foreboding, Kevin pressed the hidden latch in the wall and then slipped outside.

# 16

# *Other Kevin*

As soon as he was outside the wall Kevin tried to calm himself. "Okay, think. First, check the sky again." Kevin searched the night's sky, but if the raven was up there somewhere he was impossible to see against the blackness. Kevin remembered that Anastasia had said her Tatsuwa had amazing eyesight, so he stepped a little away from the wall and waved his arms around over his head.

Still no damn bird.

"All right. Plan B. What the hell do I have left that they'd want?" He searched through the almost empty satchel. All the blood was gone, but there were two cookies left. There was also the jar of disgusting blood goo. "Well, let's hope they want one of these two things." He moved over closer to the wall so that he could hide in the shadows again, and then made the call. "Old Magick sprites of air, I am Kevin Redbird, and with the power in my blood, and the power Nyx has gifted me with, I call you to me! Again!"

With little popping sounds, the air sprites materialized hovering in the air around him.

"*Redbird Boy! What payment do you bring us for which task you would ask of us?*"

Kevin thought, but couldn't be sure, that he was speaking to the same sprite who had come when he'd called the night before. He smiled and tried to act more enthusiastic than nervous. "Hi there! Thank you for coming again. I really appreciate it."

"*What is the task and what is our payment?*"

"Okay, well, I don't have much time for small talk anyway. What I need is for you to find a raven named Tatsuwa. He belongs to the vampyre priestess from the ridge where you first came to me. Can you do that?"

> "*There is much we can do*
> *If we get payment from you.*"

Kevin relaxed a little when the sprite's voice slipped into the singsong rhythm that marked the beginning of making a deal.

"Okay, well, I can give you some of my blood. Or I do have a couple more of those cookies you liked so much yesterday."

> "*If you want us to do this thing*
> *Your payment must not bore us*
> *It must make our hearts sing!*"

"All righty." He reached into the satchel and pulled out the jar of stinking blood goop. "How about this? It's red vampyre blood."

The sprite's reaction was instantaneous. She grew in size. Her eyes bulged and she bared her teeth, showing disturbingly pointed fangs.

"*That is abomination, not payment!*"

Kevin hastily put the jar back in his satchel. "Hey, okay, okay, I get it. I think it's disgusting too. I'm sorry. I really don't know much about air sprites. Um, why don't you tell me what you'd like for payment?"

That calmed the sprite, and she went back to being about

hummingbird-sized and looking like a cross between a big bug and a very small, winged woman. The other sprites circled around her, whispering in that strange, almost birdlike language of theirs. When they were done speaking, the entire group approached him, hovering and pointing.

Kevin looked down at himself, trying to figure out what they were pointing at.

> *"We will take those threads of gold*
> *Then no more payment from you will be owed."*

Baffled, Kevin looked down at himself again. "Gold thread? I'm sorry, I don't know what you mean."

The lead sprite flew to him, reached out one delicate hand with impossibly long fingers, and gently touched a long strand of hair that had caught on his shirt.

"Aphrodite's hair! Damn, I *was* pulling her hair, even though I didn't mean to. No wonder she yelled at me." Once he knew what he was looking for, he quickly found three other long strands. He pulled them from his shirt and held them up. Even in the darkness, they glistened. "You're right. They do look like gold, but you should know that they're not really. They're just strands of blond hair."

> *"From a Prophetess filled with power."*

She licked her lips and Kevin got another glimpse of needle-like teeth.

> *"Delicious to devour.*
> *With this payment do you agree?*
> *Or shall we fly free?"*

"Um, no! I mean yes. Yes, you can have the hair. It's not like Aphrodite's still using it." He held the four strands between his thumb and forefinger, offering them to the sprite.

> *"With this payment we do agree*
> *Offered by thee and accepted by me*
> *Our deal is sealed—so mote it be!"*

The sprite took the strands of hair from Kevin. She tossed them into the air, where they suspended, floating without moving, but stretched out like four thin ribbons of silk waiting to be threaded through the eye of a needle. Then the sprites descended upon them, one sprite for each end of each strand, which they sucked into their strange mouths, finally coming together in the center like a totally bizarre version of the spaghetti scene from *Lady and the Tramp* before they took off, disappearing into the sky.

"That was crazy. Seriously. I wish Zo was here so that she'd seen it too. I'll bet it'd crack her up that the sprites ate Aphrodite's hair." He was chuckling to himself when a loud croak had him squinting up into darkness that moved, shifted, and finally turned into a raven, circling to land on the brown winter grass beside him.

"Tatsuwa! Man, I'm glad to see you!"

"*Redbird Boy!*" the raven said.

"Yeah, that's me. Okay, you gotta get a message to Dragon. Like, now." Kevin squatted beside the big bird. He was relieved to see that Tatsuwa had a leather thong around his neck, and from it dangled a small plastic container, the kind you might store salt in. He slid it from around the bird's neck and opened it. Inside was a piece of folded paper and a small pencil.

Using his satchel as a desk, he sat on the ground and wrote quickly.

*Neferet has a stash of modern weapons in the basement of the HoN. Ten crates of grenade launchers. Ten crates of M16s. Ammo for everything. She's planning to attack soon to the south. Don't know when yet.*

He paused then, chewing the end of the pencil. He had to tell them about Aphrodite's vision and the danger the Resistance was in, but he didn't want to make her a target. Deciding quickly, he continued to write.

*Neferet has intel about Resistance hiding people in round bales. Red Army heading to Lone Star Rd. and the hayfields there tonight. If you are sneaking people out that way, you only have an hour or so to get them away. I'll be with the army.*

He paused again, and then added, *Had to use Old Magick to call the bird. We need to find a better way ... K*

He reread the note and then, satisfied, he folded the paper and put it back in the jar with the pencil. The raven croaked at him, and then hopped to his side, lifting his head so that it was easy for Kevin to slip the leather tie around his neck.

"Hey, I don't know if you can understand me or not, but if you can you've got to keep a better eye on me. I don't feel right using Old Magick as much as I've had to. Plus, I'm running out of things to pay the sprites with. Uh, hang on. Mind if I borrow a feather of yours?"

The big bird cocked his head to the side, studying Kevin.

*"Bird Boy!"* he said, and then turned, obviously offering him a tail feather.

"Dude, you're pretty cool for a bir—I mean raven." With a quick pull, he yanked out one of Tatsuwa's long, black tail feathers.

The raven's squawk of protest echoed off the stone wall as the bird took flight. He circled Kevin once, neatly dropping a warm, wet blob of bird shit on his head.

171

"Hey, thanks a lot!" Kevin shouted at him, trying to wipe the mess from his hair. "Well, at least it doesn't smell as bad as the blood perfume."

(

## Zoey

"Okay, so, let's review. Who can tell me why Thanatos died when Neferet broke the protective spell she'd cast over the Mayo Hotel?" I asked and then paused, glad to see several hands go up.

You never know about teaching. Some days everything goes smoothly and the students do their homework and act right. And sometimes it's like every brain cell in their heads has been turned off—unless you mention boobs or accidentally cuss. I'd been surprised that I actually liked teaching because, well, teenagers are as unpredictable as cats and often have less sense.

(Yes, I'm eighteen, so I'm still technically a teenager. But I'm also their High Priestess and sometimes their professor—so I'm pretty sure my teenagehood doesn't count. Unless I mess up. Then *everyone* remembers how young I am. It sucks.)

I shook myself mentally and nodded at one very enthusiastically raised hand. "Samantha, what's your answer?"

The girl was a fourth former, or, as we would've called her in human public school, a sophomore. Easy to tell by the wings of Eros embroidered on the breast pocket of her school sweater.

"Ma'am, Thanatos died because she'd put too much of herself in the spell, so when Neferet broke it, she also broke Thanatos."

Internally cringing at the kid's use of the word *ma'am*, I managed to smile. "Yes, that's right. So, do you think Thanatos should have protected herself more by putting less into the spell?"

"No," Samantha answered right away, without raising her hand. "If she'd done that, Neferet would've gotten free of the

172

Mayo before Kalona's sacrifice and before you and your circle figured out how to stop her, and we all would've died or become her slaves. Thanatos is a hero. I admire her."

"There was a lot to admire about Thanatos. Who can tell me what affinity Nyx gifted her with?"

I was getting ready to call on another kid when I gasped instead, as heat bloomed across my upper body like someone was pointing a hair dryer set to high heat directly at my naked chest—though just to be clear, I was not teaching naked. We're different here at the House of Night, but not *that* different.

"Ma'am, are you okay?" asked Samantha.

"Yeah. Yes. I'm fine. I, uh, need to step out for a second. Samantha, you're in charge until I get back. Continue the discussion about Thanatos, please." And then I sprinted for the classroom door, hand pressed to the burning in the middle of my chest.

I barely made it outside before I barfed my brains out in a recycling bin in the hall.

And then the heat was gone, leaving me limp and panting.

"Zoey!" Stark raced around the corner of the hallway, sliding up to me. "My Goddess, that was fucking awful this time!" He was feeling all over my chest—not in a sexy way, but in a holy-shit-what's-broken way.

"I'm fine now. It's over." I tried to sound normal, but my voice was as trembly as my hands. "I'm sorry I took you out of class."

"Never be sorry. *You're* my life, Z. If anything happened to you ..."

"Hey." I took his hands in mine. "Nothing is happening to me. It's happening to Kevin. That's the problem."

"No, the problem is that Kevin isn't here, so I can't knock the crap outta him for using Old Magick."

"He can't know how dangerous it is, Stark."

Stark sighed. "I know, I know. Sorry. I wouldn't really knock the crap outta him. I like him."

"Yeah, me too."

"I think you're going to have to find a way to tell him to stop using Old Magick. The irony is that you'll probably have to use Old Magick to do that," Stark said.

I avoided eye contact with him. "Yeah, that sucks. But I'm working on figuring it out."

"That's good and bad news. Look, Z, I know this is really wearing on you, and you're super worried about your brother, but I want you to promise me that you're not going to go off alone and mess with Old Magick."

I put my arms around him and rested in his embrace. "I promise. I learned my lesson about that. I won't sneak away alone and use Old Magick."

I could feel him relax, which added to my guilt. When he tried to kiss me I leaned back, covering my mouth. Against my palm I said, "You don't want to do that. I just puked."

"Ah, Z, I'm sorry. What can I do?"

"Nothing. I really am fine now. I'm going to end class early and send them to study hall so that I can go to our room and brush my teeth. Puke breath is just disgusting."

"Okay, it's almost lunchtime. Will you be okay to eat?"

"Sure! I'll meet you in the dining hall. And stop worrying. I'm fine."

Stark kissed me on my forehead. "I love you, my Queen."

"I love you too, my Warrior," I said. Then I watched him walk away, my heart squeezing in my chest. When he was gone, I fished my cell phone out of my pocket and punched the right contact.

"'Sup, Z?"

"Kramisha, I need you to do something for me."

"Your wish be my command."

"Do you still have a copy of that old prophetic poem—the one about how to get Kalona to rise?"

"I do. It's in my file labeled, 'Shit no one should mess with.'"

"Good. I need it. Would you email me a copy?"

"Is you gonna mess with it?"

"Kramisha, Kalona already burst out of the ground. It can't happen twice." *At least not in this world it can't*, I added silently to myself.

"True that. I'll email it."

"Thanks, bye."

I went back to my classroom and stuck my head inside the door. "Guys, I'm cutting class short today. For the rest of the period you may go to the Media Center for study hall." Then I closed the door on their jubilation and headed to the parking lot.

My Warrior had been 100 percent right. Kevin had to be told how dangerous it is to wield Old Magick, *and* he had to understand how to control the urge to use it again and again.

*I am going to tell him.*

*I am going to teach him.*

*In person.*

But first I needed to think—really reason through the *how*s and *when*s and *with whom*s—alone. Without looking over my shoulder for whoever was going to either stare at me like a chemistry project that could explode at any moment, or worse, ask me over and over if I was okay.

So I headed to my current favorite alone spot …

# 17

## *Stark*

As soon as the bell rang to release classes for lunch, Stark sprinted from the Field House to the Professors' Dining Hall. He didn't give a shit that he drew the attention of every fledgling, vampyre, and human he passed. Stark had a *feeling*. A damn bad *feeling*. And it had something to do with Zoey.

Sure enough, she wasn't in the dining hall.

He slid into the big booth where he and Z and their friends usually ate and waited.

And waited.

And waited.

When thirty minutes had passed, he flagged down a waitress.

"What may I bring you, Stark?"

"I'm good. I'm just waiting for Zoey. But maybe I missed her. Did she already eat?"

"No, I haven't seen her at all today. Would you like me to take your order anyway?"

"No, I think I'll wait a little longer. Thanks, though." She left, and Stark checked his phone. Again. Nothing from Z. He texted her. Again.

> You're still not here. Did I get the placed mixed up?

He pressed **SEND**, and then quickly texted again.

> I'm starting to worry. Call me.

"Hey there, Stark. What looks most delicious for lunch today?" Damien asked as he slid into the booth across from Stark.

"Oh, hi, Damien. I don't know. I'm waiting for Z."

"Yeah, I'm waiting for Jack. He's putting in extra time in the Media Center, trying to catch up on what he didn't learn back in that wretched Other World." The waitress came back, and Damien smiled at her. "I'm going to order the tacos for Jack and me. But give it about ten minutes before you put the order in. He's Other Jack, but he's just as late as the original Jack was." Then Damien turned his attention back to Stark. "Did you say you were waiting for Z?"

"Yeah. She's late too."

"That's because she's not here. I saw her bug pull out of the parking lot about midway through last hour, and I haven't seen her come back yet."

"Shit! Are you kidding me?"

"No. Stark, is everything okay?" Damien asked.

"No. Nothing is okay. Sorry, Damien. I gotta go." It took a lot of effort for Stark not to slam the door behind him when he left the dining hall.

*She just drove off and didn't say anything to me? Again.*

This was the third time in just the past few days that Z had told him she was going to be somewhere—or meet him to do something—and she was either a no-show or late. Really late.

Sure, she always had an excuse, like she had to check Neferet's tomb to be sure nothing weird was going on out there. He understood that. He also understood that Zoey could send someone else to do that. Someone like him. Or Darius. Or Rephaim. Or one of a dozen other Sons of Erebus Warriors who would report to Zoey and otherwise keep their mouths shut should they discover something crazy.

And, of course, she said she kept going to the Depot Restaurant to help with the renovation there. But between Damien, Other Jack, and Stevie Rae, there were already lots of helping hands.

Even worse, whenever Stark tried to check on Z—tried to see what was taking her so long—she wasn't ever actually where she said she was going to be when she said she was going to be there.

Stark went to the rooms he shared with Zoey first. She wasn't there. Then he hurried down the stairs and out the arched wooden door that always reminded him of a castle. He paused, his eyes sweeping the school grounds. There were fledglings and human students everywhere. Some were sitting in little groups under the flickering gaslights, sharing lunches. Some were hurrying to the dorms. Others were playing a weird tag game the current senior class had created that somehow involved cats.

His eyes were drawn to the statue of Nyx that stood in the center of the main courtyard. When he recognized one of the High Priestesses in the little group at the Goddess' feet, he felt a wave of relief and rushed across the brown, winter grass. *There she is! Let's hope she knows something.*

"Stevie Rae! Hey, we need to talk," Stark said as he joined her at the statue. Beside Stevie Rae were two young fledglings who had just finished lighting the myriad of votive candles that flickered cheerily around the base of the Goddess. They bowed nervously but respectfully to greet Stark. "Hi, yeah, hi. Nice job with the candles and whatever. Okay, time to get to lunch. Or your next class. Basically, it's time for you to *get!*" Stark waved his hand dismissively and shooed them away.

Stevie Rae watched the two fledglings scurry toward the rear entrance to the school. She scowled at Stark. "Great. You just scared 'em. Don't you remember what it was like to be newly Marked? Those two have only been here for a week. They're still cryin' in their pillows at night for their mamas."

"They'll be fine, just like we were fine. Who's *not fine* is Zoey."

"What in the Sam Hill are you talkin' about?"

"Have you seen her lately?" Stark fired the question at her.

"Yeah. No. I saw her for just a sec a little while ago. It was the middle of last hour, and she said she was headin' to the depot to see if Kramisha needed any help packing. You know Kramisha's leavin' for Chicago tomorrow, right?"

"Yeah, yeah, I know about Kramisha. And Z said she was going to the depot? Are you sure?"

"'Course I'm sure. It wasn't that long ago."

"Okay, hang on." Stark pulled his phone from his pocket and punched Kramisha's number, putting her on speaker so Stevie Rae could hear too.

Kramisha—unlike Zoey—answered on the first ring. "What you want, Stark? I's busy packing."

"Sorry to bug you. Hey, is Z with you?"

"Nope."

"Have you seen her today?"

"Nope."

"Okay, thanks."

"Hey, is everyth—"

Stark hung up and gave Stevie Rae a pointed look. "Zoey lied to you. She lied to me. She's been doing that lately. Has she been talking to you at all?"

Stevie Rae hesitated before she answered. "I started to say, 'Sure! Z's been talkin' to me every day.' But when I really think about it, she hasn't actually been sayin' much."

"Yeah, not since she started feeling Other Kevin using Old Magick."

"I know she's worried. Heck, Stark, I'm worried about Kev too."

"The problem is I'm pretty sure it's not just about Other Kevin."

"You're gonna have to give me more to go on than that. Since Z told Rephaim and me that we get to stay in T-Town I've been super crazy busy getting settled *and* figurin' out lesson plans for this dang Vamp Sociology class I was moronic enough to volunteer to teach. Jeesh, who knew teaching was so hard?"

"Every real teacher in the world knows that, but that's not the point. Stevie Rae, you need to listen to me—*I do not think Z is okay.*"

Stevie Rae motioned for Stark to join her on an ornately carved iron bench perfectly situated near the Goddess statue.

"Now, tell me what's stuck in your craw about Z."

Stark blew out a long breath as he sat beside her. "She's going to his grave. Every day. And she's lying about it."

Stevie Rae moved her shoulders. "That's not real bad. I mean, Z misses Heath. We all know that, and maybe she's not telling the truth because she doesn't want you to feel bad. Hey, if she's lying, how do you know where she's going?"

"I followed her. And before you give me crap about that let me say that I only did it because I'm worried. Real worried."

Stevie Rae held up her hands in surrender. "Hey, I'm not judging, but you do have my full attention now. Go on."

Stark ran his fingers through his thick hair and sighed again. "So, I followed her," he repeated. "And watched her. She sits there. On his grave. And talks to him. A lot."

"She talks to his gravestone?"

Stark shook his head. "No. She leans against his gravestone, but she stares to the side of it, like he's sitting there—beside her—somewhere close, and by close I don't mean Nyx's Grove."

"Well, okay, so it's weird and sad, but maybe that's how Z deals with her grief. You know it took a long time for her to even go to his grave. She's never even let me go with her. She told me once that it was something she needed to do by herself, and that I should just leave it alone. She said she likes to think there 'cause it's real quiet. Maybe that's all there is to it. Z wants some alone time. What do you think?" Stevie Rae shook her head, making her blond curls bounce around her face. "Part of this is my fault. I'm sorry that I've been so dang busy that I didn't realize she's depressed or whatever."

Stark waved away her apology. "This isn't on you. It's on all of us. I think we've left her alone too much since Kevin went back to the Other World."

"But we're givin' her space. Hey, I do know that she's been talkin' to her brother. This world's Kevin. The one who isn't a red vampyre. I thought that was helping her deal with Other Kevin not being here." Stevie Rae sighed and ran her fingers through her hair. "I haven't asked her hardly anything about how she's been feelin', especially after she kept tellin' us how *fine* she was, in spite of that dang Old Magick messin' with her and Other Kevin. Like Kramisha always says, it's not cool to be all up in Z's business."

"Yeah, well, space time is over. Since she's started 'talking,'" he air-quoted, "to Heath, she's stopped *actually* talking to me. And, obviously, you."

"Z's not talkin' to Damien or Aphrodite either?" Stevie Rae asked.

"Oh, sure. Z talks to Damien and Aphrodite, you and me. But she never says how she's feeling—except to say she's *fine*. Stevie Rae, she's pulling away from me. And from you, Aphrodite, and Damien. She's only *really* talking to dead Heath."

"You seriously don't think this is just Z dealing with her grief?"

"No, because this dead-Heath-talking crap didn't start until *after* Kevin came from the Other World and—"

"And told her about Heath being alive over there," Stevie Rae finished for him as her eyes widened with understanding.

"Exactly," Stark said.

"And then she felt Kevin using Old Magick."

"Yep. Which happened again today. Right before she took off in her bug, even though she told me we were meeting for lunch."

"Ohmygood*ness*, Z's gonna go to the Other World!" Stevie Rae said.

"Yeah, that's what I'm starting to think too," Stark said.

"Ah, hell!" Stevie Rae said.

(

# Zoey

I checked the time on my phone as I pulled my bug off Seventy--First Street onto Aspen, and then took the immediate left to enter through the somber gates of Floral Haven Cemetery. I was pretty sure I could make it back to the House of Night without being too late to meet Stark for lunch.

"I should just tell him that I like to come out here," I muttered to myself. "He'd understand. Right?"

*Um. No. I did tell him—once. Almost a year ago. And he asked me a zillion questions and said that maybe I should talk to someone. As in a* shrink *kind of someone. About my grief.*

"I tried to explain that's kinda what I do when I visit the grave. I talk. Sure, it's not to a shrink, but talk is talk, right?"

Apparently not to Stark it wasn't. Not that I really blamed him. Losing Heath had been horrible. Worse, even, than losing my mom, because the truth was that I'd been way closer to Heath than anyone in my family except for Grandma Redbird.

As if it knew the way without me steering, my little aqua-colored bug wound around the curving roadways to what had become a familiar section of the graveyard. I stopped where I always did—by the big juniper tree that marked the beginning of the path I'd followed countless times over the past year.

I always felt sad when I first got there. Floral Haven wouldn't have been Heath's first choice. Not because it was a bad cemetery or anything like that. I just knew that Heath would have liked somewhere more ... well ... colorful. Heath had liked crazy, and Floral Haven was immaculate, structured, organized, and well regulated. The opposite of crazy.

But as I walked down the path that led to the Luck family grave, my sadness lifted a little—then more than a little when I caught sight of my neighborly addition to the Luck plot. I went to Heath's proper, modest, *boring* tombstone and sat right on top of his grave, which I knew he would've appreciated. I leaned against the cold gray stone that said in block letters: **HEATH REGINALD LUCK— BELOVED SON**, and looked to the side at the next family plot closest to the Lucks', where there was only one tombstone—the one I'd purchased immediately after I'd purchased the family plot. It was as unboring as the very proper rules of the cemetery had allowed. I'd commissioned a stone made from smooth blue marble, the exact color of a perfect fishing hole. On it I'd had the artist carve a scene of Heath sitting on a small wooden dock casting his rod out into the water. I'd had them make it so that Heath was looking right at me, grinning like he always did when he went fishing.

"Hey there. How ya doin'?" I asked the carving of Heath. "Yep, it was one of those awesome Oklahoma winter days today when it's not too cold to be outside, but also not hot enough yet to bring on the Okie triple threat: ticks, ragweed, and snakes. I'll bet you'd say it was good fishing weather, but then again you thought every day was good fishing weather."

Okay, let me be clear. I hadn't lost my mind—at least not totally. I was not under any delusion that Heath was actually there, listening to me. I knew where he was … or at least one version of him. I'd been with him there—in the Goddess' Grove—after he died and my soul had shattered from grief. He's probably fishing up there somewhere right now.

But I liked pretending to talk to him.

I needed to pretend to talk to him.

Especially now.

"Hey, so, remember the other day I told you about that weird burning in my chest? Well, surprise! It *wasn't* a heart attack. It's something worse. It's Other Kevin, over there in that Other World, wielding Old Magick." I paused and rested my head

183

against his tombstone. "Yeah, that's bad. Really bad. And he's been wielding it a lot." I sighed. "Yeah, right? I know he's gonna get himself into some deep bullpoopie. Why are little brothers always such a pain in the butt?"

"Zoey? It *is* you! I thought I saw your bug turn in here."

I jumped at the voice and spun around on my butt to see my brother, Kevin, walking toward me.

"Sheesh, you scared the bejeezus outta me, Kevin. Like, make some noise next time."

"How about you tell me when you're gonna visit Heath's grave next time and I'll meet you here? I was just lucky that I was passing by when you pulled in." Kevin looked at me and grinned. "It was luck! Get it?"

I smiled up at him. "I get it." Then I patted the place beside me, and Kevin sat.

We didn't say anything. We just sat. Since Other Kevin had left, I'd been talking to this Kevin—a lot. But mostly on the phone. First, because he has a super busy school schedule and it was hard for him to get away—especially without the step-loser, my mom's awful husband, knowing that Kevin and I had reconnected.

The second reason was harder. Seeing Kevin, like right now, made me miss Other Kevin. I mean, I liked talking to this Kevin. He'd grown into a nice guy, and he'd actually traded in his video game obsession for a wrestling obsession, and he'd made the varsity squad at Broken Arrow this year, which was cool. But he wasn't a vampire. He couldn't understand me like Other Kevin could. It wasn't his fault, but that didn't make it any less true.

"Hey, don't you ever find this creepy?" Kevin interrupted my thoughts with a shoulder bump.

"What? Sitting on his grave? Nah, Heath would love it," I said.

"Well, that, and *that*." He pointed to the carving of fisherman Heath.

"Heath would love that too," I said. "Do you not remember he had a sense of humor?"

"Sure. Do you not remember he's dead?"

I jerked back as if Kevin had slapped me. "Of course, I remember. I was there. Losing him almost killed me. Why the hell would you ask me that?"

"Because of what Other Kevin told you."

I didn't say anything. I couldn't say anything. This Kevin—this human brother of mine—couldn't possibly understand about Old Magick. Nor would he understand about the dream I'd had, I was sure hadn't been a dream, but a message from dead me. He'd think I was just making excuses if I told him what I'd decided—what I knew I had to do.

*I'm not making excuses.*

My brother—my *other* brother, needed help with Old Magick and help getting rid of Neferet. Neither of those things had anything to do with Other Heath Luck.

"Zoey, I'll go with you. All you have to do is ask," Kevin said into the silence that had settled between us.

My gaze snapped to his. "You can't! I'm not alive in that world, so I can get away with sneaking over there, but you are—and you're a rogue red vampyre who has become allied with the Resistance against Neferet and her armies. It's not safe for you over there."

"Z, according to what you've told me, it's not safe for *anyone* over there."

I looked away from Kevin and my gaze found Heath's smiling image again.

"I understand that," I said.

"Do you really?" my brother asked as he cracked his knuckles and flexed his fingers—a sure sign he was stressed.

"You know I'm going, don't you?" I answered my brother's question with one of my own.

"Yep, I do. And, Z, if I know it, so do your friends."

I felt a terrible chill of foreboding. "No! I haven't said one word to any of them."

"You haven't said one word to me, either. I figured it out."

"Which means they will too," I said.

"Uh, yeah. For sure."

"Well, it's not like I was going to sneak away by myself," I said. "I've learned my lesson about thinking I can handle a major crisis all by myself—that's just stupid."

"That makes me feel better, but only a little. Z, are you sure you have to go?"

I turned from Heath's image to meet my brother's gaze. "Another version of you is in big trouble. I can help him. If you were him, what would you want me to do?"

He grinned, and I suddenly saw him as a boy, about seven, with a terrible buzz haircut and a gap in his smile where his front teeth should be—and my heart squeezed.

"Z, I can't lie. I'd totally want you to come save my butt."

*This is going to break Stark's heart*, I thought, but all I said was, "Yeah, and that's exactly what I'm going to do."

# 18

# *Other Aphrodite*

Aphrodite zipped up her sleek leather bombardier jacket and lifted her chin as she went out the front doors of the school and headed to the first vehicle in the army convoy. She could feel the eyes on her, but that was nothing new. Males had been watching her since before she'd grown boobs. Of course there was a difference between regular males and ravenous, stinky, eating-machine males, but as Neferet would say, *Not that much difference.*

She shook that thought out of her head. *If I'm quoting Neferet it's time for a serious reality check. I can do this. I can go with the army to the stupid field outside stupid Sapulpa, and then I can come home. Neferet will be pacified. I'll be back on her good list, and everything can return to normal.* The problem was that thought didn't bring Aphrodite much comfort. *Normal* at the House of Night had become almost unbearable. For the zillionth time since Neferet had started her horrid war, Aphrodite wished she'd gotten out—gotten away to Italy and San Clemente Island before the damn thing had started. She was a Prophetess. Surely the High Council would've given her sanctuary and not put her on the next flight back to Tulsa when Neferet demanded she return.

Because Neferet would have demanded it. She only had one Prophetess. For the first time in her life, Aphrodite was sorry she had been so damn gifted by Nyx that she couldn't pass for an average priestess.

"Who am I kidding. I could never pass for average."

"Gotta agree with you there, gorgeous!"

Aphrodite looked to her right. There was a young blue vampyre lieutenant leaning against the lead vehicle giving her a smile that was way too much like a leer.

"What did you say?" she asked in a deceptively sweet voice.

"I agreed with you. You're way too gorgeous to ever be average." He winked at her.

She caught his gaze with her own. "Did I ask for your opinion?"

"Nah, but I—"

"But you what?" her voice sharp enough to skewer him. "You have no manners? You have no sense?"

"Hey, look—"

She sliced through his words again. "No, *you* look. Do you want to know when you're going to die?"

"No!"

"Do you want to know *how* you're going to die?"

"Hell no!"

"Then treat me with the respect a Prophetess of Nyx deserves, or I may feel the need to enlighten you. Goddess knows you could use some enlightening."

"Uh, yeah. Okay."

"Let me fix that for you. The correct way for you to respond is, *I apologize, Prophetess. It won't happen again, Prophetess. Let me get that door for you, Prophetess.*" Aphrodite paused while the annoying little ass just stood there, his mouth opening and closing like a ferret-faced carp. She sighed and put her hands on her hips. "Is this General Stark's truck thing?"

"Yeah, it's his Hummer. Uh, I mean, yes, it is, Prophetess."

"See, you *are* capable of learning. Then open the damn door for me."

"Problem, Lieutenant Dallas?" Stark came from behind her and strode to the front passenger's side of the vehicle. He wasn't alone, but Aphrodite didn't need to look to see who was with him. She could smell him.

"Nope, sir!" The moronic lieutenant instantly opened the Hummer door for Stark.

"Good to hear it. Let's get moving." Stark glanced at Aphrodite and Kevin, who had stopped beside her. "What are you two waiting for, a written invitation? Get in the back seat." Stark shook his head, muttered something indecipherable, and Lieutenant Dallas closed his door with a firm slam.

Kevin stepped to the backseat door on their side of the vehicle and opened it. "After you, Prophetess," he said.

"The only one with manners stinks. Fantastic." She moved past Kevin and got inside. Kevin jogged around to the other side of the Hummer and took the seat beside her.

"All ready back there, *Prophetess*?" Dallas asked with just a touch of a sneer as he grinned into the rearview mirror.

"Just drive," Stark told him sharply. As they led the convoy out of the House of Night, Stark turned in his seat. "Now, tell me what you didn't tell Neferet about your vision."

Aphrodite raised one brow at him. "I have no idea what you're talking about." Then she reached into her extra-large Louis Vuitton bag and pulled out one of three bottles of Veuve Clicquot, pleased to see she'd chosen the one rosé she'd brought. Without looking at him she handed the bottle to Kevin. "Open this. Don't spill it. Don't get any stink on it, either."

Stark shook his head. "You brought champagne to a battle?"

"No, I brought *good* champagne to the *pre*battle. Kinda like tailgating, only less sports and more killing. Do you want a glass?"

She lifted one pretty little flute she'd stashed in the side pocket with her emergency bottle of Xanax.

"No. I do want an answer to my question, though."

Kevin popped the cork and Aphrodite held her glass out to him to be filled. "I did answer you."

"A *real* answer."

Aphrodite glanced at Kevin. "Cover the top of the bottle with the foil so it stays a little fizzy. Do you know nothing about champagne?"

"Nope. I've never tried it. My step-loser—uh, that's what my sisters and I call my step-dad—is too religious to—"

"Boring!" Aphrodite looked at Stark. "I didn't think they could talk."

"You mean red vampyres?" Stark asked, sending Kevin an amused look.

"Yes, of course that's what I mean."

"Aphrodite, Kevin is an officer. They talk. You just heard him talking to Neferet in the briefing."

"That wasn't talking. That was reporting. Whatever." She sipped her champagne and stared out the window as they took the turnpike toward Sapulpa.

"Still waiting for you to answer my question," Stark said.

"Sorry. What was the question again?"

Stark sighed heavily, and Aphrodite noticed Lieutenant Dallas was grinning like she was his personal entertainment.

"Lieutenant Dickless, do you always find your amusement at your general's expense?"

The grin instantly slid off his face, and his eyes went back to the road.

"Great. The only lieutenant who speaks also stinks. And to answer your question, General Bow Boy, I told Neferet everything. Well, except details like how the Red Army soldiers lost whatever might be left of their minds, and didn't stop their disgusting killing spree with the humans they found in the bales. They also ate the fledglings—*blue* fledglings who could have grown up to be big boys like you. Oh, and they ate the blue vampyres too. Basically, your disgusting Red Army massacred everyone. How's that?"

"Why didn't you tell Neferet about that?" Kevin asked.

"Because she wouldn't care. It wouldn't have changed anything. She'd still send her Red Army. Everyone would still be slaughtered. The end." She downed the rest of the glass and held it out for Kevin to refill. *And I'm going to have to watch it happen. Again.*

"Neferet might not care, but I do. We need those people alive. Especially the blue vampyres. They can give us intel on the Resistance," Stark said.

"Oh, goodie. So, instead of being torn apart and eaten, they get to be tortured."

"I didn't say anything about torture!"

"You're going to ask them nicely to give up their people and their headquarters, and when they say no thank you, you'll—what? Give them a pat on the back and let them go?"

"Whose side are you on, Aphrodite?" Stark's look had gone dark and angry.

"Nyx's, of course."

"That's the same side we're on," Stark said.

Aphrodite snorted, but said nothing else. Bow Boy could run to Neferet and say she'd been Super Bitch on this little foray. That'd be fine. Actually, that'd be great. Less chance Neferet would send her out again. What he couldn't do was run to the High Priestess and tell her Aphrodite was sympathetic to the Resistance. That wouldn't be fine. That would be deadly.

*What the hell do vamps like Stark and the Sons of Erebus Warriors think happened to all those High Priestesses Neferet demoted and then ordered to shut their mouths? That they really just disappeared to some crappy country House of Night to pray out the rest of their days in solitude?*

Aphrodite knew better. She'd witnessed what Neferet had done to them. Nyx had sent her that vision. And that was one vision Aphrodite had shared with *no one*.

"Would you like more champagne?"

Aphrodite automatically held her glass out for the refill. Then she looked at the stinky kid sitting beside her. She was surprised to realize that he was obviously Native American. She hadn't noticed that before. And if he changed his crappy, ill-fitting clothes and took care of some personal grooming—like, he really needed a haircut … and a destinking—he might even be cute. Real cute. She hadn't noticed that before, either. Well, in all fairness, once she'd smelled him, she hadn't really looked at him.

But he hadn't smelled when he'd talked to her in the garden that night.

"How old are you?" she asked him.

He looked surprised at the question. "Sixteen."

"Isn't that young to be a lieutenant?"

He nodded. "Yeah. I'm the youngest lieutenant in the army."

"When did you Change?" she asked.

"Almost a year ago." He paused, and then added, "When did you Change?"

"When I was older than sixteen," she said. Aphrodite wanted to ask him why he hadn't smelled like death the night before, but no way was she going to let Dickless and Bow Boy hear that. No way did she want them anymore up in her business than they already were. "You're a child. No wonder you haven't had champagne." She turned her head dismissively to stare out the window and wish she were anywhere else.

(

## Other Kevin

The conversation stalled after Aphrodite called him a child. She didn't look at him. She didn't talk to him. She did, of course, hold out her glass from time to time for a champagne refill.

*Man, she drinks champagne fast!*

All Kevin could do was to sit and watch with growing dread as the Hummer ate up the miles and they got closer and closer to what most likely would be a terrible tragedy.

*What if that bird didn't get to Dragon?*

No, he wouldn't let himself think about that. All he could do was what he was doing. He sent the information. He was with the soldiers because maybe there could be something he could do in the middle of battle to help people get away from the Red Army. At this point Kevin didn't give a damn whether he was discovered or not. He wasn't going to stand by and watch innocents being slaughtered by monsters.

"Here, open another one."

Aphrodite shoved a new bottle of champagne at him. He hadn't even noticed she'd drained the other one. As he coaxed the cork out of it, he threw glances at Aphrodite. She looked bad.

Well, that wasn't entirely true. She was beautiful. That hadn't changed. But she was so damn thin and pale! Dark circles were showing through whatever she'd tried to cover them with, and when she wasn't gulping champagne, her mouth was set in a hard line.

"How far are we from Lone Star Road?" Aphrodite asked as he filled her glass again.

Stark pointed to the light about a block in front of them. "We turn there, on Hickory. Then in about a mile and a half we'll take a right onto Lone Star. That's when I need you awake and aware."

Stark looked over his shoulder at her and frowned. "So, lighten up on that champagne."

"Oh, relax, Grandpa. I'm a vampyre, remember? I can't get wasted. I can't even get very high. Well, unless I mix a bunch of Xanax with this booze—which reminds me." She reached into the giant bag that sat on the seat between them, pulled out a little pill bottle, and shook out a few tiny oval pills, which she washed down with a big swig of champagne. "And, I'm a professional at this."

"You'd better be. Neferet is counting on it," Stark said.

"Yeah, yeah, yeah. I'll recognize the damn field. Worry about your zombie army—not me."

Stark turned back around and rubbed his forehead.

Kevin kept staring at Aphrodite until she met his eyes. Then, in a voice low enough that it wouldn't carry to the front seat, he said, "You know how bad this is going to get. I don't blame you for drinking and taking those." He pointed a finger at the pill bottle that was sticking out of the top of her purse.

She looked like she was going to make another snarky comment, but then her face changed. Her shoulders slumped, and she nodded sadly, whispering, "It's going to be worse than bad."

"I won't let you get hurt," he said softly.

She stared at him with big, beautiful, haunted blue eyes. "They ate kids. Younger than you. I know. I saw it all. And now I'm going to see it again." She shook her head and wiped angrily at a single tear.

He held her gaze and very distinctly but quietly told her, "Not if I can help it you won't."

Surprise flashed in her eyes, then Stark interrupted.

"Okay, this is Lone Star Road. Time for you to do your job."

"I already did my *job*. I prophesized. This is not about my job. It's about Neferet punishing me. But whatever. I'm a big girl. Tell Lieutenant Dickless to slow down so that I can check out these fields. The one I'm looking for is big. I remember a grove of pecan trees across the street. Oh, and there are trees lining the field, though a lot of the road side of it is open, so we should be able to see into most of the field."

"Which side of the road is the field on?" Stark asked.

Aphrodite thought about it, then said, "It's on our left." They'd only driven about a mile down the windy road when Aphrodite pointed. "That's it! I recognize that clump of trees."

Kevin breathed a tiny sigh of relief. The field was still a couple of miles away from the ridge where the Resistance was hiding. That was one small good thing in a giant pile of bad.

Aphrodite was looking out the window to her right. "And there's the pecan grove. Okay, keep going just a little. There should be a … yep, there's the gate. Turn in there."

Dallas guided the Hummer through an open gate and into a big, newly cut hayfield. And, sure enough, parked just inside the gate was the flatbed part of a semitruck's trailer, filled with enormous round bales.

"Stop!" Stark snapped. "Make sure the convoy blocks the gate so they can't get out that way." He started to open his door before the Hummer had come to a complete stop, commanding, "Dallas, get those soldiers off the convoy and have them circle the flatbed. Lieutenant Heffer, stay in this vehicle with Aphrodite. Your job—your *only* job is to make sure she's not accidentally eaten tonight. Can you do that?"

"Yes, sir!"

Without another look, Stark and Dallas got out of the Hummer. Kevin could hear Dallas calling commands down the convoy. Stark had taken out his bow and kept a nocked arrow aimed at the round bales. "He can't miss. Did you know that?" Aphrodite's voice cut through the stillness in the half-empty vehicle.

"General Stark?"

"Yeah, Bow Boy."

"Uh-huh, I knew. The whole army knows. He's a legend."

"In his own mind," Aphrodite said. "They say he killed his mentor."

"I didn't know that."

"Yep. It's why he's all broody. Most women find it attractive. I find it tedious. But he's not my type anyway."

Kevin couldn't help himself. "What is your type?"

"Someone with less broodiness and more heart. And muscles. I like muscles. Fill 'er up, Kev. I'm finally starting to catch that buzz."

"Do you really think that's a good idea?"

"Honestly?"

"Yes. I like honesty."

"Okay, I'll be honest. It doesn't matter whether I drink or not. It won't change what's going to happen, and it won't make me forget that I'm going to have to watch it happening *again*. And since we're being honest—nobody gives one good shit about whether I'm wasted or not except me, and if I have to watch kids being eaten by monsters, I prefer to be wasted."

"That's a good point." Kevin refilled her glass. "But I care whether you're wasted or not."

She met his gaze. "Why?"

"Are we still being honest?"

"How 'bout this—as long as we're alone let's be honest. Deal?"

"Deal," Kevin said, and his heart gave a weird little flutter beat when her gaze didn't leave his, and for the first time she looked exactly like *his* Aphrodite. The one who had kissed him in Zo's world and had told him to find her in his world.

"So, why do you care whether or not I'm wasted?"

"Because I know you're better than this."

She snorted. "That was a crazy thing to say."

"Why?"

She opened her mouth to answer him but was interrupted by a stream of red vampyres rushing past their vehicle to surround the flatbed.

"Shit. It's starting. I can't look." She bowed her head, staring down at her feet. "Tell me when it's over."

"Okay, but I'll also tell you what's going on. It's how my sister used to watch horror movies with me when we were little."

Her eyes cut to his. "What are you talking about?"

"Well, I used to love horror movies. My sister hated them, but she wouldn't let me watch them alone because then I had bad dreams and got into bed with her. So, she'd sit with me, but she'd cover her eyes with her hands. She asked me to describe what was going on because she said it was less scary when I told the story to her."

"Okay, I'm willing to give it a try. If you keep filling up my glass."

"Will do." Kevin refilled her glass and began his commentary. "They've surrounded the round bales. Stark's keeping his arrow aimed at the first one, and Dallas—" Kevin paused then and grinned at Aphrodite. "Hey, even though I couldn't laugh when you said it in front of Stark, I want you to know your nickname for him cracks me up."

"Oh, you mean Lieutenant Dickless. I don't consider it a nickname. I consider it a fact."

Kevin snorted a laugh, then went back to describing what was happening. "So, Lieutenant Dickless has a longsword and is approaching the first bale. Ah, shit. He's going to stab it into—!" Kevin sucked in a breath.

"What? What happened?"

"He stabbed it into the bale and nothing happened. Now, he's stabbing it over and over again. It's just a bale of hay. No one's inside!" He thought Aphrodite would be glad, but she kept drinking and looking down at the knee-high boots she was wearing. "Um, did you hear me?"

"Yeah, I heard. Keep watching. Not all the bales have people in them. The Resistance wouldn't be such a pain in Neferet's ass if they were stupid."

"Oh, good point. Okay. Watching. They're moving to the next bale." Kevin held his breath, then let it out on a sigh. "That's just hay too. Now they're going to a bale on the end."

"That's not good news. I know. I was hiding inside that one."

"You?"

"Not literally. When I have a vision I always see it from the point of view of someone who is dying—usually horribly. That's why it's hard for me to give specific details, because I feel what the dying person feels."

Kevin's stomach roiled. "That must be awful."

"It's worse than that."

He looked up. "Crap. They're at the next bale. Okay, he's stabbing it and—shit. He hit something."

"Not a person, though."

"No. He hit something hard, and just the tip of his sword disappeared into it."

"It's because it's not a real bale. The inside is hollow and wheel-like. There's a door on the side to get in and out. They somehow stuck the hay to the outside of the wheel. Inside can hold, oh, about four big people, or a couple of adults and three or four kids. Hey, I'm going to close my eyes and cover my ears when they start screaming."

"They found a latch and they're opening it." Kevin swallowed down the urge to puke. He wanted to cover his eyes too. And then relief flooded him. "It's empty!"

"Seriously?"

"Yeah, look!"

"Nope. Not until they check them all. At least half of the bales on this flatbed and the other one are filled with people."

"The other one?"

"Yeah, there are two of them."

"Not today. Today there's only one. Aphrodite, look. They're opening the others. They're all empty!" Kevin made no attempt to hide the joy and relief he was feeling.

"Why are you happy?"

He turned his gaze from the empty bales to Aphrodite, who was staring at him, and not the scene unfolding with zero violence in front of them. He met her eyes. And he told her the truth.

"Because I don't want anyone else to die."

"But you're a red vampyre. All you care about is eating and death."

"Is that really how you see me?" Kevin asked.

"Why didn't you stink yesterday?"

"Because I—"

*Knock! Knock! Knock!* Kevin and Aphrodite jumped when Stark banged on his window.

"You two can come out. Looks like we're early," Stark shouted through the window before turning back to the group of soldiers who were trying to reassemble the hollowed-out bales.

Aphrodite sighed. "Bring the bottle."

"Hey, why don't you stay in here? I'll go out and say something about you not feeling great."

"And have Bow Boy squeal to Neferet that I hid in the Hummer even when no battle was going on? That would be the perfect excuse for her to send me out with the Red Army again. No, I'll get out."

Kevin hurried out of the Hummer and jogged around to her side, opening the door for her.

"Thanks. I appreciate the good manners. Someone raised you right."

"You're welcome. Mostly my sister."

"There's that sister again. Maybe I'll meet her someday," Aphrodite said as she held out her hand.

Kevin took it and held it carefully in his as he helped her out of the vehicle. "I have a very good feeling you two would be friends."

Aphrodite snorted. "Then she must be a pain in the ass."

"Oh, you have no idea," Kevin said.

# 19

# Other Aphrodite

"You're sure that this is the right field?" Stark asked Aphrodite.

"Positive."

"And this is the only flatbed you saw with hay bales?"

"This flatbed is the one I saw during my vision. I was inside that middle bale there." She pointed. "I don't know what else to tell you. I don't know why no one's inside. We must be early." Aphrodite chose her words carefully. Contrary to what Neferet and Stark and the rest of them might think, she despised liars. She'd been raised by one, and at an early age had sworn that, if nothing else, unlike her mother she would try to always tell the truth. And that's what she was doing. Technically telling the truth. Sure, she was leaving out some things, but Stark would have to get a lot more specific with his questions for her to divulge *everything*.

"All right then. Lieutenant Dallas, first get the vehicles and men hidden in that pecan grove across the street. Keep every damn Red Army soldier *inside* those vehicles. We don't want the Resistance smelling them. And no lights—no noises. None. Remind those soldiers the only way they're eating tonight is if the Resistance springs our trap. Then get back over here with a few of the other officers and make those bales look right again—or at least right enough that the Resistance won't notice they've been disturbed until it's too late. We'll wait 'em out and capture them when they finally show up." He turned his gaze to Aphrodite. "Could you tell what time the attack happened?"

"No. Sorry. I was too busy being eaten to look at a watch."

Stark frowned at her and then continued to Dallas: "Okay, we'll wait as long as we can, but the Red Army has to get back to the tunnels before dawn. And remind those soldiers that they can *only* eat the humans. Blue fledglings and blue vampyres are to be captured alive."

"Yep. I'll tell 'em, sir. But they're stupid, so don't expect much." Dallas gave him a sloppy salute and started shouting orders.

Aphrodite found it difficult to stop staring at the soldiers of the Red Army. She'd never been around this many of them before. She pitied them almost as much as they disgusted her. They were milling around the flatbed and the empty hay bales. They looked agitated and confused. She thought several were actually drooling.

"Aphrodite, you can get back in our lead vehicle with Lieutenant Heffer. Heffer, you can drive, right?"

"Sure, yeah," the kid said.

"So, drive her across the street and wait."

"Actually, I need some fresh air first," Aphrodite said. "I'm taking a walk."

"Not a good idea," Stark said. "If the Resistance is around here you're not safe."

She raised her brows at him. "Not safe? There's a whole herd of ravenous red vampyres within screaming distance. Plus, you're here. With your unmissable bow. I'm pretty sure I'll be fine."

Stark's sigh was filled with annoyance. "Heffer, follow her. Aphrodite, do not be gone long. The Resistance could show up any minute, and I promise you won't want to be out here when the fighting starts."

"Oh, please. I was already out here when the fighting started. That's why I had to join you on this shit show, remember?"

She turned her back to Stark and Dallas and the horde of red things, and began to pick her way carefully through the field to the trees lining its far side. She didn't need to look behind her. She was certain Kevin would be following. She didn't care. The sense of relief that had been flooding her body since she saw only one flatbed with no Resistance members hidden inside those bales was dizzying.

*There were two trailers in my vision. I was in this one, but there was another. Filled with even more fledglings and young humans. But it's gone! Goddess, please let them have gotten away. Please don't let them return tonight. Please, please, please.*

She heard rushing water as she approached the tree line. The underbrush went from neatly cut hay to tall winter grasses and what looked like blackberry bushes. Aphrodite picked her way around a sticker-filled cluster of sleeping plants and a wall of evergreen juniper trees to look down on a lazy creek.

And then her mind didn't understand what she was seeing.

*Are there people down there?*

*In the water? Just below me?*

*What the hell?*

She must have made some sound. Must have gasped in shock, because the person at the rear of the line that was sloughing their way downstream in hip-deep water turned his head and looked up at her.

The moon shined off the water, intensifying its wan light so that the ornate sapphire tattoo of dragons breathing fire at a crescent moon in the middle of the vampyre's forehead was clearly visible.

*Ohmygoddess! It's Dragon Lankford!* Aphrodite's gaze swept the silent line of people and she recognized several of them from her vision. *It's the Resistance! They were tipped off! They didn't get slaughtered!*

She didn't have time to overthink it. Aphrodite acted on instinct. She rushed down a few feet more to come close to the edge of the bank. Staring at Dragon she mouthed, *Go! Get away!* as she made a shooing gesture at them.

And then everything happened really fast.

Dragon Lankford surged out of the creek, bounding up the bank. She tried to scramble back. Tried to run away, but the heel of her Jimmy Choo boots found a hole and snapped off. Aphrodite went down hard on her butt, dropping her bottle of champagne as the air was knocked out of her.

Dragon reached her easily. He grabbed her, lifting her to her feet and putting his hand over her mouth. He pressed a dagger against her throat as he whispered directly into her ear. "If you make one sound I will slit your throat. You're coming with me." He turned so that the line of retreating fledglings, vampyres, and young humans could see him. Dragon made the same kind of shooing gesture Aphrodite had just made at him as he called across the water in a low voice, "Go! Get to safety!" He began dragging her backward, toward the creek.

And then Kevin was there. First, coming through the line of junipers and glancing around, obviously looking for her. Aphrodite's heart slammed against her chest, filling her bloodstream with adrenaline and panic. *But I tried to help them! And now they're going to kill Kevin and probably call the attention of Stark and the wrath of the Red Army down on themselves! They're all going to be slaughtered like they were in my vision!*

But that's not what happened. Something much weirder happened.

Kevin looked down. Aphrodite knew the instant he saw her and Dragon and the escaping line of fledglings, humans, and vampyres trudging through the water. Kevin didn't draw a weapon. Kevin didn't yell for Stark. Instead he rushed down the bank to them.

"Dragon! No! Don't hurt her!" Kevin whispered frantically as he got close to them.

"I'm not hurting her. I'm kidnapping her," Dragon said.

"Why?" Kevin asked.

"Come on, Kevin. You know why. If I don't she's going to give us away to the Red Army. And she's a Prophetess of Nyx. She has visions. Even if she won't share them with us we can use her. Neferet will do just about anything to get her pet Prophetess back."

Aphrodite smacked the back of the hand Dragon was holding over her mouth.

"Um, I think she wants you to take your hand away from her mouth," Kevin said. "And it'd be nice if you'd put the knife down too."

"I'm assuming the Red Army's up there?" Dragon jerked his chin in the direction of the hayfield.

Aphrodite nodded as vigorously as she could with a knife against her throat, then she tried to say, "I was telling you to get away from here!" but, of course, the words turned into angry mush-mumble against his hand.

"Yeah. Stark's up there with about fifty red soldiers and several officers—red and blue." Kevin's gaze went to the creek and the line of people who were continuing to retreat toward the ridge and safety. "You got my message."

"Yeah. And now I've got this Prophetess too. I'll take her to headquarters. Join us when you can."

"Dragon, seriously, if you kidnap Aphrodite how are you any different than Neferet?"

"How can you ask me that? If we were like Neferet I would have already slit her throat. And, anyway, I can't let her go. She knows you're working with us, which puts us all in danger."

Kevin met Aphrodite's gaze. "Will you give us your word not to scream or do anything to draw Stark's attention if Dragon takes his hand from your mouth?"

Aphrodite nodded.

"I trust her," Kevin said. "If she says she won't yell, she won't. Aphrodite tells the truth. Right?"

Aphrodite nodded again.

"It's not wise to trust her," Dragon said.

Kevin grinned. "That's what you said about me at first too."

The Warrior sighed. "All right, look. I'll take my hand from your mouth." Dragon spoke into Aphrodite's ear. "But I won't take my knife from your throat. If you do *anything* to bring soldiers down on us, you'll be the first to die. Understand?"

Aphrodite nodded once more. Slowly, Dragon took his hand from her mouth.

"You asshole!" Aphrodite whispered at him. "You saw me tell you to get away. You knew I wasn't going to call the army. You're just acting like a fucking douchebag coming up here and grabbing me!" She turned her attention to Kevin. "I knew you were different. What the hell is going on here?"

"It's a long story," Kevin said, "but I promise I'll tell you everything. First, Dragon and the rest of his people have to get away."

"And she still needs to come with us," Dragon said.

"I am not fucking going with you." Aphrodite glared at him. "So, you might as well slit my throat right now."

"And if you do that you're just like them," Kevin said. "Plus, I'll bet Anastasia will be super pissed at you."

"Not to mention what will happen if I don't go back up there very soon. Stark will come down here looking for me. And what the hell do you think he's going to do if he finds me missing? Just let you and your group swim home?"

Dragon frowned at Aphrodite, but he took the knife from her neck.

"Now what?" Dragon asked.

"Now you need to get out of here. Fast. Stark's going to—"

"Aphrodite! Heffer! Dammit, where the hell are you two?" From above them, Stark's annoyed voice drifted down.

Aphrodite didn't hesitate. She cupped her hands around her mouth and yelled up the bank. "Go away! I'm peeing! As if it's not bad enough that a stinking red vampyre is following me around and I broke my fucking Jimmy Choos out here in this stupid wilderness. Can I get not one tiny bit of privacy?"

"She's fine, General!" Kevin added. "She's just around the other side of a clump of bushes. I can almost see her and—"

"Do not fucking look!" Aphrodite shrieked, making the whole line of retreating people freeze and stare back at them. "I swear to Goddess, if you two do not get off my last nerve I'm going to report to Neferet that you treated me like shit—with zero respect. No matter how pissed she may be at me, she's definitely *not* going to tolerate her Prophetess being disrespected!"

There was a pause while all three of them held their breath, then Stark's voice—just as annoyed—finally answered. "Just hurry up! This isn't a damn picnic."

"I will not hurry up! I will take my time peeing! And you can take the stinky lieutenant back there with you!" Aphrodite shouted, then she whispered to Kevin. "Get up there quick and be sure he doesn't come down here."

"Got it." But before he left he looked at Dragon. "You're going to let her go, right?"

"Yes. I'll let her go," he said with obvious reluctance.

Then Kevin scrambled up the bank and sprinted through the junipers. Aphrodite and Dragon remained very still until they heard the sounds of two men moving away from the creek.

Aphrodite breathed a long sigh of relief and then realized Dragon was staring at her.

"What?" she snapped.

"Why did you do that?"

"Because I don't want anyone else slaughtered by those damn red vampyres."

"Aren't you on Neferet's side?" Dragon asked.

"No. I'm on my side."

"Then how can I trust you won't betray us?"

She shrugged. "I have no idea. You'll just have to take a leap of faith. My guess is it's the same kinda leap of faith you took to trust Kevin."

"He proved himself trustworthy," Dragon said.

"Isn't that what I just did?"

They stared at each other until finally Dragon looked away. "I'm leaving now. With my people."

"Fine. I'll wait as long as I can push Stark, and then go back to the field. Oh, the Red Army is hiding in the pecan grove across the street, so don't come back."

"We won't."

"Did you get one truck out of here before the soldiers showed up?" she asked.

He hesitated, but answered, "Yes."

"Good. That's what I hoped when I only saw one up there."

"Did you tell them that there was another?"

"Oh, for shit's sake, no. Like I said, I'm tired of people being slaughtered by the Red Army," Aphrodite said.

"But you are still telling Neferet about your visions," Dragon said.

"I'm doing what I have to do to survive. Just like you." Aphrodite paused and then had to ask, "Is Anastasia okay?"

"Yes. She is safe."

"Tell her I'm glad."

He kept staring at her before saying, "You could join us, you know. After what you did here today, we'd accept you."

Aphrodite ignored the flutter of hope she felt. *What would it be like to be part of something noble like the Resistance? To have friends? To not be so alone all the time?*

But they wouldn't want her. Not if they knew the truth.

"I'll keep that in mind. And, um, thanks for the invite."

He nodded with a grunt before turning away and getting back in the creek. He motioned for the line to get moving again, and Aphrodite watched them disappear as the water curved to the right. Then she brushed dirt and leaves and Goddess only knew what off her butt and limped back up the bank and out into the hayfield.

Stark and Kevin were standing in front of the lead Hummer. The rest had disappeared—presumably into the grove across the street.

With no hesitation Aphrodite marched up to Stark.

"I'm leaving."

"Sorry. No. This night's just getting started," Stark said.

"Oh, you misunderstand me. I didn't ask your permission. I don't *need* your permission. I am a priestess and a Prophetess of Nyx. Our society is still matriarchal, correct?"

Stark looked surprised at the question. "Yes, of course it is."

"Exactly. So, I outrank you. Actually, I outrank *all of you* except for Neferet. So let me repeat. I'm leaving. Oh, and this stinky kid is going to drive me home. I am feeling the Xanax and booze—best I don't drive."

"Look, Aphrodite, Neferet said you are supposed to—" Stark began, but Aphrodite shut him up with one abrupt gesture.

"I know exactly what Neferet said. I was supposed to join you on this mission. I did. I was supposed to locate the correct field for you and your red creatures. I did that too. And now I'm done. I did not come here to camp. I did not come here to sit around and 'Kumbaya' with a bunch of soldiers. *And I just broke a boot that cost almost two thousand dollars trekking around in nature.* Goddess! I just can't with this anymore. I'm leaving. And you, General Bow Boy, may go straight to hell." She looked at Kevin. "Let's go, Stinky."

Kevin glanced at Stark. Stark ran a hand through his thick hair and sighed. Again. "Fine. Go. But I'll let Neferet know that I advised you stay."

"Whatever. Like you think Neferet would stay out here all night if there wasn't any action?" She turned her back to them and went to the passenger's side of the Hummer, where she waited, foot tapping manically, for Kevin to open the door for her, which he did before jogging around to get behind the wheel.

She let him maneuver out of the field and start down Lone Star Road before she spoke.

"Tell me everything. Now."

## 20

# *Other Kevin*

Kevin told her everything. He started with the fact that he'd been different since he was Marked—that'd he'd managed to retain some of his humanity even after he Changed into the youngest red vampyre in history. He told her about getting pulled into an alternate House of Night world, and what happened to the other red vamps and red fledglings who went over there with him.

And then Kevin told her about her own Other World twin—or at least as much about that other Aphrodite as he knew—that it was her sacrifice that had saved the red fledglings in her world, and that it was her gift from Nyx that saved him and the red vampyres who were still alive and in Zo's world.

Kevin also told her about Neferet—how she'd become immortal and almost destroyed first Tulsa, and then that entire world—and how Zoey and her group had outsmarted and imprisoned her. For good.

Then silence filled the inside of their vehicle. He glanced at Aphrodite. She wasn't drinking. She was staring at him with an expression that was wide-eyed but indecipherable.

Finally, she spoke. "So, the Zoey who is your sister over there, she and I work together at the Tulsa House of Night?"

"Well, yeah, but it's more than that. You two are friends. Good friends."

She kept staring at him, and as he took his gaze off the road for another quick glance, he saw a grimace of pain flash across her face. Then, very quietly, Aphrodite said, "That's why Neferet thought you looked familiar. And now that I'm looking—I see the resemblance too. You're Zoey Redbird's brother. *The* Zoey Redbird who was killed more than a year ago."

"Yep, that's what I've been telling you. Only she's alive in that Other World. So, you knew her before she died?"

"No. Not really."

"But you say we look alike—and Neferet kinda recognized me too. Zo must have made some kind of impression on you."

"Yes. She did. Or at least her death did." Then Aphrodite pointed to the Quick Trip on the corner of Fifth and Denver. "Pull into that parking lot. I need to tell you something and I don't want you to freak and cause a wreck."

"Hey, you don't need to worry about me. I don't freak easily."

"Just do it," she said.

He pulled into the parking lot.

When he put the Humvee in park, Aphrodite turned in her seat so that she could look into his face. "Okay," she said, "I don't want to tell you this, but chances are you're going to find out anyway. I'm pretty sure Anastasia knows." Aphrodite shrugged, and looked defeated. "And I hate lying. I don't even particularly like omitting. So, here goes. I didn't know your sister. Neferet disbanded the Dark Daughters before Zoey came to the House of Night. I didn't have any reason to get to know her because once the Dark Daughters weren't a thing, there wasn't any reason for fledglings to suck up to me. Then I made the Change and didn't have any reason to hang out with fledglings anyway. But I remember her face because I had a vision about her. And Neferet remembers her face because I told her about the vision." Aphrodite paused as if she was having difficulty choosing her words. Then she blurted, "In the vision I was Neferet. I saw a fledgling, one that wasn't even a vampyre yet, cause Neferet's death."

Kevin felt sick. "That fledgling was my sister?"

"Yes."

"So, Zo was right when she told me that she was sure the Neferet in our world had killed her and made it look like human People of Faith did it as a hate crime."

He hadn't phrased it as a question, but Aphrodite answered him. "Yes. Neferet killed Zoey because of my vision."

Kevin didn't know what to say. He looked away from Aphrodite, focusing on the steady flow of mostly trucks that pulled in and out of the Quick Trip.

"Did you like me over there?"

Aphrodite's question surprised Kevin into an automatic response. "Yes. I more than liked you."

"And I'm assuming I liked you too?"

"You kissed me goodbye and told me to find you over here."

"Okay, look, you must be telling me at least *mostly* the truth. You're obviously different than the rest of the red vamps. And you didn't stink last night, so you must also be telling the truth about that." She shuddered delicately. "And that nasty blood crap you use as perfume. But you're sixteen. A kid."

"I'll be seventeen in August," he added quickly.

"Whatever. You're still a kid. And you're telling me your sister and I are friends over there *and* you and I had a thing. That just doesn't sound like me. Any version of me. No offense."

"I'm not a kid. I'm a lieutenant in the Red Army who has seen more death than even you have—only with me it was *real* death, happening in front of me. I stopped being a kid a long time ago. And you need to define *thing*. We didn't hook up or anything like that. But we did have a connection, and I promise you that kiss was more than just a peck on my cheek. Oh, and over there you're not just friends with my sister. You're respected and loved by a lot of people. You're friends with everyone."

"Are you super sure about that? I don't make friends very easily. Mostly because most people are peasants."

Kevin was surprised to hear himself laugh. "I don't know the full story about how it happened. I didn't have time to get it from Zo, but you're definitely part of her group, and it's a pretty big group. Actually, you're friendly with all the High Priestesses I met."

"Wait, what? I thought you said your sister was High Priestess."

"She is, but there are lots of High Priestesses at her House of Night—Stevie Rae, Shaylin, Shaunee, Kramisha, Lenobia—"

"Lenobia? The equestrian professor? She's alive over there?"

"Yep. So is Travis and all their horses."

Aphrodite wiped a shaking hand across her face. "I'm glad they're alive somewhere."

Kevin studied her. "Ah, I get it. No one from the Resistance leaked the Keystone location. You had another vision. You told Neferet. And Neferet sent the Red Army to wipe them out."

"Yes. Do you want to turn around and take me back to Dragon for retribution?"

She spoke steadily—she even sounded haughty. But Kevin saw the way her face paled and her hands trembled so badly that she had to clutch them together in her lap.

He didn't answer her question. Instead he asked one of his own. "Actually, I don't think you like all this killing. So, why did you do it?"

"I told Neferet about Zoey because back then I still believed Neferet was doing Nyx's work. I mean, smacking down some humans sounded good. Who doesn't get sick of their idiotic racism and misogyny? Please. That shit needs to become as extinct as the dinosaurs."

"What does that have to do with telling Neferet to kill my sister?"

"That's my point! I still believed that Neferet was basically good. And I didn't know she was going to kill your sister."

"But you knew she'd kill Lenobia and Travis. You had to have seen that in your vision."

"I did. I also had that horrific fucking vision when I was with Neferet. I—I was Lenobia. I spoke as Lenobia. I died with Lenobia. I experienced everything with her. The death of her mate. The death of her horses. The death of her friends. It was beyond awful. I didn't even realize I was describing everything to Neferet until after—after I'd recovered from the vision and she'd already sent the Red Army to wipe them out." Aphrodite drew a deep breath and wiped away the tears sliding down her pale cheeks. "But you're right. I'm responsible for their deaths. I'm responsible for all of their deaths."

"I don't get it. If you know how awful Neferet is, why do you keep telling her about your visions?"

"I try not to! And when I can't hide that I've had one I try to leave out any detail that can lead that fucking army of monsters to the people I see them slaughtering—but I want to survive too! I hated telling her about the Resistance hiding people in those bales of hay, but I knew I'd pushed Neferet as far as I could. *She was going to make me live in those tunnels with those creatures.* I can't do that. I just can't."

Kevin couldn't say anything. He wanted to tell her she *could* stand up to Neferet. She *could* be that strong. He knew an Aphrodite who was that strong, but as he watched her he realized that she wasn't *that* Aphrodite. Not yet she wasn't.

He put the Hummer into gear and pulled out of the parking lot, turning north toward the heart of downtown.

"You're not taking me to Dragon?"

"No."

"Where are you going?"

"To the depot. You can drive the Hummer back to the House of Night," he said.

"You're seriously not going to turn me in to the Resistance?"

"Seriously."

"Why aren't you?" she asked.

"Because I'm not a monster," he said. "I have the capacity to love and to forgive. I forgive you. You did what you thought you had to do to survive. You're still doing that. I guess we all are."

"Is it as bad in those tunnels as I think it is?"

"Worse," Kevin said.

"Will they be able to tell you're not like them?"

He sighed. "I hope not."

"But if they find out you're different they'll probably kill you. Or eat you." She shuddered. "Or something hideously awful."

"Well, I do have that blood goo stuff, and I'm used to hiding how I really feel when I'm around other red vampyres. You say I stink, right?"

"Yes. Absolutely. Can't you smell it?"

"I try not to."

Aphrodite snorted a laugh, then as Kevin was getting ready to take the turn that would lead them to the depot, she said, "Don't turn here."

"But it's the quickest way to the depot."

"I know. Turn right instead."

"That's not the way to the depot."

"Again. I know. Go to Saks instead."

"Huh?" He was gawking at her in surprise and almost hit the curb.

"Oh, for shit's sake! Watch where you're driving and close your mouth," she said.

"Why do you want me to take you to Saks?"

"Ssh. I'm thinking. Just drive."

Kevin did as he was told, making his way to Utica Square and the Saks Fifth Avenue that was the cornerstone of the outside shopping square. "Park over there in the shadows on the side, not in the front," Aphrodite told him.

He pulled into a dark spot and put the Hummer in park. "So,

I guess I'll wait out here while you're shopping, then drive back to the depot?"

"No." Aphrodite dug through her giant bag, causing the remaining untouched bottle of champagne to clank against one of the crystal flutes. "Here it is—come to Mama," she murmured as she pulled out a platinum credit card and handed it to Kevin. "Take this in there. Buy yourself new clothes. Nonstinky, non-ill-fitting clothes. And none of those skinny jeans either. That hipster look is ridiculous. Get some T-shirts too. Nothing flashy. Just clean and, again, *not ill-fitting*." She gave his clothes, borrowed from Dragon—who was decidedly shorter and more muscular than Kevin—a disgusted look. "Get enough to fill four or five big bags. Oh, and don't forget some boy pajamas. Keep this in mind when choosing pj's—I do *not* want to see your flopping wiener through them, so get something lined."

"I'm so confused." Kevin stared at the credit card. "Why are you giving me this?"

"Do you have enough money to buy four or five big bags of clothes from Saks?"

"Hell no."

"That's why I'm giving you my card."

"Aphrodite, I really appreciate it, but what I have on is fine for the tunnels."

"Yeah, I get that. But it's not fine for being around me," she said.

"Huh?"

She sighed dramatically. "I. Have. A. Plan. Now go in there and do what I said and let me think it through."

"What if they notice I'm not Aphrodite LaFont?"

She rolled her eyes skyward. "Use your red vamp mind trick thing on the simpletons."

"Oh, yeah. I forgot about that. Okay." He started to open the door and paused. "Um, do you need anything from in there?"

She shuddered. "No. It's not Nordstrom. I prefer Miss Jackson's."

He grinned mischievously at her. "Hey, in Zo's world the Miss Jackson's closed."

Aphrodite held up her hand to stop him from saying any more. "Do not blaspheme like that. Now, be gone. And hurry up. I only have one bottle of champagne left."

"Yes, ma'am." He saluted her, and then did exactly as she commanded.

# 21

# *Zoey*

> Nerd Herd and our Warriors and lovers! Meet me at
> the broken tree. Bring circle candles & sage. Lots of
> sage. I'll be there in 10 min.

I didn't give myself time for second thoughts. I pressed **SEND**
for the group text and then turned my attention back to the media
room table in front of me and the open, musty-smelling old book
titled simply *Old Magick*. I flipped back a few pages and reread the
end of the previous chapter.

> *Remember, when asking for the aid of Old Magickal beings,*
> *especially elemental sprites, there is always a cost. Often they are*
> *satisfied with blood, but the Ancients are easily bored and capri-*
> *cious. They tend to value payment that is unusual or difficult to*
> *acquire. Be quite certain that the method of payment is specific,*
> *and be even surer that the payment is made. Do not make the*
> *mistake of believing you can escape the debt you incur to the*

Ancients. You will not—even should the payment required be your life. You will die. Of that there is no doubt whatsoever.

"Hell," I said to the book and the long-dead vampyre High Priestess who had written it centuries ago. "Hell, hell, hell. I hate how that sounds."

But there wasn't anything I could do about hating it. I'd made my decision. I even believed it was a smart decision. Well, I *hoped* it was a smart decision. Smart or not, I thought it was the right decision.

"Stark's going to be so pissed," I murmured to myself.

"Why am I going to be pissed?"

I jumped and turned in my chair. "Goddess! You scared me."

"Because you're hiding in here and didn't think anyone could find you?" He sat beside me and gave the open book a distrustful glance.

"I'm not hiding. I'm researching. Alone."

"Sorry. Didn't mean to bother you."

He started to get up and I grabbed his hand. "Don't go. I'm sorry. That sounded mean and that's not how I wanted it to sound." I drew in a long breath to steady myself. I didn't want to have this talk with Stark. Ever. But I'd done enough childish avoiding. I'd made my decision, so it was time to tell him the truth. "I need to talk to you."

He turned in his chair to face me. "Finally!"

His look of relief made my stomach clench.

Stark touched my cheek in a sweet, intimate gesture that always made me feel fluttery inside, and he smiled that cocky smile of his that I've loved since the day I met him. "Hey, whatever it is, we can handle it. Together. Just tell me what's wrong and then we'll figure out how to fix the problem."

I leaned forward and kissed him—softly, slowly. He pulled me into his arms and returned the kiss, and for that moment I let my world be filled with my Warrior, my lover, my Guardian, and my friend.

When we finally parted his smile went cocky again. "If the

problem is you need to be kissed like that more often, I have your fix. It's a tough job, but you can definitely count on me, my Queen."

I mock-punched his shoulder. "A tough job?"

"Yep, but someone has to do it."

I shook my head at him, and then sobered. *Stop procrastinating! Just tell him.*

"I'm going to the Other World after Kevin," I blurted.

"Yeah, well, I figured as much. When do we leave?"

I took his hand between both of mine. "I leave tonight. You're staying here."

He didn't say anything for several long seconds. Then, slowly, he pulled his hand from between mine.

"Why?" His voice sounded flat, but his eyes filled with pain.

"Well, Neferet has to be stopped and I can't let Kevin destroy himself with Old Magick, which it seems he's on the road to doing. He's using it. You can feel how often. He must believe he has to. I know I did. We all know that. Neferet is a nightmare. But Kevin understands nothing about Old Magick, or Neferet, and that's going to—"

"Not why are you going," Stark interrupted. "I already figured that out. Why am I not going?"

"Oh. Sorry. Because you can't."

"If you can cross over to another world, why the hell can't I?"

"I don't mean you physically can't. I mean you can't because there's already a James Stark over there. He's a general in Neferet's army. Kevin said he's even Neferet's lover." I grimaced. "Which is so damn gross I can hardly stand to think about it, and believe me—I'm going to try my best to do something about that. Goddess, can you imagine how—"

"I don't care about that. That's not *me.* I care about *you.* This you— my Queen, who I am Oathbound to as her Warrior and who I protect as her Goddess-given Guardian. Z, I understand why you have to go. I've known you've been thinking about it—worrying about Other Kevin—I even expected you to go. But I have to come with you."

219

I shook my head. "I'm sorry. I wish you could, but it doesn't make any sense. *You're already over there.* And you're super visible. I need to sneak over—tell Kevin he has to quit using Old Magick—help him defeat Neferet, which I think I have figured out—and then get back here." I met his anguished gaze and said what I had to, said what he wouldn't want to hear but must hear. "Stark, you wouldn't be helping me if you went. You'd be adding to what is already going to be a really difficult thing to do. I'm sorry," I repeated. "But I've made up my mind. I'm going, and you're not."

The pain flashed to rage. "You think I don't know the real reason you don't want me to go? It's because you're going to see Heath and you don't want me being a third damn wheel!"

I'd expected him to say that. I'd expected his hurt and his anger. But it didn't make this any easier.

"No, Stark. That's not why you can't come with me. If you got caught, which would be easy to do because *your alter ego over there is a powerful general who everyone knows*, you would be killed. Or tortured. Or something awful. And I couldn't bear that. But it's about more than what I can and can't bear. It's even about more than what you can and can't bear. If they caught you it would be bad for Kevin and his world for sure, but bad for our world as well. Stark, think. What would happen if Neferet found out there's a whole other world over here—one she's *not* in charge of? And then think about what she'd do if—no, not if—*when* Other Kevin and his Resistance turn the tide and actually start to defeat her. What would Neferet do?"

"I don't fucking know!"

"Yes, you do. We all do. She'd run. And she'd run here." I took his hand in mine again. "Stark, I love you. I hate hurting you. And I'm *not* going over there just to see Heath. But this isn't about you and me. It's about two whole worlds and being sure Darkness doesn't ever win."

"Did you hear yourself? You're 'not going over there *just* to see Heath'! 'Just'!" he air-quoted. "But you are going to see him, aren't you?"

"I don't know. Kevin told me he's at OU. I'm not going there, Stark. I'm going to Tulsa."

"I don't believe you."

"Please don't do this. Don't be jealous of someone who isn't even alive," I said.

"But that's the problem, isn't it? He *is* alive over in that world you're just dying to get to."

This time I let go of his hand myself. "You actually think I want to go? That I want to fight Neferet again? That I want to leave my home and my friends and *you*?" I shook my head. "You're jealous and you're wrong." I stood. "Everyone's meeting me at the messed-up tree. I have to go."

"Yeah, I know. I got your group text. It was super intimate." He turned in his chair so that he was facing the book and not me. "Is that how you were going to tell me?"

"In a text? No!"

"I didn't think that. I meant were you going to tell me you're going and I'm staying in front of everyone?"

I chewed my cheek. Actually, I'd planned on telling everyone together that I was going—and who was and was *not* going with me. *Good job, Z. Stark thinks you're willing to insult and embarrass him—as well as leaving him for Heath.*

"I—I didn't mean to hurt your feelings. I just know I have to go, and I have to tell everyone. I didn't think about it making you mad that I was telling everyone together," I said lamely.

He looked up at me then. "I'm not mad that you were going to tell me with everyone. I'm sad. Sad that that's all I mean to you."

"Stark! You mean everything to me!"

"That's bullshit."

I went to his side and put my hand on his shoulder. I wanted to touch his hair—his face—to kiss him and hold him and never let him go. But he flinched away from my hand and turned his sad, angry gaze to the old, open book in front of him.

"I love you. That's not bullshit. You know that. All you have to do is feel it—feel our bond."

"You think I'll be able to feel it when you're over there?" he asked woodenly.

"I don't know," I said. "I hope so. I think I could feel my bond with you in any world."

"I hope not."

Those three words sliced into me, cutting through skin and muscle and bones, leaving me speechless and so, so sad. I picked up my backpack and slid it over one shoulder. Then I turned away from my Warrior and left the Media Center.

(

They were all there—my circle: Aphrodite, Damien, Shaunee, Shaylin, and Stevie Rae. And their Warriors and lovers: Darius, Jack, Erik, Nicole, and Rephaim.

But no Stark. He hadn't followed me from the Media Center. I swallowed my sadness and approached the blackened, broken tree, treading quietly so that I could watch my friends before they knew I was there.

Aphrodite was obviously in charge. She was pointing at places around the messed-up tree, and Other Jack, looking super cute in a pale violet tee tucked into adorably distressed jeans, was carrying the ritual candles to the areas she'd chosen. It was easy to tell what Aphrodite was doing, and I was filled with gratitude for her. She was setting up a circumference around the tree, readying everything for the casting of our circle.

Stevie Rae was holding a big pile of sage smudge sticks, of which she passed out one each to Damien, Shaunee, and Shaylin.

*Good. That'll be the easy part. I hope they're ready for what will come next.*

"Hey, Z! There ya are!" Stevie Rae dimpled at me. "I brought the sage."

"And I brought the candles," Other Jack said, beaming a sweet smile at me.

"I'm assuming we're cleansing this disgusting tree?" Aphrodite said.

"Yep, we are," I said. "At least for starters that's what we're doing. But first I need to talk to all of you."

My friends moved closer, forming an attentive half moon before me. I studied their faces, thinking about how much we'd all been through and how close it had made us. I didn't want to leave. I didn't want to go face a Darkness we'd already defeated. I felt sad and scared and very alone.

"It's okay, Z," Stevie Rae said. "Whatever it is, we're here for you."

"Just tell us," Damien said. "We'll figure it out."

"Your aura is strong. Whatever it is, you're at peace with it," Shaylin said.

"Remember you're not alone," Shaunee said. "We've got your back."

"And so does Nyx," Aphrodite said. "The Goddess is with you too. Always, Z."

The rest of my friends nodded agreement.

I blinked real fast, determined not to let my tears spill over. "Thank you. That means a lot to me, and I really needed to hear that I have your support. I hope I still do when I tell you what's going on."

"You will," Stevie Rae said. "You're our High Priestess. We trust you, Z."

When I knew I could speak without bursting into tears, I began. "First, we're going to cleanse this tree. We're not going to do anything too crazy—just a basic smudging and cleansing, though I am going to ask that everyone join in and help us smudge. It needs *lots* of cleansing."

"Do you want us inside or outside your circle?" Erik asked.

"Good question," I said, smiling at him as he stood beside Shaunee, one arm draped intimately around her shoulders as she leaned into him. "I want you with us in the circle, like you would be if we were doing a school-wide ritual. So, Jack, could you please move the element candles out so our circle is a little bigger?"

"Absolutely!" Jack immediately began scampering around the circle, placing the big pillar candles so that they included everyone.

"I'm going to call the elements and cast the circle. Those of you who represent the four elements, please light your sage sticks from your elemental candles. The rest of you can light your sticks from my spirit candle." A thought struck me, and I decided it was a perfect addition to a simple smudging. "I want to make this more than just a smudging, though. This tree—this place—has so much sadness and Darkness attached to it that we need to do something extra with the smudging. We need to bring joy back here. What if we smudge to a song?"

"I'm all for that!" Stevie Rae said. "How 'bout using—"

"Oh, for shit's sake, no!" Aphrodite interrupted. "No Kenny Chesney songs."

Stevie Rae frowned at her. "You're hurtin' my heart."

"It needs to be a super happy song," I said. "One we all know, and one someone has on their phone."

"'When the Sun Goes Down' by Kenny Chesney is super happy," Stevie Rae said.

Aphrodite snorted.

"Well, according to a group of researchers at the University of Missouri, 'Don't Stop Me Now' by Queen, with the ever-fabulous Freddie Mercury, is neurologically the happiest song in the world," said Damien.

Everyone stared at him.

"How the hell do you know that?" Aphrodite said.

"I'm smart and I actually read," Damien said.

"When he fences he listens to that song. A lot," Jack said,

hurrying back to Damien's side. "And you know what an awesome fencer my Damien is!"

"That's the truth," I said. "So, you have the song on your playlist?"

"Correct," Damien said.

Before I could ask if everyone knew it, Jack's hand went up like a perfect little student. "Yes, Jack?"

"Um, I just thought of a song. A really, *really* happy song I'm sure everyone knows. And it's on my playlist." He leaned into Damien. "Sorry, Damien. I hope you don't mind."

"I don't mind. What's the song?" Damien asked.

Jack sang his answer. "'Raindrops on roses and whiskers on kittens …'"

Stevie Rae picked up the next line. "'Bright copper kettles and warm woolen mittens!'" "'Brown paper packages tied up with strings,'" Shaunee sang.

"'These are a few of my favorite things!'" Aphrodite totally surprised me by chiming in. "What?" she frowned at everyone staring at her. "Who doesn't like Julie Andrews?"

"What do you think, Damien?" I asked.

"I think I love cream-colored ponies and crisp apple strudels! It's not scientific, but I vote for 'My Favorite Things.'"

"Sounds great to me. Um, everyone knows it, right?" I asked the group, and everyone except Rephaim nodded.

"I'll just try to follow along," Rephaim said.

"It's okay, babe," Stevie Rae said. "I know all the words. I'll help you."

"Okay, perfect. So, when the song is over, we'll end the smudging by making a minipyre there, in the middle of the circle, right in front of the tree." I pointed to a place in front of the center of the dark, twisted oak. "I'll go around the circle and get the smudge sticks from Damien, Shaunee, Shaylin, and Stevie Rae—and then I'll add them to the rest of the sticks. Shaunee, then I'll ask you to add some fire to the pile so that it'll burn right."

"Easy-peasy," Shaunee said.

"That means you're leaving the circle open after the smudging," Aphrodite said. "So, what's next?"

I met her gaze. "Next, I summon Oak, the Old Magick tree sprite who answered my questions before."

"Why are you messing with Old Magick again?" Aphrodite asked.

"Because I'm going to ask her to lead me to the Other World where my brother needs my help." I spoke quickly and was instantly filled with a wave of relief for finally having told everyone.

"That's fucking nuts," Aphrodite said.

"No!" Other Jack's eyes had gone huge. He looked absolutely terrified. "Don't go, Zoey! That world is horrible." He shuddered, wrapping his arms around himself. "I know your brother told you some things about it, but you can't possibly understand. You just can't. *Don't go!*" He started crying softly, and Damien took him in his arms.

"Why do you believe you must go there?" Darius asked me.

"Several reasons," I said. "Kevin's been using Old Magick. A lot of it. And he doesn't have any idea how dangerous it is, or what it can do to him. I have to tell him before it changes him."

"He's using it because that's the only way to defeat Neferet," Aphrodite said.

"No, it's not," I countered. "It was the only way to defeat *our* Neferet, because she'd become immortal."

"Well, doesn't it make sense that becoming immortal is the path she's on over there, just like it was over here?" Shaunee said.

"Yes. And that's another reason I have to go over there. Right now Neferet is just a vampyre. Who knows what'll happen if I wait? Plus, I have a plan to turn the Blue Army against her."

"How?" Aphrodite asked.

"Jack, correct me if I'm wrong, but from what my brother told me the Warriors believe Neferet is still in the service of Nyx, right?"

Jack sniffled and nodded vigorously. "Oh, yes. Neferet's their only High Priestess. They count on her to know Nyx's will."

"And what would happen if there was absolute proof Neferet wasn't following the will of Nyx anymore?" I asked.

"The Warriors wouldn't follow her. Well, some might. Like, some of her lovers. And there are many of them. But the majority would stop fighting for her, and that includes a bunch of the Blue Army," Jack said.

"That's my plan," I said. "I'm going to show everyone at the Other World Tulsa House of Night that Neferet is a fraud—that she's using her powers for Darkness and isn't following Nyx anymore."

"Good plan, Z, but how ya gonna do that?" Stevie Rae asked.

I smiled at my bestie and at her mate. "Well, for that I am going to need the help of Rephaim."

"Me? Of course I'll help you." Rephaim spoke with no hesitation. Then he blinked and I saw understanding bloom across his face. "You're going to free my father in that world!"

"Yep, that's part one of my plan. What better way of showing that Neferet isn't following Nyx than having her winged Consort denounce her in front of the entire House of Night?"

"But Kalona was a real asshat when he first was freed over here. What the hell are you going to do about that?" Aphrodite asked.

"I'm going to count on his son to get through to him," I said. "And me. Remember that I still have a piece of A-ya within my soul. Rephaim and I—together—have to be able to reach Kalona, especially since we know that deep inside he still loves Nyx and was so awful because he didn't think the Goddess would ever forgive him."

"And we're going to convince Father he's wrong about that," Rephaim said.

"Hopefully a lot faster than he was convinced of it over here," Aphrodite muttered.

"So, you want Rephaim to go over there with you," Stevie Rae said.

"Yes, I do."

"But even if that works there's still the Red Army to deal

with," Jack said, his voice sounding shaky. "And they're monsters. They don't care about who Neferet follows. They don't care about Darkness or Light. All they care about is feeding their hunger."

"And that's why there's a second part to my plan. Stevie Rae, I'm sorry, but I need to ask you to please come with me too."

Her look of relief made my heart squeeze. "Oh, Z! Of course I will!"

"If I'm getting this plan of yours, you'll need me too," Aphrodite said.

"Yep, but not this you. The Other Aphrodite," I said.

"Okay, look, it'd be lots easier if I went with you," Aphrodite said.

"You can't. You're already over there, and you're a Prophetess, but you're also a fully Changed blue vampyre. Not the first blue *and* red vampyre there ever has been," I said.

"So what? Erik can give me some of that crap they use on actors to cover their Marks so that humans can forget they're watching vamps," Aphrodite said.

"Yeah, I can. There's a bunch of it in the Drama room," Erik said.

"Even though my man doesn't use it," Shaunee said. "Because if those asswipe human bigots can't grow enough empathy to identify with someone who looks different, then that's their problem and they can stop watching his movies."

"But they all want to watch your movies," said Jack, sounding adorably starstruck.

Erik turned his movie-star megawatt smile on Jack. "Then I guess they'll have to accept who I really am, or they're shit outta luck."

Jack giggled.

*Man, Erik's grown up!* I thought. *Good for him.* "Erik, would you go get the cover-up for me?"

"I'm on it. Be back in a sec." Erik sprinted away.

"See, I can cover the red in my Mark and go over there with you. We'll do our thing again, and the red fledglings and vamps will get their humanity back. No biggie," Aphrodite said.

"And what about the Other Aphrodite?" I turned to face my friend, hating that what I had to say to her was going to cause her pain. "What does you stepping in do to her? Will that mean she never grows up? Never learns to care for more than herself? Never learns empathy or that sometimes love means sacrifice? Never learns to stop self-medicating and to stand up to her mother?"

Aphrodite stared at me, her face going pale. "What if she's not capable of learning? I asked Other Jack about her. She's definitely not with the Resistance. She's in league with Neferet. What if the me in the Other World is already lost to Darkness and you can't reach her like you reached me because Neferet killed you too damn soon?"

"At your core—in your souls—you two are the same. I know what that core is, and it's not Darkness. You have more Light in you than any of us—Nyx showed us that by the gifts she's given you. I can reach the Other Aphrodite."

"I wouldn't bet my life on that," Aphrodite said.

Without any hesitation I said, "I would. Over and over again."

"I would too," Darius said, putting his arm around Aphrodite.

"Me too," said Stevie Rae. "Even though you and I seriously disagree on my music choices."

"And your fashion choices," Aphrodite added.

"I believe in you too, Prophetess," said Rephaim.

"We all do," Shaunee said.

"Z will reach you because you're not the only one of us greatly gifted by Nyx," said Shaylin. "So is Zoey Redbird."

I watched Aphrodite wipe away tears before she said, "If it's not for me, why is Erik getting the cover-up crap?"

"It's for Stevie Rae!" Jack spoke like a light bulb had just lit over his head. "You gotta cover her Mark because there are no female red vampyres in my old world."

"Exactly right, Jack." I patted the backpack still slung over my shoulder. "Which is why I have sapphire makeup pencils in here. Stevie Rae, are you ready to be a blue fledging again?"

"Sure! Hope it turns out better this time around, though."

"You can bet on that," I said. "Because I'll be joining you. And this time as a normal blue fledgling."

"Seriously?" Shaunee said.

Instead of answering her I asked a question. "Jack, are there other High Priestesses in your old world?"

"No. Not anymore. Neferet is the only High Priestess there," he said.

"And my guess is Neferet keeps a close eye on the remaining priestesses—just in case one of them begins developing into a High Priestess. Am I right?"

"Well, it's not like I was close with her or anything like that, but everyone knows Neferet doesn't allow any other priestess to perform rituals for the school. She has to lead everything. But she doesn't let red fledglings or vampyres attend rituals anyway."

I shook my head. "She must have done something terrible to the High Priestesses to get them to shut up and step aside."

"I don't know about that, but there are rumors—only whispered in the tunnels where Neferet would never go. Some say she killed them."

"Goddess, no!" Shaylin gasped, and Nicole took her hand reassuringly. "That's horrible! Nyx's heart must be breaking!"

"And that's a third reason we have to go over there. Nyx needs us. We all know the Goddess won't manipulate the actions of mortals, but we know her will—Stevie Rae, Rephaim, and I—and we'll make sure to end the atrocities Neferet has committed in Nyx's name."

My circle nodded somberly in agreement as Erik jogged up, handing me a bag filled with makeup bottles and sponges. "Everything you need's in there. I brought you the waterproof kind. It's hell to get off, but you won't have to worry about any Marks showing through it, not even if you get caught in rain or snow."

"Thanks, Erik."

"Break a leg over there. I believe in you," he said.

I stuffed the bag in my backpack and had to clear my throat

before speaking, but I finally was able to say, "Okay, I think that's everything. Are y'all ready?"

I asked the group, but I only watched Stevie Rae and Rephaim. They were the first to respond.

"Yes. I am ready," Rephaim said.

"Me too, like a hog's ready for his mud wallow!" Stevie Rae said as everyone (except Aphrodite) laughed and nodded.

"Where's Stark?" Aphrodite said, shutting everyone up.

"The last time I saw him, he was in the Media Center," I said.

"And why is your Warrior not here at your side?" asked Darius.

"Because I won't let him come with me."

"He can't!" Jack blurted. "Everyone knows General Stark. Even with his red Mark covered, anyone who saw him would know in an instant who he looks exactly like, and they'd grab him."

"I know, and that's what I told him, but he can't stand the thought of me going into danger without him." I drew a deep breath and spoke the rest of the truth. "And he thinks I'm going over there to see Heath, which hurts him. Real bad." I hesitated and then added, "Guys, after I'm gone, would you all please stay close to Stark? Help him through this? I'll be back, and when I am I'll make this up to him. I'll make him understand, but until then I just ..." Then I lost my words as grief and loss overwhelmed me. *What if Stark never forgives me?*

"We'll help him," Damien said. "Don't worry about that. Just focus on what you have to do over there to come back here. I'll talk to Stark."

I went to Damien and hugged him hard. "Thank you," I whispered. "Tell him how much I love him."

"I will, but he already knows, Z," Damien whispered back.

I stepped out of Damien's comforting embrace. "Everyone be sure you have a smudge stick, and then take your places. Let's get this over with!"

# 22

## *Zoey*

It was cool having my friends join me inside the circle, and I realized how long it'd been since I'd led a major ritual. *I'll have to fix that when I get back*, I promised myself, because I *would* get back—and so would Stevie Rae and Rephaim.

Damien, Shaunee, Shaylin, and Stevie Rae took their places at each of the four quadrants of the circle, picking up their ritual candles. Their Warriors and lovers spread out with them, filling in the circle. I went to the center, where Jack had placed my purple spirit candle and a box of long, wooden matches. I paused long enough to draw several deep, cleansing breaths. Then I opened my backpack and easily found the bell I'd put in the front flap. Holding it carefully so that it didn't start ringing, I picked up the matches and moved to the eastern edge of the circle where Damien stood expectantly with his yellow air candle in one hand and his smudge stick in the other.

"Air gives us breath and so much more. Without it we wouldn't be able to shout or laugh, cry or scream. It is the first element we know when we are born, and so we always begin the circle by calling it. Air, please come and help blow away the Darkness that has tainted this tree. I welcome you to our circle!" I lit Damien's candle and a rush of warm breeze lifted my hair. As soon as I felt the air, I held the bell high and rang it loud and clear, three times.

Then I moved deosil, or clockwise, to stand before Shaunee in the south.

"Fire warms us. It nurtures us by cooking our food, and it cleanses by burning away that which is no longer useful. Fire, please come and help this sage burn away the Darkness that has tainted this tree!" I didn't need to touch my match to Shaunee's red candle. It burst into cheery flame instantly.

"Burn, baby, burn," Shaunee whispered.

I smiled and lifted my bell, ringing it sharply three more times, then I moved deosil to the west and Shaylin, who waited there expectantly holding up her blue candle.

"Water is us, just as we are water. Without it would we turn to dust and dirt and die. With it, we are quenched and cleansed. Water, please come and help us wash away the Darkness that has tainted this tree!" I lit Shaylin's candle and the scent of the ocean filled the air around us as I lifted the bell again and rang it three times before continuing my trek around the circle to Stevie Rae in the north.

"Hey there Z!" she dimpled at me.

"Hello, earth," I smiled back at her. "Earth is our home. It sustains us. It feeds us and holds us close, and it is to earth our bodies eventually return to rest within her. Earth, please come and strengthen us so that Darkness no longer taints this tree!" Stevie Rae's green candle burst into flame and we were surrounded by the delicious scent of night-blooming jasmine. I inhaled deeply as I lifted my bell and rang it three more times.

Then I moved to the center of the circle and picked up my purple candle. "Spirit, you are who we are at our purest. You are what lives on when our bodies can live no longer. You fill us each uniquely and set our personalities—our loves, our hates, and our desires. Spirit, please come and fill this place that has been abused by Darkness so that Light may shine here once more!" I rang my bell three final times, and as its clear echo faded, I placed it on the ground and picked up the thick smudge stick of fragrant white sage.

I faced my circle, loving the silver thread of light that bound us. It was so bright that it illuminated the tree, making it appear as if Darkness had already begun to be cleansed from it.

"Okay, elementals, light your smudge sticks. The rest of you light your sticks from each of theirs. Jack, are you ready with a few of your favorite things?"

"I am! Just tell me when to press play!"

I waited for a few breaths until everyone's sage was lit and gray-white smoke began to billow lazily around the circle.

"Okay, when the song begins everyone join in. Dance and draw shapes in the air with your smudge stick—be joyful—think nothing but good thoughts. Just be careful not to step outside the circle," I said.

"And don't worry, we all love Julie Andrews. It doesn't matter who you are—sing, sing, sing!" Jack said gleefully.

"That's right!" I smiled at him. "Press play, Jack!"

As "raindrops on roses and whiskers on kittens" played, my circle and my friends joined in. At first we were all a little tentative, but by the time we got to "when the dog bites," we were all singing and laughing and dancing around the circle.

"Ohmygoodness, look!" Stevie Rae pointed up at the smoke lifting in swirls and eddies above us, and we all gasped together.

Moving in and out of the smoke, firefly-looking sprites darted like sentient diamonds, glittering and glowing—and changing the smoke to form the shapes we were singing about. I saw kittens with big whiskers, sleigh bells, and what I was pretty sure were wild geese flying with the moon on their wings.

It was one of the most magickal moments of my life, and I wished with everything inside me that Stark was there, laughing and singing and dancing at my side.

"Z! Look at the tree!" Jack shouted.

I did—and had to tell my mouth not to flop open. More firefly sprites swarmed it. Starting from its splinted, broken base they flew in time with our music, around and around, up and up, and as they moved, the tar-like blackness that had tainted it washed away, until all that was left was a kinda strange-looking, splintered, lopsided tree that began sprouting tiny buds along its once-ruined limbs.

"It's going to have leaves on it again!" Stevie Rae shouted joyously over the music.

Twirling and laughing, we sang the last lines with Maria and the Von Trapp family, "'I simply remember my favorite things, and then I don't feel soooooo bad!'"

Breathing hard and grinning, I said, "Jack, would you gather all the smudge sticks and put them here in the center of the circle by the tree?"

"Me?"

I nodded.

"Ohmygoddess, yes!"

Jack hurried around the circle, collecting the sage sticks and placing them, with mine, in a smoking pile.

"Shaunee, anytime you're ready," I said.

"Easy-peasy. Burn, baby, burn!" Shaunee flicked her wrist at the pile and it instantly blazed with light and the scent of sage.

"Perfect," I said. "Thank you." Then I sobered, and my gaze went to Stevie Rae, still standing in the north, with Rephaim beside her. "Are you two ready?"

Rephaim nodded nervously.

"As I'll ever be," Stevie Rae said.

"We're going to have to offer a payment to the sprite," I explained. "I have an idea for it, but you two need to be okay with it. I'm going to need some blood from each of you."

Stevie Rae and Rephaim exchanged a look.

"Okie dokie, Z. We're cool with that," said Stevie Rae.

"Thank you," I said sincerely before getting into my backpack again and carefully pulling out the sharp athame. Surrounded by the magickally cleansing smoke of sage and the support of my circle, I called. "Oak, ancient, Old Magick sprite, with the power in my blood, and the gifts given to me by the Goddess Nyx, I summon you to this circle. Oak, please appear!"

And then I held my breath.

She didn't make me wait long. In seconds the center of the newly cleansed tree began to shimmer and with the sound of a sigh, Oak emerged from the broken trunk.

The sprite didn't come to me. She didn't acknowledge any of my friends or me. First, she turned to the tree. She placed her delicate hands on it and slowly, intimately, leaned forward until her forehead rested against it. I could hear that she was speaking, but I couldn't understand the language. When she finished, she kissed the gnarled bark softly, sweetly, before finally turning and gliding to me.

*"Redbird Girl, I am glad that you completed your payment."* Her darkly beautiful, almond-shaped eyes looked around our intact circle, taking in each of the vampyres standing there. *"The strength of your circle is pleasing to me. It feels of love and laughter, friendship and sacrifice. I approve."*

"Thank you. And thank you for answering my call."

She bowed her head slightly in acknowledgment. *"I find that I am enjoying this rare awakening. Between you and the Redbird Boy, the days and nights have become more interesting. What is it you wish of me now?"*

I didn't hesitate. "I want you to take me and two of my friends with you to the Other World where my brother, who you call Redbird Boy, lives. And I want you to bring us back too. When we're ready."

In a birdlike movement, the exquisite sprite cocked her head and studied me. For too many long, uncomfortable moments she said nothing at all, and when she finally spoke, I felt like I'd been waiting for time to unfreeze.

*"I can do what you ask, but the payment will be great."*

"How about blood from three kinds of beings?"

Her mossy brows shot up to the ivy that was her hairline. *"Which type of beings?"*

"One is me, a blue vampyre and High Priestess who has an affinity for all five elements. The second is Stevie Rae, a red vampyre and High Priestess whose affinity is also yours—earth. And the third is Rephaim, Stevie Rae's mate, a being who—"

*"Was created by Old Magick,"* she finished for me, swiveling her head like an owl to peer at Rephaim and Stevie Rae. *"Do the two of you give this offering freely?"*

"Yes, ma'am, I do," said Stevie Rae.

"Yes. I give my word that I do," answered Rephaim.

Oak's gaze returned to me. *"That payment is interesting. It will get you to the Other World. It will not return you, though.*

> *"For that a new payment must be*
> *And what that is we shall see*
> *We shall see ... "*

My stomach clenched even though the sing-song rhythm in her voice said she was going to make a deal with me. But this was exactly what the old books had warned about. I needed to set both payments or Stevie Rae, Rephaim, and I could be in deep bull-poopie when we tried to come home.

"Let's set the return payment now. Things will be easier that way. I mean, what if we have to come back in a big hurry?" I said.

> *"That is your problem not mine*
> *Agree to my rules or stop wasting my time."*

"This isn't good," Aphrodite said. She'd been standing near Damien during the ritual, and Oak turned to the east and focused her gaze on my friend. "The payment shouldn't be left undecided. That's just asking for trouble."

*"The Prophetess speaks truth*
*In spite of her youth."*

Oak paused, sniffing the air like a hound.

*"The scent of your blood is unique.*
*Pledge it, and your friends' return shall*
*not be so bleak."*

"Fine!"
"No!"
Aphrodite and I spoke at the same time. Oak's gaze found mine again.

*"Blood payment by a powerful Prophetess is one way*
*Unless in the Other World you shall wish to stay."*

"They're not staying. I'll pledge my blood as payment to you to bring them back." Aphrodite spoke quickly so that I couldn't interrupt her. "But I'm not going with them. So, how will I know when to pay you?"

*"Mighty Prophetess there is nothing you need do*
*When payment is required I shall find you."*

"Aphrodite, I don't like this," I said. "Don't make this pledge. Between Stevie Rae, Rephaim, Kevin, and me, we'll figure out a payment Oak will accept."

*"Risk your life on that, would you?*
*It seems a silly thing to do."*

"Silly or not, it's my choice."

"Actually, no. My blood. My body. My choice," Aphrodite insisted. "Oak, I give you my word. When it's time for Zoey and Rephaim and Stevie Rae to return I will pay the blood price for them."

*"I accept your price tonight*
*A blood payment and promise, strong and bright*
*I seal this deal with thee and thee, thee and thee."*

Oak's gaze trapped each of the four of us in turn as she completed the binding.

*"So I have spoken—so mote it be."*

My stomach was so messed up I wanted to barf. This felt wrong—dangerously wrong. But it was done.

I looked at Aphrodite. She was standing so straight and strong and proud, but I could see the fear in her eyes, and I promised myself that I would do everything I could to be sure she wouldn't regret giving her blood to get us home.

"Thank you, my friend," I told her. "I love you."

Aphrodite's lips twitched, but she didn't sneer or smile. Instead she fisted her hand over her heart and bowed respectfully to me. "You are welcome, High Priestess. And I love you right back."

Blinking my vision clear of tears I turned to Oak. "Can you take us anywhere in that world?"

*"Within reason,"* Oak said. *"Queen Sgiach does not appreciate interlopers on her isle, so you would not receive a pleasant welcome there."*

"Oh, no. I don't need to go to Skye. I want to go someplace closer to here. It's a lavender farm, and the woman who owns it is—"

*"Oh, I know this place of which you speak. The woman who tends the land there is delicious."* Oak smiled, showing way too many sharp white teeth.

But I grinned anyway. "'Delicious,'" I repeated. I looked at Aphrodite. "Tell her bye for me, okay? Tell her not to worry." I paused and added, "And tell her the sprite called her delicious. She'll love that."

"She'll worry less when she knows you went to her first. Maybe," Aphrodite said.

"Maybe-not worrying is better than for-sure worrying. Take care of yourself. You are High Priestess until I return."

I saw the surprise in Aphrodite's eyes before she bowed her head and fisted her hand over her heart again. "It will be as you say, High Priestess," she said solemnly.

My eyes caught movement in the circle, and I saw that each of my friends had followed Aphrodite. They were all bowing to me, hands fisted over their hearts.

"Thank you," I told them. "I'll be back soon." My gaze found Damien. "Tell Stark I love him."

"You can count on me, High Priestess."

"Stevie Rae, don't blow out your candle. Aphrodite, close the circle after we're gone."

"I will."

"We're ready," I told Oak.

*"Then link hands, you three, and follow me!"*

Stevie Rae put her green candle on the ground. She held one hand out to me—the other was already linked with Rephaim's. I took it and as we turned with the sprite toward the tree, which had begun to glow, a shout came from behind me.

"Zoey Redbird! Stay safe. Stay strong. And come back to me!"

My head whipped around, and I looked over my shoulder at Stark. He was standing just outside the glowing circle. Our eyes met.

"I love you, my Warrior, my Guardian. I always will."

"And I you, my Queen, my High Priestess, my heart. Remember, we're bound by blood and love … always love."

Then the glow expanded and I followed the tug on my hand. I stepped into the center of the blazing opening and the world around me exploded into light.

# 23

# Other Kevin

"How's this?" Kevin opened the driver's door to the Hummer and held up four big bags full of tissue and clothes.

Aphrodite glanced at the bags. "Not bad for a novice. Get in."

Kevin tossed the bags in the back seat and got behind the wheel. "Where to now?"

"Home." Aphrodite made a show of holding her nose as he got in the vehicle.

"Home?"

"House of Night home. Sheesh. Promise me that smell washes off."

"Yep, I promise. Want to see the dead blood goop I have to smear on myself to smell like this?"

"That would be a hard pass."

"So, I'm going to drop you off?"

"Nope. You're coming with me."

"Where?"

"Oh, for shit's sake—*home*."

"What about the tunnels?"

"Do you want to go to the tunnels?"

"No. Absolutely not. They're the worst." He started the Hummer. "But what else am I supposed to do?"

"Well, I've been thinking about that. Your general is gone, right?"

"Yeah, like I said—he died in Zoey's world."

"Along with all of your flight, group, squad—or whatever they call it, right?"

"Almost right. Three of them are still alive, but they stayed in Zo's world."

"So, you're really not attached to any general except Stark."

"I suppose you could say that."

"And he's assigned you to me."

"I suppose you could say that too."

"Good. Then consider yourself my personal soldier."

"Which means what exactly?" he asked.

"Well, for starters it means you're not going back to the tunnels, and you need to dress better. Do you think lavender would help cover that nasty stink smell?" she said.

"I don't know. It'd probably help, and I could smear less of the blood goop on me so that it'd help for sure. But you mean I'm going to stay at the House of Night?"

"Yep."

"Wait, I don't have to live in the tunnels?"

"Not as long as you're my personal soldier, you don't."

Kevin felt like his heart was going to explode with gratitude. "Aphrodite, thank you. Thank you so much!"

She waved away his thanks. "What can I say, I'm a giver. Plus, I want to know more about this other world and your sister, and I can't do that if you're stuck in the middle of a horde of smelly monsters." They'd made the short trip from Utica Square to the House of Night, and Aphrodite pointed at a parking spot that was up front and well lit. "Park there."

"Okay, but no way we can sneak onto campus from there."

"We're not sneaking," she said.

"But everyone will know I'm here."

"Everyone will definitely know, and they'll get used to seeing you around. That'll help you and the Resistance, won't it?"

"Yes! Definitely."

"Good. Maybe it'll also help balance out some of the bad that I've done by telling my visions to Neferet."

"It's a start, that's for sure," Kevin said. He parked and looked at her. "What now?"

"Now is the easy part. I'll handle everything. You just follow my lead. *Literally.* Walk behind me and be sure you stay several feet behind. Look subservient and not too bright. And when we get stopped, because I promise you we will, I'll do the talking. You don't even look up. Pretend you're a clueless, but not too feral, red vampyre. Can you do that?"

"I've been doing that for about a year now," he said.

"Then you've had plenty of practice." She sat and stared at him, and when he just stared back she rolled her eyes. "Kev, you're supposed to be grabbing all of 'my' bags," she air-quoted. "And then opening my door for me. Remember, you're my personal soldier. I should never touch a door, lift a thing, open a bottle of champagne, blah, blah, when you're around."

"Oh, sorry. Okay, got it!" He jumped out of the Hummer, grabbed the four bags, and juggled them awkwardly as he rushed around to open her door.

She stretched her long legs out and then frowned at her knee-high Jimmy Choo boots. "Fuck! I forgot I broke that heel. Well, I'll just use it to help my acting. Here." She surprised him by holding out her hand, which he took and helped her climb out of the Hummer. Then she wiped her hand on her skinny jeans. "You're going to have to get a lot better at personal hygiene."

"I'm actually a clean, neat person. I had to pretend not to care about dirt and grime and dried blood and other gross stuff when I lived in the tunnels."

"You don't live in the tunnels anymore. Clean up," she grumped as she started hobbling toward the sidewalk that curved through the little side courtyard where a fountain musically cascaded and eventually opened to the main schoolyard.

"Will do," he said, hurrying to catch up with her.

She shot an annoyed look at him. "You're supposed to be behind me looking subservient."

"Oh, right. Forgot. Won't happen again, Prophetess," he bowed several times and backed up.

"That was good. Keep that bowing stuff up."

"Do you want me to call you mistress, or is Prophetess okay?"

"Don't be ridiculous. Prophetess is fine. Mistress sounds entirely too old. Now shush and look pathetic."

With Kevin following, Aphrodite clomp-limped through the courtyard, exiting into the schoolyard. It was just after dinnertime. Fledglings were scattered about the school grounds. Gaslights domed in art deco copper cast dancing shadows across wide sidewalks and winter grass. Cats trotted around, some stalking mice, some following their chosen fledgling or vampyre. Students lit candles at the feet of Nyx's statue and prayed to the Goddess. A group of female fledglings were getting a fencing lesson from a vampyre Kevin didn't recognize.

Everything seemed normal, but the difference between this heavily controlled, segregated House of Night and Zoey's school was enormous. Everyone here looked subdued or worried, frightened or desperate, and Kevin's heart ached with homesickness for a place he'd barely known, but which had felt so right.

Aphrodite turned to the right, heading to the part of the cluster of castle-like buildings that made up the professors' quarters. She followed the gentle curve of the sidewalk, approaching two fledglings who had spread yoga mats on the grass and were in the middle of a graceful flow.

As Aphrodite got closer to the two fledglings, their heads

turned in her direction. They recognized Aphrodite—that much was clear—and they put their heads together as they stared at her.

Then they saw Kevin and their eyes widened. One was a spectacularly beautiful black girl he recognized instantly as Shaunee, and the other a sexy blond wearing nude-colored yoga tights and a tiny, bright red sports bra. Both left zero to the imagination. *Holy crap! This has to be that Erin fledgling Zo told me about—the water to Shaunee's fire!* They gawked at him as Aphrodite walked past them, whispering back and forth to each other, giggling under their breath. When he drew near them Kevin clearly heard what they were saying—which meant so did Aphrodite.

"Hey, Twin, check it out," said Erin.

"What is it, Twin?"

"Aphrodite's new lover!" finished the blond, pointing at Kevin. Then they both dissolved into mean laughter.

Aphrodite stopped. She turned, barely glancing at Kevin as she limped past him. "Just one moment."

Kevin wanted to shout at her, *No! Don't kill them with your laser vision! I might need them later for a circle!* But he had to shut up. He had to play his part, so he ducked his head and surreptitiously watched as Aphrodite walked straight up to the two fledglings, who automatically stumbled a couple of steps back. "Repeat that to my face and not to my gorgeous backside." The Prophetess' voice had gone to ice.

"Hey, we didn't mean anything," said Shaunee.

"Yeah, we were just kidding around," said Erin.

"You're the two who call yourselves Twins, aren't you?" Aphrodite asked.

"Yes," they answered together.

"I'll call you Brain Sharers. And because you share one small brain between the two of you, I'll give you one small break. But next time you insult either me or my personal soldier slash servant, I'm going to volunteer both of you for dinner duty at the tunnels."

"Dinner duty?" asked Erin.

"What's that mean?" asked Shaunee.

Aphrodite stepped forward, invading their personal space. "It means you'll give the feeder humans a break and offer your own blood to red officers—personally—*from your necks*, though I hear the vein that runs up your thigh is also a very popular feeding spot of choice." The two fledglings looked horrified, which Aphrodite waved away. "Oh, don't be so dramatic. They won't be allowed to drain you completely. Just almost completely."

"N-Neferet wouldn't let that happen!" stuttered Erin.

"Want to bet your blood on that, Thing One?"

Erin quickly shook her head.

"What about you, Thing Two?"

"No, thank you."

"No, thank you, *Prophetess*, is what you Brain Sharers meant to say."

"No, thank you, Prophetess," they intoned nervously together.

"Better. Much better. Now, I think it best if you never speak to me again."

"Hey, we didn't mean anything. Really," said Shaunee.

"Bullshit," Aphrodite said. "Spineless little girls like you always simper and say you didn't mean anything when you get caught being bitches. Grow the hell up. You're not in middle school anymore. This is real life—not the internet, where you can say stupid, hateful crap without any consequences. And, for shit's sake, do the world a favor and come out as big ol' lesbians already."

Erin blushed like crazy as Shaunee's mouth flopped open in shock.

"Huh. Never mind. Looks like only one of you would be down with that. Or should I say, only one of you would *go down* with that." Aphrodite laughed gaily, flipped back her long hair, and managed to twitch away, even with a broken heel. As she passed Kevin she spoke loudly enough for the Twins to hear. "Come on, Stinky. Finish schlepping my stuff upstairs. And then you need to scamper off and get me some more champagne. Tragically, I think I'm out, and dealing with the Brain Sharers has made me thirsty."

"Yes, Prophetess. Of course, Prophetess!" Kevin ducked his head and waited for her to get a couple of yards in front of him before he began walking again, thinking, *Looks like I'll have to find another fire and water. Ah, hell …*

And as he followed her into the professor's building, he heard croaking overhead, and looked up in time to see a giant raven circling above him. He opened the thick wooden door and paused. Sure enough, the raven landed on the sidewalk, cocking its head at him.

*"Redbird Boy!"* it croaked.

"Come here! Hurry!" Kevin motioned at the bird, who hopped inside the little foyer with him.

"Kevin, what the hell is taking you so long?" Aphrodite called from the winding stairway.

"Sorry, be there in just a sec!" He opened the raven's tube and took out the little pencil and paper, hastily scrawling, *I'm with Aphrodite at the HoN. Staying here during daylight. More soon.* Then he stuffed the paper and pencil back in the tube and opened the door for the raven, and it took off skyward.

(

"Want me to go get the champagne for you now?" Kevin stood uncomfortably just inside the closed door of Aphrodite's opulent bedchamber.

"Hell no. I have plenty of champagne. I'm not a barbarian." She nodded to the kitchenette off the sitting room exquisitely decorated with an amethyst velvet couch and matching chairs embroidered with silver thread that depicted a triple moon. "Well. Don't just stand there. Get in the shower and wash that nasty stink off. Put on those new pajamas. Then we'll talk."

"But. Um. It'll be dawn in …" he paused, connecting to his internal clock. "Less than two hours. I need to go somewhere safe to sleep."

She sighed. "I said you're my soldier now. You stay here."

"*Here*, here?" Like his eyes had a will of their own, his gaze went to the huge canopy bed clearly visible through open French doors.

"Seriously? You think you're sleeping in my bed?" Aphrodite rolled her eyes.

"No! No way. I wouldn't presume. Ever. But where am I sleeping?"

"I have a super luxurious walk-in closet. There aren't any windows in there. Or, you can sleep in my soaking tub. Take your pick."

"How about the couch?"

"There are windows out here."

His gaze went to them. "Aren't those purple velvet curtains black outs?"

She sighed. "Fine. Yes. This once you can sleep on the couch *if* you really don't stink and *if* you don't snore. I can't stand a snorer."

"I promise I don't stink, and I don't think I snore. But I've never slept with anyone, so I can't promise that."

Aphrodite's cornflower blue eyes found his. "So, you're a virgin."

Kevin's cheeks flamed hot. "Well, yeah. I am."

"Huh. Interesting. Get in the shower."

She shooed him toward a closed door, through which he gladly escaped to find himself in a marble bathroom that was so white and so clean that he didn't want to touch anything.

"Do you want something to eat? I'm going to call the kitchen," Aphrodite called through the door.

"Um, yeah. I'll eat about anything. And, uh, could you get me a bottle of—"

"Blood. I figured as much. Oh, and put those awful clothes you have on in a laundry bag under the sink. Tie it tight and remember to throw it away tomorrow. Super gross."

"Yeah, okay. No problem." Kevin didn't know what else to say to that, so he stripped, easily finding an empty laundry bag, and pulling the drawstring tight.

Then he entered heaven.

Her shower was enclosed in circular glass, and it had one of those giant round showerheads that made it feel like Kevin was in a fantastical rainstorm. There were also showerheads that spouted from the walls, and when he flipped a switch, streams of hot water cascaded at him, hitting all over his body. She, of course, had soap that felt like silk and smelled like almonds and honey.

He wanted to stay in there for hours, but he could almost feel Aphrodite's impatience, so he forced himself to hurry as he quickly lathered again and again, until every trace of the stinking blood goop had left his skin.

Kevin dried with a violet towel so big and so fluffy he could have used it as a blanket. Then he put on the new sweatpants and T-shirt and stuck his damp head hesitantly out into the room.

On the glass coffee table in front of the couch, Aphrodite had put a tray filled with a big sandwich, chips, and a tall glass of warm red blood that had his mouth watering.

"Come on out; it's just me. I never let any of the servants in here while I'm home. They clean and whatnot only when I'm out. And I make them leave my food deliveries outside the door on a silver tray table." She shrugged. "Yes, I know. I like decadence. Not apologizing for it."

On sock feet, Kevin padded into the sitting room to find Aphrodite dressed in comfy-looking yoga pants and a white sweatshirt with **WILD FEMINIST** blazed across her chest. She was curled up on one of the embroidered velvet chairs, sipping champagne and nibbling on a cracker that had little black balls on it.

He sniffed in her general direction. "That smells fishy. What is it?"

She gave him a long-suffering look. "Caviar, peasant. Your upbringing was severely lacking."

"Agreed." Kevin sat and drained the blood in one long gulp. He put the glass down to find Aphrodite staring at him. "I was thirsty," he said lamely.

"Tell me the truth. Do you have your hunger under control?"

"Absolutely. It's no different now than a blue vampyre's need. I was just really thirsty because I was wounded a few nights ago and I'm still recovering." *Not to mention my stress level has been off the charts*, he thought.

"Do you give me your word on that?"

"Yes, Prophetess. You have my word that my humanity is completely returned to me, and my hunger is under control."

She studied him for several minutes before going back to her caviar and champagne. "Do you need more blood?"

"No, but I do need this food. Thank you."

"No problem. Though I really confused the kitchen. I don't eat many sandwiches."

"Do you eat much of anything?" Kevin asked through a big bite.

She frowned. "I'm eating right now."

He snorted.

"Just worry about yourself. I'm fine. I'm always fine."

"Don't believe you," he muttered.

"I heard that. Okay, first, I'm glad you don't stink anymore."

"Me too. I hate the smell of that stuff. And your shower is awesome."

"Yes, I know. Second, I want you to tell me what happened to the other Aphrodite when she sacrificed part of her humanity to save the red fledglings in your sister's world. I realize she didn't die, but what exactly happened to her?"

The question surprised him, but after a moment of reflection Kevin decided that it shouldn't have. He'd been curious about what the other version of him had been doing in Zo's world, and that other version wasn't a Prophetess or a tool of Nyx. So, between bites he told Aphrodite what Zoey had explained to him, ending with, "When

Stevie Rae and the rest of the red vampyres over there regained their humanity you'd lost your Mark, but not your prophetic gift. Until the red vamps and fledglings from here got pulled over there with me, I don't think anyone really knew exactly what you were."

Aphrodite looked perplexed. "But why? Why would I willingly sacrifice myself like that? I *could have died*, or lost everything—*all* of my gifts. It makes no sense. The me over there is an idiot."

"That idiot saved a whole race of vampyres."

"Why?"

"For love, of course. The other you is surrounded by people she loves. She may act like a heartless bitch sometimes, but only half of that's true, which is cool because I happen to like bitches."

She rolled her eyes. "And you say that over there I'm now a weird red-and-blue hybrid vampyre as well as a Prophetess?"

"Yep."

"How did that happen?"

"Not sure. There was a lot going on and I didn't have much time to ask questions. What I do know is that Nyx gifted you with the ability to give people—humans as well as vampyres—a second chance after they've messed up, like, tragically-in-a-big-way messed up."

Aphrodite snorted. "That's probably because I know a lot about messing up tragically in a big way."

He grinned. "Could be. Other Aphrodite's Mark is just like yours, only there's more of it, and half of it's red. Nyx said that every time you use your gift and grant someone a second chance, part of your Mark will disappear until eventually it'll be gone completely, and then you'll be human and live out a normal human lifespan."

"That sounds bizarre. I'm not sure I'd like that."

"I'm pretty sure Other Aphrodite felt like that when it happened too. But then she saw the difference she made with me and Other Jack, and the rest of them—and I'm one hundred percent sure she decided she was glad for the gift."

"So that Aphrodite is good. Really good," she said.

"Yep, absolutely," he said.

"You sound pretty stuck on Other Aphrodite."

Kevin met her gaze. "I'd say Aphrodite is spectacular—in any world."

Aphrodite snorted and then was silent for a while, sipping champagne and nibbling caviar and crackers. Kevin finished his sandwich and was mowing through the mound of chips when she spoke again.

"It must be a lot different over there." She'd lit the fire and was staring into the fireplace like she could see the other world within the controlled flames.

"It is. And then it isn't. That world feels different because it's a lot less scary. Neferet's defeated. Zo and her friends run the New North American Vampyre High Council, which means they're in charge of the House of Night sites in the US, and they've started these awesome programs where humans can take classes with fledglings."

She looked at him like he'd lost his mind. "Human teenagers. At the Tulsa House of Night. Taking classes." She shook her head. "It's hard to imagine."

"It's not happening just in Tulsa. Humans and vampyres are coming together at a bunch of the schools. It's cool."

Aphrodite went back to being silent. Kevin was going to ask her for a pillow and a blanket when she spoke again.

"We're all so damn isolated over here. But your sister's world doesn't sound like that at all."

"It's not, but not *all* of us are isolated here, either. Not Dragon and Anastasia—not my g-ma. Actually, not any of the Resistance fighters. They're friends, but more than that."

"Bleeding hearts," she said.

"Friends with a cause," he corrected. Then he met her gaze again. "You don't have to be alone. Not even here. You aren't alone in Zo's world."

"This isn't your sister's world."

"No, it's not. It's mine. And I'm going to change things."

"You?"

"Me."

"All by yourself?"

"Well, no," he smiled. "I'm not by myself. You're helping me."

"I think you're an idealist," she said.

"Probably."

"Idealists get people dead."

"Sometimes, but while they live, they live magnificently. Join me. Join the Resistance. You might as well—you already kinda have. You saved Dragon and all those people today."

"I'm also the one who put them in danger," she reminded him.

"Did you want to? Did you want to be the reason the Red Army killed them?"

"No! I hate all this death and killing. And I hate that Neferet uses me like a weapon."

"Then help me find a way to change things for the better in this world."

Instead of answering she got up and disappeared into her room, returning with an armload of blankets and a fluffy goose-down pillow, which she plopped on the couch beside him.

"Hey, thanks. This is really nice of you. I'll clean up the dishes before I fall asleep," Kevin said.

"Don't be ridiculous. You're my soldier, not my housekeeper. There's a silver cart just outside my door. Stick the dirty dishes out there. The minions will take care of them." Then she hesitated, and her hand reached out, for a moment like she was going to touch his hair. "Before you pass out you might want to dry your hair more. Sleep on it like that and it's going to stick up—"

"Like a duck's butt," he finished for her. "I know, I know. Zo used to tell me that all the time."

"Yeah, well, it's distractingly tousled and shaggy and even kinda ..." Her words trailed off and she shook her head like she wanted to dislodge her last thought.

He couldn't help it. He looked up into her gorgeous eyes and said, "Were you gonna say kinda sexy?"

"Must be almost dawn. You sound delirious."

"Other Aphrodite likes me, you know," he grinned cheekily.

"Other Aphrodite has issues. Lots of issues."

"But excellent taste," he said. "She would've done what you did today. She would've made sure Dragon and the rest of those people got away."

"Goodnight, Kevin. Tomorrow we'll figure out a more permanent rooming solution for you," was all she said before she disappeared into her bedroom.

"Goodnight, Aphrodite," he called through the closed door.

Kevin put the dishes outside the door on the silver cart that waited there, banked the fire, and made up his bed on the couch. Then, exhausted and feeling safe for the first time in his world since he'd been Marked, Kevin slept.

(

"Kevin, come on! You need to wake up!"

Kevin swam his way up from the depths of a deep, beautiful dream that had him back in Zo's world laughing with her as he held Aphrodite's hand and she accepted his proposal to be his mate.

"Huh? What? You will?!" he said sleepily, reaching for Aphrodite's hand.

She actually let him take it, and then she pulled him to a sitting position.

"Wake! Up!"

Kevin blinked and rubbed a hand across his face. "I'm up. Sorta. What's wrong?"

"There is a big black bird pecking at my window. I was going to throw something at it, but it said 'Redbird Boy.' Um, might I assume that's you?"

"Yes! Is it still there? Let it in!" He'd taken off his shirt to sleep, so he hastily pulled it over his head and hurried after Aphrodite into her bedroom.

Aphrodite's raised hand stopped him. "Stay there! My drapes are totally open and the sun is definitely up."

Kevin only had a moment to pace back and forth, then the big raven flew into the sitting room, landing on the glass coffee table.

*"Redbird Boy!"*

"You found me! Good job. Okay, okay, I'll read it."

Aphrodite peered over Kevin's shoulder. "What is that thing around his neck?"

"It holds notes." Kevin pulled the leather thong over the bird's head and opened the little tube, taking out the paper inside.

"Ohmygoddess! That's how you warned the Resistance about the bales of hay."

"Yep."

"What's the note say?"

He turned and looked up at her. "It's Zoey! She's here!"

## 24

# *Zoey*

"It's super weird how much it looks the same, isn't it?" Stevie Rae said when the three of them had stopped blinking spots from their vision and could see again.

"Yeah, it looks like home," I said. Then I looked closer. "Well, almost." The lavender fields were the same. The house was the same. With one major difference—from all the eaves on the porch, as well as the windows of Grandma's house and the surrounding trees, hung strands of beads. Hundreds and hundreds of beads.

"Those decorations are beautiful," Rephaim said.

"They're more than that," I said. "They're made of turquoise—lots of turquoise."

"A strong protective stone," Stevie Rae said.

"Yeah, and see the bundles of sweet grass, sage, and …" I paused, studying the clusters of herbs closer as we approached the front porch. "Cedar. She has those hanging everywhere too."

"More protection?" Rephaim asked.

"Yep." I led my friends up the porch stairs and drew a deep breath. "She must be burning myrrh and frankincense in her fireplace with the wood." I identified the distinctive scents easily, although smelling them drifting around Grandma's house was a surprise.

"They smell good. What do they do?" Stevie Rae asked.

"Protect, but also cleanse the spirit and heighten intuition," I said.

"Wow, Grandma Redbird brought out the big guns," Stevie Rae said.

"So much turquoise and such powerful cleansing and protecting herbs! Your grandmother must feel she is in serious danger." Rephaim said what I'd been thinking.

*Please be okay … please be okay … please be okay …* was the prayer to Nyx that played over and over again in my mind as I raised my hand to knock on the front door.

Which opened before I touched it.

Grandma Redbird was there—wearing a long, comfortable-looking skirt and a simple cotton shirt. She had a colorful shawl wrapped around her shoulders and her long dark hair, frosted with beautiful sliver, fell free around her shoulders. She stared at me through eyes huge and dark and filled with shock, and I suddenly realized that maybe Kevin hadn't found her. Maybe she didn't know about the Other World.

"Grandma, it's me. I'm not a ghost. I promise."

Like my words had flipped on a light within her, Grandma's shocked expression changed instantly. She gasped and tears filled her eyes to overflow as her smile radiated such joy and love it was a benediction.

"Oh, u-we-tsi-a-ge-ya! My girl—my heart—it is you! It is you!" She flung open the door then, sobbing and laughing at the same time, Grandma Redbird took me into her arms.

I inhaled deeply. It didn't matter what world we were in or what version of my grandma this was—her scent, her touch, her love—they were all the same.

"I have missed you so much," she said through her tears as she kept hugging me.

"I'm so sorry, Grandma. My death must have been awful for you."

She laughed then, and held me out at arm's length, using the end of her shawl to wipe her cheeks. "I think it was much worse for you, u-we-tsi-a-ge-ya."

I shuddered and nodded, remembering every instant of that Zoey's death. *Don't say anything to Grandma about it. She doesn't need to know the awful details I know. Ever.*

Grandma glanced behind me. "A female red vampyre? She must be from your world, Zoeybird."

"She is! This is my bestie, Stevie Rae, and her mate, Rephaim."

"Greetings, Stevie Rae, and osiyo, Rephaim," Grandma said.

"It's real good to see you in any world, Grandma Redbird," Stevie Rae said.

Rephaim looked clueless.

"Oh, sorry, Grandma. Rephaim's mother was Cherokee, but he doesn't speak any of our language."

"Well, then, hello, Rephaim," she corrected.

"Hello, Grandma Redbird. As Stevie Rae said, it is really good to see you."

Grandma was looking around over my shoulder. "Is Kevin with you? I didn't hear a car pull up, but I had the feeling I used to get when you'd visit me." She smiled gently at me and touched my cheek. "That is why I believed you were a spirit when first I saw you."

"I didn't mean to scare you, Grandma."

"Oh, you could never do that, Zoeybird. Your spirit is as welcome here as you are. But is your brother not with you tonight?"

"Kev's not with us, and we didn't drive here. But I'm real glad he's already talked to you. Do you know where he is?"

"Not exactly, but I know someone who does. Come on in, Zoeybird." She motioned for me to come inside, which I did. But, of course, Stevie Rae couldn't follow me, and Rephaim waited on the porch with her.

"Uh, Grandma, you have to invite Stevie Rae into your home."

"Cross my heart and swear that I'd never hurt you," Stevie Rae said.

"Of course you wouldn't, my dear. Please, come in. You are welcome in my home."

"Thank you! Grandma—hey, you don't mind that I call you that, do ya? All Z's friends in our world call you Grandma," Stevie Rae said.

"I don't mind at all. Actually, I rather like it."

"Good! So, Grandma, you wouldn't have any chocolate-chip lavender cookies, would ya?"

"I absolutely do. The three of you make yourselves at home by the fire and I'll get you some. This is such a blessed, wonderful night!"

Grandma hurried into her kitchen while we made ourselves comfortable in her living room. I gawked around. It was crazy how familiar yet how different everything was. Grandma had the same bookshelves, but different books were on them. Art filled her walls, just like back in my world, but there were subtle differences in the pieces she displayed. And the couch and comfy chairs were in the same place, but totally different colors and styles than the ones I was used to. It was strange, but perfect, like another onion layer exposed of the woman who had been grandma, mother, and best friend to me for most of my childhood.

"Here you go." She put a plate of fragrant cookies and three glasses of sweet tea on the coffee table before us—and we dug in. "So, Zoeybird, did you reverse the spell again and reopen the divide between worlds? Is that how you got here?"

"No," I said through a mouthful of delicious cookie. "This time I got help from a tree sprite."

"An Old Magick tree sprite? She didn't give her name, did she?"

"Yep, she did, Grandma," Stevie Rae said. "Her name is Oak, and we think she knows you."

"She does indeed." Grandma looked grim. "Your brother and I met her a couple of days ago. The sprites seem to have taken a liking to us."

"So, you were with him when he used Old Magick?" I asked.

"Yes, twice."

I blew out a long breath. "That's the biggest reason I'm here. Kevin has to stop using Old Magick. It's super dangerous."

"Anastasia warned him that there must always be payment made for the use of Old Magick," Grandma said.

"That's true, but it's also true that Old Magick can change whoever wields it."

"Change them? How so?" she asked.

"It's not good, Grandma. And I'm no expert. There's still a lot about Old Magick I just don't understand, but I had to wield it to defeat Neferet in our world, and it almost turned me into someone you wouldn't have recognized."

"Z got angry," Stevie Rae said softly. "And she stopped depending on her friends."

"And you're worried that will happen to our Kevin?" Grandma said.

"I'm worried that worse will happen to Kev," I said.

"Then we must get to him and warn him," Grandma said. "Zoey, pack up the rest of those cookies. I'll get my basket. It'll only take me a moment to get ready."

"Where are you going, Grandma?" I asked.

"With you, of course."

"But where?"

"To the headquarters of the Resistance. Kevin is spying for them, so they'll be able to reach him."

Rephaim, Stevie Rae, and I exchanged a look. I cleared my throat and said, "Um, Grandma, how about you tell us where they are and we'll go. From what Kevin told us, it's really dangerous out there."

Grandma stopped just before climbing the stairs to her room. "U-we-tsi-a-ge-ya, am I a frail old woman in your world?"

Stevie Rae snorted a laugh and answered before I could.

"No way, Grandma! You're awesome. You were even captured by Neferet once, put in a cage, and tortured, but you survived."

"And thrived!" Rephaim added.

"Of course I did. Because I am not a frail old woman. Children, this world is filled with danger, but I am part of the Resistance. I stand up and fight Darkness. Anything else is unconscionable. And, besides that, you need my help to get to their camp."

"Okay, you're right. I'm sorry I doubted you," I said.

"Grandma, how far away is the Resistance camp?" Stevie Rae asked.

"Oh, it'll take about an hour and a half."

"That might be a problem. It's gonna be dawn in an hour and forty-eight minutes," Stevie Rae said.

"Oh, that's right, child. You're a red vampyre and sun is deadly to you. Well, let's see. We'll take my delivery van. There are no windows in the back and I'll bet your young man is handy enough to rig a blanket as a curtain to keep out the sun in the rear from the front window, and we'll hurry. The Resistance is situated in a cave, so you'll be fine once we reach them."

Stevie Rae looked at Rephaim and then back at Grandma.

"Is there more I should know? Are red vampyres from your world especially susceptible to the sun, even if they're protected from it?"

"No! Actually, if it's overcast and we're covered up, we can go outside during the day," Stevie Rae said.

"But it's uncomfortable for them," I added. "Go ahead, tell Grandma about Rephaim. She'll understand."

"Okay, here goes—Rephaim used to be a Raven Mocker, but he turned from Darkness to follow the Goddess, and Nyx forgave him, giftin' him with a human body."

"But only between sunset and sunrise," Rephaim continued. "While the sun is in the sky I take the form of a raven. It is my penance for the terrible things I did before I met and loved Stevie Rae."

Stevie Rae took his hand. "It's okay. Everybody messes up. It's just that your saying sorry is complicated because your mess up was super bad." She looked at Grandma Redbird. "But he really is sorry. And he really does follow Nyx now. Promise."

Grandma was staring at Rephaim as if she was just now really seeing him. "Raven Mocker—I haven't heard that terrible name spoken for many decades."

"It is a past I regret," Rephaim said.

"Raven Mockers are half-man, half-raven creatures of Darkness who target the weak and helpless, or the sick and dying. They are vile. You must have great good within you for Nyx to have forgiven you," Grandma said. "And if Nyx can see that great good, then so shall I. So, young woman, what you are saying is that we must also be prepared for your mate to transform into a raven at sunrise?"

"Yes."

"Well, then we best hurry. That's something we must let the Resistance leaders know about, preferably *before* it happens. I do have a request, though."

"Name it," Rephaim said.

"I would like to hear the story of how you came into being. Raven Mockers are only spirits in this world, not flesh—not something anyone could ever love."

Rephaim smiled at Grandma Redbird. "It is a long story, but I will be happy to share it with you during our drive."

"Excellent! Now, Zoey, I imagine you know enough about my kitchen to find the Tupperware so we can take the rest of those cookies with us. Correct?"

"Yes, Grandma." I got up and started for the strangely familiar kitchen.

"Good. We leave in five minutes." But before she climbed the stairs she came to me and took my face between her age-weathered hands. "To see you again before I join my Zoeybird in the spirit world is truly the greatest gift of my lifetime." She kissed me softly, and I hugged her again before she hurried up the stairs, taking them two at a time like a woman decades younger.

"Same Grandma—different world," Rephaim said.

"It's pretty cool." Stevie Rae nodded and wiped away happy tears.

"Same Grandma—same love," I agreed. And, feeling more confident than I had since I'd told Stark my plan, I began looking through kitchen drawers. And Grandma was right, as usual. It took me no time at all to find her Tupperware.

(

It was crazy how the weather changed when we got to the Sapulpa ridge. The night had been cold but clear—not so as we got farther and farther down a windy road called Lone Star, which wasn't nearly as strange as the convoy of military vehicles that pulled off Lone Star as we turned onto it.

"Stay down in the back!" Grandma told Rephaim and Stevie Rae. "Turn your head away, u-we-tsi-a-ge-ya! I don't want them to glimpse your Marks."

I did as she said, pretending to be very interested in the scenery as I let my long, dark hair fall over most of my face. After the column of transport trucks went past us, Grandma kept nervously checking her rearview mirror for several long, silent minutes.

Finally, she breathed a relieved sigh. "It looks like they're in too much of a hurry to bother with us."

"Is that normal?" I asked Grandma.

"To pass a military convoy? Yes. Out here? Not particularly, though there were red vampyres under Stark's command searching the ridge the night I brought Kevin to meet the Resistance."

"Bet that didn't go well for poor Other Kev," Stevie Rae said from the rear of the van.

"At first, no. But when it was Kevin who called the sprites, and Kevin who convinced them to veil the ridge and protect the

Resistance from Neferet's armies, well, then Dragon was more receptive to believing he was on the side of Light."

"I'd forgotten that Kevin said Dragon and Anastasia are alive in this world! Ohmygood*ness* I can't wait to see them again," said Stevie Rae. Then her expression changed. "Oh, no. Dragon!"

"And Anastasia," added Rephaim, looking pale and sad.

"What is it? Why would Dragon and Anastasia upset you?" asked Grandma, glancing in the rearview mirror at Stevie Rae and Rephaim.

When they didn't answer, but turned to look at me instead, I told Grandma the truth, even though I seriously didn't want to. "When Rephaim was a Raven Mocker, before he knew Stevie Rae and was still under the influence of Darkness, he killed Anastasia. Dragon knew that. He had a hard time forgiving Rephaim, even after Nyx forgave him."

"I never blamed him for that," Rephaim spoke up quickly. "He is stronger than me. I don't believe I could ever forgive if someone killed my Stevie Rae."

Stevie Rae touched his cheek. "Course you could. You'd know I'd want you to, and so would Nyx."

"I do not believe telling this story to this world's Anastasia and Dragon would benefit any of us," said Grandma firmly.

"I agree with Grandma," I said.

"Is it not being dishonest to keep this from them?" Rephaim asked.

"No. It happened in another world, and you weren't even *you* when you attacked the House of Night and killed Anastasia," I reminded him.

"Z's right," said Stevie Rae. "There's no point in upsetting Anastasia or Dragon in this world. They're alive and well—and you're going to be their friend and ally."

"Rephaim, you cannot undo what you did in another world— at another time. All you can do is to move forward in love and Light," said Grandma Redbird.

Rephaim bowed his head, looking sad but not defeated. "Then that is what I will do. And I will protect this world's Anastasia with my life."

That settled, my mind was still whirring because of another name. "Grandma, you said Stark led the red vampyres who were searching the ridge the night Kevin got here. So, he really is a big deal in the army?"

"He's a general—one of the main commanders. Apparently Neferet counts on him quite a bit. Do you know him in your world, Zoeybird?" She took her gaze off the road briefly to meet mine.

I sighed. "Intimately. He's my Oathbound Warrior and much more. We're in love."

"And in our world, he's not a blue vampyre. He's red. Like me," said Stevie Rae.

"His heart is good. Very good," said Rephaim.

"In your world that might be true, but in this world he is a force for Darkness," said Grandma, gripping the wheel until her knuckles turned white.

"It's not a 'might be,' Grandma. We're bonded. I know his heart as well as I know my own, and I don't believe that Stark knows he's being used as a force for Darkness," I said firmly. "I'm no expert on alternate dimensions, but the three people I've met from this world—Kevin, Jack, and you, Grandma—are all more similar than different from who they are or were in my world. That's another reason I had to come. I think Neferet is manipulating him. I believe I can reach Stark."

Grandma studied the road silently before she relaxed a little and said, "I hope you're right. If Stark turned against Neferet, it would be a major coup for the Resistance."

"Well, my Stark is as devoted to Nyx as he is to me. Maybe he just needs to know that Neferet has turned from the Goddess. I know *my* Stark stood up to Neferet and Kalona when it would've been much easier for him to do what those two told him to do."

"I believe in him too, Z. There's no way Stark would knowingly take a side that's against Nyx," said Stevie Rae.

"I would trust him with my life," said Rephaim. "In any world."

About then Grandma turned onto a lane barred by a massive iron privacy gate. She reached out her window and pressed the intercom, and a woman's voice answered, punctuated by what sounded like a mob of barking dogs.

"It's too damn early to be selling anything and I'm not buying. Go away!"

"It's Sylvia Redbird, Tina," G-ma said, speaking to a small camera. "I called you about the puppies. I hope you don't mind that my friends and I want to take a look."

"You said you'd be in a hurry, so I left the keys in the Polaris. It's parked beside the car castle," Tina replied. "I've also packed it with a few supplies. Since they built that cave the Resistance has quadrupled in size."

"Thank you, my friend. I am sorry to bother you at this hour. Go back to your rest. I shall take it from here."

"I don't need to send Babos out again, do I?" Tina asked.

I watched Grandma smile into the video intercom. "Not if you trust me."

The gate buzzed open. "That I do. Good day, Sylvia."

"Wado, Tina," replied Grandma.

"What does *wado* mean?" asked Rephaim as Grandma drove through the gate and down a long, tree-lined lane.

"It means *thank you*," said Grandma. "Child, I hope you are here long enough for me to teach you some of your language, but if not, would you do me a personal favor?"

"Anything, Grandma Redbird."

"Get my double in your world to teach you, and tell her she's been errant in her tribal instruction."

"I will do that!" Rephaim said.

"Ooooh! Can I learn too?" Stevie Rae asked.

"Is she family?" Grandma asked me.

"Absolutely," I said.

"Then yes, you may," Grandma said, pulling in next to the Polaris, which was parked right where Tina said it would be.

"'Car castle' sure fits it," Stevie Rae said as we looked up at the stone garage with a pergola on the top of it as well as balustrades.

"Well, Tina is nothing if not interesting," Grandma said. "Hurry, now. Dawn isn't far away. Oh, can any of the three of you drive one of those things? I can in a pinch, but we'll be going fast over unpaved, bumpy paths, and my skills aren't up to that."

"Heck yeah, I can drive any ATV. I have brothers," said Stevie Rae, and we all climbed into the Polaris, which I discovered was basically a tricked-out golf cart that could go fast.

"I have a brother, but I couldn't drive this thing," I said.

"Z, not to be mean or anything, but I might be a better Okie than you."

"I don't doubt it."

Grandma chuckled and said, "Head up that dirt road. Take a left when we get to the top of the first ridge and then turn right and keep turning right as the paths split. I'll tell you when to slow down."

"Easy-peasy!" Stevie Rae said. "Hang on, y'all!"

The Polaris roared to life and we hung on. Dodging spiderwebs and giant ruts like a pro, Stevie Rae guided it up, up, up, winding along the face of a ridge as the weather got colder, foggier, and just plain weirder the farther we climbed. When the poor visibility caused Stevie Rae to slow way down, Grandma shouted over the engine.

"Stop for a moment, please, child!"

Stevie Rae put the ATV into park. Then Grandma did something very strange. She stood up so that her head poked through the roll bars that pretended to be a roof, and shouted into the grayness that foretold dawn.

"Oak! It is me, Sylvia Redbird! I give you my promise that those with me mean no harm to my grandson or his people."

There was a pregnant pause, and then Oak's gentle voice replied from within the rustling winter-brown leaves of the trees surrounding us.

*"I see you, Wise Woman, and I recognize those who are with you. You may pass in peace."*

And, just like that, the night warmed, and the icy fog surrounding us lifted, though mere yards from us I could see the fog thickened again, hiding the ridge in ice and mist.

"Okay, it's safe to go on now," said Grandma. "It's not much farther, though. Keep a lookout for a large tree fallen across the path."

"Will do!" Stevie Rae put the Polaris into gear and floored it.

I leaned close to Grandma so she could hear me over the engine. "So, Kevin did this? Protecting this ridge was one of the reasons he used Old Magick?"

"Yes. He had to. Stark was leading the Red Army directly to the Resistance. There were innocents here. They would all have been slaughtered."

I nodded, beginning to understand the depth of Kevin's need. I couldn't blame him for calling the sprites. I probably would have done the same had I been in his place.

"Fallen tree, dead ahead!" Stevie Rae called as our headlights illuminated the felled log. "And we have about fifteen minutes before it's dawn."

"Go ahead and put it in park close to the tree," Grandma said. Then she stood again and shouted, "I'm trying to harvest mustard plants by the light of the moon. That's when they are most potent!"

"Huh?" I said.

"Sssh, we shouldn't have to wait long before—"

From the trees above us, camo-wearing vampyres repelled to the ground. All of them had crossbows, with arrows nocked and pointed at us. One vampyre separated himself from the group. I recognized him before I could see his Mark. There was only one Warrior who held himself with that confidence, moved with that controlled, lithe grace, *and* held a huge longsword as if it was a feather.

"Dragon!" I couldn't stop my mouth from shouting.

"Ohmygood*ness!* It's so great to see you!" said Stevie Rae. She actually started to get out of the Polaris, no doubt to give him a big ol' Oklahoma hello hug, but Dragon's narrowed eyes and the longsword he kept trained on her definitely dampened her enthusiasm. It also had Rephaim moving protectively to his mate's side.

But it was my grandma who beat all of us out of the vehicle. She went to Dragon, ignoring his longsword.

"Merry meet, friend Dragon. I bring allies from another world—the world Kevin told you of." Grandma half turned, motioning for me to join her, which I did—moving carefully so I didn't accidentally provoke anyone to shish kebab me. "This is my granddaughter—"

"Zoey Redbird!" Stepping from the thick forest shadows, Anastasia Lankford walked to me, smiling brightly. "Merry meet. It is lovely to see you alive and well."

"Right back at you, Anastasia." My eyes began filling with happy tears, and I couldn't stop myself from hugging her tightly. "I've missed you."

"Me too!" said Stevie Rae. "Can I have a hug?"

Anastasia looked from me to Stevie Rae, her eyes widening at the intricate red Mark that framed her face.

"Oh, sorry. Maybe you didn't know me in this world? My name is Stevie Rae Johnson."

"I do recall a young fledgling, but she rejected the Change early in her first year at the House of Night and was not in any of my classes."

"Yeah," Stevie Rae sighed. "That happened in my world too, but then I came back."

"A female red vampyre. It is very odd," said Dragon.

"Well, Dragon, if ya think I'm odd, just wait a few minutes till sunrise and check out what happens to Rephaim!" said Stevie Rae.

"Stevie Rae, I will hug you," said Anastasia.

"Yeah!" Stevie Rae flew into her arms, and as she held Anastasia tight, she grinned over her shoulder at Dragon. "You're next, Swordmaster."

Dragon's reply was a grunt.

Then Rephaim stepped before Anastasia and I held my breath. He knelt to one knee and gazed up at the priestess with eyes that were shining with unshed tears. "Anastasia Lankford, I pledge my protection to you."

"Why, thank you, young man." Anastasia smiled down at him, though I could see she was confused. "You and I must have also known one another in your world."

"We did. But not for long. I should have protected you there. I will protect you here."

"That's great, boy. But you will have to stand in line behind me," said Dragon.

"Oh, Bryan. A priestess can never have too many protectors, especially not in these very dangerous times." Anastasia held out her hand, and Rephaim took it, kissing it formally. "I gladly accept your offer of protection, though I hope I never have to use it."

"Thank you, priestess. Thank you," said Rephaim, getting to his feet.

"I hate to break up this lovely reunion, but dawn is almost here and we really need to get Stevie Rae inside and Rephaim somewhere he feels safe to make his change," I said.

"All right." Dragon spoke with his familiar grumpy reluctance. "Johnny B, conceal the Polaris."

My grandma pointed to the back of the ATV. "Tina sent supplies. They are in the container in the back. And, before you ask, yes—I brought more cookies."

Dragon smiled then. "Sylvia, you are Goddess-sent."

"I am, indeed," Grandma said cheekily.

"Drew, help Johnny B unload and carry the supplies to the

cave. The rest of you stay here and be sure the Red Army doesn't get past the sprites."

"We saw them leave," I said, trying not to gawk at this world's version of Johnny B and Drew.

"Yes, a convoy passed us just as we were pulling onto Lone Star," said Grandma. "What happened here today?"

"It's what *didn't* happen that's important," Anastasia said. "Your grandson saved two groups of human refugees and blue fledglings."

"Oh, thank the Great Earth Mother," murmured Grandma prayerfully.

"Exactly," agreed Anastasia. "Now, please follow me. As your grandma knows, it isn't far to the cave from here, but it is a steep climb."

We trudged along after Anastasia and Dragon. I kept staring at the two of them, thinking how unbelievably awesome it was to see their linked hands and their heads tilted toward each other. For a moment I wanted nothing more than to summon the sprite and figure out a payment that would allow them and Other Kevin, Other Stark, Other Aphrodite, and the rest of the good guys here, to go back to my world with us and forget about all the death and Darkness over here.

But I knew that wouldn't be right. This world needs good guys too.

"It's tempting, isn't it, Z?" Stevie Rae spoke softly from beside me.

"Are you reading my mind?"

She grinned. "It's not hard to do. I'm thinkin' the same thing— how great it would be to have Dragon and Anastasia back with us."

"It would be, but only for us. For this world—not so much."

"Sometimes it sucks to not be selfish," she said.

"Yep," I said.

Then we didn't talk at all because we had to climb single file up a rocky path that seemed to end nowhere—until we turned a narrow corner and saw the opening of a cave. Scents of simmering stew drifted from within, along with the muffled voices of women and children.

"Wow, this is awesomesauce!" said Stevie Rae. And then she

gasped and turned quickly to Rephaim. "Uh-oh! And I didn't even warn them."

"Warn who about what?" Dragon said, instantly alert.

"Well, um, remember when I told you to just wait and see what happens to Rephaim at sunrise? Okay, don't freak. I'll explain everything after he flies away."

"What is happening!" Dragon spoke forcefully, moving to stand protectively to block as much of the cave entrance as he could, longsword raised.

"There is no danger, friend Dragon," Grandma said. "Rephaim is simply not quite as he seems—like most of us."

"Sun's rising now!" Stevie Rae ducked her head, cringing against a sun I couldn't even see yet.

"She needs to be inside that cave!" I said.

I was taking off my jacket to throw over Stevie Rae's exposed head when Dragon moved so that she could duck past him, where she stopped just inside the cave and turned to stare at Rephaim.

We all turned to stare at Rephaim.

He'd taken off his shirt and was looking around frantically, which made me wonder what happened to his pants and underwear if he was still wearing them when he changed into a raven.

But nothing happened. Nothing at all.

"I am not judging you, but your mate strips every sunrise? Why?" Anastasia asked Stevie Rae.

Stevie Rae didn't answer. All she could do was stare at Rephaim.

"Are you sure it is sunrise now?" Grandma asked gently. "It is difficult to tell with the tree coverage."

"Yes." Stevie Rae's voice was shaky. "There's no doubt. Sunrise happened three minutes ago."

Rephaim held out his arms, staring at his very human hands. "It is not happening. I am not changing!" He looked up, meeting my eyes. "Why? I do not understand."

"Neither do I," said Dragon.

"Rephaim changes into a raven every sunrise to sunset," I explained, though my voice quivered, as I felt shaky too.

"Why? What type of creature is he?" asked Dragon.

"He used to be something called a Raven Mocker," I said. "But they are ancient, evil creatures, and he turned from Darkness when he fell in love with Stevie Rae. Nyx forgave him, giving him the body you see him in now."

"But I had a penance to pay for the evil deeds I once did," Rephaim said. And though he answered Dragon, his gaze had found and remained on Stevie Rae. "So, when the sun is risen I return to the form of a beast. Only not here. Not now."

"Perhaps that is because you committed no evil deeds in this world," Anastasia said. "Nyx has no reason for you to serve penance here."

I wish I could've explained to Anastasia how ironic her words were—and how cathartic for Rephaim—but I knew I couldn't. So, all I did was watch through very watery eyes as Rephaim went to Stevie Rae, took her into his arms, and held her tightly as she cried happy tears all over his very bare and very human chest.

# 25

# *Stevie Rae*

"Ohmygood*ness,* Kev made all of this?" Stevie Rae gawked with Rephaim and Z as they followed Aphrodite into the cave. The opening was modest. Only about half a dozen people could fit comfortably there—*if* they weren't too tall or big. But step beyond the entrance and suddenly the cave became a huge underground cathedral with hearth fires burning cheerfully in several places all around the circumference.

"Yes and no," said Anastasia. "He summoned the Old Magick sprites and paid them with medicine bags from both Sylvia Redbirds—the one in this world and the one in your world. The sprites did the rest."

"It was a miraculous thing to witness. I am so pleased I played even a small part in it," said Grandma Redbird.

"Sounds like you played more than a *small* part, Grandma," said Zoey. "You paid the price."

"Ah, but the cost was not high, and I'm sure my counterpart in your world would agree with me that it was well worth it."

"Well, it's super cool!" said Stevie Rae. She was holding

Rephaim's hand as if she'd never let him go, and still could hardly believe it was daylight outside, yet there he was—beside her and in human form—smiling down at her. She felt beyond giddy. As the Frankie Ballard song said, it felt like a jolt of sunshine and whiskey.

"*Croak! Croak!*" From the entrance, a huge raven dive-bombed toward them, swooping low and circling to land on Anastasia's raised arm.

"Oh, Tatsuwa! I am so glad you're here." The priestess stroked the bird's dark head as he leaned adoringly into her hand.

"You own a raven?" Rephaim said.

Stevie Rae felt the tension in his body through their joined hands, and she looked up at her tall, handsome, very human lover. She'd never seen him around any other raven, and he was staring at this one with an expression of mixed curiosity and fear.

Anastasia smiled kindly at Rephaim. "Own him? Oh no! One cannot own another being. I simply found Tatsuwa when he was a fledgling. I helped him, and he has chosen to remain close to me."

"That's not quite accurate, my love," said Dragon Lankford. "He hadn't fledged yet when you found him."

"You're right, Bryan. This lovely boy was knocked out of his nest during a terrible storm almost a year ago. I found him and cared for him until he could fledge."

"And he repays your kindness with absolute devotion," finished Dragon.

"I believe I understand how he feels," Rephaim said, sharing an intimate look with Stevie Rae.

"Well, you weren't a baby when I found you," she said.

"No, but I was hurt and helpless and couldn't fly." He looked at Anastasia. "Do you think he would mind if I touched him?"

"Tatsuwa belongs to himself. I do not answer for him. Ask him yourself."

Rephaim squeezed Stevie Rae's hand before letting it go. Then he approached the big bird. He'd moved his perch from Anastasia's arm to her shoulder, and he was watching Rephaim with a bright, intelligent gaze. "Hello, Tatsuwa. I am Rephaim. I believe you and I have much in common." He lifted his hand, offering it to the big bird as if he were a dog. Tatsuwa cocked his head, studying Rephaim, and then he leaned forward, allowing Rephaim to stroke his folded feathers.

"He likes it if you pet him right above his beak," Anastasia said.

"He's beautiful." Rephaim spoke in a hushed voice as he stroked the raven.

"That's how you look," Stevie Rae said, coming up beside Rephaim. "Only you're bigger."

Rephaim sent her a shocked look. "Bigger? But he's enormous!"

Stevie Rae grinned. "Do you understand now why Aphrodite is always teasing us about getting you a giant cage?"

"Aphrodite ..." Dragon grumbled.

"Uh-oh, what did she do?" Zoey asked.

Before Dragon could answer, his mate spoke. "Just a little thing. She made sure a whole group of fledglings and human children didn't get slaughtered by that Red Army convoy you passed on the way here. And your brother was with her as well."

"Yes. He kept me from capturing her and bringing her here," said Dragon.

"But wait, that's good, right?" Stevie Rae said. "Kev found her, and she has to be on our side or she wouldn't have saved those people."

"Exactly," Anastasia said firmly.

"The only side Aphrodite is on is her own," Dragon said. "We all need to remember that."

"Not to be mean or anything, but that's what we used to think in our world too, and we were wrong," said Stevie Rae. "Without Aphrodite I'd be as gross as all the red vamps here in your world. Well, all the red vamps but Kev."

"There's a lot more to Aphrodite than what she shows the public," Zoey said.

"If my opinion counts I'd like to say that even though she takes some getting used to, and I don't like that she calls me Bird Boy, Aphrodite has far more Light in her than Darkness."

Dragon stared at Rephaim for several long breaths, then said, "Your opinion counts very much, as I believe you have known Darkness intimately."

"I have, Swordmaster." Rephaim bowed his head slightly to Dragon. "As have you, though perhaps not in this world."

Dragon bowed back to Rephaim. "There is much you and I could discuss."

"I look forward to it," said Rephaim.

"See! I knew you and Dragon would've been real good friends!" Stevie Rae said, resting her head on Rephaim's shoulder and yawning loudly.

"I look forward to hearing the story of your courtship," said Anastasia. "But I imagine Stevie Rae would like to be shown to a sleeping chamber first."

Stevie Rae tried unsuccessfully to stifle another yawn. "That would be awesome. I can stay awake when the sun's up, but it's not easy."

"Hey, go ahead and sleep. I'll fill Dragon and Anastasia in on our plan and then grab a few hours of sleep myself," said Zoey. "Um, can you guys tell Kevin I'm here? I don't think it's smart for me to just walk into the House of Night and start looking for him."

"Tatsuwa can help you! Can't you, handsome?" Anastasia cooed at the big bird, who actually purred back at her as he rubbed his head against her cheek. "Sweet boy!" she laughed softly.

"The bird knows Kevin?" Zoey asked.

"Oh, absolutely. And he can get your brother a note from you," Anastasia said.

"Like a carrier pigeon?" Stevie Rae asked.

"More like a Saint Bernard," said Dragon. "Anastasia will show you."

"But first, are you hungry, darlings, or would you like to be shown to your rooms?" asked Anastasia.

"I'm pretty full of cookies," said Stevie Rae, rubbing her eyes sleepily. "Rephaim, do ya need something to eat?"

"All I need is to have you sleep in my arms." He wrapped his arm around Stevie Rae's shoulders and held her close.

"That sounds better than a Kenny Chesney love song," she said.

"If Zoey and Sylvia remain here with Bryan, I will show Stevie Rae and Rephaim to one of our empty bedchambers," said Anastasia. Then she stroked the raven's head again and told him, "I would like for you to remain here as well, my friend. Zoey will need you to get her message to Kevin."

"*Redbird Boy!*" Tatsuwa croaked.

"Wait, y'all can *talk* when you're ravens?" Stevie Rae said, butting Rephaim with her shoulder.

"I had no idea," said her shocked-looking mate.

"We'll need to work on that," said Stevie Rae. Then she hugged Grandma Redbird and Z. "See y'all at dusk."

Z hugged her back before saying, "Hey, you guys wouldn't happen to have any brown pop, would you? Anything with caffeine and sugar in it will work. I need to stay awake and focused."

"Yes, there are several coolers in the main hall of the cave," said Anastasia. "It's just inside here and on the way to the sleeping chambers. I can show you, and you can return here."

"Awesome!" said Z.

Then the four of them entered the enormous cavern that reminded Stevie Rae of the time she'd gone on her eighth-grade field trip to Missouri's Meramec Cavern—minus the cool stalactites and stalagmites.

The main part of the sprite-made cave was a huge underground circle, and dotting the circumference of it were groups of people—mostly fledglings and blue vampyres, but Stevie Rae noticed that there were several humans among them, mostly either young or very old. Each of the groups were positioned around a hearth fire, and they were all busy. Some were cooking food, some were mending clothes, and others simply appeared to be telling stories. Cats padded around the cave as well, finding the best laps to rest in or the coziest spots close to crackling hearth fires. Stevie Rae thought the whole place was awesomesauce.

"It is bedtime," Anastasia explained as they moved across the wide circle. "So, not as busy as usual. Typically, the Warriors will be practicing sword fighting or archery and teaching the young ones ways to protect themselves."

And then Anastasia paused in her explanation, as one of the blue fledglings had noticed them, and was pointing at Stevie Rae with a shocked, open-mouthed expression.

"Uh, Anastasia, that girl over there looks like she just saw a boogerman, and that boogerman is me," said Stevie Rae.

"Indeed," said Anastasia. "I will handle this now." The lovely priestess motioned for Stevie Rae to walk with her, and together they strode to the center of the cavern. Anastasia clapped her hands several times, focusing everyone's attention on her. When she spoke, her words were clear and sharp and filled the cavern. "Everyone, I want you to meet our newest members of the Resistance. This is Stevie Rae. Yes, she is a red vampyre, but like Kevin, she is also our ally. Treat her as you would a friend. Her mate is Rephaim, and her other companion is Zoey Redbird, sister to our Kevin."

Everyone stared, but there were several greetings offered, and to Stevie Rae's surprise, people soon stopped staring and went back to whatever they had been working on—well, everyone went back to what they'd been working on except one tall, dark, and very handsome blue vampyre. He approached their little group, but he only had eyes for Zoey.

"Oh, lordy," Stevie Rae said under her breath—then she and Z said his name together.

"Erik!"

"Hey there, beautiful. I don't think I know you, and thought I'd introduce myself." His grin was double-watt, movie-star brilliant. "But it seems *you* already know *me*."

"Yepper, we sure do," Stevie Rae said, stifling a giggle.

"At least he's part of the Resistance," Z said to Stevie Rae, ignoring Erik's seductive smile.

"Well, Z, he mighta grown up," Stevie Rae said.

"You stay positive, Stevie Rae. That's one of the things I love about you," Z said.

"Sorry, I'm confused," Erik said.

"We know!" Z and Stevie Rae said together before they dissolved into girlish giggles.

Rephaim stepped up, offering his hand to Erik. "I am Rephaim. It is good to meet you. Again."

Erik took his hand but frowned slightly. "'Again'? I don't remember meeting you." Then his confusion cleared. "Oh, I get it. You're a human fan."

"Something like that," Rephaim said.

Then Erik turned to Zoey. "You do seem familiar to me, though. Have we met?"

Z laughed softly. "Not in this world, Erik. But it is good to see you here, with the Resistance."

"Yeah, well, this war is crappy for Hollywood. My career sucks right now, so this fighting stuff definitely needs to end."

"What'd you say about him growing up?" Z asked Stevie Rae.

"I take it back," Stevie Rae giggled.

Erik opened his mouth to respond, but Anastasia spoke first. "Erik, Johnny B, and Drew are bringing in new supplies from the main trail. Could you be a darling and see if they need your muscular help?"

"Anything for you, milady!" Erik bowed to Anastasia with a flourish. Then he winked at Zoey—"I'll see you later, Miss Zoey."—before striding away.

"Not if she sees you first," Stevie Rae said, sotto voce.

"I take it you know Erik in your world," Anastasia said.

"Very well," Z said.

"He is very, um, *young*," Anastasia said carefully.

"Yep, but he gets better," Z said.

"*If* he's forced to," added Stevie Rae. "Don't let him get by on his looks. There's really a lot more to him, but right now *he* doesn't even know that."

"I'll keep that in mind," said Anastasia.

"Hey, why isn't it smoky in here with all of those fires?" Zoey asked.

"Actually, we aren't sure. All of this, except that small entrance up there, was created by sprites, so we're just grateful for a safe haven, and the fact that it isn't filled with smoke." Anastasia headed to the left side of the big room where a stream bubbled musically from somewhere in the stone floor and ran deep and long down the side of the cavern before disappearing into the stone again. Floating in the stream were lots of cans and bottles, all held together with netting. "There you can find cold brown pop, bottled water, and even wine."

Zoey went to the stream and fluttered her fingers in the water. "Wow! That's really cold!"

"Yes, and it runs in and out of this whole network of tunnels and caves. There is even a branch of the stream we use as our bathrooms."

"Good job, Kev!" Stevie Rae gushed as Rephaim fished a couple of bottles of water from the stream, and a can of brown pop, which he tossed to Z.

"Thanks! See you two at sunset."

Stevie Rae blew Zoey a kiss, and then turned back to Anastasia. "This cave is beautiful. It's like it's been here for centuries."

"I think of it the same way—as ancient as the sprites who carved it. And perhaps it is. Perhaps it was just waiting for them to reveal what time had covered."

"That's a nice thought," said Rephaim, putting his arm around Stevie Rae's shoulders and holding her close.

"Come, your room is not far from here."

They followed Anastasia from the main cavern. There were several tunnel choices, but each was marked with different colored chalk lines that looked like arrows—some pointed toward the main cavern, and some away.

"We all have excellent night vision, but as there are humans here," Anastasia paused and added, "and other types of beings ..." Rephaim nodded in recognition that she was referring to him. "You'll find lit lanterns hanging from the walls, as well as a lantern in your room. You only need to remember to follow the red chalk arrows to return to the main cavern. The other colors are coded as well. We're following blue arrows. They lead to the sleeping rooms. Yellow lead to the bathroom area, where you can relieve yourself as well as freshen up, but be forewarned: the water is always cold," Anastasia said with a shiver.

"That's no problem. When we first moved into the tunnels under the depot they were way grosser than this," said Stevie Rae.

"So, you use the old Tulsa tunnels in your world too?"

"Yes, but from what Kevin told us, ours are different than the tunnels the Red Army inhabits," said Rephaim.

"I would imagine so, as the red vampyres in your world are so much different than ours."

"Hopefully not for long," said Stevie Rae.

"That seems an impossible dream," responded Anastasia.

"But I'm livin' proof it's not impossible!"

"And that is very true. You and Kevin are hope personified for us." They'd come to a narrow tunnel and an area that reminded Stevie Rae of Swiss cheese, with lots of little alcoves holed out of each side of the tunnel. Several were hung with blankets that were closed, blocking the view inside them. Anastasia stopped before one that had a blanket pulled back. "You should find this comfortable. And, as I said, if you need to freshen up, follow the yellow arrows, and then return by following the blue. Is there anything else you need?"

Rephaim and Stevie Rae shared a long, intimate look as she said, "No, thank you, Anastasia. We already have everything we need."

"Then I will wish you only the pleasantest of dreams."

Finally alone, Stevie Rae and Rephaim entered the little carved-out space, untying the blanket from the side of the entrance and letting it fall closed behind them.

The room was tidy and cozy. A lantern sat on the flat top of a chair-sized mound of Oklahoma sandstone. Its light flickered across the curved stone walls, giving the effect of a fireplace. Not far from the lantern a thick pallet had been made up with two side-by-side sleeping bags. The pillows and comforter were fluffy and clean and smelled like lavender soap.

Stevie Rae picked up a pillow and sniffed. "I'll bet Grandma Redbird has something to do with this."

"I have learned never to bet against you."

"I always say you're a quick learner," Stevie Rae said. She put the pillow down and stood awkwardly beside the bed, suddenly and unexpectedly nervous.

"What is it? Why do you look uncomfortable?" Rephaim asked her.

"Well. Um. We've never slept together like this before."

"But isn't this a thing to celebrate—not a thing to be nervous about?"

"Yeah, but tell that to my heart. I think it might beat outta my chest." She took his hand and placed it over her heart.

He smiled down at her and drew her into his familiar embrace. "Remember what you used to tell me when I was frightened by new things?"

She nodded, suddenly breathless. "Yes. I said just hold tight to me and it'll all be okay."

"Stevie Rae, my only and forever love, just hold tight to me and it will all be okay."

He bent and kissed her, and Stevie Rae felt her bones go liquid.

His kiss blotted out their surroundings, and he became her world. Carefully, Rephaim guided her to the sleeping pallet, cradling her against him so that their bodies pressed intimately together, and the kiss went from soft and sweet to hot and insistent. Time seemed to pause. Sunrise always made her languid, and Stevie Rae had often wondered what it would be like to make love with Rephaim when she was so vulnerable. She'd dreamed about it while he was soaring through the sunlit sky. She'd longed to feel his strong arms around her, and his beautiful body enter hers—joining them fully before they drifted off to sleep together.

Soon Stevie Rae realized reality was much, *much* better than her dreams had been.

Slowly, gently, Rephaim took off her clothes, and then, just as unhurriedly, Stevie Rae undressed him, taking her time to run her hands and her lips down his lean, muscular chest. She reveled in his beauty and the smoothness of his brown skin.

In turn, he took his time exploring her body. They had made love many times, but never during the day—and Stevie Rae felt suspended in time and pleasure. His touch was like fire. It made her smolder and glow. She loved how they were able to take their time. She gasped with the pleasure his hands and mouth brought her, and she made him tremble with desire as she touched him intimately, thoroughly. Stevie Rae covered her lover with kisses until neither of them could bear it any longer. Then their bodies joined and they moved together in a dance as ancient as love itself.

And at the moment of release, Rephaim called her name, and she his, while their lips met and their breath mingled. Then, wrapped in Rephaim's very human embrace, Stevie Rae sent a prayer of thanks to Nyx for allowing them this magickal time together before they drifted off to sleep—finally, finally *together*.

## 26

## *Other Kevin*

"I'm coming with you," said Aphrodite firmly. "And stop pacing. You're making me unattractively dizzy."

"You couldn't be unattractive," Kevin said, and then added quickly. "But no, you're not coming with me."

"Uh, I'm way too used to compliments to be thrown off by one. And I didn't *ask* to come with you. It was a statement."

Kevin stopped pacing and faced her. "What if Dragon doesn't let you go?"

"Then you'll make him."

He ran his hand through his hair and stifled the urge to shake her. "Dragon is a Swordmaster. And an extremely experienced Warrior. I can't take him. Not even to protect you."

She rolled her eyes. "Kev, I didn't mean you should fight him. I meant that you'll help me reason with him—again. And, honestly, being 'caught' by the Resistance can't be any worse than living with the stress of Neferet's unending threats and the way she uses me."

Kevin studied her, noticing again the dark circles under her eyes and the dull look of her skin. And she was so thin! It worried him. Did she never really eat or sleep?

"The Resistance will want to use your visions too," he said honestly.

She shrugged. "So? At least then they'll be used for good." Aphrodite held up her hand to stop Kevin from replying. "Yes, I have come to the realization that Neferet is no longer following Nyx's will. Yes, it took me too damn long to face that realization. But now I have, and I need to do something more than sit here and wait for my next vision to show what horrible thing Neferet is going to do. You're responsible for that, so it's only right that I go with you to the Resistance."

"I'm responsible?"

"Of course. If a red vampyre can come back from being a monster and actually turn into a good guy, then I can stand up and do the right thing too."

His smile was slow. "You think I'm a good guy."

"Don't get a big head. I didn't say great. How long until sunset?"

"Fifteen really long minutes."

"Okay, so, here's what we're going to do. As soon as the sun sets we'll go to Neferet's office. I'll tell her you're going to drive me to Dallas because I need some Nordstrom shopping therapy to replace the boot I broke out there in that damn field in Bugtussle. There's no way we can make the trip in one day, so that'll give us plenty of time to meet with your sister and the Resistance and get back here—*if* we're getting back here."

"What if Neferet says no?"

"She won't. She can threaten and bully me, but she knows she can only push me so far. And she'll see this shopping trip as typical for me. She won't even question it. She *will* question you driving me, though. But I'll handle that."

"Aphrodite, are you really sure about this? I can go to my sister and come back quickly. You don't need to be involved in this at all."

"Kev, I've been involved since I didn't tell Stark about Dragon or turn you in for being a weird red vamp. It's too late for me to turn back now, and I don't want to. I'm done hiding behind my visions." She stared into the fireplace. "I can't stand being the cause of death anymore."

He sat beside her on the couch. "Hey, you didn't cause any deaths. Neferet and her armies did."

Her gaze met his, and Kevin could see such misery within her eyes that it made his breath catch.

"But I didn't do anything to stop them, and I could have."

"You did last night. You saved Dragon and all those other people."

She shook her head. "I was the reason the Red Army was out there in the first place. Kevin, was I a selfish, egotistical waste of space in Zoey's world?"

"No! Of course not!"

"Well, I am here. And I don't want to be anymore. You don't have to help me be better. I have to do that myself. But please don't get in my way."

Slowly, Kevin took her hand. "I'll help you. I'll always help you." He lifted her hand to his lips and kissed it softly.

One perfect blond brow lifted, but she didn't pull away from him—which Kevin definitely thought of as a victory.

"Now, go smear some of that disgusting blood crap on yourself, but not too much of it. I'm going to try to cover the smell."

"Huh?"

She sighed. "Kevin, Neferet would never believe I'd let a stinky red vamp drive me all the way to Dallas and back, even in the town car with the glass partition. So, I'm going to attempt to cover the stink."

"Town car? Glass partition?"

"Were you raised by wolves?"

"No. An elder of the Children of Faith," he said.

She shuddered delicately. "Worse. No wonder you're such a barbarian. Goddess, you have so much to learn. But, first things first. *Sparingly* put on your disgusting blood perfume and grab my overnight bag. It's just inside the bathroom door."

He did as she asked, grimacing and holding his breath as he unscrewed the top of the jar that held the gelatinous, disgusting mixture and smearing it—*sparingly*—under his clothes. When he was done he grabbed Aphrodite's suitcase, which was decidedly more than an overnight bag, and his own satchel, and rejoined her in the sitting room.

"This isn't an overnight bag."

"Oh, you know nothing, Kevin Snow."

"Hey! I got that reference!"

"Well, there's hope for you yet." Then she grimaced. "Eww! I can smell you! Goddess, that's disgusting."

"I know. I hate it."

"Okay, come here."

Kevin walked over to her. She lifted a pretty purple crystal bottle that had a weird-looking rubber bulb thing attached to it, and she squeezed the bulb, which sprayed a fine mist of lavender-scented water on him. He breathed deeply and then sneezed.

"You don't like it," she asked, eyebrow raised again.

"Yeah, I do. It smells lots better than that blood gunk."

"Boy, cat shit smells better than that blood gunk." She tucked the bottle into her giant Louis Vuitton purse. "Is it time yet?"

"Yes. The sun set forty-nine seconds ago."

"That's a real weird talent." She stood by the door waiting for him to open it.

"But a handy one," he replied.

"True. All right—remember to—"

"Walk behind you. Carry your stuff. Look subservient and stupid."

Her smile had the blood rushing through his veins hot and hard. "You *can* learn! Well done, you. And let's go."

She twitched away and he followed her, trying not to grin at the view.

"I can feel you looking at my ass," she said without even

glancing over her shoulder. "Stop it. You're supposed to be *subservient*. Plus, that's a little pervy."

"Oh, right. Sorry."

She'd come to the outside door and stopped, waiting for Kevin to rush past her and open it. As he did so he asked, "So, just for the record, is there ever a nonpervy time for me to look at your ass?"

This time she raised *both* of her perfect brows. "If there is, I'll be the first to let you know."

"Thanks." He grinned at her.

"Don't thank me until it happens. *If* it happens." She patted his cheek as she breezed past him.

"Oh, it'll happen," he muttered under his breath.

"Heard you!" she said.

He stifled his smile and let her get several paces ahead of him, then he bowed his shoulders and put a blank but hopefully stupid expression on his face and followed her.

The campus was starting to stir, as professors and upperclassmen hurried about, preparing for a new school day. They looked at Aphrodite. Of course they did. She was striding across campus with her head high and her thick, blond hair flowing behind her like a cloak. Kevin thought she was magnificent.

She was also pulling all eyes away from him.

When she stopped before the door that led to the school's administrative offices, Kevin hurried past her again and opened it for her. Aphrodite marched inside and turned to the left. Just off the main hallway were Neferet's luxurious offices. Aphrodite didn't hesitate. She raised her hand to knock on the thick door and glanced back at Kevin.

*Ready?* she mouthed.

He drew a deep breath and nodded, hoping he was a good actor.

Aphrodite knocked twice.

"Enter!"

Kevin had, of course, never been in Neferet's office suite until then, and it definitely wasn't an act that had him stopping just inside the door and gawking around like a brainless tourist.

Everything inside the suite of rooms was beautiful. Had he ever imagined how Neferet would decorate her offices, which he hadn't, Kevin would've guessed that she'd have drenched everything in gaudy gold and marble and crystal. He would've been wrong.

The main room, which held Neferet's desk, was almost completely decorated in white. On the walls hung beautiful black and white photographs of Neferet—in each of them she looked like a version of Nyx come to earth. In one she'd even mocked up a headdress of diamonds to look like the Goddess' headdress of stars.

It was super unsettling.

The desk was a piece of art. Made entirely of green onyx—the exact color of Neferet's eyes—and lit from within, it was the perfect frame for the preternaturally beautiful High Priestess, who sat elegantly behind her desk in a throne-like chair. In front of her desk were two velvet chairs the same color as the desk.

James Stark was sitting in one of the chairs. As they entered the office, Stark turned, his eyes widening in surprise when he recognized Kevin. Kevin saluted him quickly and then stood at parade rest, his gaze on nothing in particular.

"Aphrodite! Your ears must have been burning. General Stark and I were just talking about you."

Aphrodite didn't miss a beat. She took the chair next to Stark, crossed her long legs, and flipped back her hair.

"Really? That's a coincidence. I was just thinking about talking to you about Stark."

"Do tell!" Neferet gushed and leaned forward as if she and Aphrodite were besties.

Kevin knew better.

"Did General Bow Boy tell you I broke the heel of my Louis Vuitton's last night tromping around in the wilderness?"

"I don't remember him mentioning that. Did you, Stark?"

Stark frowned at Aphrodite and then returned his attention to Neferet. "I didn't mention it because it isn't important. The fact that we caught no members of the Resistance last night *is* important."

"Not my fault the Red Army is so loud and stinky that they can't manage to set a trap. Ugh, speaking of." Aphrodite's hand disappeared into her purse to reappear with the purple perfume bottle, which she squirted absently over her shoulder in Kevin's general direction. "Next time you assign a soldier to me could you please choose one who doesn't reek?"

Stark just stared at her. Aphrodite shrugged and ignored him. "Anyway, I wanted to let you know that I'm going to Dallas for some retail therapy. And to replace my boots, which I really should charge to Bow Boy here, but I'm a giver so I'll take care of the cost myself."

"Wait, so somehow she's blaming *me* for her stupid broken boot *and* the fact that her vision was bullshit?" Stark barked.

"My vision wasn't bullshit. It was real. It was true. They all are."

"Then, my dear, why did Stark not kill one Resistance member last night or capture one single blue vampyre traitor trying to flee?" Neferet asked in a winter-cold voice.

Aphrodite didn't seem ruffled at all. "Simple. Changing the outcome of a vision is easy. All it takes is one person to do one small thing different than they potentially would have and, *voila!* Vision changed. Example—if just one member of the Resistance had a decent nose they would've smelled the Red Army and warned the others. Not my fault *he* was too early."

"You didn't give me a time!" Stark said, thoroughly exasperated.

"I gave you a place and a very bloody outcome. Must I do *every-thing* for you?"

"Enough!" Neferet raised her hand. Kevin felt the room change, become thick, heavy, oppressive. He couldn't help himself. He looked directly at the High Priestess.

From behind and beneath her, Kevin saw the shadows begin to pulse and move. One of the shadows detached from the others, slithering across Neferet's arm to wrap around her waist and disappear out of view.

Neferet's green eyes found his.

Kevin lowered his gaze instantly, tasting the bile of complete terror in the back of his throat.

"I am not a child, Aphrodite. I do not need an explanation about how prophetic visions work. I am Nyx's chosen one on earth. Do not forget that."

Aphrodite bowed her head slightly. "I never forget that, High Priestess."

"Good. General Stark, perhaps next time you should be sure all red vampyres remain inside closed vehicles until *after* the Resistance members are trapped."

"Yes, High Priestess," Stark said expressionlessly.

"Now, Aphrodite, you may go to Dallas, but be quite sure you return in time for the football game tomorrow night. General Stark and I are planning a little New Year's surprise, and I would hate for you to miss it." She fluttered her well-manicured hand dismissively at Aphrodite. "You are excused."

"Thank you, High Priestess," Aphrodite said formally. She stood, and began a traditional bow, fisting her hand over her heart, but suddenly Aphrodite stumbled and would've fallen had Kevin not moved quickly forward and caught her elbow. She instantly jerked her arm away from him and tossed back her hair. "Eww! Didn't I tell you never to touch me?"

"Yes, Prophetess." Kevin rounded his shoulders and backed away from her.

"Aphrodite, are you quite well?"

Neferet's sharp eyes were dissecting the Prophetess.

Aphrodite tossed back her hair and sighed heavily. "I'm fine. It's probably his stench that's making my stomach feel so sick. Stinky!" She glared over her shoulder at him. "Did you get those bottles of blood-laced wine I ordered from the kitchen?"

"Uh, n-no. I, I didn't know you—"

"Oh, please. Just don't speak." Aphrodite narrowed her eyes at Stark. "Thanks *so much* for shackling me with that one."

"But I—"

"Come on, Stinky! Must I always do everything? Now I have to wait for you to go to the kitchen. Goddess! As my mother says, good help is impossible to find."

"Your mother is wise for a human," said Neferet. "Aphrodite, you will take special care, won't you? I'd hate for anything untoward to happen to you—especially before my surprise tomorrow night."

"Oh, I'm fine. And I have Stinky here to protect me if we run into any Resistance members shopping at Nordstrom." Aphrodite turned and met Kevin's eyes—and he had to stop himself from gasping.

Her blue eyes were bloodshot. He was sure they hadn't been when she entered the office.

Aphrodite went to the door, which Kevin opened quickly for her, and followed her out.

The instant the door closed behind them Aphrodite stumbled back, falling against Kevin.

"What is it?" he whispered urgently, putting his arm around her.

"Kev, get me to the town car. Now. It's in the front row of the parking lot. Here're the keys." With trembling hands, she took them from a side pocket of her purse and handed them to Kevin.

Kevin grabbed her elbow, steadying her again, and they hurried down the hall away from Neferet's office.

"This isn't like any vision I've had before. There's something wrong with my eyes!" Aphrodite tripped and almost fell.

"Here, hold onto me." Kevin wrapped her arm through his. "Oh, shit! Your eyes. They look like they're filling with blood!"

"Goddess! If I collapse—if Neferet realizes I'm having some kind of strange vision, there is no way she'll let me leave. And I don't want to tell her whatever I'm going to see—I don't want to tell her ever again! Help me. Please."

"I've got you. It's going to be okay. Do you have sunglasses in that purse?"

"I—uh—yes. In the big middle pocket."

Kevin took the purse from her and grabbed the Chanel box, opening it and putting the dark glasses on her face. "Now hang onto me. Don't let go. I won't let you fall."

"P-people will see me holding onto you. They'll talk."

"It'll be fine. It'll be like I'm escorting you. You can make up something hateful to say about how I failed miserably at it because of how bad I smelled." As he spoke he kept them moving forward, practically carrying her now.

"Kevin! Oh, Goddess! It's bad. Everything is turning red! I can't see anything!" she sobbed softly.

"Close your eyes. I've got you. We're almost there." Kevin propelled them forward as quickly as possible. "Turn your head to the right, like you're looking out of the window. Now!" he whispered urgently. She did and he breathed a small sigh of relief as a group of curious fledglings approached them on his left. Kevin stood tall, squared his shoulders, and skewered each of the young House of Night students with his best terrifying red vampyre glare.

They hastily looked away, barely noticing Aphrodite.

Then they were outside, and he slid his arm around Aphrodite's waist as her knees crumbled. He punched the red button and a black town car just in front of them bleeped. Half carrying, half dragging, he got her to the car, threw open the door, and gently helped Aphrodite lay inside across the luxurious black leather seat. He tossed the suitcase in the trunk, got behind the wheel, put the car in gear, and drove as quickly as he could without throwing gravel all over the school.

"Aphrodite? Are you okay back there? What can I do?"

"Get me to the Resistance." She spoke between great, wrenching sobs. "I—I just saw what Neferet's planning at the football game tomorrow!"

## 27

## *Zoey*

"When is he going to get here? Should we meet him halfway? Why can't we call him?" I felt like I was going to crawl out of my skin as I stood just inside the mouth of the cave and watched night descend on the ridge.

"The note Tatsuwa carried from your brother said he would leave the House of Night at sundown. That should put him here at any moment," said Anastasia.

"If he didn't run into any trouble," Dragon added.

"Do not fret, u-we-tsi-a-ge-ya. Your brother is a capable young man. He will be here soon," said Grandma Redbird.

"What did we miss? Is Kev here yet?" Stevie Rae rushed up with Rephaim, they were both holding mugs of steaming coffee and looking a lot happier and better rested than me. I tried not to be envious. It had, after all, been my choice to leave Stark behind.

"Not yet," I said, trying not to sound as stressed and bitchy as I felt. "I wish he'd hurry."

"I'm sure he is doing his best. Just be a little patient and—" Grandma began.

There was a series of owl hoots that carried from somewhere in the distance, answered by another series of similar hoots, closer.

"There," Anastasia smiled. "That must be him now. That is the Warriors' call for an incoming friend."

She was right. It was only a few more (unbelievably long) minutes, and then Kevin rounded the corner that led to the cave.

"Ohmygood*ness!* Is he carrying—"

"Aphrodite!" I cried and rushed out to meet my brother and the woman he carried in his arms.

"Zo! It's really good to see you!"

"Are we there yet?" Aphrodite said weakly.

"Kevin, what do you mean bringing her here?" Dragon pushed his way in front of me, reminding me of what a judgmental ass he'd become after Anastasia had died.

So I shoved right back. Hard. I moved around him and got a good look at Aphrodite. My brother cradled her in his arms and moved slowly and carefully. She had a folded T-shirt covering her eyes and I could see dark splotches on it, as well as bloody tear tracks on her pale cheeks.

"She's had a vision," I told Dragon with a hard look. I touched her arm gently. "How are you feeling, Aphrodite?"

"Worse than I look. Assuming I still look as gorgeous as usual. Who are you?"

"That's my sister, Zoey," Kevin said, grinning at me.

"Hi. I hear we're friends in another world," she said.

"We are. Good thing too, because I know exactly what to do to make you feel better."

"Booze and pills?" she asked hopefully.

I easily recognized her attempt to hide the fact that she had a debilitating migraine and was probably still blind.

"She sounds like our Aphrodite, that's for sure," Stevie Rae said.

"I don't know who that is but I know where she's from," said Aphrodite. "Nowhere, Oklahoma—right?"

"Different world—same person," mumbled Rephaim.

"This isn't a family reunion—it's a Resistance," Dragon grumped. "Kevin, you understand that as she has now been here, to our headquarters, she cannot leave."

"I thought about that, Dragon. And you need to understand that first, this *is* a reunion. Being part of a Resistance doesn't mean we also can't be part of a family. Second, Aphrodite is blind. She hasn't been able to see anything since we left the House of Night. There is no way she could find her way here again. Now, do I need to go down to the ranch house and have Aphrodite cared for there, or are you going to let us into the cave *that was built because of my connection to Old Magick?*"

I'll admit that I was shocked that Kevin stood up to Dragon. The Swordmaster could absolutely kick my brother's butt, yet there he was, holding Aphrodite in his arms, going toe-to-toe with him.

"Bryan, Kevin is one of our own. And he is right—we are family." Anastasia put her hand on her mate's arm gently. "My love, do you not trust him?"

"Yes. Kevin has proven himself," Dragon said reluctantly.

"Then we must trust his judgment too."

"Bring her in," was all Dragon said, and then he moved aside.

"Anastasia, I'll need something cool and damp to put over her eyes, and she needs something to drink." I remembered that in this world Aphrodite was a fully Changed blue vampyre and added, "Wine laced with blood would be perfect."

"We have those things. I'll be back in just a moment." Anastasia hurried away.

Kevin went to the interior of the cave and the closest hearth fire, where he knelt and gently place her on the stone ground where she could lean against the rounded rock wall.

"Rephaim, would you run back to our room and get Aphrodite one of our sleepin' bags? That'll help her be more comfortable," said Stevie Rae. He nodded and hurried away.

Aphrodite cocked her head to the side. "Am I friends with a bumpkin in that other world?"

"Yepper," said Stevie Rae. "But don't worry. You're still nuttier than squirrel turds in our world too."

"Squirrel turds? Really? I'm feeling like I need to go there and have a serious talk with myself," Aphrodite said, pressing a shaking hand against the T-shirt that covered her eyes.

I sat beside her. "What's it been, about forty-five minutes since your vision?"

"Yes," said Kevin. "She had it just as we were leaving the House of Night. She was so brave. It hit her hard. Her eyes filled with blood and she went blind, but she kept walking—kept moving forward so Neferet wouldn't know. She's like a superhero."

"Kev, you sound besotted. Stop it." But Aphrodite's soft tone took the sting out of her words.

"I'm not one hundred percent sure I know what that is, but I think I might be cool with it," Kevin said.

"It kinda means you'd drink her bathwater, Kev," Stevie Rae said with a big grin. "And like it."

"Hum. Aphrodite, would you like me to like that?" he asked.

I punched his arm. "You're gonna make her roll her eyes, and that'll hurt."

"Sorry." Kevin looked chagrined.

"Aphrodite will be better soon. She just needs to rest," I said. "Thank you, Anastasia." I took the clean, wet strip of a linen bandage from the priestess. "Aphrodite, I'm going to take the shirt from your eyes and replace it with a damp cloth. It'll feel good."

"Okay," she said, nodding shakily.

"Keep your eyes closed. Our Aphrodite says that helps," Stevie Rae added.

"Just breathe, child," Grandma Redbird said.

"Who's that?" Aphrodite asked.

"Our grandma," I said. "You'll love her. We all do—in whatever world."

"That's sweet, Zoeybird. I'll go see if I can find some nice, hearty soup. That will also help." Grandma disappeared farther into the cave.

"Okay, here goes," I said. Gently, I took the bloody T-shirt from Aphrodite's face. I knew what I was going to see. I mean, I'd helped Aphrodite through the aftermath of more visions than I could count. Still, it was awful. Blood had crusted in the corners and edges of her eyes. Her eyelashes were matted with it. Blood, mascara, and eye shadow had tracked down her face, making her look like a macabre clown.

"Don't open your eyes. I'll clean you up a little." I looked at Anastasia, who was staring in shock at Aphrodite's face. "I could use another of these cloths."

"And I could use that blood-laced wine," Aphrodite said.

"Of course! I'll be right back."

"Here's the sleeping bag," Rephaim said.

"Aphrodite, I'm gonna lift you up again so that they can put the sleeping bag under you. Is that okay?" asked Kevin.

"Yeah, but don't go fast. My head feels like it's going to burst."

Kevin couldn't have been gentler with her had she been a newborn. *He's got it bad for her.* And that thought was followed by, *I wonder where Darius is in this world?*

Anastasia hurried back, just in time for me to finish cleaning up Aphrodite's face. "Okay," I said, "press this against your eyes, and then I'll help you drink the wine."

Instead of doing that, she turned her head toward me—bloody eyes still closed. "We are really good friends, aren't we?"

"Absolutely," I said.

"You and I might fight some," said Stevie Rae, touching Aphrodite's shoulder gently and then sitting on the other side of her, "especially 'cause you do not like my fashion sense—but you almost died for me. We're friends too. Real good friends."

Aphrodite pressed the damp, cool bandage against her eyes and let me guide her hands to the mug of blood-laced wine, which she drained in just a few gulps. Then she settled back against the side of the wall and sighed.

"Better. It is getting better." Her chin lifted and her head turned toward me again. "Wait. You've done this before."

"Yeah, a lot," I said.

She smoothed back her hair and drew a deep but shaky breath. "So, how does your Aphrodite cope with being blind?"

"She's not blind!" Stevie Rae and Kevin said together.

"Then why the hell am I?"

"Aphrodite, is this the first time your eyes have bled during a vision?" I asked.

"Yes. I usually pass out, but not always. Nothing like this has ever happened to me. Is this what happens to your Aphrodite during *all* of her visions?"

"Yes. Well, all of them since she ..." and my words trailed off as I realized what must be happening. "Dragon, you told me Aphrodite didn't betray you to the Red Army last night, right?"

"That is right." The Swordmaster came over to crouch near us.

"Of course I didn't. I'm not a damn monster. I hate this fighting crap."

"And she hates that Neferet uses her visions as weapons," Kevin added.

"Kev, I can speak for myself. But, what he said."

"How long?" I asked.

"I don't know what you—"

"Sorry, I'm not being clear. How long have you hated the way Neferet uses you?"

She shrugged a shoulder. "I don't know."

"Yes, you do," Kevin said. "Tell her. Zoey will understand."

Her head turned in Kevin's direction. "She might, but no one else will."

"I did," he replied.

"I'll try my best to understand," said Stevie Rae.

"As will I," said Rephaim. "Oh, I'm Rephaim. Stevie Rae's mate. I'm not sure if we're actually friends in our world, but you do call me

Bird Boy, which I like to think of as a nickname rather than slander."

"No clue what you mean by that," Aphrodite said. "But hello. You sound tall. That's one thing in your favor." Then she cleared her throat before she continued. "I have hated how Neferet uses me since I had the vision of Lenobia and Travis—their friends and their horses—all being murdered."

"It was you! You are the reason they're all dead!" Dragon glared from Aphrodite to Kevin. "And you brought her *here*?"

"Hey, wait. You don't have the whole story. Aphrodite—"

"Kev! I said I can speak for myself. Dragon Lankford and anyone else listening—I had a horrible vision that showed Lenobia's death. I *was* Lenobia. I felt everything she felt as she lost her lover and her friends and the horses she loved more than life. Did you know Lenobia was the last of them to die? That she watched the entire slaughter? I did *not* go to Neferet with the vision. I was *with* Neferet when it happened. She acted like she cared for me. She helped me through it. All the while she was only gathering details so that she'd know where to send her awful Red Army. And that's when I started hating her."

"But you didn't leave. You didn't join the Resistance," Dragon said.

"No. I didn't stand up like I should have. I was complacent. I did avoid her. I started spending a lot of time alone, just in case I had a vision. And when I couldn't avoid her, when she knew I was having a vision, or when she bullied me into admitting I'd had one, I only gave her confusing details and convoluted truths. It's only recently that I've realized that still makes me complicit. So, I decided to stand up when I saw you in the creek. And I'm going to keep standing up. I don't want more blood on my hands." She sighed. "Could I get another glass of wine, please? There's champagne in my suitcase. You did bring it, didn't you, Kev?"

"Prove it," Dragon said.

Aphrodite's full lips twisted into a very familiar sardonic half smile. "Well, I can't get it myself right now, but I can prove I brought champagne if someone gets the damn suitcase for me."

"You know that is not what I meant!" Dragon yelled. "I'm asking for proof that you've changed sides."

"Bryan, let the girl rest first," said Anastasia.

"No, my love. We are at war. There is no 'rest first' when you're at war. Aphrodite, if you have turned against Neferet, prove it."

"Uh, Dragon, I can prove it," I said.

"This should be good," Aphrodite said.

I bumped her leg with mine and whispered, "Not helping." Then I faced Dragon, feeling a little like my brother. "Our world's Aphrodite only started having bloody-eye visions *after* she made the decision to become a force for good—a decision *Nyx* approved of. I know because the Goddess has appeared several times in our world. Aphrodite has made a change. I'd bet my life on it."

"So would I," said Kevin.

"That happened in your world. Not ours," said Dragon stubbornly.

"Fine. How about this—do you know that Neferet commanded the Bedlam football game to take place tomorrow night at Skelly Stadium?"

"Everyone in Oklahoma knows that," said Dragon.

"And most of Texas too," added Anastasia.

"Figures. Bumpkins really like their football." Aphrodite shook her head in disgust and then grimaced at the pain the movement caused. "But what you don't know is what I just saw in a vision. As her idea of a New Year's Day celebration, Neferet is going to command her Red Army to slaughter the losing team. All of them. Players—cheerleaders, which I find really unacceptable—and coaches. Every single one of them. And after that *no one* will dare cross her."

"That's horrible!" Stevie Rae said.

"Oh, Goddess! That's so bad!" said Anastasia.

"Wait, Bedlam?" My shocked gaze found my brother's.

He nodded. "Yes. Heath will be there as starting quarterback for OU."

303

# 28

## *Zoey*

Aphrodite's vision sent shock waves through the Resistance. Dragon and Anastasia instantly went into motion, herding all of us—Kevin, Anastasia, Stevie Rae, Rephaim, Grandma Redbird, and me into a place they called the briefing center—an oval-shaped room with a low ceiling and only one entrance and exit. Someone had placed flat-topped rocks, big enough to be makeshift chairs, in a rough circle. We all sat. Even Aphrodite, who was just beginning to get her vision back.

"I'm assuming you came here with a plan." Dragon turned his attention to me as soon as we were all seated.

"I did," I said.

"Now would be a good time for you to share that plan," he prodded.

"Okay, but I'm going to tell you a lot of stuff about my world, and I know you'll have questions, so please just let me get finished before you start asking them."

"That sounds reasonable," Dragon said as Anastasia nodded.

I wiped my sweaty palms on my jeans and launched into my two-part plan, explaining as quickly and thoroughly as I could about Kalona—who he really is, what he did in our world—and I even told them about my circle and how I'd need the power of those with elemental affinities to help contain him when I free him until we can convince him to work with us to sway vampyres everywhere into believing the truth—that Neferet is not following the will of Nyx. I told them about how Aphrodite's sacrifice in our world had allowed our red vampyres and fledglings to maintain their humanity. I also told them about our Neferet. They'd already read her journal. Kevin had brought it with him from our world, so they knew her origins, but I gave them the rest of the details—how she'd embraced Darkness and the White Bull, and become a Tsi Sgili witch, immortal and so completely in league with evil that she considered tendrils of Darkness her children.

When I finished, the room was completely silent, and into that silence Aphrodite's words cut like a boat through placid waters.

"Good plan, but if we're going to stop the slaughter tomorrow there's only time for the part where I somehow give the Red Army back their humanity."

"Yeah, I realize that," I said miserably.

"Tendrils of Darkness?" Kevin spoke up. "What do they look like?"

Stevie Rae shivered. "They're super disgustin'. Like giant black snakes with no eyes and big ol' nasty teeth-filled mouths. In our world Neferet kept them hidden for a while from blue vamps, but they can't hide from anyone who's trafficked with Darkness."

"What does that mean?" Dragon asked.

"It means that Neferet could hide them from me or you or Anastasia, but she couldn't hide them from Stevie Rae or Rephaim, because Rephaim used to be a creature of Darkness and Stevie Rae was allied with Darkness before Aphrodite's sacrifice saved her."

"Oh," Kevin said, looking sick. "That's why she couldn't hide them from me today in her office."

"You saw something?" I asked.

He cracked his knuckles and then wiped a hand across his face. "Yeah, I did. They slithered from the shadows behind her. I didn't know what the hell I was seeing. I actually thought I was imagining it, and then I kinda forgot about it when Aphrodite had her vision. But they were what Stevie Rae described. Horrible snake things. They didn't look very solid, though. It was like they were still part of the shadows—as weird as that sounds."

"Doesn't sound weird at all, Kev," Stevie Rae said. "Sounds like she's just started manifesting them."

"Wait, what?" Aphrodite took the cloth from her eyes and squinted at Kevin. "I didn't see anything."

"Which is further proof that our Aphrodite has been immature and selfish, but never been allied with Darkness, isn't it, Zoeybird?" Grandma asked.

"Definitely," I said. Aphrodite frowned and started to protest, so I hurried on. "And it's also proof that we have run out of time."

"You think our Neferet is becoming immortal," Anastasia said.

"Yeah, that's what I'm afraid of," I agreed.

"Then we have to take as much power as possible away from her *now*, before it's too late," said Aphrodite. "She's already so fucking awful. She almost took over your world, and there she didn't even have a Red Army."

"She'll be unstoppable as the leader of those creatures once she fully manifests the powers of Darkness and becomes immortal," Dragon said grimly. "We won't stand a chance."

"It is all quite horrible," Grandma said, shaking her head in disgust. "Neferet has upset the balance of Light and Darkness by using those poor, tormented red vampyres. It is a true abomination of nature."

With a jolt I sat up super straight. "Grandma! What did you just say?"

"That Neferet is an abomination of nature?"

"No! No, not Neferet!" I could barely contain my excitement. "Red vampyres! Her Red Army is an abomination of nature—a twisting of us, of blue vampyres. That's good. That's really, *really* good."

"Your sister is making no sense," Dragon said to Kevin.

"Yeah, she is!" Stevie Rae's blue eyes were sparkling with excitement. "You're thinkin' 'bout what the sprite said about Old Magick, aren't ya?"

"Yes!" I tried to explain. "I'm no expert in Old Magick, but I've wielded it successfully and I do know some truths about it. First, it's capricious—changeable. Old Magick doesn't take sides. It didn't just work for me because I'm one of the good guys, same as it didn't work for Kev because he is too. It worked because they recognized our ancient blood and because we gave them acceptable payments."

Grandma Redbird nodded. "Old Magick works for Neferet, and she is definitely not good."

"Exactly. Somehow it recognized her," I said.

"That probably happened when she was a young girl and was somehow tied to the abuse she suffered at her father's hand," said Anastasia.

"And who knows what horrible price she pays them," Kevin said.

"Right. Neferet just followed their rules, and because they don't take sides in the struggle between Light and Darkness, they have no ethical problem helping her. That's how Old Magick works—*unless* an abomination of nature has occurred and needs to be put right. I know this because Oak made me cleanse a tree on our school grounds that had been ruined by Darkness. Oak said it then. She wanted it cleansed because sprites will not tolerate something they consider an abomination of nature."

"Oak? My Oak, the earth sprite? You know her?" Kevin asked.

"Yes, and don't call her yours. Don't ever forget that she's dangerous—they all are. Everyone here needs to understand this—wielding Old Magick changes the user. It's addictive. It's destructive. The *only* vampyre I know who has done so successfully is Queen Sgiach on the Isle of Skye, and I'm pretty sure she isn't really a vampyre anymore."

"Queen Sgiach is in this world as well," Anastasia said. "Though no one has spoken to her or entered her island for more than a century."

"That's how it was in my world too, before I went there."

"She allowed you on her island?" Dragon sounded incredulous.

"More than that," Stevie Rae said, smiling proudly at me. "She and Z became good friends, such good friends that Sgiach named her a Queen as well."

"That is truly amazing! Perhaps we should get you to Skye," Anastasia said. "We could definitely use Sgiach's help."

"I'd be happy to go and talk with her," I said.

"There's no time for that," Aphrodite said. "Not before tomorrow night's slaughter."

"I can't go to Skye in time to stop that, but I can call on Old Magick. All I have to do is to convince the sprites that red vampyres in their present state are an abomination of nature and get their help putting them to right."

"Won't using that much Old Magick change you?" asked Kevin.

"No. I won't actually be wielding it. The sprites will be on their own—not working through me."

"But they will still require a payment," said Rephaim. "Old Magick *always* requires a payment."

"I'll pay them."

Everyone stared at Aphrodite.

She shrugged. "What? The other me did it in Zoey's world. Why the hell wouldn't I do it in this world?" Aphrodite met my gaze. "Your Aphrodite lost her Mark when she saved the red vampyres, right?"

"Yes, she did."

"But she wasn't a fully Changed vamp, like me. Right?"

"Right again," I said. "She was still a fledgling, though she was already having visions."

"Well, then, I'll probably lose part of my Mark. It didn't hurt your Aphrodite, and she eventually became a High Priestess *and* a Prophetess of Nyx with special powers, didn't she?"

"Well, yes," I said. "But it wasn't that simple. Our Aphrodite had to go through *a lot* to become that. There is really no way to know what it will cost you."

She shrugged again. "Less than the deaths of hundreds of innocent people."

"Aphrodite, how are your mama and daddy doin' over here?" Stevie Rae asked her.

Aphrodite looked surprised by the question but answered easily. "My father died a year ago of a heart attack. My theory is my mother finally bitched him to death. She is now the mayor of Tulsa."

Dragon snorted in contempt. "Frances LaFont is firmly in Neferet's camp."

"Not literally, though," Aphrodite said. "She'd never step foot on the House of Night property. She prefers to remain safe in the luxury of the Skelly Mansion and just agree with everything Neferet commands. Why do you ask, Stevie Rae?"

"Well, your daddy's dead in our world too." Stevie Rae glanced at me and I nodded. "And so's your mama. But before she died you had words with her, and whatever happened between you pretty much pushed our Aphrodite over an edge."

"So? My mom's a bitch. In any world, we don't get along."

"You almost drank and drugged yourself to death," I said. "And when you hit rock bottom, that's when you finally were able to get free of your crappy parents and get over the crappy things they'd done to you. You finally grew up."

Aphrodite narrowed her eyes at me. "I am a grown-up blue vampyre and a Prophetess of Nyx."

"I wasn't talking about that. You were that in my world too."

"No. You said I lost my Mark. I wasn't a vampyre yet."

I sighed. "Okay, yeah. What I'm trying to make you under-stand is that—"

"I get it. It's dangerous. I'm going to lose something in exchange for doing this good thing. Fine." Aphrodite turned to meet Dragon's gaze. "If I do this will you believe I'm different? Will it make up for Lenobia?"

"It will not bring her back, of course," Dragon said. "But it is a sacrifice worthy of her, and she would appreciate it."

"Good. Then it's settled. We're going to the football game and I'm going to make sure the Red Army gets woke."

(

That night sped by. The cave—which I didn't get nearly enough time to explore, but could tell by just the little I saw was completely amazing—was filled with energy and movement as Dragon had the entire Resistance headquarters scrambling to get ready to mobilize.

"But how are you going to sneak all of these Resistance fighters into the game without Stark and the rest of them getting suspicious?" Aphrodite asked.

We'd moved from the briefing room to cluster more comfortably around the main hearth fire near the entrance of the cave. Aphrodite's sight had returned and I kept getting taken aback by how familiar she was—yet different from my Aphrodite. This one was thinner and somehow looked older, though they were exactly the same age. And she seemed sadder and more vulnerable, which she definitely tried to hide under a typically arrogant Aphrodite facade. That was, of course, a lot like my Aphrodite had done when I'd first met her, but she'd been better at it than this one.

After knowing her for less than a day it was pretty easy for me to tell that this Aphrodite was lonely. Very lonely. It made my heart hurt for her, and it also made me understand, again, just how important friendship is. Without us—the strength and friendship of our Nerd Herd—Other Aphrodite was sad and lost.

I was determined to help her find herself.

"Easy-peasy!" Stevie Rae said. "The answer's in Z's backpack. All we need to do is make sure it stretches far enough to cover everybody who needs it."

"What is she talking about?" Aphrodite asked me.

"I brought a big tub of professional cover-up for vamp tattoos with me. We thought we'd need it for Stevie Rae, and probably me too." I held up my hands and then pulled aside the collar of my T-shirt to let them glimpse some of my extra tattoos.

"You went to a tattoo artist?" Aphrodite wrinkled her nose.

"Nope. Nyx gave me these. And more. Before I made the Change she used to give me an extra tattoo every time I did something major to show that I was walking her path."

"I thought they were lovely before I knew they were a gift from the Goddess," said Grandma, running her finger lightly over the intricate design on my palm. "Now I think them exquisite."

"Thanks, Grandma. But it only takes a little dab of the cover-up stuff and a vamp becomes a human—even if it rains," I finished.

Dragon nodded. "That is an excellent idea, though it will not work for Anastasia and me. Our faces are too well known."

"Oh, I think you'd be surprised," I said. "Cover your Marks. Change into some Eskimo Joe's sweatshirts and OU hats and carry some pom-poms or whatnot, and I promise you no blue vampyre, especially a general or High Priestess, is going to pay any attention to you at all."

"She's right," Aphrodite said. "You'll just be another walking refrigerator to them. They'll barely look at you."

"This might actually work," Dragon said.

"It has to," I said.

"How will you call the sprites?" Anastasia asked.

"Together!" Kevin and I said at the same time.

"Jinx!" he said and punched my shoulder.

"Stop! Plus, I'm pretty sure I beat you. Again," I told him. "But yeah. We'll call the sprites together. They should hear us and come."

"Can't you call them here and explain what's going on?"

Aphrodite said. "Leaving the most important part of your plan up to last-minute chance with a magick that's—like you said—capricious, doesn't sound smart."

"My gut says we wait until the game and call them only when Neferet gives the order for the Red Army to eat the losing team," Kevin said. "Zo said they don't take sides, but abominations of nature piss them off. Well, a salivating horde of zombielike red vampyres is a pretty damn big abomination."

"I think Kev's right," I agreed. "The sprites have to understand how bad it is with the red vamps, and the best way to do that is to show them getting ready to slaughter a bunch of innocent people. But I see what Aphrodite's saying. We need to talk about our circle."

"What circle?" Aphrodite said.

"Exactly," I said. "We need one. A strong one. If we spread out around the circumference of the stadium and cast a wide circle around it, we'll pretty much be guaranteed the sprites will hear our call."

"That sounds reasonable," said Anastasia. "But you also explained that you need a circle made up of those who have elemental affinities, and we have none of those type of gifted vampyres here."

"I said I'd need that kind of circle power to contain Kalona—an angry and kinda crazy immortal." I glanced at Rephaim. "No offense."

"None taken. My father was crazed when he was entombed by the Wise Women."

"But," I continued, "for a regular circle that's strong enough to focus our call to the sprites, we shouldn't need more power than we have right here." Then I smiled at Anastasia. "And you *do* have at least one vamp with an elemental affinity—or more specifically, elemental affini*ties*." I pointed at Kevin. "My brother, like me, has affinities for all five elements."

"That is right! You are so young that I keep forgetting what a powerfully gifted vampyre you are, Kevin," Anastasia said.

"Hang on, what?" Aphrodite looked utterly shocked. "Why didn't you tell me anything about that, Kevin?"

He shrugged and his cheeks blazed pink. "I guess it didn't come up."

"And I've been gifted with earth," said Stevie Rae.

"So, we have three of five with true elemental connections, correct?" Dragon said.

"Correct," I said. Then I grinned at him. "Dragon, I believe you would be perfect to invoke fire."

He blinked in surprise. "Me? But I am not a priestess."

"No, but you're definitely fiery," said Kevin. "And I mean no disrespect by that."

Anastasia stifled a giggle, which made her look like an adorable little girl. "Bryan, Zoey is right. You have the dragon within you, and that is definitely fiery."

I smiled at Anastasia. "Which makes you the perfect choice to invoke air. You'll always be able to stoke the dragon's fire, *and* you'll always know when to blow it out."

Her smile blazed as Anastasia bowed her head slightly to me. "High Priestess, I acknowledge your wisdom and I agree. I will be air tomorrow night."

"Thank you, High Priestess," I tipped my head to her in return.

"Oh, Zoey. I am not a High Priestess," she said quickly.

"Sure you are," I said. "That's not a title that can be taken away by anyone but Nyx, and I happen to know that you and the Goddess are very close."

"That makes my heart sing," she said, with happy tears standing in her eyes.

"Which am I supposed to be?" Kevin asked. "Water or spirit?"

"Your choice," I said.

He thought for a moment, and then I saw his gaze find Aphrodite. "Water," he said. "I like the thought of washing away sadness."

I nodded and didn't say anything more because I knew it would just embarrass him again, but at that moment I couldn't have been prouder of him and I hoped if Darius wasn't still alive in this world that maybe, just maybe, Kevin and Aphrodite could find happiness together.

"Johnny B!" Dragon shouted, making me jump and my thoughts scatter. The kid ran up, and I tried not to gawk. In this world, he was a fully Changed vampyre with a tattoo that was made up of strong, sapphire-colored geometric lines that formed cool-looking triangles.

"Yes, Dragon," he jogged up from where he'd been flirting with a fledgling at a neighboring hearth.

"Borrow Tina's truck. Then cover your tattoo with the concealer Zoey brought with her. Go into town and buy as many OSU and OU shirts and game paraphernalia as you can find. Enough for each Warrior to wear something."

"And us," Anastasia added. "Each of us as well."

"Yes, exactly. Get enough for Anastasia, Zoey, Stevie Rae, and Aphrodite too," Dragon said. "And be sure you go to several stores. Don't buy too many from one place. Draw no attention to yourself."

"Yes, Dragon!" he hurried off.

"How will we get weapons into the stadium?" Dragon asked. "They'll have metal detectors. They always do."

"We won't take them in. The Red Army will," Kevin said.

"Which will help us how?" Dragon asked.

"It'll help us a lot when we take them *from* the Red Army. One at a time. As the game is being played. Solitary Red Army soldiers will be super easy for any *human* to lure into a shadowy spot—a bathroom stall or really anywhere they won't be in view of any of Stark's blue Warriors. And when the *human* turns out to be a disguised Warrior for the Resistance, the red vamp won't stand a chance."

"But try not to kill 'em," Stevie Rae added. "They'll be back to themselves as soon as Aphrodite fixes 'em, and they all deserve a second chance."

"They've done terrible things," Dragon said.

"But not because they wanted to," Stevie Rae countered. "They

314

have no will of their own. They only have hunger and anger. I know. I've been there. Give 'em a second chance, Dragon Lankford."

The Swordmaster nodded slowly. "Agreed. I will give the order to render them unconscious."

"You are a good Warrior, Bryan, and an even better man." Anastasia leaned over and kissed him softly.

"Only because I am your Warrior and your man."

I had to look away because they were choking me up. It was great to see them again—together and happy. But it also made me remember how much I missed them, and that was something I had to take back to my world with me. I glanced at Aphrodite. She had her blond head tilted toward Kevin and was smiling at something he was saying to her. And suddenly I realized that I was going to miss this Aphrodite too.

## 29

## *Zoey*

"It's only three hours until sunrise." Dragon spoke in a voice that carried across the great entrance chamber of the cave system where the Resistance members had gathered. "All of you going with us know our plan. Finish readying yourselves. Eat. And then sleep. Those of you remaining here must also be on alert and be ready to move and move quickly. If things do not go in our favor, Anastasia will send Tatsuwa here with a warning." Dragon looked around until he spotted my grandma. "Sylvia Redbird, I would like to ask if you would take charge of those we must leave behind. Will you?"

Grandma bowed her head slightly. "It would be my great honor."

"Thank you. Tatsuwa will be told to find you. If he comes bearing a dire message you must evacuate immediately. Lead the people to Polecat Creek. We have hidden rafts in the underbrush near the old wooden bridge. Drew!" Dragon called.

The short but powerfully built young vampyre stood. "Yes, Swordmaster!"

"I want you to be the Warrior who remains here. Sylvia will

need help getting the young ones to the creek, and you know exactly where the rafts are hidden."

"I do, and I will watch over those left in my charge—I swear it to Nyx."

"Excellent. Sylvia, if it comes to that, you'll float the rafts to where Polecat Creek drains into the Arkansas River just outside the Oklahoma Aquarium in Jenks. You'll be met there by a barge owner who will hide all of you inside transport cartons until you get to Fort Gibson. From there the Arkansas Resistance will take you to their hidden caverns."

"But we have faith that we will be victorious!" Anastasia said, lifting her fist in a victory salute while everyone cheered. "Rest now. Spend time with loved ones, as that is never time wasted. And may the blessing of Nyx be with us so that we shall all blessed be."

"Blessed be!" the crowd responded, and then people broke off into couples and small groups.

I liked their energy. We were all worried, of course, but there was no frantic nervousness here. There was only a calm feeling of determination. Everyone understood that we all might die or be captured tomorrow, but we had the same focus—ending Neferet's reign of Darkness and abuse, and that shared focus was also a shared strength and comfort.

Kevin tapped my shoulder and motioned for me to go with him to the mouth of the cave. "Hey, come here for a sec."

We went to the cave opening where it was cooler and darker than it was inside.

"It's always freezing out here," I said.

"It's the sprites," Kev explained. "They keep this ridge cold and foggy, and if someone sketchy gets too close it starts to sleet. It's awesome, really."

"Old Magick." I sighed. "It's crazy cool, but also just plain crazy."

"That's true." He turned to meet my gaze. "Thank you. I know you're here because you were worried about me."

"Yeah, well, I didn't want you to turn out like Neferet."

He shuddered and cracked his knuckles. "I'd never really had anything to do with her until I came back from your world, and let me tell ya, Zo, that is one creepy vampyre."

"Hey, before she channeled her powers into being a batshit cray immortal with snakelike children, she could read minds in my world. *That* was a pain in the butt."

"Seriously? She doesn't seem to be able to in this world—thank the Goddess for that. How did you get around it?"

I grinned. "Well, she could never read my mind, but Damien made everyone memorize vocab words and definitions whenever she was around. It was super educational and super annoying."

"Bet he had fun doing it, though."

"Yep, he sure did. Damien is really happiest when he's teaching. And that's something I need to remember when I get home. So, note to self—be sure Damien has his own classroom and can teach whatever makes him happy."

"You're a really good High Priestess."

His compliment gave me a rush of joy. "Thanks, Kev! Hey, you're doing awesome here. Because of you the Resistance has all of this, and Aphrodite is heading down the right path."

"I just hope she's strong enough to walk it," he said softly.

"She is in my world. You know that. She'll be strong enough here too."

He nodded. "You're right. One of the things she hates is to be underestimated. I won't make that mistake."

"Just like you won't make the mistake of falling for her?" I said, only semi-teasing.

"Too late for that."

"Yeah, I figured as much. Just watch your heart, Kev. Darius is her Warrior. They fit together. You've seen them, so you know it's true. When he shows up in this world, you will probably lose her, and I don't mean to hurt your feelings or make it seem like you don't matter. I just mean to remind you of the truth."

"I know," he said, staring out at the night. "But I can't help it. I love her, Zo."

I was afraid of that, so his announcement didn't shock me. "I get it. Just be prepared. Kev, does she know about Darius?"

He shook his head. "I don't think so. She hasn't mentioned him and I don't know any Darius in this world." Kevin sighed. "Warriors are scattered all over the Midwest holding the states Neferet controls. He could be anywhere. Or he could've died in battle."

"And you haven't told her about her Warrior in my world?"

"No, Zo, because she's not in your world!" he snapped. Then he sighed again and ran his hand through is thick, dark hair. "Sorry. I didn't mean to sound like an ass. I'm just trying to do my best. A lot's happened in a really short time."

"I get it. Just be careful of your heart, 'kay?"

"'Kay. So, we have a few hours until sunset and I thought I'd see if you wanted me to take you home."

I blinked at him. "Home?"

"Yeah. Home. Um, our old home. 1405 East Fargo in Broken Arrow. Do you want to see Mom?"

I felt like he'd knocked the air out of me. "Mom?"

"We can take Tina's truck. I'll bet G-ma would go with us too. You know—as a buffer."

"Mom's still married to the step-loser here?"

"Yep."

I chewed the inside of my cheek. "How was she at my funeral?"

"Hysterical. That stupid pastor talked shit about what a shame it is that you chose a pagan demon over Jesus Christ or some other such nonsense, and she lost it."

"Wait, at my funeral the pastor said I went to hell?"

"Yep. You know how those People of Faith are. If you don't believe exactly as they do, you're doomed to hell or worse. Zo, that idiot pastor actually said that if you're not a believer and you don't follow the Bible—and of course, by the Bible he means his interpretation of it—that you have no … um … wait, how did he put it? Oh, I remember! He said if you don't follow the Bible you have *no moral boundaries* and no way of knowing that being a pedophile or rapist is wrong."

"You have got to be kidding."

"Nope. It sucked. Big time."

"Wow. That's one of the stupidest, most narrow-minded things I've ever heard. Kev, was that my eulogy?"

"Yep. And that was the nice, least judgmental part."

"Gross."

"Yep again."

"No one else said anything?" I asked, not sure why I felt so upset. I mean, *I* wasn't dead, and the dead Zoey was hanging out with Nyx in her Goddess Grove in perfect peace. But still. It pissed me off.

"Are you kidding? The People of Faith don't even let anyone take communion who hasn't taken all their classes and kissed the rings of the male leaders of their church enough. Oh, and by *rings* I mean *asses*."

"Right, I got that."

"So, no. They didn't let anyone else speak."

"That doesn't really surprise me." I glanced at my brother and then blurted what I hadn't told anyone. "I saw Neferet kill her."

"Her?"

"Me her. Other Zoey. Your sister over here."

"What? How?"

"I don't know how, but she reached me through a dream. That Zoey let me watch what Neferet did to her." I shuddered and wiped my suddenly wet palms on my jeans. "It was awful, Kev. But fast. She didn't suffer. And in the dream vision thing, she looked right at me and told me I needed to get over here and help you defeat Neferet."

"Damn, that musta been horrible."

I nodded. "Yep. Even worse than my sucky funeral."

That lightened the mood and made him chuckle. "Hey, you will be happy to know that Heath and a whole group of us walked out of your sucky funeral when they did their call for us sinners to come forward and accept Jesus Christ as our savior crap."

"They turned my funeral into an event to proselytize?"

"Pros ... what?"

"Kev, you really gotta read more and increase that vocab of yours. Proselytize—save, redeem, preach to recruit—in other words, to convert people to the way they believe."

"Oh. Yep. That's what they did. And that's when a big group of us walked out."

"Well, that was nice of you. Thanks. Uh, where did they bury me?"

"Floral Haven. They cremated you. You have a little drawer-like cubby thing that says your name on it—Zoey Heffer."

"Oh. My. Goddess! Zoey *Heffer!* That is *not* my name."

"Exactly what I told Mom. The step-loser overruled me. He said he was paying for it, so it would say what he wanted it to say."

"I'd like to slap that bastard's face."

"Get in line. Hey! Want to go do that? I can use my cool red vampyre mind-control thingy on him and you could slap him as much as you want. I could even zap Mom into being nice to us. Temporarily."

"Did she come see you after you were Marked?" I asked.

"No, but, you know—the red fledgling thing is scary."

"Okay, I get that. But how about this—did she come see me after I was Marked? Even once before I died?"

He shook his head. "Not that I know of, and I'm pretty sure I would've known, because she and the step-loser would've argued about it."

"Yeah, they always thought we couldn't hear them because their room was on the other side of the house."

"They were wrong."

"Massive parenting fail on their part," I said.

"So, wanna go?"

I didn't need to give it any more thought. "Nope. But thanks for asking. They'll just hurt my feelings, and they did enough of that in my world. I don't need it in this world too."

"Okay, I get it. How about Heath?"

"Heath?" My stomach clenched.

"Yeah, Heath. Your childhood and teenagehood—and I'm pretty sure if you had lived he would've been your adulthood—sweetheart. You know he's alive here. He lives in Headington Hall on the OU campus. He's super easy to find because he's a big-deal quarterback."

"Wait, he's a freshman. He can't be a big-deal quarterback. Not yet."

"Oh, yeah he is. He's kicking ass. OU is undefeated this season with him leading the team."

"Holy crap! That's awesome. His dreams are coming true."

"Yeah, it's cool. So, wanna head to OU?"

"Um, well, um, we can't get to Norman and back in three hours," I said lamely.

"I know, but you can drive back, right? I'll bring some blankets to cover up with. It'll be fine."

"You're serious?"

"Yeah, Zo. Of course. He was your guy. I figured you'd want to see him."

I breathed out a long breath. "Not before the most important game of his life. It'd mess up his head, and you know Heath." I added with a shaky smile. "It doesn't take much to mess up his head."

"Very true," he agreed.

"So, no. That's really nice of you to offer, but I don't think it'd be the best thing for Heath."

"Okay." He gave me a contemplative look. "That's real grown-up of you, Zo."

"Well, I'm trying," I said.

Then from somewhere just outside the mouth of the cave I heard the strangest thing. Kevin had started to say something else, but I put up my hand and shushed him.

"*Me-uf-ow!*"

"Kev, did you hear that?" I walked a few feet outside the cave, trying to see through the darkness and fog.

"Sounded like a cat. Not surprising, Zo. There're lots of cats around here."

"No, not *a* cat. *My* cat. Kitty-kitty-kitty! Nala? Is that you, baby girl?"

"*Me-uf-ow! Me-uf-ow! Me-uf-ow!*" Grumbling like a fat little old woman, an orange cat leaped from one of the boulders and rushed up to us.

I dropped to my knees, holding out my hands for her. "Oh, Nal! You look so wet and cold—*and skinny!* Come here to me!"

She did, briefly rubbing against my legs. But she didn't let me pick her up. Instead she padded directly over to Kevin. She circled around and around his legs, rubbing against him and complaining over and over in her old-woman voice.

"Hey there, Nala," Kevin said, bending to pick her up. "How did you get here?" He sent me a confused look over the top of her wet head as she turned on her purr engine and snuggled in his arms. "Could your cat have followed you?"

I shook my head, feeling happy and sad—and a little jealous—all at the same time. "No, Kev. I promise you *my* Nala is curled up on my bed probably complaining at Stark right now. This is obviously *your* Nala."

He blinked in surprise. "Mine? Seriously?"

I smiled and reached out to stroke her damp fur, feeling her body rumble with her magnificent purr. "Seriously. In this world, you are her person."

"Wow! That's really cool. I've never had a cat. Animals hate red vamps over here."

"Not your kind of red vamp. Congratulations, Kev. She's an awesome cat. She can be kinda grumpy, and she'll sneeze cat snot in your face, but if you need a snuggle she'll always be there for you. And she has the *best* purr engine in any world."

"Hey! There y'all are!" Stevie Rae rushed up like a mini Oklahoma tornado with Rephaim and Aphrodite following in her wake. "Ohmygood*ness!* Nala! What are you doing here?" Stevie Rae scratched the top of her head, which made her purr even louder.

"This is Other Nala, and she just showed up, and she chose Kevin as her vampyre," I said.

"That is wonderful news," said Rephaim, petting the little orange tabby.

"How do you know this cat?" asked Aphrodite, looking over Kevin's shoulder at Nala.

"I'm her vamp in my world. So, it totally makes sense that Kev is hers here," I said.

"She's a ginge," said Aphrodite. "Which is unfortunate, but she's still cute. No cat has ever chosen me, but I do like them." She reached out tentatively to pet Nala, who flopped over on her back in Kevin's arms so that Aphrodite could pet her belly.

"Does anyone know if this Tulsa has a cat-rescue group called Street Cats?" I asked as Stevie Rae, Rephaim, and I shared a conspiratorial look.

"Yes, they do. The House of Night supports it. Or they used to before Neferet started her annoying war," said Aphrodite, still petting Nala.

Stevie Rae's grin was gleeful. "Well, after we get this Neferet mess fixed maybe you should take a trip to Street Cats. And that's all I'm sayin' about it."

"You're a strange one, aren't you?" Aphrodite said. When Stevie Rae opened her mouth to answer, Aphrodite held up her hand. "No, that was rhetorical."

Steve Rae frowned at her, and then turned to me. "Z, Anastasia said she'll show y'all to your rooms now so you have plenty of time to eat, clean up, and then get a good day's sleep."

Rephaim slid his arm intimately around her waist. "I am finding that sleep is underrated," he said, as Stevie Rae blushed up at him.

"Oh, for shit's sake—get a room. Sheesh."

Aphrodite sounded so exactly like my Aphrodite that I snorted a laugh.

"Finding our rooms sounds good to me. And it looks like I'm going to need some cat stuff too," Kevin said. "Right, Nala? Right, little girl cat?" He made kiss noises at her, which had me smiling. "Plus, I need to clean up. I wiped off that gross stinking blood crap I have to wear at a gas station on the way out here, but I swear I can still smell it somewhere under all that lavender Aphrodite squirted on me."

"Is that what that is? And all this time I thought you were just farting!" giggled Stevie Rae.

"And you're very, *very* sure the bumpkin and I are friends in your world?" Aphrodite muttered to me.

"Yep," I said. "You're why she's like this. If our Aphrodite hadn't sacrificed for Stevie Rae, she'd be a stinky monster and definitely not here with us."

"Again, I'd really like to have a talk with my other self," Aphrodite said.

"Hey, I grow on you," Stevie Rae said. "You'll see, if we're here long enough."

"You mean like a decade or so?" Aphrodite deadpanned.

I stifled a laugh by clearing my throat and quickly changing the subject. "So, where are we meeting Anastasia? I could use some food and a clean-up before bedtime too."

"This way, Z. Anastasia's sorting the OU and OSU shirts Johnny B brought back from T-Town. Man, I love me some football. I hope we get to watch at least a little of the game. *Boomer Sooner!*" Hand in hand, she and Rephaim started walking to where we would find Anastasia.

"She makes my head hurt," Aphrodite said.

"Sometimes things are freakishly the same in both of our worlds," was all I said.

"Come on, Zo. Let's go find our rooms," said Kevin.

"You guys go ahead. I need a few minutes to myself out here. Praying seems a good idea right now."

"Okay, no problem. Anyone can tell you where to find Anastasia," Kevin said.

Aphrodite and Kevin walked away, their heads together as they continued to pet and fuss over Nala. And I felt a jolt of surprise. *When had Kev gotten so tall? He looks all grown-up!* And that thought made my heart squeeze.

He and Aphrodite followed behind Stevie Rae and Rephaim, who were holding hands and sneaking kisses. I watched the two couples—because they were obviously *couples*. Aphrodite's gaze sought out Kevin wherever he was in the cave, which was usually not far from wherever Aphrodite was. He was totally crushing on her, which was no surprise at all.

It made me lonely.

It made me miss Stark. Not Heath. Not anyone else. Stark. And with every bit of spirit and will and love within me I thought, *I'm coming back to you, Stark! Please know how much I love you. Please believe in me like I believe in you.*

I waited, hoping I'd feel something back—even a tiny echo of our connection. But all I felt was empty, and all I heard was the lonely beating of my solitary heart.

"Zoeybird? May I join you?"

"Sure, Grandma. Wanna sit out here with me for a little while?" I pointed to a couple of flat-topped rocks that didn't look too wet.

"Yes, I would."

We sat in companionable silence for a while. The night was beginning to turn from black to the predawn lightening that made me think of a dove's feathers. The ridge was beautiful. I loved that it hadn't been developed and basically looked like it had one hundred or more years ago.

*Thank you, Nyx, for places like this that remind me of my connection to the land and to my ancestors who cared for it. Help me find strength through that connection for whatever comes tomorrow night. Help me do the right thing and to walk your path with integrity and kindness. Whatever happens, please comfort Stark and let him know that I do love him—so, so much.*

"U-we-tsi-a-ge-ya, you seem very far away, and very troubled. Would it help to talk about it?"

"Well, it usually helps for me to talk to you, so yeah, I would like to. Grandma, I'm worried that Stark will always resent me for coming here. He thinks I'm here because of Heath."

"Oh, because in your world Heath is dead."

"Yeah. But that's not the main reason I'm here. I tried to explain that to Stark before I left, but he didn't believe me. I hurt him—I'm hurting him right now. And I hate it."

"Yet you came anyway. Why?"

"To help Kev, of course. And, I dunno, Grandma—maybe also to say goodbye. But why would that take anything away from Stark? It doesn't change how much I love him. I don't think anything could ever change that."

"Zoeybird, it is difficult to love anyone else properly or even fully if you do not truly know yourself. So, perhaps you should spend less time worrying about Stark, and more time looking within and learning what, *or who*, you truly want."

"As usual, you make a lot of sense," I said.

"I believe I just say aloud what you already know within your heart."

"Thank you for always believing in me." I slid my arm around her and we leaned into each other.

"It is a great gift to see you again, u-we-tsi-a-ge-ya. One I will eternally thank the Great Earth Mother for."

"Well, Grandma, someday—hopefully not very soon, because

Kev definitely needs you—you'll be able to thank her in person. Nyx knows you well, whether she's had a chance to tell you that in this world or not."

"And that is another great gift I have been granted. Thank you, child. It will be very difficult for me to say goodbye to you again."

I tightened my grip on her, holding her close. "Then don't. Let's just say, 'See you later,' instead."

"That, my Zoeybird, sounds like a wonderful idea."

Grandma and I sat there, arm in arm, watching the sky ready itself for the sun and talking about nothing and everything—and just before we went inside to find Anastasia I realized that my spirit wasn't frantic or sad anymore. My spirit was calm and ready. Ready to do everything I could to help my brother defeat Neferet—*and* ready to go home to my world, my House of Night, and my Stark.

# 30

# *Other Stark*

"Neferet, I mean no disrespect, but I really don't think it's a good idea to let the Red Army inside the stadium." Stark paced back and forth in front of Neferet's green onyx desk. "It's asking for trouble—even if you have them feed before the game. So many humans together in such a small space is just too much temptation."

"Oh, Stark, you do worry so! But that is part of your charm. Only part of it, though. That beautiful young body of yours is the other, much *bigger* part." Neferet let one sharp, scarlet-painted fingernail trace seductively down her neck to the plunging V of her emerald-colored silk dress.

He pulled his gaze from her breasts and frowned. "I'm not kidding. This is a serious situation."

"Really? Are both teams here?"

"Yes. The buses arrived hours ago. The players will sleep, or at least rest, today. The sun sets at five twenty, which is about when they'll go from the dorms you emptied for them to the stadium to dress and warm up. We'll open the stadium to fans at eight. Kickoff is at ten o'clock sharp."

"They did bring cheerleaders and their bands as well, did they not?"

"Yeah, yeah. And their booster clubs too. You said you wanted the full Bedlam spectacle, and that's what you'll have."

"And the Blue Army will be there, with my Warriors in attendance as my personal guard, correct?"

"Of course. Someone has to keep the Red Army from eating everyone," he muttered.

"Then I'm not seeing a serious situation. I'm seeing one you have in order."

"But, Neferet, what I'm trying to make you understand is that having red vampyres in attendance is dangerous for every human in that stadium—and you have commanded that the stadium be full of humans."

"Exactly. Tell me this, my dear young vampyre, which are more expendable—blue vampyres, red vampyres, or humans?"

"I don't understand."

Her sultry tone changed instantly. "Of course you do. It is a simple question. Answer it."

"Red vampyres, I suppose." He spoke hesitantly, not sure about the point she was trying to make.

"I would argue that my Red Army is *not* expendable, because they are my army. That leaves humans, because, of course, *we* are not expendable."

"But humans feed us. We do need them, Neferet." Stark felt chilled by her tone. She was so callous—so absolutely uncaring, that she was becoming unrecognizable. Stark even thought she was changing physically, though when he tried to identify specific differences he seemed unable to hold the thoughts in his mind. *Something strange is happening to Neferet—something strange and Dark.*

"Of course they feed us!" she was saying. "But they also procreate at a ridiculous rate—so making more of them is rather easy, wouldn't you say?"

"Uh, I've never thought about it like that."

"Well, do. And while you're thinking, be quite certain that the Red Army is armed."

"No, Neferet! That's not—"

"*Never tell me no!*" She stood as she shouted at him, and Stark thought he saw strange, writhing movements in the shadows around her desk. "You are my general. You do my will."

"Neferet, I do the Goddess' will. That is what I have sworn to do." Stark spoke carefully, calmly, though he did take several steps back, away from Neferet, her desk, and whatever creepiness she was hiding beneath it.

Her demeanor changed instantly. Her grin was a satisfied cat licking cream. "Well, then, that makes everything easier, doesn't it? Who on this earth knows the Goddess' will better than her one chosen High Priestess?"

"No one, High Priestess," he answered automatically.

"Exactly. And Nyx has been very clear about what must happen at the game tonight. You know that. You know I've told you I am planning a New Year's Day surprise that the Goddess has fully blessed. Now, run along, General Stark. Be sure the Red Army is fed and watered at sunset—and then be quite sure each of them has weapons. Nothing elaborate, mind you. Simple knives and swords are fine. No need for arrows. They can so easily go astray, can't they? Well, unless *you're* firing them. So, do be sure you bring yours, won't you?" She didn't wait for his response but settled herself back into her chair. "After they are armed, take them to the stadium. Station them at field level near each exit—all the way around the stadium, so that it appears to be held by a ring of scarlet. Isn't that a lovely visual image?"

"I'm not sure I understand. You want the Red Army by each exit from the field? By the players and cheerleaders? Not far from about thirty thousand humans in the stands?"

Neferet sighed. "Yes. That is exactly what I want. An exquisite blood-colored ring around the field."

"Neferet, even if fed, the Red Army will be difficult to control."

"This is *your* problem, General Stark! You have your bow and arrows. You cannot miss. If a soldier tries to eat a human, skewer it. Even the most feral red vampyre understands self-preservation. Show them that to preserve themselves they must not eat humans. Well, unless they are commanded to, of course."

"But why would you command them to eat anyone at the game? Isn't it just a game? Just entertainment for humans and vampyres?"

"Because, my dear, sometimes a few must be sacrificed to save many."

"But what does that have to do with the game?"

"Well, let's say the humans get out of hand. You know how these awful bumpkins can be about their ridiculous patriotism. What if they decide to rise up and try to push back against our rule? Examples must be made to stop the destruction of many."

"Okay, I do understand that, but we've been to a lot of college football games, and the human audience has not once tried to rise against us. Neferet, I'm not sure you completely understand what football is about—it really is *just a game*."

"Oh, my dear, *nothing* that pits one group of humans against another is *just a game*, but it is highly useful that their silly squabbling and prejudices keep them separate and weak. Imagine if they all stood together against us." She shuddered delicately. "They outnumber us. They out-weapon us. We would go back to being vulnerable, second-class citizens. I, for one, shall *never* go back."

"So, basically, the Red Army is there only in case humans try anything."

Neferet laughed, and the sound was like fingernails on a chalkboard, sending terrible shivers of foreboding down Stark's spine. "Oh, silly Stark—they are there for so much more. They are there to show my power and our dominion over the human infestation of this planet. You are there to keep them in order unless I need them released. Can you handle that, General? Or shall I look for your replacement?"

"I will follow your orders. I'm here only to serve the Goddess."

"Excellent! Wasn't that easy? You really should stop worrying so much. All will be well—as long as you are allied with my will—and the will of the Goddess, of course."

"*Of course*," Stark said, though he was certain Neferet did not catch the sarcasm in his tone.

"You know, my dear, you really should smile more. You're much too handsome to scowl. Try it. Give me a smile. Just a little one."

Stark forced his lips up, though he felt like his face might crack.

"See, that is so much nicer, isn't it? I do prefer a smiling male to a pouty one. Now, run along. You have much to do. Send Artus to me. He and I need to discuss my Warrior escort. You are dismissed."

Stark fisted his hand over his heart and bowed to Neferet before leaving her office. It wasn't until he had closed the door that he felt like he could take a deep breath.

Reluctantly, Stark headed to the Field House where he knew he'd find Neferet's ancient, gnarled Swordmaster, Artus. Then he'd have to go to those Goddess-be-damned tunnels and get the Red Army ready for whatever show Neferet was putting on. Beside the pain-in-his-ass addition of the Red Army, this game should be little more than the usual vampyre entertainment. Neferet was wrong about humans. There was no way they were going to rise up and attack at a football game. Everything should go smoothly tonight, so Stark couldn't figure out why his gut refused to unclench. *Probably because this feels like a clusterfuck in the making. I will be so damn glad when this night is over . . .*

(

## Other Kevin

"Look, I'm not going to wash you, little Nala, but you have to let me dry you with this towel. You're still looking pretty wet and scraggly." Kevin resumed toweling the complaining orange fur ball off, determined to ignore her yowling.

"Kevin Redbird, are you killing that kitten?"

He looked up to see Aphrodite standing at the entrance to the little bedroom Anastasia had assigned to him. She was wearing a very large T-shirt and even larger socks, and her hair was pulled back in a ponytail that was letting blond tendrils escape to curl around her face.

He thought she was the most gorgeous girl he'd ever seen, and he had to clear his throat before he could coax any words out.

"I'm drying her, not killing her. But she's definitely not happy with me. Wanna help?"

"Sure, but you might not want me to help. I told you before that I like cats, but what I didn't say is that they usually don't like me back."

"She doesn't seem to be liking me much right now, so I'm guessing that won't matter. Come on in."

Aphrodite padded on silent sock feet into the little hollowed-out room, which kinda reminded Kevin of a bubble, closing the blanket that served as a door behind her. Kevin was sitting on the bedding pallet with a complaining Nala balled up on a towel in his lap.

Aphrodite sat beside him. She crossed her legs and arranged the big T-shirt to drape over her knees. "Here, you hold her and I'll take a corner of the towel and dry her with it."

"Good luck. She has claws," Kevin said.

"Of course she does. She needs those claws for climbing and mouse catching, don't you, pretty girl?" She cooed to Nala, who stopped complaining and arched her back as Aphrodite used the corner of the towel like a brush, rubbing it gently down her body.

"Hey, she likes that!" Kevin said.

"Yeah, she does. Maybe she just needed to get her hair done. Is that it, Nala? I know all about needing a day of beauty."

Nala looked up at Aphrodite and sneezed into her face.

Kevin held his breath, waiting for Aphrodite to freak out, but she didn't. *She laughed.* Musically, joyously, she giggled and wiped her face with the other end of the towel as she baby-talked Nala.

"Did you catch a cold out there looking for your Kevin? Poor girl. We'll keep you warm and dry now. You don't need to worry."

Nala revved up her purr engine, and she made three little circles before curling up on Kevin's lap and closing her eyes while Aphrodite finished drying her.

"I thought you said cats don't like you."

"No, I said they *usually* don't like me. Nala is obviously smarter than most cats and has better taste."

"I couldn't agree more." They smiled into each other's eyes, and Kevin felt his heartbeat throughout his body. She was so close! And so, so beautiful.

"Well, she seems pretty dry now," Aphrodite said. "She also seems like she's asleep."

"You tamed the wild beast!"

"She's hardly wild. She's sweet." Aphrodite looked around the room. "So, they put you across from me. Better you than Stevie Rae and Rephaim. I walked past their room on the way back from the bathroom and all I can say is Rephaim is a screamer and I swear I heard the bumpkin yell '*Yee-haw.*'"

Kevin snorted a laugh. "I could've gone my entire life without knowing that."

"That makes two of us."

The soundtrack to the silence between them was Nala's purr quickly dissolving into a snore, which had Kevin and Aphrodite grinning at each other.

"I'm going to move her over there to the little cat bed Anastasia gave me," Kevin whispered. "Don't breathe." He carefully carried her to the donut-shaped bed, depositing her in the middle of it. Then he came back to sit beside Aphrodite. "I think you lulled her into a cat coma. She's still snoring."

"It's nice that she likes me. That's never happened to me before. My mother, who is horrible, by the by, refused to let me have any pets. She said they were all soulless creatures who wasted oxygen." Aphrodite

335

snorted. "I used to think she was describing herself." She leaned back against the side of the cave and gave Kevin a contemplative look. "Did you meet my mom when you were in your sister's world?"

"Nope. But I do know she was a nightmare over there too."

"Well, at least she's consistent. She'd like knowing that, and she doesn't like much." Aphrodite paused and then said, "Kevin, would you tell me the truth—no matter what I asked you?"

"That's the deal we made."

"You're right, it is. I like that I can trust that with you—that we'll tell each other the truth. It hasn't happened much in my life."

"I'd like to change that," he said.

"You already have." Then she hurried on. "So, am I a lot different in that other world?"

Kevin took his time answering. He was determined to tell her the truth, but he also knew that she was letting her guard down around him, and he wanted that—wanted intimacy with her, so he was determined not to say something stupid that would mess it up.

"It's weird. You're alike, but different. I'm pretty sure you both had awful childhoods. You're both Prophetesses. You're both beautiful and kinda bitchy."

She raised her brows at him.

"It's a compliment," he said.

"Whether it is or not, it's the truth. Go on."

"But Zoey's Aphrodite is part of a big, close family."

"I thought you said she has the same awful parents I do. Uh, I do not have any siblings. My mother refused to be pregnant twice. She said it made her body too unattractive for too little return."

"Goddess, she's a crappy mom—even crappier than my ultra-religious mess of a mom."

"That's one contest I wish I didn't keep winning. Anyway, how could I be part of a big family?"

"Because Zo's House of Night and what they call their Nerd Herd are family."

"Wait, go back. Did you say *Nerd Herd*?"

He grinned. "I did. When I was there I asked how they came up with that name. You named them."

"Oh, for shit's sake! I named the nerds and then I joined them?"

"Yep, that's the story."

"And I thought I had issues in this world."

"So, that's the biggest difference. You're happy over there. You're surrounded by friends and family. You're valued by Zoey as a great prophetess. And, of course, you have that extra red added to your Mark, and those extra powers too."

"And you swear that Nyx gave me that power."

She hadn't phrased it as a question, but Kevin knew she needed to hear the answer. "Yes. Absolutely. I give you my oath that Nyx gave you the power to grant second chances."

"It's just so weird. Sure, I have visions, but I've never, not one time, heard the Goddess' voice or even felt her presence."

"Maybe Nyx is waiting for the right time."

"And when would that be?"

"When you're ready to hear her voice, and be in her presence," Kevin said.

"Have you ever heard or felt her?"

Kevin's gaze went far off as he remembered entering Nyx's Temple and, for the first time, feeling the presence of his Goddess. He had to clear his throat before he could speak, and when he did the words sounded rough with emotion. "Yes. I know Nyx. I've felt her. She's touched me."

"What was it like?"

"Pure love," he said. And his gaze found hers again. "You'll see someday."

"How can you be so sure?"

"Because you're Nyx's Prophetess. And because I believe in Nyx and her love."

"That's a good story, Kev."

"That's a true story, Aphrodite."

"Are you scared about tomorrow?" She abruptly changed the subject.

"Well, yeah. Of course," he said honestly.

"Because you don't think I can do it?"

"No way. I know you can. I'm scared because the Red Army is a fucking nightmare. And I'm scared that innocent people will probably get hurt because Neferet is an evil bitch. Zoey might get hurt too, which scares the crap outta me, and not just because she's my sister and I don't want her to die. Again. If anything happens to her, Other Stark will come over here and rip my heart out of my chest, which will not be cool."

"Definitely not. So, Zoey and her Stark are seriously in love?"

"Yep, but it's more than love. They're bonded. He's her Warrior and even more than that. They fit together. I'm happy for them. It's what I want. Someone I fit together with."

"It's what I want too. But don't tell anyone. Everyone thinks all I want is a different hot guy in my bed every night. Or maybe every other night."

"And that's not what you want?"

"No. It's exhausting. But it's less scary than loving someone."

"Unless you love the *right* someone."

Aphrodite sighed and flipped back her ponytail. "But how the hell do you know when someone is the *right* one? I'm sure my father thought he loved my mother, like, a zillion years ago. But their marriage was a sham. By the time he died they hated each other. I decided right then that I'd rather be alone than take a chance at that kind of living nightmare. So, what about guys? Do I have a lover or whatever over there?"

Kevin's chest suddenly hurt, but he couldn't—*wouldn't* lie to her.

"Yeah, well, that's another thing that's different about that Aphrodite and you. In Zoey's world you have an Oathbound Warrior named Darius. He loves you. You love him. You two fit together."

He couldn't look at her, so instead he stared down at his hands.

"Wait, I thought that Aphrodite and you kinda had a thing over there."

Kevin smiled sadly at his hands. "No. Well, only a little. Only what your heart had room for. You didn't love me. You liked me." He felt his cheeks getting warm and wished he hadn't turned the damn lantern up so high when he was trying to dry Nala. "You did kiss me and tell me to find you in this world, and to just be myself because you'd love me in this world too."

"*Too*? Sounds like I mighta kinda loved you a little."

"Maybe a little."

"And what about you? How did you feel?"

He swallowed hard and moved his shoulders. "How could any guy *not* fall in love with you?"

She didn't say anything for so long that Kevin's cheeks went from blazing hot to cold with the kind of embarrassment that comes from heartbreak.

And then he felt her move. She slid over so close she could touch him. Aphrodite reached out and took his chin in her hand, gently lifting it and turning his face so he had to meet her eyes.

"No guy has *ever* loved me. Not one. They've wanted me. Lusted after me. Tried to use me. Feared me. Hated me. But never loved me."

"Then every one of them was a fool."

"But you aren't. Kevin Redbird, you are no fool," she said.

His laugh was humorless. "I think the definition of a fool is someone who falls in love with a woman who is not his to love."

"That Warrior isn't here, Kev," she said softly, looking from his eyes to his lips. "What if in this world *you* are my Darius?"

Aphrodite leaned into him, pulling him down to her. She kissed him, long and deep and hot. Their tongues met, touched, teased. Her arms went around his shoulders and suddenly she was in his lap and his hand stroked the length of her smooth leg.

"I want to stay with you tonight," she whispered against his lips. "I *need* to stay with you tonight."

"You can stay with me forever," he murmured back—lifting her, turning her, so that their bodies pressed together as they explored the secret, beautiful places only lovers share.

And then finally they fit together. Perfectly.

# 31

# *Zoey*

"What happened to TU?" Stevie Rae asked as they pulled into the already packed parking lot. They'd timed it so the Resistance Warriors, who all had their tattoos covered and were wearing either OU or OSU paraphernalia, would enter late, just before kickoff, so that they had an excuse to rush in with the other humans who had to wait for the last minute because vampyres were always seated first—and always in the best seats.

"What do you mean? This is how TU has always been," said Dragon from the driver's seat of Grandma Redbird's van.

"In our world, the campus is a lot bigger and, well, nicer," I tried to explain as I looked at the sparse old stone buildings that surrounded a super high-tech stadium. "But your stadium is nicer, even after we updated ours."

"Not much happens academically at TU," said Anastasia. "It was a wonderful university a few decades ago. Only the brightest and best attended. But they couldn't compete with OU and OSU's sports programs, so the university went into decline. Well, as you already noted, except for the stadium. Other teams use it, so that rich man—Bryan, what was his name?"

"Boone Pick, Pick Boone, or something like that."

"Yes, thank you, my love, him. He donated money to the school, but not for academics, of course. To redo the stadium so that they could host semipro teams. I believe the new stadium seats thirty thousand."

"Dang," said Stevie Rae. "Makes me sad. I always wanted to go to TU. They have—well, *our* TU has an awesome film studies program."

"I didn't know you liked that kind of stuff," I said.

"Yeah, in high school I really wanted to be a director—you know, like Patty Jenkins. Then I got Marked and died. And undied, and Changed into the first red vampyre High Priestess, so I got kinda sidetracked."

"If you want to go to TU when we get back, you totally can," I said.

"Z, that would be awesomesauce! You think I'll have time, what with being sure the Depot Restaurant gets up and running?"

"We'll make time. No one should ignore their dreams."

"Okay, everyone ready?" Dragon asked. He swiveled in his seat to look back at us. Stevie Rae, Rephaim, Anastasia, Dragon, and I all decided to arrive together. The rest of the Resistance, including Kevin and Aphrodite, had divided themselves up in cars and trucks that Tina had supplied from local Resistance members. Kevin and Aphrodite had driven together in their town car, pretending to go straight from their shopping trip in Dallas to the stadium.

"I'm ready!" I mustered as much confidence as I could, though worry gnawed at my stomach. There were just so many things that could happen in such a giant space filled with so many people and an army of ravenous, inhuman vampyres. I mean, what could go wrong besides everything? Then I shook myself mentally. *Get it together, girl. Act like a High Priestess.* "We're going to do this," I said firmly. "Everyone totally understand their parts?"

"We separate and head to the top of the bleachers, each in the direction of the elements we represent," Anastasia said.

"And then we watch the game and wait," Dragon said.

"That's my favorite part!" Stevie Rae gushed. "Boomer Sooner!" Then she looked chagrined. "Uh, I didn't mean that Aphrodite saving all the red vamps wouldn't be as cool as a football game, though."

"They understand," Rephaim said, kissing her gently.

"I don't like that we're all separated," said Dragon.

"We have these." I lifted the high-tech walkie-talkie from my pocket. It looked like one of those old flip phones, only it didn't flip open. There was a button on the side, and when I pressed it I could talk to the others. Each of us had one: Dragon, Anastasia, Stevie Rae, Kevin, and me. I was supposed to give them the signal, and Anastasia would open the call to the elements with air.

"I wish we coulda given one to Aphrodite. She is the one who has to make the sacrifice," said Stevie Rae.

"It was too risky. She has to report to Neferet. If Neferet makes her stay there in the press box with her, we'd be discovered the second her walkie-talkie bleeps," said Anastasia.

"But she'll know when we cast the circle. It should be obvious," I added.

"I hope so," muttered Dragon.

I grinned at the grumpy Swordmaster. "You just wait and see. Everyone will know when we cast the circle."

We climbed out of the van and joined the stream of humans wearing OU red and OSU orange. It was a less rowdy crowd than what was normal for a Bedlam game, but that was no big shock, especially as we all had to pass silent, glowering blue vampyre Warriors. The good news was no one had to pay to get into the game. And I decided that was the only good news, as we entered the stadium and got our first glimpse of the field—*and the red vampyres that were grouped around each field exit forming a bizarre blood-colored circle around the players and cheerleaders.*

"Oh, Goddess!" Anastasia gasped beside me. "She has them down there on field level."

"Ready to eat anyone who tries to leave," said Rephaim.

"This is bad, Z," said Stevie Rae.

"Maybe not." I motioned for my group to follow me to one of the concession stands, where we huddled in a tight circle, pretending to try to decide between hot dogs and nachos. I spoke quietly and urgently. "At least they're all together down there."

"But how are we going to get weapons from them if they're on the field and our Warriors are scattered around the stadium?" asked Anastasia.

"Our Warriors won't be able to be armed," said Dragon darkly.

"All that means is that we have to be fast," I said. "We know the slaughter won't happen until after the game. Aphrodite saw that much. I'm assuming Neferet will make some sort of ridiculous speech first."

"That sounds right," said Dragon.

"So, as she starts her speech, we prepare to call the elements."

"Maybe we should start the call as soon as the game's over," Rephaim said.

"That will only work if no one can tell we're casting a circle," Dragon said, looking at me. "And you're sure people will be able to tell?"

I nodded, still speaking low. "There should be a ribbon of light that connects us. People are definitely going to notice that—especially Neferet."

"All right. Then we wait until she gives the command," said Dragon.

"Anastasia, be ready to call air," I said.

"I will be. Do not worry about me."

"You'll be next, Dragon," I reminded him, trying not to sound as nervous as I felt.

"I know the order of the elements, Zoey," he said, though not unkindly.

"We all do, Z. It'll be fine," said Stevie Rae.

"Okay. I'm going to take a seat down as close to the fifty-yard line as I can get. That'll be where I call spirit. Blessed be, everyone."

"I shall be in the east," said Anastasia. She kissed Dragon. "Blessed be." Then she hurried away.

"I go to the south. Blessed be," said Dragon. I saw him begin to make a fist as he automatically was going to show me the proper respect as a High Priestess and bow, but he caught himself in time, and with a wry smile he actually winked at me before he also left, heading to the southern end of the stadium, leaving me alone with Stevie Rae and Rephaim.

"Z, is this gonna work?" my bestie asked.

"It has to, but if something awful happens, you and Rephaim get out. Don't wait for me. Don't wait for Kevin or Aphrodite or anyone. Just get out. And don't go back to the ridge. Take the van. Go to Grandma's farm. I'll meet you there."

"Got it," Rephaim nodded soberly. "I'll keep her safe."

"At least we're wearin' the right shirts." Stevie Rae pointed to the matching red OU sweatshirts my group had all opted for. "OU almost always wins."

"Boomer Sooner!" I said. "And blessed be, you two."

We had a brief group hug, and then they headed for the north end of the stadium. I drew a deep breath, trying to ready myself. I turned to head into the stadium when I heard a voice that stopped me dead. I looked frantically around. Stark was standing near the men's bathroom, talking to—and another jolt of shock hit me—he was talking to *Dallas!* In this world Dallas was a blue vampyre, but he looked exactly like he had last time I'd seen him … just before he died.

I ducked my head and hurried past them, like I had to get to the ladies' room really, *really* fast. Then I paused just around a cement wall, where I pressed into its shadow, listening intently.

"Dallas, stop complaining and get your ass field level," Stark said. "I need you and every officer who isn't in the press box with Neferet down there. Keep those red soldiers together. Keep them under command. Make them stand at parade rest. Hell, make them stand on their fucking heads for all I care. Just keep them from eating the cheerleaders!"

"Hey, I hear ya. I'll do my best, but that's a lot of red soldiers. We're way outnumbered."

"Then kill one of them if you have to. Make them more scared of you than they are hungry. Shit, Lieutenant, they just fed!"

"Right?! Their hunger is annoying as hell."

"Well, get them under control! The last thing we need is a slaughter down there."

*Stark doesn't know what Neferet's planning!* The realization soared through me. *I knew it! I knew he couldn't be like Neferet. She's using him and his devotion to Nyx.* And that thought had my spirits lifting and my attitude shifting.

Stark and Dallas separated. I watched Stark disappear into a curtained, guarded entrance that read **PRESS BOX** over it.

*Good. At least I know where he is. Stark's not going to be cool with Neferet commanding the Red Army to eat innocents. He's going to stand up. He's going to speak out. And when he does—we'll be his backup.*

Feeling way more confident, I readied myself, and then entered the stadium. The game had already started and the bands—in the stands at opposing ends of the stadium—were playing some kind of battle song that had lots of people on their feet. I kept my eyes on the stands, trying to find a single seat as close to the fifty-yard line as possible. At row twenty-five I finally spotted a space and pushed myself through a sea of red toward it, where I tried to sit—but the ref had just called holding against OU, so, of course, all the Sooners around me were standing and booing.

So I stood. And finally I let my gaze go to the field.

Heath was there. He'd jogged to the sidelines, whipped off his helmet, and was having a very arm-waving discussion with the ref, who was shaking his head and pointing back out on the field at the OU huddle where Heath should be.

I stared and pressed my hand against my chest because my heart felt like it would beat out of my body. He was wearing number three on his jersey, like always. I had to blink hard to keep from bawling. Number three wasn't for Daryle Lamonica, Oakland's famous "Mad Bomber" who'd played football a zillion years ago, like in the 1960s. (I only know about him because Heath knew *everything ever* about football.) Anyway, Heath always wore number three because that's when we'd met. When I was in third grade.

I wiped my eyes and kept staring at him. He was so cute! His hair looked like a baby cow had held him down and licked all over it, making it stand up in adorable sandy blond tufts. He had those dark quarterback lines drawn under his eyes, which totally took me back to high school, and I had to stifle the urge to yell his name and give a big ol' Broken Arrow "Go Tigers!" shout.

The ref made a shooing gesture at him again, and he crammed his helmet back on and rejoined the huddle.

*He looks so grown-up!* I realized as I watched his team—his older, more experienced team—look to him as he called the next play. It hurt my heart, but I swear I could've watched him for days. I'd grown up watching him play football—getting better and better—growing into an outstanding athlete and finally an outstanding leader. I was glad to see he'd kept himself together. Obviously, he hadn't crawled into a case of beer and given up after I died.

Sure, part of me was a little resentful—the selfish, immature part of me. But the rest of me—well, the rest of me loved watching him living his dream. And when he threw the first touchdown of the game I was on my feet too, joining in with the die-hard OU fans and their new chant of "We've got Luck! We've got Luck! We've got Luck!"

He came off the field with the offense, and that's when I saw her. One of the cheerleaders—a hot black girl wearing OU's tiny little cheer uniform—rushed up to him, wrapped her arms around him, and kissed him smack on his lips. While the crowd cheered, Heath totally kissed her back.

"Touchdown for OU!" bellowed the announcer. "And their

quarterback gets an *Oklahoma hello* from Jenn Amala, one of OU's cheerleaders. Looks like his *luck* is a lot more than a name."

I threw up a little in the back of my throat as I watched him smile that sweet Heath smile at her as she skipped (Skipped! Seriously!) to rejoin the rest of her scantily clad squad. Heath waved at the crowd.

Then the little walkie-talkie in my pocket crackled.

"Zo. Come in, Zo!"

I sat down, covered one ear, cupped my hand around the walkie-talkie, and tried to pretend like I was talking on a phone.

"Kev?"

"Are you all here?"

"Yes. We're in place."

"Ignore that girl. He'll always love you."

I sighed. "Not important right now. Where are you?"

"Nosebleed section in the west. Ironically just below the press box. Fifty-yard line, but waaaaay above it. Ready to call water when you give the word."

"Hey, that means you're up there behind me. I'm in row twenty-five at the fifty-yard line. Where's Aphrodite?"

"Press box with She-Who-Must-Not-Be-Named."

"Got it," I said.

Then his voice got all echoey as he must have covered the walkie-talkie to whisper, "Hey, we can't get any weapons because the red vamps are all on the field."

"Dragon knows. They'll have to improvise."

"Which means we'll have to work fast."

"That's the plan." The stadium roared again as OSU fumbled and OU recovered. "Gotta go. Can't hear you very well."

"*Boomer Soo—*," Kev yelled before the walkie-talkie cut off.

Heath ran back on the field and my eyes followed him. Well, when I wasn't staring at his girlfriend. I had to admit Jenn Amala was pretty. And I was glad she wasn't some ordinary blond chick—like

Kayla. I shuddered at the thought. Shaunee would be glad Heath was getting some black-girl magic. I tried to be glad too.

And when that failed, I went back to watching him and trying to control the bile that kept rising in my throat.

## (

## *Other Aphrodite*

"This game is a bore," Neferet pouted, sipping from a crystal goblet filled with red wine and even redder blood. "I thought the Bedlam thing was a magnificent rivalry."

"Well, it is," Aphrodite said reluctantly, waving away one of Neferet's Warrior guards who tried to pour her more blood-laced wine. "But OSU isn't very good, that's all."

"*Not very good* seems an understatement. It's intermission and the score is thirty-eight to three. *Three*. A field goal is all that orange team could manage."

"Halftime," Aphrodite corrected.

"What?" Neferet's head swiveled, owl-like, to look at Aphrodite. "And why are you dressed so plainly?"

Aphrodite looked down at her jeans, her favorite pair of silver sparkly Jimmy Choo heels, and the red OU tee she'd tied up to show a little of her flat, gorgeous belly.

"Neferet, I'm dressed for a football game. And this pause in the game isn't called an intermission. It's called halftime."

"Semantics." She waved away Aphrodite's comment.

"The marching bands are good," Aphrodite said, attempting to make safe small talk.

"Good? They're dreadful. Too much brass and noise and not enough finesse." She drummed her long red fingernails on the press box window as she held out her empty goblet. "Artus. Refill."

The grizzled Warrior moved with the speed and grace of a

predator, refilling his High Priestess' glass. As he did, Neferet ran a sharp nail up his arm, tracing his bicep and leaving a painful-looking pink trail.

The Warrior had to stifle a moan of pleasure.

Disgusted, Aphrodite averted her gaze.

"Did you have something else to say? Perhaps a thank you for these outstanding seats?" Neferet asked Aphrodite.

"These are great seats. I used to come up here with my father. He was a TU alum," Aphrodite said.

"Again—boring. Human fathers are so overrated. I thought you understood that."

Aphrodite shrugged. "Compared to my mother he was father of the year, every year." She noted Neferet's dark look, and quickly changed the subject. "But he never had the power you have. It's amazing that we have the press box all to ourselves. Thanks for the invite, Neferet. These really are great seats."

Aphrodite glanced around, plastering a grateful smile on her frozen face. The only other person in the box with them, besides Neferet's Warriors, was a very sweaty human who was commentating the game. Neferet had shoved him over to the far side of the room and had ignored him completely. Aphrodite noted that he'd started stuttering halfway through the second period when Neferet had started complaining about being bored.

"What did you do with that young red vampyre who was following you around?" Neferet had turned away from the huge wall of windows and was studying Aphrodite with disconcerting concentration.

"Who? Oh, you mean Lieutenant Stinky." She shrugged. "I told him to go find his flight or squadron or whatever it's called. I don't care what Stark says, I can't stand his smell anymore."

"Stark says he *didn't* assign that soldier to you."

Aphrodite's heartbeat began to hammer, but she'd spent her entire childhood hiding her fear from her mother—and that skill had never left her. She rolled her eyes. "Oh, right. It was *my* choice to have a rancid red vampyre follow me around. Wait! I thought Stark was following *your* command." She sat up straight as if the thought had just come to her. "You mean you didn't tell him to shackle me with that stinky creature?"

"No, my dear. I did not."

She snorted. "Well, I'm going to have words with General Bow Boy. Where is he, anyway?"

"Fussing with the Red Army. He should return any moment," Neferet said.

"Good. I'm going to tell him if assigning Stinky to me was his idea of a joke, *I am not amused.*"

"Hm. That's interesting." Neferet's gaze went back to the field below them where the bands had finished and the players were warming up. "Unlike this game. But I know how I can make it much more interesting. Artus, get that microphone from that inconsequential human over there and give it to me. It's time."

Aphrodite felt sick. "Time for what?"

"Aren't you the Prophetess? Can't you tell me?" Neferet's sharp eyes trapped her.

Aphrodite did her best to look confused. "No. I haven't had a vision since the one about the hayfield."

"Well, then, watch and learn." Neferet took the mic her Warrior had taken from the commentator. "I need that camera on me. It should play on that screen with the score so everyone can see me."

"Human! Turn the camera on the High Priestess!" Artus commanded.

The poor guy was trembling so badly that he almost couldn't get the camera turned around to face Neferet.

"What are you going to do?" Aphrodite's stomach flipped around so hard she was finding it difficult to breath.

"Why, I'm simply going to liven things up. Is it ready?"

"Y-y-y-yes, ma'am."

"High Priestess!" Neferet shrieked. "How many times do I have

351

to tell you ridiculously simple humans, especially you *males,* that my title is High Priestess, not sweetheart, not honey, and not ma'am!"

"I-I'm s-sorry, High Priestess," he groveled.

"Of course you are. I forgive you." Her smile was reptilian. "Now turn that thing on."

The red light blinked, and the man nodded to her. Aphrodite glanced at the field to see Neferet's face suddenly being broadcast on each scoreboard and every video monitor in the stadium.

"Good evening, everyone. I am Neferet. Your High Priestess. I am *thrilled* you accepted my invitation and came to celebrate Bedlam with me. Now, I am quite sure that many of you—especially those of you wearing orange—are feeling disappointed and, perhaps, a little bored with how the game is going. I know I certainly am. Thankfully, I prepared a solution, though I was going to save it until the game was officially over. But, no matter. Now is the perfect time.

"Perhaps you noticed my lovely Red Army is field-level, guarding every exit. With their smell they are certainly difficult to miss!" She laughed at her own joke before continuing. "Well, as with everything I do, stationing them there was purposefully done, and here is why. The winning team will take home that silly glass bell. The losing team—their cheerleaders, their band, and their coaches—they will all be fed to my Red Army. I do despise losers, don't you? So, carry on, and do your best. Half of you have a very short time left to live."

# 32

# *Zoey*

As Neferet's image went blank on the video monitors, the stadium erupted in panic. Humans everywhere shot to their feet and began pushing to get to the exits. I fought to stay in my seat as people shoved around me, cursing and crying. Terrified, I looked down at the field. Heath had ripped off his helmet and was facing the OSU team. I watched in horror as he strode over to them and dropped to his knees. Then, turning so that he faced the press box, Heath raised his hand in defiance. Slowly, his OU teammates joined him, surrounded him, and did the same.

I could see the tears in the eyes of the OSU players as they followed suit. Coaches, cheerleaders, referees—they all took to their knees and held up their fists in protest.

And, just like that, the people surrounding me changed as well. The panic stopped as first one person halted and raised their fist to the sky, turning to face the press box defiantly. Then another stopped, and another, until the seas of orange and red rippled together in protest.

Neferet's face flashed back on the video screens, only this time she didn't look serene and beautiful. This time she looked more like the

Neferet I knew too well—totally insane. Her green eyes were tinged with red and spittle flew from her lips as she shrieked at the camera.

*You will play this game or I will loose my Red Army on all of you! You have until the end of halftime intermission to decide!*

That sent a ripple of fear through the stadium, but Heath didn't move. And the rest of the field held strong as well.

I keyed the walkie-talkie.

"Anastasia!"

"Here!"

"Call air!"

I concentrated and felt a gush of warm night air rush past me as it headed to the east, answering Anastasia's call.

"Dragon—go!"

I paused until I felt the heat of flame, like someone had just turned on one of those outside propane heaters that restaurants like to use. Then I keyed the walkie-talkie again.

"Kev, your turn!" I shouted into the walkie-talkie, knowing he was somewhere at the top of the bleachers directly behind me.

As soon as I smelled the ocean I said, "Earth! Your turn, Stevie Rae!"

"Easy-peasy!" came her answer, followed by the scent of fresh-cut grass.

I drew a deep breath and concentrated on my intent—casting an Old Magick–ready circle.

"Spirit, I need you! Please come and complete my circle!"

The people closest to me had started to stare, so I did the only thing I could think to do. I took the sleeve of my sweatshirt and wiped off my forehead and face, exposing my adult vampyre tattoo. I smiled at the people around me.

"The Resistance is here. We're going to help you. Spread the word. Try to stay calm."

"But what can you do against the Red Army? They're monsters! And if they bite us we die!"

"Look," I pointed up and in a circular motion, following with my fingertip the glowing silver rope of light that ringed the entire stadium. "That's my circle. We have more power than you know. Trust us. We're here to stop Neferet for good."

The people around me gasped. One woman stepped forward.

"Good luck. We're counting on you," she said. "And blessed be. My sister was Marked a long time ago. I still miss her."

"Thank you!" I said.

"What can we do to help?" asked the man at her side.

"I need to get up there. Fast." I pointed at the stadium seats above us and just below the press box.

The woman who'd spoken to me turned and called down the row to our right. "Jeremy! Help this young woman out, would ya, please? She needs to get up there real quick." The woman pointed.

A giant of a man stood and started toward me. I could see his resemblance to the older woman.

"Sure, Mama," he said. Then he looked at me. "Well, sis. Stay behind me and let's get to gettin'. Best hold onto my belt so I don't lose ya."

I didn't question him. I just did as he said. He turned. I grabbed his belt, and then he started climbing, taking giant steps up and over each row as people either parted to let him through, or he simply pushed them aside like they were curtains and he was determined to step through them onto a stage.

I followed in his wake, gratefully gripping his belt with both hands so that he almost carried me like a tail behind him.

"Sis, there's a kid yellin' and wavin' at us. Is that who I'm takin' ya to?"

I peeked around the mountain of a man to see Kev, flailing his arms over his head at us.

"Yep, that's my brother."

"Hang on!"

I hung on, and soon Jeremy deposited me right in front of

Kevin. He was alone in the top row of the bleachers. Everyone else had fled toward the exits.

"Dude, that was seriously cool!" Kevin reached out to shake the giant guy's hand.

"No problem. Need anything else?"

"No," I said. "Go back to your family and keep everyone calm and together. We'll take it from here. And thanks. Thanks a lot."

"Welcome, sis." And just as easily as he'd climbed up, Jeremy the Giant made his way back down.

"Okay, we're calling Oak and the sprites now, right?" Kev asked.

"Not yet. First we need to get up there to the press box." I glanced at the scoreboard. "We have exactly one minute and twenty-two seconds before halftime ends. That's not enough time to negotiate with Oak to fix this mess, and if we don't stop Neferet's 'Eat them all' command, a lot of innocent humans will be killed."

"How the hell do you think you're gonna stop Neferet from commanding the Red Army to start killing?"

"I saw Stark go up there earlier. Hopefully, he's still up there. I'm not going to stop Neferet. He doesn't even have to stop her. All he has to do is—"

"Counter her command!" Kevin grinned. "That'll at least confuse the armies and make them hesitate."

"Yep, long enough for us to call the sprites and have them heal the red vampyres."

"Good plan, Zo, but how do we get up there?" He pointed above us at the giant glass box.

"Well, as Stevie Rae would say, since we have all five elements here that should be easy-peasy. Trust me. This isn't my first rodeo." I keyed the walkie-talkie. "Anastasia! We're going to need air. That means you have to concentrate and help us control your element. Ready to do that?"

"Yes, I am!" she said.

"Okay, here goes!" I held my hand out for Kevin's, which he

took without hesitation. "Focus on air—on how strong it is, how it surrounds us, fills us, and is always here for us." Then I turned so that Kevin and I faced east. "Air! Hear my call! I am Zoey Redbird. This is my brother, Kevin Redbird. Nyx has gifted us with air affinities, and we need you to hear us. For the good of this world, we must be lifted up there." I pointed to the very top section of the press box, knowing Neferet would never settle for seats that were anything but the best. "Air, take us there!" I squeezed Kevin's hand tight. "Focus! And don't let go of me!"

Kevin and I closed our eyes. I imagined air swirling around us, becoming tangible, like a gust of wind turned into the hand of the Goddess—cupping us in her palm and lifting us. In my mind's eye I suddenly saw a clear image of Anastasia. She was sitting cross-legged at the top of the eastern bleachers, her eyes closed and her head tilted back. Her face was absolutely serene. Her long gray-streaked blond hair floated around her in invisible air currents. She was more radiant and beautiful than I'd ever seen her look.

And then Kevin and I were surrounded by a funnel of air. But this funnel wasn't Oklahoma tornado crazy. It was soothing, serene, and warm. Safe within its eye, we began to lift.

"Wow! Hell yes, we have juice!"

I could hear the crowd below exclaiming in surprise, but I stayed focused thinking about air and how much I appreciated the invisible but powerful element. In seconds we were floating in front of a wall of windows behind which Neferet stood, glaring at us. Aphrodite was there too, watching us with wide-eyed surprise. There was also an ancient-looking Warrior—scarred, gnarled, and mean-eyed, watching us with a flat, calculating expression.

And there was Stark, who had just sprinted into the press box, mouth open, staring.

"How do we get in?" Kevin shouted over the funnel of air.

"The same way we got up here. Air can lift us, so air can also smash that glass." I caught Aphrodite's shocked gaze and mouthed,

*Get down.* She didn't hesitate. I saw her drop to the floor and then I raised both of my hands, taking Kevin's with me. I turned my head to look at him. He met my eyes. "Imagine what we want, and then we ask air to push." He nodded. I closed my eyes again, concentrating on a vision of air smacking against the glass and shattering it into a zillion tiny pieces that rained harmlessly to the empty top bleacher seats below us. Then I opened my eyes and told Kevin, "Push! Now!"

Kev and I pushed and, miraculously, air responded, smacking against the glass and shattering it into diamond dust before lifting us through the empty window frame and depositing us gently inside, just feet from Neferet.

# 33

## *Zoey*

"Thank you, air!" I said before facing a glowering Neferet.

"Hi, Neferet. Remember me?"

"Insolent child!" she shouted. "I have never seen you before in my—" Her words broke off abruptly and I saw recognition flash across her face.

"That's right. You thought you killed me. Guess what? *I'm back!*" And without thinking, my body did something I'd wanted to do for ages. I closed the few feet between us and slapped her—hard—across the face.

"You little *bitch*!" Neferet's hand flew to her cheek as from the shadows around her tendrils of Darkness began to hiss in anger and slither toward me.

"Ah, hell no! I've been through this crap before." I glanced at Kevin, who was just behind me. "Focus on spirit!" I saw him nod and then I raised my hands. "Spirit, shine the Goddess' Light on these creatures of Darkness!" A ball of brilliant purple light formed in my hands and I threw it into the writhing shadows.

Neferet's scream mirrored the inhuman shrieks of the tendrils.

As I'd hoped, this Neferet hadn't managed to fully manifest her "children" in this world yet and, unable to bear the Light of the Goddess, they retreated back to the Dark void—or wherever the hell (literally) they came from.

"Artus, my Warrior. *Kill them!*" Neferet commanded.

I was frantically trying to think about what element I could call to help us against her Warrior when Kevin stepped in front of me and, in one swift motion, he pulled a strange-looking knife with a white blade from a leg sheath. He shouted, "Air, guide this true!" He threw the knife. With a howling gust of hurricane-strength wind, the dagger imbedded itself to the hilt in the Warrior's throat. Artus clawed at it for a moment, then his eyes showed white, and, like a tower in an earthquake, he fell.

"You got a knife in here?" I asked, stunned.

Aphrodite grinned. "It was my idea. It's made of porcelain. Didn't show up on the metal detectors."

"General Stark! Protect your High Priestess! Kill these assassins!"

Stark lifted his bow and nocked an arrow.

I knew we were screwed if Stark fired. My Guardian, my Warrior, my lover who can never, ever miss.

Aphrodite was on her feet and rushing to stand in front of Kevin and me. "Don't do it, Stark. They're the good guys—not Neferet."

"You would betray me? My own Prophetess?" Neferet's face had gone pale. Her eyes blazed with a strange red light.

Totally unaffected by Neferet's hatred, Aphrodite flipped her hair back and faced the crazed High Priestess. "Oh, for shit's sake! I am not *your* Prophetess! Just like Stark is not *your* general. First and forever we swore to serve Nyx, and it's been obvious to me for a while now that you're not serving the Goddess. You're allied with Darkness." Aphrodite's gaze went from Neferet to Stark. "You know it too. Stark, you and I aren't friends, but you're not like her. You still follow Nyx. Neferet does not."

"Kill those insolent children! All of them! And while you do that I'll command *my* Red Army to teach those pathetic humans a lesson they will never forget." She moved to grab the microphone, but Stark intercepted her, getting to it first.

"What are you doing?" Neferet's voice was filled with loathing. "Do you wish to give the kill command, or will you betray me too, and be proven a liar and Oathbreaker like Aphrodite?"

I spoke up quickly. "Stark, I'd say don't listen to her, but you need to. Listen very carefully to Neferet. Study her. Think. I'll bet you've been studying her for some time now because you're none of those things. You're not a liar. You're not an Oathbreaker. You take your vows very seriously and you have to know Neferet has not been following Nyx for a very long time."

"General Stark, shut this ridiculous child up!"

"No, Neferet. You did that once already, when you killed me to start this damn war. You'll never do it again."

"Zoey Redbird?" Stark's eyes went wide with shock as he finally recognized me. "You're the fledgling that was killed by the People of Faith more than a year ago."

"Well, yes. Sorta. One version of me was killed but not by the People of Faith. Neferet killed me and set the murder up to look like radical humans did it. Neferet was broken as a child before she was Marked. Instead of healing, she chose vengeance and anger. She hates all humans. This whole war is nothing more than Neferet getting back at her father for raping her."

"You *cunt!* You know nothing about me!"

"You're absolutely wrong about that. I probably know you better than you know yourself. I know that soon you'll be attempting to free a winged immortal from his eternal prison so that you can pretend he's Erebus. I know that you've been studying the evil Tsi Sgili. I also know that you're playing with the idea of being consort to pure Darkness—the White Bull." As I spoke I watched Neferet's eyes and saw the truth within as they registered shock at my understanding. I turned my focus on Stark. "Stark, do you really believe there is any way Nyx would approve of red vampyres murdering a stadium full of innocent humans?"

"Of course Nyx approves," Neferet said. "And why not? The time of humans is over. What have they done in the centuries since we allowed them to usurp our rule of this world? They have poisoned this precious earth, warred unendingly against themselves, and committed atrocities in the names of their various gods. The Goddess knows they are only good for food and labor. Why else would she have created red vampyres except to give *us* victory over man. Now, do as the Goddess and I command—kill them all!"

I met Stark's gaze. "You know she's wrong, but I can prove it to you. Just tell the Red Army to stand down and I will show you."

"Is that not the red vampyre lieutenant you trusted?" Kevin flinched as Neferet gestured toward him. "The one that lying bitch of a Prophetess said you assigned to her? No wonder your last mission failed, General Stark. He's not a red vampyre! He doesn't even have a Mark. He's part of the Resistance!"

I couldn't stop my gaze from going down to the field. The Red Army hadn't attacked, but they had moved out on the field. I could see blue vampyre soldiers trying to keep them contained as they waited for Neferet's kill command. The two football teams had formed a circular group in the middle of the field—players on the outside, cheerleaders, referees, and coaches on the inside. I couldn't find Heath, but I was absolutely certain he would be one of the first to meet his death if Stark didn't side with us.

Beside me Kevin wiped the cover-up off his red Mark. "Wrong again, Neferet. I'm what all those soldiers down there could be if their humanity was returned to them, which is exactly what Zoey, Aphrodite, and I intend to do today." He turned to Stark. "I'm sorry I lied to you, but I have a message for you from William Chidsey. He's ashamed you're siding with Neferet. He knows you know better."

Stark's face blanched white at the mention of his beloved mentor's name. "William is dead."

"In this world, yes," I said. "But that only means he's joined the Goddess. Do you really think he'd be proud of the things you've done in Neferet's name?"

Without replying Stark lifted the microphone to his lips and pressed the speak button.

"This is General Stark. Neferet's kill order is rescinded. I repeat—stand down. Stand down now. Maintain control of the Red Army and await my orders. Wave if you copy!"

He paused, and we all stared down at the field where first one, then another and another blue vampyre officer standing between the humans on the field and the milling red soldiers stepped forward and waved their acknowledgment.

I was watching the officers when a jolt of recognition hit me. I was sure I knew one of them. Even from this distance his powerful body and the way he carried himself was obvious. *That's Darius. I know it is!*

Stark keyed the mic again. "Excellent. New orders will come shortly. Humans—remain where you are. You are safe." He released the button. "Prove that you're telling the truth, Zoey Redbird."

"No!" Neferet shrieked. Raising her hands in claws she rushed at Stark, who easily sidestepped, trapping her arms behind her back as he shoved her into a chair.

"Be quiet and sit there or I'll gag and tie you. I've been listening to your will and following your orders for months, believing I was doing the will of our Goddess. Now it's your turn to listen. Let's see once and for all exactly who is following Nyx and who is a lying Oathbreaker." He nodded to me. "Show me."

"Let's face the window and call them together," I said to Kevin.

"I'm with you, Zo."

"Me too," said Aphrodite.

We walked to the wall that used to be glass and was now open to the magnificent sky.

"You start," I told Kevin. "They know you better in this world."

I felt him draw a deep breath and let it out slowly, then his strong, confident voice echoed from the room out into the night.

"Old Magick sprites, elemental beings as old as the earth, I am the one you know as Redbird Boy. I need your aid. Oak! I ask that you and your elementals come to me. There is an abomination you must make right!"

"Good job," I whispered to him.

"Thanks. Aphrodite helped me practice." He grinned down at her and it made my heart squeeze to see the love that blazed between them.

I drew a deep breath, just as Kevin had done, and let it out slowly. Then I raised my voice to join my brother's call.

"Old Magick sprites, I am the one from far away that you call Redbird Girl. I join my brother in beseeching your aid. Oak! I ask that you and your elements of air, fire, water, and earth come to me. You must know about this abomination of nature!"

We waited and my stomach turned upside down a few times. I had enough time to think about IBS and wish that being a fully Changed adult High Priestess cured it.

Then the sky in front of us began to shimmer and—with a strange sounding *Pop!*—sprites suddenly materialized. I sucked air and heard Kevin and Aphrodite's gasp echoed by the full stadium below us.

I'd never seen so many sprites—not even on Skye when I conjured them with Queen Sgiach's help. They filled the sky over the stadium, and they were glorious. They came in so many shapes and sizes that my mortal mind couldn't process them. Many of them looked like birds—with the heads of women. Some seemed more insectile, like enormous butterflies and dragonflies—every bit of their bodies were iridescent and glistened like wet pearls.

From the middle of the enormous group, Oak drifted to us as the sprites parted to allow her through. She was bigger than she'd been when she'd led us to this world, and she looked wilder, somehow less humanoid and more the personification of a tree.

"Redbird Boy and Redbird Girl, your call is a surprise. I find that intriguing. What is this abomination of which you speak?"

"Look down on the field," I said. "And really *see* the red vampyres. Smell them. Observe their insatiable hunger."

"And why should I do that?" the sprite asked.

Aphrodite spoke before I could. "Because they are an abomination of what is natural. They are missing their humanity."

The sprite startled in surprise, which sent ripples through the other Old Magick beings. Then her almond-shaped eyes narrowed suspiciously.

"Truly? Or are they simply a force that opposes you? We do not meddle in the squabbles of mortals, even should those mortals be as long-lived as vampyres—red or blue."

"I was once one of them," Kevin said. "My humanity was returned to me through great sacrifice in my sister's world. But even with my blood, which ties me to the land, I felt their hunger and their never-ending rage. It is not natural. It is not in opposition to us. It is in opposition to nature and the world."

"Go down there and see for yourself," I said. "You'll understand once you look more closely at them."

"Don't listen to these children." Neferet stood, smoothing back her long auburn hair and straightening her shoulders. For that moment she looked every bit like a High Priestess, beloved of Nyx. "The red vampyres are simply my soldiers. They are, indeed, less evolved than blue vampyres, but they are mine. Given to me by Nyx. I speak for the Goddess—not these Oathbreakers."

Oak's laughter was visible, sending glittering tendrils of lilting sound all around us.

"Neferet, I see you. I know you. You have not spoken for Nyx for more than a century." The sprite turned and commanded. "Air sprites! Go to the red ones on the field. Fill them. Know them. Then tell me what you learn."

Like a mini fireworks explosion, a group of the sprites shot off, falling down to the field and onto the milling groups of red vampyres, who began shouting in anger and fear, and trying to swat them as if they were insects.

It only took seconds. The air sprites returned and Oak met them. They engulfed her, obscuring the tree sprite from our view. And then she was back, floating before us, her expression grim. When she spoke I could see her sharp, pointed teeth. Her eyes blazed with anger.

> *"Abomination of nature indeed!*
> *Your call to make right this horror we*
> *shall heed."*

Kevin and I breathed twin sighs of relief as we recognized the singsong tone the sprite used whenever she had decided to make a deal.

"Thank you so much—" I began.

> *"But as the abomination is not of our making*
> *There must be a payment for our taking."*

"That's me," Aphrodite said. She took a step toward the glassless window and the hovering sprites. "I will pay the price to return humanity to the red vampyres."

> *"Prophetess, there is much here that must*
> *be made right*
> *And though your humanity shines bright*
> *It might not bring with it enough light."*

"Aphrodite, be careful." I spoke to her low and fast. "Be sure you know the exact price you have to pay."

Her blue eyes found me, and I saw the lonely truth within

them. This Aphrodite seemed like mine, but I suddenly understood that inside she was much, much more broken.

"I know what I have to do and I'm fine with it. I'm better than fine with it. I'm glad of it." She turned to Kevin and stepped into his arms, tiptoeing to kiss him. I heard her whisper, "I love you. Forgive me." Then she moved away from him and even closer to the window. "I understand. I'll pay the price. You have my oath as a Prophetess of Nyx. Isn't my blood enough to fix them—all of them?"

*"It is, indeed.*
*You are all that we need."*

"Hang on. Wait. No. This doesn't feel right," Kevin said.

He started to reach out to Aphrodite, but I snagged his wrist first. "You can't stop this," I said.

Aphrodite looked over her shoulder at me. "Tell your Aphrodite that I made it right."

My eyes filled with tears that leaked down my cheeks. "I will. Thank you."

"Zo, wait," Kevin said. "We need to stop her before—"

Oak held a glowing, delicate hand out to Aphrodite.

*"Come, Prophetess, our deal has been made.*
*Now the price must be paid.*
*I seal this deal between thee and me.*
*So I have spoken—so mote it be."*

"Aphrodite! Don't!" Kevin lunged for her, but she moved more quickly and with no hesitation. Aphrodite stepped through the broken window and grasped Oak's hand. I held my breath, sure we were going to watch her fall to the bleachers far below, but it didn't happen like that.

Aphrodite floated with the sprite. They hovered in the air

together as the people below pointed and cried out. I could see Aphrodite's face. She was radiant. Her smile was filled with joy and I thought she looked like a young girl who had never known abuse or sadness, heartache or loneliness. Then the sprites surrounded her, engulfing her in a ball of brilliant silver light.

"What's happening?" Kevin rushed to the window, staring out.

I couldn't say anything because I knew what was happening. Aphrodite was sacrificing everything to save this world.

The glowing silver ball drifted slowly down toward the field, and as it got closer and closer, the light changed from silver to something that looked like ballerina-slipper pink, then a lovely salmon color. When it finally came to rest in the middle of the fifty-yard line, making both teams scatter to the sidelines, it changed color yet again to its final shade—the perfect red of fresh blood.

The instant it touched the field the ball of light exploded, sending scarlet beams away from it. Like waves crashing against a beach, the bloody light washed through the humans and the blue vampyres and found the Red Army. It crashed against them as they cried out, covered in brilliant, blazing red so bright that we all had to look away.

Then everything went dark. I was blinking spots from my eyes when the keening began. It lifted from the field, carried on the night wind like smoke. I rubbed at my eyes, frustrated that it was still so difficult to see. Then my vision suddenly cleared, and I understood the sound. On the field the red vampyres were sobbing. Some had fallen to their knees. Some were standing with their arms wrapped around themselves. Still others were laying on their sides in the fetal position. But all of them, every single man, was sobbing uncontrollably.

I whirled to face Neferet. "You did this. You used them instead of trying to help them. Their agony will forever be tied to you—so I have spoken. So mote it be!"

Neferet stood, her face completely expressionless—almost serene. Then she smiled, and I have never seen such evil reflected from another's soul.

"And why should I care about those men? Men are all the same, no matter what skin suit they're wrapped in. They are abusers and users. They have subjugated women for centuries. Raped us. Bought and sold us. They live to control us. Any agony those men feel is less than every one of their gender deserves."

"I pity you," I said.

"Neferet, High Priestess of the Tulsa House of Night," Stark said formally, "I am going to escort you back to your chambers. There you will be held until the Vampyre High Council decides your fate."

"No, boy. You will not." With a movement so preternaturally swift that no one could stop her, Neferet hurled herself out of the glassless window.

We looked down, expecting to see her bloody and broken body on the bleachers below—but there was nothing. No body. No Neferet.

"Crap!" I said. "I should've known! I should've brought turquoise to tie her up with. Crap!"

"What happened to them?" Stark asked as he stared down at the field of keening red vampyres.

"They're mourning," Kevin said. "Their humanity has been returned and they understand exactly what monstrous things they've done."

"That—that's terrible," Stark said, wiping a hand over his face. "Are they dangerous?"

"Only to themselves," I said.

Stark picked up the microphone and commanded, "Blue officers—escort all humans from the field and the stadium. Leave the Red Army where they are. We will deal with them after the humans are safely outside the stadium."

The blue officers and soldiers instantly did as Stark commanded, ushering humans to the exits.

"What is Neferet?" Stark turned to me and asked.

"Well, she's not immortal. Yet. Or she wouldn't have been this easy to defeat. But she's definitely heading that way. Stark, you need to talk to my grandma, Sylvia Redbird. She can help you learn about the Tsi Sgili."

"The what?"

"It's what Neferet's becoming. And it's real bad," I said. "But you can defeat her. You just have to work together with my brother, Kevin." I nodded to Kev, who paid no attention. He was staring down at the field—at Aphrodite. "Also Dragon and Anastasia Lankford, and all the rest of the High Priestesses and Warriors Neferet banished or forced to flee and become the Resistance. They'll help you—and you'll need them."

"Zo, we gotta go. The sprites are gone and Aphrodite is alone down there," Kevin said.

"I know. Air will take us back down."

Kevin held his hand out to me, but before I could take it Stark stepped between us.

"Wait, don't go yet. Who are you? No, *what* are you? Why do I feel like I know you? I met the other Zoey once, just before she was killed, but she didn't have your powers—or at least I don't think she did. I didn't get to know her hardly at all."

"You do know me, but not in this world. In this world Neferet ruined that for us. I'm the same Zoey you met, just older and I hope a lot wiser. What am I? A High Priestess who believes we're stronger, better, more *humane* together—and that means red vampyres, blue vampyres, *and* humans. They aren't our refrigerators. They're not that different from us. Hell, Stark, we used to be them. But you already know that because you are a good man—a truly good man. Nyx knows you. She trusts you. You can do great things in this world. You can be a big part of the healing that needs to take place between humans and vampyres. You have to listen to your gut, though. And trust the Goddess."

"You'll help me too, right?"

I smiled sadly at him. "No, Stark. I have to go home."

"But will I ever see you again?"

"Look for me under the Hanging Tree in the Goddess Grove. But don't be in a rush to get there. Live a long, happy life. Love passionately and often. And may you always blessed be, my love." I put my arms around him and pulled him into my embrace, kissing him like I wanted to kiss *my* Stark.

Then I went to Kevin and took his hand. I didn't look at Stark again. I couldn't—not if I was really going to leave. "Air! Come to us again please. Take us down to the football field."

Together, Kevin and I stepped out into the arms of the night air where it held us close until gently placing us on the field.

"Aphrodite!" Kevin cried, as he caught sight of her. She was crumpled on her side and laying there very still while a Warrior stood over her, keeping the gawking crowds back as the other Warriors hurriedly helped the teams and the cheerleaders from the field.

Kevin sprinted to her, getting there first. I could have run with him, but I knew what I was going to find and, perhaps selfishly, I wanted just one more moment not to feel the heartbreak.

When I reached them, I wasn't shocked to recognize that the vampyre Warrior who had been standing over Aphrodite was Darius.

Kevin had pulled Aphrodite into his lap and was cradling her like a child. I knelt beside him.

"It's okay. It's okay. I've got you. Everything's going to be okay now." Kevin was talking to her softly as he rocked back and forth, and tears slipped silently down his face.

Aphrodite's eyes fluttered open. I couldn't believe she was still alive. She was so pale her skin seemed translucent. Her breath came in wheezing gasps.

"Kev." Her voice was so soft we had to lean in to hear her.

"Ssh, don't talk. I'll get you some help," Kevin said.

"Too late. I was waiting to say goodbye to you." Her face crumbled then. "Don't want to go, but I have to. Scared, Kev. I'm scared."

"Hey, hey! No. You're gonna be—"

I touched his arm. "That won't help her. She's dying, Kevin."

Raw despair shimmered in his eyes, but he nodded and lifted Aphrodite in his arms until she was almost sitting.

"You don't have anything to be scared of. You did it. You saved all of them."

"It worked?"

"Yeah, you were fantastic. And now you're going to go see Nyx. Zoey says it's great there with her, right, Zo?"

I leaned close and took Aphrodite's cold, limp hand. "It's more beautiful than I can describe. You're going to love it. I promise. The me from this world is there. Find me, 'kay?"

Aphrodite nodded, tried to smile at me, and failed.

"And I'll come find you someday—just in case your Darius isn't up there waiting for you," Kevin said.

From the corner of my eye I saw the tall Warrior's body jerk in surprise, but Kevin and Aphrodite were in a world of their own, and for just a few moments more, no one else was alive except them.

Aphrodite tried to touch Kevin's face, but she couldn't. Kevin caught her hand and pressed it against his cheek.

"Silly Kev," she said. "Don't you know by now that *you* are my Darius in this world? That's what I've been trying to tell you."

"I love you, Aphrodite. Always," Kevin said.

"Me too. You're my person … who fits together with me perfectly. Kiss me goodbye, Kev."

Kevin bent and kissed her. Aphrodite breathed one long sigh— and then she breathed no more.

Darius approached us slowly, respectfully. He reached out and touched Aphrodite's golden hair.

"I did not know her, yet she seems so familiar. And so very spectacular," he said.

Kevin looked up at him. "Her name was Aphrodite, and she *is* spectacular. In any world."

Darius nodded, bowed respectfully to me, and then rejoined the other Warriors trying to figure out what to do with an army of hysterical vampyres.

I knew they needed help. I knew I should figure out something to do for them, but at that moment I felt so numb—so empty—that all I could do was sit there with my arm around my brother as his cries joined with the red vampyres, lifting into the heavens.

"She did it! Those sprites were amaze—" Stevie Rae was shouting, as she and Rephaim ran us to us.

And then she saw Aphrodite.

"Oh, Goddess. No." Stevie Rae dropped to the grass beside us with Rephaim staying close to her. "Why?"

"I don't know," I said.

"It worked!" I heard Dragon's voice behind me.

"Aphrodite was incredible!" Anastasia's voice came from over my shoulder as well.

I turned to see them jogging up to us, smiling victoriously—until they saw Aphrodite.

"Oh, Aphrodite." Anastasia crouched beside me, gently closing Aphrodite's eyes. "May your reunion with Nyx be filled with joy."

"I don't understand. This sacrifice did not take her life in your world," said Dragon.

"No, it didn't." I wiped my nose with the sleeve of my sweatshirt. "I don't understand it either."

*"Then let me explain, Daughter."*

Chills cascaded over my skin as the Goddess' familiar voice filled the air around us. As one, the stadium gasped and then went completely silent as every vampyre, red and blue, fell to their knees and bowed their heads.

Standing just a few feet from us was Nyx. In this incarnation she looked like an exquisite Cherokee maiden. I instantly recognized the tear dress she wore—it was a glistening calico print in all the colors of the rainbow. Glowing ribbons decorated the quarter-length sleeves, and around the skirt, just above the flounce, were shining diamonds creating the design of our people's seven-pointed star. She wore her hair long and free, and it floated in a dark waterfall around her waist.

"Hello, Nyx." I bowed my head and fisted my hand over my heart. "Merry meet."

She drifted to me and lifted my face, kissing each of my cheeks, instantly drying my tears.

*"Merry meet, u-we-tsi-a-ge-ya. You did well in coming here, though I know the cost to your heart has been great."* Then she turned her radiant gaze to Kevin, still holding Aphrodite's body in his arms as his head bowed.

*"U-we-tsi, you may lift your head."*

My brother did. His face was ravaged by grief and tears, but he smiled at his Goddess. "Merry meet, Nyx."

*"I want you to know why Aphrodite's life was sacrificed here today. In this world she was not strong enough to withstand the loss of her humanity. She did not have friends here. She only knew love briefly, with you, Kevin Redbird. Her loneliness broke her."* The Goddess' gaze included Dragon and Anastasia. *"Learn from her loss. You need each other. It matters not the color of the Marks on your face—or whether you are vampyre, fledgling, or human. You need each other to truly live. And you will always be stronger together."*

Then the Goddess turned in a slow circle, her dark eyes taking in the red vampyres where they knelt or lay. All were staring at her as they continued to weep silent, soul-shaking tears.

*"Oh, my poor children."* She spoke softly, but her voice carried to every corner of the stadium. *"You are not responsible for the atrocities you committed. You were used by someone in my name, as if I approve of pitting my children against one another. I do not! No god or goddess worthy of worship approves of war and violence and killing. No, this sorrow must be mine and not yours to bear."*

Then the Goddess began to weep, and, as tears cascaded down her smooth cheeks, the sky opened and a warm, gentle rain began to fall—just over the stadium. As it soaked us we didn't get wet. Instead it absorbed through our clothes, through our skin, and poured into our bodies to find our hearts—our souls—and it washed the sadness, grief, and pain completely away.

The red vampyres' tears changed as well, from despair to joy, as they hugged each other and shouted praises to the Goddess.

I looked at Kevin. He was still crying, but he was smiling down at Aphrodite's still body as he stroked her hair and held her close one last time. And then I saw him grimace and jerk, as if something had just smacked him across his back. He turned his head and pulled at his shirt and I saw his fresh sapphire tattoo, which looked exactly like the one that stretched from one of my shoulders to the other.

He looked up and met my eyes.

"Really?" he asked incredulously.

"Really." I nodded.

We both looked to the Goddess, but she was staring up at the night sky.

*"Oak! Return,"* Nyx commanded.

The tree sprite instantly materialized, bowing low to the Goddess.

*"Dear sprite, you have my gratitude for righting the terrible wrong that was done to my red vampyre children."*

*"Anything for you, Great Goddess,"* Oak said.

*"Then I do have one request."*

*"Name it, Nyx, Goddess of Night."*

*"Let this child's sacrifice be payment enough to return my three children to their rightful world."*

*"So you have spoken, Immortal Earth Mother. So mote it be."*

Nyx came to us. *"You must return now, children. There is only so much meddling that can be allowed from one world to the next, and your time here is over."* She paused, catching my gaze. *"Zoey Redbird, would you like to say a final goodbye before you return?"*

I knew what she was talking about—or rather *who* she was talking about. And my answer was easy.

"No, thank you. I know my heart. We said our goodbyes in your grove." Speaking those words gave me the greatest sense of relief I'd ever felt in my life. I loved Heath. I would always love Heath. But the man who wore his face in this world wasn't *my* Heath. He didn't share my memories, and he couldn't share my future. Seeing me now, so briefly, would only cause him confusion and pain. "But does he know I'm here? Does he know this was me?"

*"No, Daughter. He saw only a dark-haired, powerful vampyre High Priestess, not his Zo. You chose wisely, as I knew you eventually would."*

"Thank you, Nyx. Thank you so much."

But I did still have goodbyes to say. Kevin looked up at me and, gently, he lay Aphrodite's body on the grass. He kissed her forehead, and then he stood and pulled me into a hug.

"I'm gonna miss you," he said.

"Me too."

"Are you being nice to the other me over there in your world?"

"Yep. You're not as dorky as I thought you'd be."

"Good. Be his friend. Don't let him be lonely," Kevin said.

"Never. I'll never let him be lonely," I assured him. "I love you, Kev."

"I love you too, Zo."

As I stepped into his arms I whispered, "You can love again. I promise. I've been where you are."

He didn't say anything, but his arms tightened around me and I hoped he would remember what I said and allow himself to be open to love again.

When he let me go I shared a hug with Anastasia and Dragon, and Stevie Rae and Rephaim also said their goodbyes.

Unable to stop myself, I looked up at the press box. Stark was there, standing in front of the broken wall of windows. Slowly, he lifted a hand in a simple goodbye salute. I touched my lips to my fingers, and then lifted my hand to him in return.

I turned to my friends and the three of us held hands and faced our Goddess.

"We're ready to go home now."

*"Then I shall say merry meet, merry part, and may we merry meet again, as I have a new Prophetess to greet in my grove. Remember that we are all linked by love ... always love."*

As the Goddess disappeared in a great burst of black glitter, Oak waved her hand in a circular motion 'round and 'round and 'round in front of us until the circle became tangible and we could see the door between our worlds.

*"Call if you have need of me again. I find you most interesting, Zoey Redbird."*

I smiled and nodded, but muttered, "Not if I can help it."

And then I led my friends through the opening, and we left my brother's world behind ...

(

I felt the difference instantly. That strange, lost feeling that had clung to me for the past several days was finally, finally gone.

*This is my world. This is where I belong.* I breathed a sigh of relief as Stevie Rae and then Rephaim appeared behind me, which instantly closed the circular opening.

"Man, it's good to be—" Stevie Rae began, but was cut off by a joyous shout.

"Z!"

I turned in time for Stark to wrap me in his arms, lift me in the air, and kiss me over and over. Before I'd even found my breath, he put me down and began to feel my arms, touch my face, even turn me around to look at my back.

"What are you doing?" I asked him breathlessly.

"I'm making sure you're one hundred percent okay! You are, aren't you?"

I opened my mouth to answer, and then what was behind him caught my eyes. There, pitched right beside the newly cleansed tree, was a tent.

"What's that?" I asked, my heartbeat racing.

"It's my tent," he said. Then he gave me his cocky, cute half smile. "You might have to leave me behind once in a while, but you'll come back. And when you do you need to know that I'll be right here. Waiting. Always."

"You asked me before if I was one hundred percent."

"Yeah, I did."

I went to him and he wrapped his arms around me.

"Now I can answer you. Yes, James Stark. Now that I'm back where I belong, I am absolutely one hundred percent." It was my turn to kiss him, and I did—like I never wanted to stop.

"Z! Hey, Z's back!" I heard Jack's shout echoed by Damien and Shaunee.

I glanced over Stark's shoulder to see the three of them, with Erik, Shaylin, Nicole, Lenobia, and Travis sprinting across the grass toward us—and my heart soared with happiness.

"Hey, Rephaim, know what's the strongest thing in any world?" Stevie Rae said.

"Yes, I do. It's love … always love …" Rephaim said.

And I couldn't agree more.


THE END … for now.

# FAN Q&A

*You have questions? P. C. & Kristin have answers for you!*

**When writing about multiple worlds, do you ever have trouble switching between them? Like something similar to a book hangover? If so, how do you overcome it?**

—LEAH GEORGE

**P. C.:** I used to, but not so much anymore. The more books I write, the more writing tools I have in my toolbox, and part of those tools help me compartmentalize worlds and characters. It's actually easy to write a book on my own (like one of my Tales of a New World books) *while* I'm coauthoring with Kristin. It gives me a break in each world!

**K. C.:** I agree! I thought it would be a lot more difficult than it is. (Not saying that it's easy. Some authors prefer to only write in one world at a time.) I welcome the break. The change in scenery, which is how I think of it, gives that part of my brain a chance to rest a little bit, and when I come back to work on the world I've left for a bit, I find that I discover things I wouldn't have if I'd just kept pushing through.

**Have you ever ditched any writing that you started because it wasn't going anywhere or because you got writer's block and just couldn't finish it?**

—VICKI RAPAGLIA

**P. C.:** Rarely. Usually I write books I'm contracted for, which means I submit a formal proposal for a new book or series and then a publisher loves it and buys it—*then* I write the entire book. So, what I'm going to write is already decided on well before the book is completed. Once in a while, I'll write myself into a plot corner and have to make some changes, but ditching the whole book isn't an option when I'm under contract for that project. Usually when I'm having a problem it's because I've tried to force characters to do something they don't want to do, and I have to step out of the way and get back in touch with them. And I don't believe in writer's block. Being a career author is a job, but people like to romanticize it into something mystical and magical, so when they can't finish a book or a short story or whatever, they scream "writer's block!" Career authors write through hardships and plot problems. We don't have time to indulge in writer's block.

**K. C.:** P. C. and I operate in the same way in that I too will already have a contract for whatever project it is I'm working on. To ditch it would mean that I'd have to pay back whatever monies I'd already received, (and then how would I make my house payment or buy food or pay for my insurance?! It stresses me out just thinking about it.) I also take a lot of pride in my work and I would never want to let my publisher down like that. If I am having a problem, that's where a good editor is truly an asset. Your editor is there to help you with these exact types of issues. I am grateful to have several who I not only work with, but who are also my friends.

Did you ever imagine that the fan base HoN has would be as big as it is? Did you think so many different age ranges would read it? I know I started the series in my thirties and instantly was hooked!

—MAUREEN GURNEY

**P. C.:** Honestly, no! I was teaching high school and simply wanted to write a series wherein I could deal with the challenges I'd watched my students face for years. Basically, I wrote the books for my students and was shocked when so many different people loved them.

**K. C.:** I was nineteen when we started working on the HoN together. I definitely did it because I just assumed it was going to be a big success. Now I roll my eyes at my younger self for not having any idea what it takes to make it in this business, but I also believe that my "we're going to be über successful!" attitude only helped us. I'll always go into my next project thinking the same thing. It's not worth doing if I don't. Only now I understand the amount of hard work and discipline it takes to create a book or series that can reach as many people as the HoN has and continues to.

When did you realize that HoN went from a "new series on the shelf" to the huge following it has become now? Once you realized it had a huge following, what was your reaction?

—AMY COPELAND

**P. C.:** I love to tell this story! It was the release week for the third book in the series, *Chosen* (and my eighteenth book in print). Our editor had been telling us for a while that the first two books kept going back to print, and that the numbers for the new book looked very good—but we never expected what happened! I remember our editor called me Wednesday midmorning and said that we were really high on Bookscan (measures books purchased in the US), and I asked, "Is there any way you think we could make the *New York Times* bestseller list? Maybe the extended list?" (The published list is the top ten books in each category. The extended list goes to twenty-five.) She said she had no idea, but that she'd call us later that day because the *Times* lets publishers know on Wednesdays if any of their authors have made the Sunday list. So, Kristin and I decided to walk our Scottie dogs that evening. Our editor called while we were on the trails. She was *shouting*, "YOU ARE NUMBER TWO ON THE *NEW YORK TIMES* BESTSELLER LIST!" I was in such shock that I could hardly speak. Our editor kept yelling and freaking out, and at the same time Kristin was asking me if we made the list. About then I started to cry. I held up two fingers and Kristin said, "Twenty! We're number twenty?!" I shook my head and mouthed, *number two* and she freaked out as well. Then we laughed and cried and called the rest of the family and our close friends. The next day my students and teacher friends snuck into my classroom early and had it completely filled with balloons and decorations. It was life-changing and magickal—as special as you can imagine.

**K. C.:** This story still makes me cry! I'll never forget this moment. (I'll also never forget how freaked out our dogs were. We kept hopping around sobbing and screaming. But I'm sure they've since recovered.)

**How do you manage day-to-day life when you get close to the deadline for your books?**

—BRITNEY SPOTO

**P. C.:** I love this question because I *don't* manage this very well! I write at night, usually ending between midnight and 1:00 a.m., unless I'm close to the conclusion of a book (which means it's deadline time). Then I write for hours and hours and go to bed when the sun comes up, which really messes up my days and nights. The only way I manage is by depending on my fantastic assistant, Sabine. She makes sure my household runs well and there is food in my fridge, even when I've totally become a vampyre.

**K. C.:** I am on the path to better managing this. I am a chronic procrastinator, so I'll be writing like a crazy person in the weeks leading up to a deadline telling myself the whole time that if I'd just written even a tiny bit more in the months before I wouldn't be killing myself at the end. Recently I decided that I absolutely *hate* living my life like that, so I've created a new system. I figure out how many words my first draft absolutely must be, and then I do math (eek!) to figure out how many words I need to write in a typical Monday–Friday workweek. Then I vastly overestimate how long that will take me each day, so when I finish early I can either keep writing and get ahead on the next day or it feels like a treat to get off work early.

**What do you and Kristin like to do after the conclusion of a coauthored book? Do you guys open a bottle of wine to celebrate? Heeheehees**

—T. J. MARQUES

**P. C.:** (Waving at Thiago!) Kristin and I like to go out for a celebratory meal at a fantastic restaurant. She rarely drinks, so that bottle of wine is for me me me!

**K. C.:** And if I do drink (bleck), it's never wine. Am I really the only person who thinks that they all taste the same?

**P. C.:** Yes, Kristin Frances. Yes, you are.

**Do you plan on letting House of Night continue as long as you guys can? I can't get enough of the House of Night!**
—ANGEL BURBULES FINNEGAN

**P. C.:** I have two more Other World novels outlined, but whether I publish them or not is totally up to fan demand. I always have ideas for several books and series whirling around in my imagination, so for me to write the next two HoN books instead of a new series fans will have to show me (and our publisher!) that they want more!

**What gets you into a writing mood? I know for me it's a song that just gets my writing juices going. Also, what's your favorite type of song or genre of music?**
—CYNTHIA MAZUR

**P. C.:** Knowing I have contracts to fulfill and deadlines to meet gets me into a writing mood. For career authors writing is a job, so while it's nice to have my candles lit and my pot of tea brewed, all that is really necessary is a computer and an idea. The only music I ever listen to while I write, and I know this is going to sound crazy, is a YouTube channel I subscribe to that plays antianxiety music for dogs. My dogs (and cat) are always around me when I write, and they like it—and I just tune it out. As to music genres, I like lots of different types of music—from pop to classic rock (Meatloaf!) to new age to movie soundtracks. And country. I heart me some country music!

**K. C.:** Same, same—but different. I can write anytime, anywhere if I'm contractually obligated to turn in a book. If I'm at home, I do prefer to light my candles, get my jug of water ready, and start burning my incense. It really tells my brain that I'm serious and it's time to write. Some of my very favorite bands/singers are Ella Vos, Nahko and Medicine for the People, Selena Gomez (she makes me feel all sassy), and Billie Eilish —who I happen to be listening to right now!

**When did you fall into the love of writing and what or who was your inspiration?**

—BETH JACOBS

**P. C.:** I wrote my first book in first grade. It didn't get published. Yet. I don't know what inspired me then, but I can't remember a time when I couldn't read and write. I grew up in a household where my parents read on a daily basis, and still do. I discovered Anne McCaffrey's Pern books when I was thirteen, and that was the first time I realized a woman could write *and* star in a fantasy novel, and I was determined to do just that!

**K. C.:** Shortly after turning in *Redeemed*, I had to make a choice. Do I go back to college (please, God, no!), or do I try to get a contract and write my own books? I enrolled in a soul-sucking higher learning institution (as you can tell, I do *not* have a lot of good things to say about college, but totally do it if you want and all that positive stuff I'm supposed to say to get you to pursue mounds of debt—I mean, a degree) and started writing a book. I was saved from going to college by a publishing house I no longer work with and did not have a positive experience with, but I learned a shit ton, so winning. I only fell in love with writing after I actually started doing it alone. And P. C. will always be inspiration. She's the hardest-working and best woman I know.

When creating a world of fiction how do you decide which parts need the research, and which parts you just have to create? In HoN what made you decide later in the books to start switching points of views?

—JACKIE GARDNER

**P. C.:** I research everything. I do extensive research to create workable ecosystems and to be sure my paranormal and/or mutated creations are credible to the world. Even pure fantasy needs a foundation in reality.

I only sold three novels when I began writing HoN. Then the series took off and my wonderful publisher, Matthew Shear, told me that I could do whatever I wanted to do with the world. I realized then that I wanted to broaden and expand the HoN storyline to include many more characters and side plots. None of those extra things could have been done if you only got Zoey's point of view, which is why I changed the books to third person unless Zoey is the focus of the scene.

**K. C.:** I hate research. I'm sure it comes from my deep loathing for school … Hmm … But I will never let that stand in the way of creating a believable world. I spent a year researching for the new solo series I'm working on because I want it to be real to my readers. It's also based in some science-y stuff, which, in my opinion, *must* be thoroughly researched to be believable.

The Nerd Herd are more than just undead superheroes, they also are icons that embody and champion cultural, religious, racial, and sexual diversity. What are some of your inspirations when incorporating social progress into the series?

—MATTHEW MADONIA

**P. C.:** In the early HoN books, my high school students inspired the issues I included, and as the series progressed I began to take inspiration from society in general, especially societal issues that affect young people the most. I have often been asked about why I "made" Zoey's mother and stepfather so horrible, and my answer is that those fictional parents reflect what I witnessed far too many times during my fifteen years of teaching. I also thoroughly enjoy creating conflicts that shake up the Bible Belt.

**K. C.:** P. C. and I will always include and represent all the different and beautiful types of amazing humans there are on this planet.

**What inspired the Other World series?**

—BRI'ANN BEAR

**P. C.:** You guys did! Kristin and I wanted to write a special surprise book for the HoN's tenth anniversary, which inspired us to brainstorm the Other World story.

**Would you ever write novellas about other characters? I love all the books and would love to have more background on certain characters. Like maybe a novella about my favorite character, Sister Mary Angela, and how she became a nun or her early life, or Grandma Redbird as a young girl? What is the best part about writing these books? Would you ever consider working on something with another person? Maybe a fan?**

—KATARINA ENNA ALEXANDROVNA DMITRIEVICH-
SHCHERBATSKAYA

**P. C.:** I very much enjoy writing novellas, so absolutely! But whether I write more or not is totally dependent upon our publisher(s). I can't write what they don't contract me for—so if you want novellas, tell Blackstone Publishing!

The best part about writing HoN is that the characters feel like family. It is incredibly easy for me to fall into their world(s). It's like coming home.

About cowriting—first, I don't cowrite HoN with Kristin. She is my editor and helps me with brainstorming. Kristin and I do coauthor books together, though, which I enjoy very much. And I have partnered with another author, Gena Showalter. We created two anthologies together and have written a duology as well—though those were collaborations and not actual coauthoring. While I enjoy collaborating with other authors, I don't have any desire to coauthor with anyone but Kristin. She and I fit perfectly together.

**When did your interest in Wicca begin?**
**—CHELSEA HAMILTON**

**P. C.:** I've been Pagan for many years. For the religion of HoN, I merged several different Pagan traditions, including Wicca, to create a unique, matriarchal society.

**We know you take inspiration for your novels from things in your life and surroundings. What one thing did you find most inspiring that would be a surprise to most people who know you personally?**
**—KATELYN RENEE SIMERSON**

**P. C.:** This might sound silly, but I think even people who know me well would be surprised by how much I'm inspired by my pets. Their acceptance, unconditional love, and joy often show up in the pages of my books.

**K. C.:** None of your friends would be surprised by that, woman. You are totally a crazy dog/cat lady. Tales of a New World was inspired solely by your animals. *And* the last time someone asked who inspired you, I puffed all up thinking you would say me, AND YOU TOTALLY SAID YOUR GERMAN SHEPHERD! So, no, not surprising.

When I listen to my Spotify playlist, I'm constantly making up music videos in my head, and they often end up morphing into entire book scenes.

**Your books touch base on a lot of issues that people don't like to talk about. Was it a way to break that barrier and bring the injustices to surface and make people really think about how we live and treat each other?**
— NINA GIBSON

**P. C.:** When I began writing HoN I was teaching public school in a high school outside Tulsa, Oklahoma, and I was determined to showcase the issues I watched my students wade through and try to deal with every day—usually without an adult in their corner or even one willing to talk frankly with them. And after living in Oklahoma for decades and observing the hypocrisy of the racism, misogyny, and homophobia that is rampant in the Bible Belt, I decided to write a YA series that brought those issues and that hypocrisy to the forefront so they could not be ignored.

**K. C.:** Yes! Yes! Yes! I (being one of just two children of color who lived in my neighborhood growing up) wasn't allowed to swim in certain friends' pools, go inside their house, or spend the night because of "rules" their parents had. And those are just some of the memories I have of growing up in an area so on fire with this passive-aggressive underground racism. (I'll spare you the details of what people would say to my mom and me when we walked through stores together.) All of these experiences have served to reinforce the importance of speaking out for (or *writing* out for) what is right. I am blessed to have this platform and will use it to talk about what's real and what's right, no matter how uncomfortable.

**WHEN ARE YOU COMING TO THE NEW ENGLAND AREA?! Lol. That has been biting at my mind every time y'all go on tour. It's never near my state and it makes me a sad panda.**

**—ALEISHA ZINTEL**

**P. C.:** I'm glad you asked that question! Most people think authors go wherever they choose to go on tour. That's not true. Publishers set up tours. We go where we're sent. If you want authors to come to your local bookstore, the best thing you can do is to get vocal with that bookstore and ask them to request publishers put them on their tour list. Good luck!

**What made you want to make the symbols on the HoN characters crescent moons on their foreheads that could turn into beautiful tattoos as their powers came to them?**

**—KRISTY YARBROUGH**

**P. C.:** That was a respectful nod to the ancient practice of physically marking a priestess who has been accepted into the service of her goddess, and I'm a big fan of tattoos!

**How did you come up with the idea of familiars? Was it a relationship with one of your own felines that sparked it?**

—BAILEY BERGMAN

**P. C.:** My pets are often in my books, and HoN is no exception! But the idea was inspired by the fact that wise women, midwives, and healers have long been associated with cats, as they understood early that cats kept down the rodent population, and that helped prevent disease.

**Do you think of an ending of a book first? Or do you just go with a flow as you go day by day?**

—MICHELLE MEYERS

**P. C.:** This question made me laugh (semihysterically)! I wish I could just go with a flow when I'm writing, but I don't think I'd ever finish anything if I did that. I do plot and outline. Even though my work is character driven, which means my characters do things that change my outlines, I know the beginning scene and the ending scene of a book when I start it. The way to the ending scene usually changes as I'm writing, but the ending itself stays the same.

**K. C.:** I write detailed outlines because I don't write in order. To be able to do this and not end up with a pile of scenes that have no way of fitting together, I have to have everything planned already. Sometimes I'll think of the ending first, but most of the time I land somewhere in the middle and that's the seed of my outline.

How can two people write the same book without the writing style changing throughout the book?

—SHAUNA LYNCH

**P. C.:** Well, in the HoN I do all the writing and Kristin does all the editing. We do cowrite other books, though, and when we do that we take turns writing chapters according to which character is in the lead during the chapter. Our editors, agent, and publishers can't ever tell who wrote which chapter and, yes, the style is the same. Part of that comes from the fact that we're mother and daughter and we sound like each other. The rest is because we are cowriting so we know the voice has to remain consistent. We're experienced authors and we're good at that. It's basically a lot of hard work and focus—and a big box of writing tools.

**K. C.:** Staying in the same lane with voice and style isn't as difficult as it might seem. It's like with anything you're submerged in. If you've been reading the same book for hours and then return to your real life, there's that small window of time when you truly feel like you're still connected to the book world. You could even sound exactly like your favorite character if you wanted to. It's a lot like that—but stretched out, since I'm not leaving the book world to return to real life.

Will there be a HoN show/movie within the next few years?

—JULIANNA BERGER

**P. C.:** In November 2011 Samuel Hadida at Davis Films purchased the film rights to HoN. Kristin and I met with Hadida in Paris and had a lovely time discussing what was supposed to be the first of five major motion pictures. Hadida hired a fantastic screenwriter, Marc Haimes (*Kubo and the Two Strings*). Marc wrote a wonderful screenplay that has my full support. Hadida has done nothing with it. There isn't anything more Kristin and I can do until the rights revert to us in 2020. Yes, we find the situation very frustrating. If you want to make your voice heard and tell Samuel Hadida you would like the HoN to come to film (or TV!), here is his contact information. He's not listening to the authors. Maybe he'll listen to the fans!

Twitter: @Metropolitan_Fr
Facebook: https://www.facebook.com/DavisFilms.us/
Email: info@metropolitan-films.com
Mailing address:
Davis Films
29 Rue Galilée, 75116
Paris, France


**What's next for you two talented ladies?**
**—SAMANTHA GREEN**

**P. C.:** *Wind Rider*, the third book in my bestselling YA fantasy series Tales of a New World, releases in October 2018, and then in January 2019 the first book in Kristin and my new coauthored YA series, the Dysasters releases! We can't wait!

**K. C.:** And we actually wrote the Dysasters together! So, check it out and see if you can tell who wrote which characters. I'm also working on adapting the first book in the Dysasters series into an amazing graphic novel (release date to come). And keep an eye out for news about my new YA series, the Key!

*And always remember*
You are powerful! Your choices matter.
Thank you for choosing us.
Sending you light and love ... always love.